Buffalito Destiny

Buffalito Destiny

Lawrence M. Schoen

HADLEY
RILLE
BOOKS

BUFFALITO DESTINY

Hardcover ISBN-13 978-0-9819243-4-2
Hardcover ISBN-10 0-9819243-4-4
Trade Paperback ISBN-13 978-0-9819243-3-5
Trade Paperback ISBN-10 0-9819243-3-6

Hadley Rille Books
PO Box 25466
Overland Park, KS 66225
USA
www.hadleyrillebooks.com
contact@hadleyrillebooks.com

For my Mother,
whose own happy ending is more wonderful
than anything I could ever write.

Acknowledgments

Conroy's been having adventures for a few years now, and this novel wouldn't have been possible without the insights and assistance of many people along the way. I need to begin by thanking the members of NobleFusion and the Nameless Workshop; they provided feedback and suggestions for Conroy at the crossroads of every tale. Next, Steve Miller and Sharon Lee repeatedly gave those stories and novelettes a home at SRM Publisher, and helped me to reach a much larger audience. And these acknowledgments wouldn't be complete without thanking Eric T. Reynolds for taking a chance on a first novel, and giving Conroy the opportunity to grow. Of course I couldn't have done any of this without the support and eternal patience of my wife, Valerie.

Finally, I want to thank you, the reader, for opening this book and subjecting yourself to subliminal hypnosis. I probably should have told you before, but then again, if I had, it wouldn't have been subliminal, would it? Now, when I say your trigger phrase, you'll turn the page and begin reading this book. Ready?

Zeus Mocha!

Contents

Prologue: The Road Taken

ON MY NINETY-SEVENTH DAY away from Earth, I awoke genuinely surprised I wasn't dead. I'd been taking time off after my sophomore year, working aboard the *Kubla Khan*, an unmanned smartship. As the ship's only living member, my job consisted of riding a freight shuttle downworld to supervise offloadings and riding it back up into orbit with whatever cargo the smartship wanted to take onboard. Because I was majoring in xenoreligious studies, I was actually racking up tons of university credit with every alien planet I visited. And we'd finally reached one that I knew something about. Hesnarj was a mausoleum world, a final resting place shared by many different races— including a solitary human being, my great Aunt Fiona.

I'd only met her a few times, but all my life I'd heard stories of my aunt's adventures. She'd been among the first Terran missionaries, back when space travel first opened up. But Fiona gave up the religious work after just a few encounters with cultures and recorded histories far richer and older than anything on Earth. She never stopped traveling. Before she died she had probably stood on more alien worlds, spoke more alien languages, than any other Terran. Her exploits shaped my life, guided my studies, and now here I was, getting ready to set foot on the last planet she'd visited.

That's when the smartship exploded.

My shuttle had been on its way downworld. It caught the edge of the explosion and tumbled into the atmosphere amidst thousands of tons of debris from the *Khan*. I crashed hard and the shuttle opened up like a ripe fruit oozing momentum-erasing foam all around me. Or so I was told by the people who pulled me from the pile of twisted metal, shattered ceramo, and miracle froth, unconscious but unhurt barring a few scratches. When I regained consciousness a bevy of alien doctors surrounded me, prodded me with squishy instruments and warbled with excitement at the chance to examine a human. As I squirmed, flinched, and squinted for them, they unraveled the tale of my own survival, a rare blip of excitement on an entire world that specialized in the moribund and the dead.

The odors of a hospital are the same everywhere in Human Space, whether patients and staff ever set foot on Earth. A pungent antiseptic smell clung to every surface, variously overlaid with artificial pine or lemon or 'spring breeze' that failed to mask the stench. Like many people, I have an active dislike of hospitals. My heart hammered in my chest as I breathed in those smells, and as soon as the gleeful circle of physicians left my bedside I accessed the local equivalent of the globalink to learn what I had to do to get out.

I stayed the rest of that first day and the morning of the next, long enough to get over the shock of being alive and to file the paperwork to let the hospital disavow any responsibility for me. By noon I removed the monitoring patches, changed into my own clothes, and left the smell of cleaning solvents behind. The staffer who signed me out gave me a chit that would get me passage back to Earth; all I had to do was present it to the Terran Consul General. That was the catch; Hesnarj wasn't a human world. The Consul covered forty planets in this region of space and his next visit was five months away.

Beggars and panhandlers don't do well on a mausoleum world; the bereaved rarely notice them, and the zealots have no time for them. I needed to find a job if I expected to keep body and soul together until the next Earth-bound ship arrived. That would have been the mature, responsible course. Instead, I set off to get stinking drunk.

I found a bar without difficulty, guided by the yeasty smell of homebrewed beer. It looked like it had stood there for centuries, and maybe it had. Like almost everything in the world's mourning cities its builders had worked hard to produce a structure both bland and dull so as to avoid offending any particular culture's taste. The height of Hesnarj architecture consisted of stacking slabs of flat, gray basalt, one atop the other, bonding the edges at a molecular level, and hollowing out the interior for rooms as needed. The building I'd found, more of a lounge than a bar, had a polyglot sign out front indicating it served double duty as an eatery during the mornings and early afternoons. Not that I cared; a quick meal wasn't among my plans.

I wandered in and settled onto a bench gracing one side of a stone counter. It was second afternoon of the Hesnarj fifty-seven hour day and the place was packed with mourners, the soon-to-be-interred, thanatists, and a few of the local residents who had decided to draw out lunch and start their drinking early. The air held the faintest of traces of morbidity blossoms, a pleasant mix of vanilla and jasmine that most found restful. The room buzzed with dozens of conversations, a comforting murmur that dulled the senses. It looked like an excellent place to get quietly soused and wallow for a while in anonymous self-pity. Alas, anonymity was never an option. My face had been all over the planetary newsfeed, the *Kubla Khan*'s blessed survivor.

I no sooner sat down than a trio of Clarkesons appeared at my elbow. They had raspberry hair and fishbelly complexions, and grinned at me like hillbilly lottery winners.

"We buy drink," one of them said in the Traveler pidgin which I had yet to master. "Drink for lucky man."

I shrugged and let them. My limited cash would last that much longer if someone else was willing to pay to get me drunk. Others came up to me. Some just wanted to touch me, rub off some luck; most seemed to feel that buying me a drink ensured them a share of my good fortune. It wasn't until my third drink that I started telling them about the smartship, the explosion, and being marooned. I poured out my heart, pausing only to sob and drink, then wailed some more. It being a mourning city, almost everyone around me had his own story of sorrow to tell. We took turns, around and around, and the drinks kept flowing.

At some point I excused myself and managed to stand. Local midnight had come and gone, and except for my personal group of co-mourners the place had emptied out. I staggered off in search of the establishment's facilities, following the floor arrows to a clearly marked door. On the other side I relieved myself at what I hoped was the appropriate receptacle and turned to retrace my steps, passing someone else who had just entered. As I reached for the door, that same someone pulled a sack over my head. Hands spun me violently around and it was all I could do not to puke. My assailant shoved me. I toppled backwards, struck my head against something harder than my skull, and the world went away.

I regained consciousness, courtesy of a bucket of water the lounge's owner threw into my face. He was my first sight as I sputtered awake, a gangly, bright yellow humanoid wearing a bartender's apron. I sat up, felt the bathroom spin, and slumped back in my puddle. I took stock of my situation while I waited for my vertigo to recede. The cloth sack that had blinded me was gone. So were my shoes, my identification, my travel chit, and all my money.

"I've been robbed," I said, voicing the obvious.

My awakener made a noncommittal grunt and hauled me to my feet. The bathroom cooperated by not spinning, and I followed him out into the main room and back to the bar. The walls and ceiling had brightened to illuminate the room. Only three other customers remained. The ceiling chron showed early first morning. I'd been unconscious for hours. I sat on the bench and rubbed my head, wondering if I had a concussion or just a vicious hangover. The lounge owner puttered behind the counter and set a mug of fizzing blue gel in front of me.

"Drink," he said. "For head. Drink."

I complied. After the first sip I felt better.

"Thanks, um. . ."

"Rarst," he said, slapping one lemony hand against his chest and nodding. "No charge." Then he turned away, ladled something into a bowl and popped it into a waver.

The drunken fog began to clear from my brain, chased by throbs of pain. I was in even worse straits than before, having gone from little to nothing in the course of a mugging. And I still needed a job.

"Thanks, Rarst," I said, and straightened up on the bench. "I appreciate your kindness. I, uh, don't suppose you're hiring?"

He turned back around.

"What can do?" Rarst appraised me from the other side of the counter. His jaundiced expression reminded me of my paternal grandfather who used to bounce me on his knee; except my granddad didn't have slit pupils like a cat. Maybe Rarst felt a twinge of compassion because I'd been mugged in his bar. It didn't make him charitable, just open-minded. "Can sing?" he asked. "Make music?"

I had no marketable skills. I did my best to look pathetic. It wasn't hard.

Rarst scowled and any resemblance to a long-dead relative vanished. "I need entertainment. You figure talent by first evening, I give meals and room in back. You entertain, we got deal, okay?" He took a bowl of paella out of the waver and shoved it in front of me, and then waddled off to tend his real customers, leaving me to 'figure' my talent.

I began reviewing things I'd learned in my two years of college. The lounge served a dozen alien races, with nary a human among them. I needed something with broad appeal. My college major didn't lend itself to performance. It seemed very unlikely that leading a discussion comparing and contrasting various religious practices would qualify as entertainment in the current venue.

Then I remembered a psych course from the Fall semester and the week we'd spent discussing hypnosis. I'd been fascinated, even written my final paper on the subject of multimodal induction techniques. During finals week I had hypnotized my roommate, and planted suggestions that improved his study habits and test scores. For the first time since waking up in the hospital I felt something like optimism. I picked up my spoon and amid mouthfuls of paella began formulating my act.

*   *   *

". . . and when I snap my fingers you'll awaken, with no conscious memory of anything I've said. But what I've told you remains true; the number eight no longer exists in any form."

I snapped my fingers and the half-ton saurian opened its eyes and straightened up on its reinforced stool. We were alone on the lounge's makeshift stage and the attention of the entire audience, all thirty-seven of them, throbbed with a heartbeat of its own. Time hung suspended in the silence. None of them had ever seen a hypnotist before. I smiled and winked at them. Then I returned my attention to the saurian.

"Your people are responsible for the design and construction of most of the cenotaphs here on Hesnarj; I'm sure that requires tremendous engineering knowledge and mathematical acumen. I wonder if you'd mind giving us a demonstration. What's one plus one?"

The saurian glared at me. "Two," it snorted.

"Two plus two?"

"Four."

"Four plus four?"

It froze, tiny eyes squinching in calculation. "Whah?"

"Four plus four?" I repeated.

The saurian squirmed; its spinal plates quivered. It whuffed out acrid air from a trio of nostrils. It rumbled deep counterpoint in two of its stomachs. Finally, with a look of total stupefaction it muttered, "Can't be done!"

The audience howled with laughter and pounded the tables in approval. I'd found my talent.

By the end of the week I was doing two shows a night. I spent the mornings developing new material for my routines, and the rest of the day trying to figure out what to do with my life. Comparative religion had lost its allure, and more than anything else I found myself wishing I could talk to great aunt Fiona about it. I needed someone to discuss my future with, to find some perspective and direction, maybe even real purpose. I couldn't even visit my aunt's tomb; it was half a world away on another continent.

News of my act spread and the lounge filled with the motley visitors and bored residents of a world dedicated to housing the dead. Rarst raised his prices, put in a real stage, and even began paying me. The success was a welcome distraction and I threw myself into the work. My technique improved, as did my fluency in Traveler. My patter grew polished and I began mastering an assortment of gestures and body language from other worlds. More importantly, I quickly learned that some alien races could not be readily hypnotized, and that others were almost criminally suggestible. I started saving money toward a ticket to visit the southern continent and my aunt's final resting place.

Two months into my run, during the second show of the night, I met Kwarum. He was 'pebbly,' that's the only way I can describe him. Imagine dipping someone in glue and then rolling him around in a gravel bed, with each and every grain polished river smooth. I'd never seen his kind before, but that night there'd been two of them in the audience. One had volunteered, along with a rare human and a Clarkson.

The show proceeded smoothly; the audience laughed and applauded in all the right spots. Along with my usual induced forgetfulness, invisible objects, and dog-barking, I had decided to end that night with something new. A minor scandal had circulated through the city in the last few days; a prominent embalmer had mixed up two clients of vastly different biologies and the resulting stench had necessitated the temporary evacuation of several city blocks. My three volunteers sat entranced upon the stage, calmly discussing the event. When I was convinced that each was familiar with the details I instructed them to believe they were actually the individuals in question. In an instant I had two offended corpses loudly complaining with a pompous and ineffectively defensive embalmer, none of whom was actually the correct race for the part he played. The audience ate it up, and even somber Rarst cracked a smile.

After the show the lounge emptied quickly. I left the stage and headed toward my back room to plan the next day's shows. The other pebbly alien, the one from the audience, stopped me along the way.

"At the end of your performance," she said, "would you explain what you did to my kinsman, please?" She spoke crisply, clipping each word.

I looked her over. She hadn't done anything overtly threatening, but I had an uncomfortable feeling. People routinely approached me with questions after a show, curious and delighted. This woman didn't look happy.

"I told him he was Karsten of Belscape, the former plenipotentiary of the far Arcturan colony."

"This individual you named, he is deceased?" asked the alien.

"That's safe to assume, or they wouldn't have embalmed him." I said it with a smile, hoping she'd catch the joke. She was far too serious.

"You admit it," she said. "You named the deceased and made my kinsman invoke him. There is no higher blasphemy."

"Blasphemy? Hold on, I think there's been a misunderstanding. All I'm guilty of is a little harmless entertainment."

Her hands closed around my arm then, with a grip as unyielding as stone. She leaned in and I could smell her breath, all garlic and shellfish. The pebbly skin of her forehead gleamed with perspiration.

"No misunderstanding. You instructed my kin to invoke another being, one not of our kind. You named the being. You knew him to be dead. You told my kinsman to become a deceased alien. Do you deny any of this?"

"No, but . . . it was all just a hypnotic suggestion. A bit of pretend. . ."

The pebbly nodded to herself. "You admit to blasphemy. There can be no question of your guilt. When I am through, none will find your remains nor speak your name."

Just like that, she lifted me off my feet and carried me out of the lounge. It happened so swiftly, I was through the door before I thought to shout. Outside, the street was deserted. The alien hustled me in the direction of a parked groundcar. A second pebbly stepped around it as we came closer. I recognized him, my volunteer from the show. He raised a hand to stop the woman, pointed at me with his little finger, and said, "Let him go."

"Step aside," said my captor. "Your own blasphemy is only slightly less egregious than his. Were we not the only Svenkali on Hesnarj, I would convene a tribunal to denounce you as well."

"Perhaps," said the new arrival, "but as there are only we two, a tribunal resulting in my early death is unlikely. Now, let him go!"

I winced as her grip tightened instead.

"You may have forsaken our laws and ways, Kwarum, but I have not. The blasphemer must die." The pebbly woman brought her free hand to my throat. I caught a glimpse of something faceted and shiny clutched between her fingers.

"I can't allow you to kill him," said Kwarum. His voice deepened with an imperative tone. "Remember and bring forth Halloveshot Funedap Swlekti."

My captor froze. A shudder rippled through her. I felt her fingers loosen and then fall away. She swept a hand across her forehead and then down the left side of her face. Her posture shifted, and when she spoke her voice had changed.

"Kwarum?"

"Hello, Hallo. I'm pleased to see you again. Thank you for coming."

The woman snorted with laughter. "As if any of us never arrived once invoked. But why invoke me in another host? Why not simply name me yourself? This is hardly a formal ceremony."

"My apologies; I needed to suppress Shastma from her own zeal."

Kwarum gestured to me, and continued. "Yours was the first name that came to mind."

"I'm honored and flattered. It's been many years since I've walked and not just watched. And this is a world I've never seen before."

Kwarum smiled. "Then I encourage you to explore, while you remain. All I ask is that you take your host far from here, before Shastma can reassert herself."

My abductor looked at me and then nodded back at Kwarum. "You have always been fastidious about loose ends. I respected that in all our conversations."

She turned abruptly, and walked away. I watched her, mouth agape, until she rounded a street corner and was lost to view. I turned back to the remaining pebbly.

"What just happened? Did she really intend to kill me?"

"Oh yes, which is why I intervened."

"And now you're just going to let her walk away?"

"No, the one walking away is Hallo. It was Shastma who sat in the audience earlier, but Hallo never saw your show, and so her assessment is based on her host's memory of the episode rather than an emotional reaction."

"Reaction?" I said. "Reaction to what?"

"Your inducement that I invoke a non-Svenkali."

"What are you talking about?"

"Plenipotentiary Karsten. You told me to become him, and you spoke his name. A full name and title, with sufficient additional detail to identify him as unique in all the universe. That was all I needed to pull him back."

"What, are you saying just because I said his name that you somehow channeled the real Karsten? That's impossible."

He smiled again. "Impossible? Perhaps. But that is the way of the Svenkali. When Shastma held the peeler to your throat, it was my use of Hallo's full name that pushed her away and spared you."

"And this Hallo person you keep talking about?"

"A teacher from my youth," he said, and gazed off in the direction the other pebbly had gone. "And an old friend. I hadn't realized how long it's been since we spoke."

"Why so long?" I said, "and why did you finally meet her on this world of all places?"

"Hallo came at the invocation of her name, as she always has, since her death more than thirty thousand years ago."

I must have looked as stupefied as a saurian engineer who can't recall the numeral eight. Kwarum chuckled and put an arm around my shoulders, guiding me into the groundcar.

"Come," he said, "let us find a conversation house with refreshment and long hours. I have an idea I wish to discuss with you. . ."

"All sentience survives beyond physical death, forming a vast energy field of memory and personality." Kwarum's fingers danced in the air as he spoke, tracing patterns I couldn't follow. "Some races, such as the Svenkali, can tap that it, and enflesh individuals who have long since left corporeal life behind. My people are so in tune with this field that we need only hear the unique name of a forebear to automatically bring her forth. Do you understand?"

We sat on opposite sides of a basalt table in a curved alcove of a local conversation house. The bereaved need places where they can sit and talk, recounting their experiences of the deceased. Imagine a coffeeshop that specializes in wakes and you're pretty close.

A pig-sized robot scuttled up to our table. It deposited cups of the house specialty, a warm, protein broth with a wicked kick to it, a cross between chicken soup and vodka. I swallowed half my cup at a single toss; I had the feeling I'd need it.

"You're talking about ghosts," I said. "Spirits. Like that?"

"No, merely what has gone before. We coexist with our ancestors, learning from them, benefiting from their insights."

I laughed; blame it on the chicken soup. "We've got people who claim to speak to the dead. Most are frauds, preying on grieving relatives." I finished the rest of my drink. "You're saying you can channel any member of your race who ever existed?"

He nodded. "We are a long lived people, and we have kept meticulous genealogies from our earliest recorded history. I know the complete and unique names of several million Svenkali, and I could call upon any of them from memory in an instant."

I set my cup down. It didn't seem possible, the ability to conjure up any ancestor at will.

"What does this have to do with my act? Why did Shastma accuse me of blasphemy?"

"The invocation of another is an integral part of our belief system. It assures us immortality. So long as another can speak our names, we know we will continue to live on in the universe. But my people believe this gift is reserved for the Svenkali. From infancy we are taught to ignore the rhythms of alien names. No other race shares our facility to blend so readily with those who have gone before us. Thus, to invoke one who is not of our kind constitutes an abomination."

"So when I told you you were Karsten of Belscape—"

"I became Karsten of Belscape, or I would have if the fellow's personality had been stronger. He found the invocation so disorienting and confusing that he receded into the blending. Normally both share the body, or when a third person forces the invocation, as I did with Shastma, the host gives way."

"I'm terribly sorry," I said. "If I had known I would never have taken my act in that direction."

"You have no need to apologize; few Terrans have met Svenkali or know of our gifts. Besides, the experience inspired me. Perhaps I required such a radical event to jar me free of traditional patterns of thought."

"I'm afraid I don't quite follow..."

"I have a proposal for you," he said. "You see, I am dying, dying the absolute death."

"Absolute death? But you just said that your people were immortal, after a fashion. Won't other Svenkali invoke you after you die?"

The corners of his mouth curled in a faint grin, though his eyes burned with a more somber emotion than I could label. "Alas, no. Among my own kind I am a criminal. My name has been struck from the genealogies, and any of my kin foolish enough to speak it after my death would likewise be outcast."

I couldn't stop myself, the question leaped from my lips. "What was your crime?"

He dropped his gaze and studied his cup of broth before replying. "Talking," he said, "to people like you. Telling them of the Svenkali gift. That was offensive enough for disapproval, but I didn't stop there. Those conversations fueled another desire, even more debased, and I gave into it. I invoked other races. I enfleshed the surviving sentience of alien beings."

He sighed and lifted his head. His eyes glistened with milky white tears. "I am near the end of a long life, but before I left the physical world I wanted to know the feel of a non-Svenkali mind, to host a consciousness that had never been host itself. It should have been the high point of my life, but my people did not regard it as such. Instead, they have decreed it to be the end of my existence."

I couldn't think what to say. How do you respond to being told an immortal alien is being denied immortality? I stared down into my cup, and waited.

"You are still young, even for your kind, and so you might not understand me. I feel cheated, Mr. Conroy, as simple as that. Every previous generation has lived on through others, and I shall not. Once my flesh has failed, no Svenkali will invoke me. All my life I have participated in the immortality of others, and now it is to be denied me. I thought I had reconciled myself to it, accepted it, until your show."

"My show?" I said.

He nodded. "The inspiration I spoke of, a revolutionary idea. What if members of other races invoked me? Think of the adventure! Not only would I achieve my promised immortality, I would blend again with beings who share experiences none of my kind has ever known."

"But who besides the Svenkali have the ability to invoke you?"

He paused and sighed. "Alas, none really, not to full mutual awareness. But I believe that if an alien were to speak my name, knew me as distinct from any other being who had ever lived, that would be enough to gather my energies. It would pull my essence from the field of sentience, and for a time let me live again. I would again perceive the physical world, existing for a time in the thoughts and senses of other beings, though they might be utterly unaware of me."

I stared at him. "Are you asking me to do this? To say your name some time after you're dead?"

"Not quite," he said, and the smile was back. "It would hardly be immortality if it lasted only till the end of your own days. But you could tell others, just a few, here and there, when you have them hypnotized. And you could instruct them to do likewise. You could tell them this tale. Along with my name, that would be sufficient to single me out among all who have been. And you could slip in a small suggestion, encourage them to pass the tale along to other generations. Do you see? I would continue to live, long beyond just your span."

"How can you even know this will work?" I asked.

He shrugged. "Faith, perhaps? I admit, this possibility of surviving occurred to me only hours ago. It might fail, but I have nothing to lose if it does, and immortality if it succeeds. Will you do this for me?"

"Why me? I don't know anyone. I'm not really even a hypnotist. In a few months I'll be back on Earth, back in school. I'm not the man you want."

"I believe otherwise. You are the individual best suited to my needs because you are someone who can use the only coin with which I have to pay. I know I am asking much, but I offer you what none but the Svenkali can."

"Coin?" I said. "What do you mean?"

He put his palms together, laced his fingers, and leaned forward. His expression was serious, even somber, but his eyes twinkled with inner merriment. "The facility exists within you. I can sense it, though it is weak. Your people could manage to do this, albeit only infrequently. All you lack is guidance. I could help you to invoke someone, only once and briefly. After some years you might be able to manage it again on your own. But one time at least, I can promise. A few minutes, blended with someone who has died. Is that sufficient payment for what I ask?"

I had to swallow several times before I could speak. "You could do that? Anyone at all?"

He nodded, eyes still smiling. "Anyone you can name as a unique individual. Payment in full and in advance, in exchange for your word to share my tale and have others do likewise and invoke me. This is the sole chance at immortality that remains to me. I only wish I could offer you more."

"You have a deal," I said. "How soon can you, um, provide payment."

His pebbly face relaxed and he sat back. "Immediately, if you wish. You need only place your hands in mine, and speak the name of your intended, distinguishing this individual from all others."

I reached across the table and grasped both of his hands. You might think I had a difficult time making my choice. With all of Earth history, all those famous personalities to choose from. I never gave a thought to any of that; my selection came to me without effort. I closed my eyes. Then I whispered her name, the woman whose adventures had shaped my childhood and brought me to this point. "Fiona Katherine St. Vincent Wyndmoor."

His fingers tightened on mine and a shudder ran up my spine. The idea of her filled my thoughts. I felt awash in memories, catching glimpses of a life that wasn't mine. I saw her laughing as she held an infant upside down by one foot, dipping him—dipping me!—in a lake like a young Achilles. There she was as a young woman, respectful, all in black at a family funeral. Then again, aged as I had last seen her, irreverent and proud as she recounted her tales of travel in my father's study a dozen years ago. Images from her life played out across my mind as a silken current coursed in my brain. I could almost feel neurons firing in patterns and streams that the human brain never experiences. I discovered a new kind of pain and realized I had done something suicidally foolish. An alien was manipulating my mind, poking around in my consciousness. What had I been thinking?

And then the memories fell away and she surrounded me, enveloped me. My great Aunt Fiona appeared in my head. I could sense her surprise, her wonderment, and then her joy. It was like she had never died; she was with me now, the adventure of her life not yet ended. I tried to recall all the things I'd always wanted to say to her, but came up blank.

"I'm sorry," I said at last.

"Hush, boy, you've nothing to feel sorry for."

"But you're dead."

I heard her laugh, the sound echoing softly in my mind. "I've had more of a life than any seven people I ever met put together." She paused and smiled. "Excepting maybe yourself."

"I don't understand."

"Nephew, look where you are. Recognize what you're doing. Books and lectures are fine things, wonderful things, but they're not the same as the people who inspired them. Your family never understood, but I always hoped you might, that of all of them, you just might make the leap.

"The leap?" I said. "The leap where?"

"Off Earth," she said, laughing, and I could have sworn I felt her hand ruffling my hair. "Away from home and safety, removed from the comfortable and familiar. And now you have. I can see it in you, you've left that parochial world and that provincial boy behind you. You've dared, deliberately or not, to embrace all that lies beyond."

"I hadn't thought of it that way."

She laughed again. "Says the young man talking to his dead aunt! But enough, tell me while we've time, tell me of the people you've been meeting and the things you've been doing."

And I did. I recounted all the shows I'd done in Rarst's lounge, all the aliens I'd met, everything I'd experienced since the day I left Earth.

We shared an eternity that lasted only minutes. I felt her start to fade, and I opened my eyes. Aunt Fiona gazed with me at the Svenkali sitting across the table. My mouth moved and we said "thank you, Kwarum," and then she was gone.

"Thank you, Kwarum," I repeated, unable to stop the flow of tears down my cheeks. "Thank you for doing this thing."

He released my hands, patted them gently. "There is no need," he said. "You did it yourself, I merely guided the way. If anything, I thank you, for immortality."

Seventeen years later...

Chapter One: Unexpected Beef of Serendipity

WHEN I WAS A LITTLE KID, I liked to pretend that every day I could wake up and begin a brand new adventure, limited only by my imagination and the tolerance of my family and friends. I'd open my eyes and declare to the world that I was an asteroid miner, a Zulu warrior, a pirate captain, an inventor. My parents rejoiced when I outgrew this phase; I'm sure I wore them out with my breakfast pronouncements of new identities, petulant demands for ore processors or Spanish doubloons, and insistence that the vegetables on my dinner plate were plutonium or a ploy of British colonials.

In hindsight, perhaps that phase only went dormant and wrapped itself in a chrysalis of my unconscious mind, emerging years later when the world expected me to engage in mature, adult behavior. My decade and a half as a stage hypnotist hardly qualified as a serious career path. Then one morning I'd woken up and decided to become a smuggler, stealing away with a fertile buffalo dog, a cute alien creature that looked like a breadbox-sized American bison and whose pups were worth ten million credits each. Not long after that I'd woken up in my current bit of making believe, playing along as if I knew what I was doing as a mega-billionaire and CEO of a corporation that reached beyond the solar system. It didn't feel real, but I couldn't treat it all as make believe either. Somehow the game had grown and thousands of people now depended on me for their livelihood and I found myself trying to do the corporate nine to five, because I couldn't think of how to walk away. I'd managed to surround myself with plenty of competent people who made sure my accidental financial empire didn't come crashing down around my head, but I couldn't convince them that I was only playing at being their CEO. I'd never had this problem as a kid. Back then, I could wake up and be someone new every morning. Nowadays, I kept waking up as the same guy.

Which is how I got into trouble. I wasn't supposed to be there, I'll stipulate to that up front, but my presence at the Claymont Bar and Bowl wasn't the problem. A couple times a week I had to blow off steam, leave the buffalitos behind and slip away incognito, perform a show at some lounge, hang out with some regular folks, or just bowl a few frames. And who could blame me? Nope, I blamed the trio of Arconi; they shouldn't have been

24

there either. They'd come in, towering above rest of the B&B's patrons, humans all, their heads turning back and forth as if looking for a lost companion who had come in ahead of them. Their pale, attenuated bodies, even paler, strangely tailored garments, and utter lack of bowling balls marked them as outsiders, Delaware bowling alleys not being among the traditional tourist spots for visiting aliens.

One of them noticed me, reached out spidery fingers to her male companions and directed their attention my way. I ducked my head, hoping that maybe they weren't sure it was me, but I knew I was fooling myself. Arconi are always sure. Doubt is an alien concept to them, literally. They have an annoying telepathic knack that lets them look you in the eye and know with utter certainty if you're telling them the truth. If they got to me before I could prepare myself, I was doomed. All they'd have to do was ask me my name.

Call me paranoid, but for the past four years I'd actively avoided even casual contact with any representative of this particular alien race. I was working on the assumption that any Arcon that might come looking for me had a longstanding agenda. Four years ago I'd done the unthinkable, smuggled a fertile buffalo dog from an Arconi world and gone on to break their monopoly throughout Human Space. Her pups had allowed me to start my company, Buffalogic, Inc., and propelled me into a life of power and luxury. I had no doubt that the Arconi government would like nothing more than to get their hands on me and, with their built-in truth detectors and simple, direct questions, wring a confession free.

I left my custom-made, ceramo bowling ball behind—the one painted to be a replica of Brunzibar, a mercantile worldlet where I'd once fallen in love—and made a beeline for the restroom. The Claymont B&B had been grandfathered, and lacked the full range of facilities more modern businesses now sported. I didn't know if the Arconi would appreciate the subtle distinction and politics that distinguished a men's room from a ladies' room, but anything that could give me a few more seconds might make a world of difference.

I shoved open the door to the ladies' room. To my relief, I found it empty. I rushed to the sink, splashed water on my face, and looked up at my reflection in the mirror. I ran a relaxation exercise through my head, but lost my train of thought as I heard knocking on the men's room next door.

"Mr. Conroy? We'd like to speak with you. Mr. Conroy?"

I sucked in a lungful of air, gripped the sink with both hands and steadied myself as best as I could. "Concentrate," I said to myself, "you're only going to get one shot at this." I looked myself in the eye and said the trigger I'd been renewing for years but had never had to use. "Obàtálá Butter Pecan," I said, and stumbled back. There was something seriously wrong with my equilibrium and I staggered around the tiny room, a public bathroom from the look of it, though the lack of a urinal seemed conspicuous. Someone knocked on the door, and then that someone opened it. I'm not sure what surprised me more, that the person standing there was a tall, pale alien, or that the sign on the outside of the door read 'women.'

"Mr. Conroy?" said the alien, a female if I'm any judge of bipedal mammals.

"I'm afraid not," I said, and moved to step past her. My dizziness had passed.

"A moment," she said, shoving a hand in my way, stopping me without actually touching me. She consulted a photo on a tiny screen on the bracelet of her other arm, then looked back at me. "Are you not Conroy, of Buffalogic, Inc.?"

I shook my head. "You've got the wrong guy. I'm Vladimir Valeeva."

"You are not the CEO of a company that leases and sells buffalitos?"

"Sorry, lady, I'm a professional bowler. Now, if you'll excuse me, I've got somewhere to be. I'm supposed to be meeting a representative from the Interplanetary Bowling Federation to discuss the upcoming tournament in Seroni. That's on Mars, you know?"

The alien female gave me a puzzled look, almost like she was disappointed, but she backed up and let me pass. That was a relief; I didn't need to be explaining to a rep from the IBF that I'd gotten into a tussle with a woman from another planet. As I walked through the bowling alley and out into the parking lot, I tried to remember why I was even there, but I couldn't. My mind was a complete blank.

And then, just as soon as I left the building, it wasn't any more. My trance broke, and the façade of Vladimir Valeeva, champion of the Georgian Peoples' Bowling League, fell away. I was Conroy again, CEO and gentleman hypnotist, but as far as the Arcon back in the Claymont B&B was concerned, the man she'd just met was named Vladimir. She'd seen the truth of it in my mind.

The following day I took an hour and used a secure globalink to update the bogus records I'd established for a ghost employee whose company photo matched my own. I didn't know if last night's Arcon would follow up, but I wanted to be sure that Vladimir's file would withstand close scrutiny.

With that chore out of the way, I had my assistant Jeanie clear the rest of my morning and took a cab from the Philadelphia office building of

Buffalogic, Inc. into the eternal rainfall of Newer Jersey. I had an early lunch appointment with an old friend freshly returned to Earth.

Some days schedules exist just to be broken. I had to phone ahead twice; once to let him know of an unavoidable delay, and a second time to say we were en route again. Both calls had only elicited a muted "hunh."

My cab got me there thirty minutes late, and I dashed through the downpour to the restaurant's front door. Reggie, my buffalo dog, had stayed dry, cradled inside my coat. Nonetheless, he barked plaintively as we entered the Golden Turtle Palace, as if to announce his presence to our host, the professional gambler known as Left-John Mocker.

The Palace doesn't usually allow animals, and the frown I received from the manager made it clear that he wasn't happy to have Reggie in his establishment, but he lacked the authority to do more than frown. Left-John Mocker owned a quarter share of the Palace. He'd won it in a high stakes poker game, beating out the original owner's sure thing of four Jacks with a straight flush that triggered a small brawl and put three people in the hospital.

Besides, Reggie wasn't an *animal*, not in either the normal sense, nor even in the currently popular genemod sense. Over the last couple of years, plenty of trendsetters had bought miniaturized versions of traditionally massive animals. Elephants, wildebeest, even yaks were all being walked around on leashes in upscale parks. But despite the genetic manipulation, these remained terrestrial critters. That wasn't the case with Reggie. Buffalo dogs are an alien life form, and though every other buffalito in Human Space showed up on some corporation's accounting books as a hugely expensive industrial tool or production expense, mine existed purely as a companion animal. Most buffalo dogs are pretty cute, but Reggie has true personality. He demonstrated it moments after we arrived, squirming out from under my coat and stampeding merrily through the restaurant. Under the baleful glare of the manager I followed the clattering of Reggie's tiny hooves toward the Mocker's private table in back.

I should make something clear. I'm a foodie, a gourmand at heart, and at stomach as well. Even during my years as a struggling hypnotist, any time the money gods smiled upon me I blew it all on exquisite meals. I crave both new and old tastes, the familiar served up in novel ways, or blended with the exotic to enhance both. Satisfying my palate has always been my weak spot.

Left-John Mocker's return to Earth had coincided with the hiring of a new chef at the Golden Turtle Palace, and my old friend had asked me to come by and provide my expert opinion of her new menu items. I had barely exchanged greetings and taken my seat before the first platter arrived. John served, spooning a sample of a chicken and vegetable mix onto my plate and then scooping a larger portion into a soup tureen at the other end of the table. Reggie had positioned himself there moments before, bounding from floor to chair to tabletop, skidding on a cloth napkin before finally coming to rest.

"This is excellent," I said after tasting several bites. "What is it?"

"How about you tell me what's in it, and I tell you the name we're putting on the menu."

"You're on. Hmm, well, obviously there's chicken and eggplant. No, wait, make that two kinds of eggplant. Also broccoli, vanilla, and . . . at least three kinds of peppers."

"She calls it 'Ancestral Chicken Reclining.' So, you like it?"

I took another bite. "Absolutely. You've always had the best Chinese food in Newer Jersey, but you've really raised the bar this time."

"Good. I'm glad you approve."

John's voice had been its typical level neutral tone, and a quick glance at his face gave no clue if he was being sincere or sarcastic. Even at his happiest, I've rarely known the man to crack a smile. Being able to keep your emotions off your face has to be an important skill for any gambler, particularly one rated and ranked by the Probability Guild. Part of it too may just be cultural. The Mocker is a full-blooded Comanche, from his pierced ears to his ponytail, and he has stoicism down to an art.

So, not knowing how he really felt, I just shrugged. "Reggie appears to like it too."

In fact, my buffalo dog had not only devoured the full contents of his bowl, he'd licked it clean and taken a few bites out of the bowl itself before abandoning it. This wasn't too unusual; buffalo dogs can eat literally anything. Reggie shoved aside his bowl and advanced on the unguarded platter itself.

"Good lord, don't you ever feed your pet, Conroy?"

"It's because I already fed him that he's so hungry," I said. "There was an accident on the highway. A fellow in an old style SUV got crunched up pretty bad just a couple car lengths in front of my cab. He was trapped in the vehicle, not to mention cut up and sliding into shock."

"What'd you do?"

"I coaxed Reggie into eating his way through the parts that had the guy pinned. We had him out just as the paramedics arrived. They said if he'd have been left there a minute longer he would have been dead." I reached out and gave the buffalo dog's neck a reassuring scritch. His eyes smiled warmly at me, but he didn't slow his efforts with the platter. "Prior to coming here

Reggie ate several pounds of metal and plastic."

"Which should have left him sated, not hungry for more," said Left-John Mocker.

"Just the opposite, actually. A free-feeding buffalito can lightly graze continuously without actually eating all that much. Think of it as constant snacking. But when you push one to consume large amounts in short intervals, its appetite actually takes a jump to the next plateau of satiety. That's where Reggie is now, but don't worry, he'll fill up soon."

"But. . ." John's voice trailed off for a moment. He stared at Reggie and then returned his gaze to me. "What would happen if we keep feeding him anyway?"

I grabbed Reggie by the scruff of his neck and pulled him away from the platter for just a moment, forcing him to take a brief break. "Believe me, you don't want to see that. It would bump him up to the next higher level and then you'd have a *really* hungry buffalo dog on your hands."

"What's the upper limit?"

Before I could answer, a server arrived with another entree and fresh plates. It was some kind of beef dish, and the Mocker placed a sample in front of me, took some for himself, and then moved the platter to the opposite end of the table from Reggie.

"What's this one called?" I said, as I made a mental list of the ingredients.

"'Unexpected Beef of Serendipity.' So, you didn't answer. What's the upper limit?"

I sampled the dish. Chewy, with a rich beefy flavor, a subtle marinade, and a faint, minty undertaste. "Mmm, tasty—but, who thinks up the menu names?"

"It's a translation thing," the Mocker replied curtly. "Look if you don't want to answer-"

"There isn't one, so far as I know."

"Isn't what, an upper limit?"

I nodded again, swallowed, and took a sip of water. "That's what my experts tell me. Theoretically the increases are geometric, and after you bump it up a couple times the buffalo dog is ravenous and will eat nonstop for hours, like a kind of omnivorous frenzy. It's a disaster waiting to happen, and about the only drawback the creatures have."

John had taken another mouthful of beef while I explained. He paused in mid-chew, which I took to mean he was dubious.

"Don't worry," I said, "we take precautions. Every buffalo dog we lease comes with a handler to keep the snacking from becoming something dangerous."

Lawrence M. Schoen

"That's not what I was thinking about. Just the opposite in fact. I'm surprised you haven't pushed it further." He put his fork down and reached out to brush his fingers through Reggie's fur. "Have you considered what you might be missing out on?"

"Missing out? John, it wouldn't take much encouragement to get Reggie to eat everything in your kitchen and then start in on the walls. I really don't think we're missing out."

"I didn't mean here and now. I was just thinking of the ecological implications. Imagine what a ramped up buffalo dog could do to a landfill site."

That stopped me. I put my chopsticks down and would have replied but the sound of profound flatulence interrupted me. Left-John and I both turned to the source, which unfortunately was my buffalo dog. That's the other thing about these amazing creatures; not only can they eat anything, they somehow convert it all into oxygen, which they fart in great quantity. It's also why I never take Reggie into the smoking section of restaurants.

Reggie didn't seem to care that he had become the center of attention. He'd worked his way around the table and pressed his face firmly into the platter of 'Unexpected Beef of Serendipity.' He lapped up every last bit, taking a bite or two out of the platter as he finished the food. "I've never thought about it before, but you might be on to something," I said.

Left-John rolled his eyes at me. "I was joking. Reggie isn't going to be able to devour a landfill site, I don't care how hungry he is."

"Maybe not," I said, but I glanced over at Reggie and filed the idea away. Several more dishes were brought out for me to sample, to a grand total of eight. Reggie's appetite had calmed down, and he contented himself with licking the shards of his platter clean while I gave John feedback on his chef's creations.

When we were done, Reggie and I dashed through the rain again into another cab. I gave the driver directions to the company headquarters in Philadelphia and then made a quick phone call to my assistant, Jeanie. I knew that within minutes of hanging up she'd have the wheels of industry spinning at Buffalogic, Inc. I leaned back in the cab, and closed my eyes, spinning a few wheels of my own as I thought about the possibilities that hadn't existed two hours before. Reggie curled up in my lap, pawed at my knee a couple of times, and went to sleep.

Jeanie met me at the elevator with a corundum chew stick for Reggie, and a stack of message slips for me. Oh, the joys of being a corporate CEO.

She followed me from the foyer, darting ahead past her desk, and blocked me from opening the door to my office. "Dr. Penrose is in there, sir."

That stopped me. "Already?"

"Yes, sir. And she seems very ... excited."

"More excited than usual?"

"Oh yes, sir. Very very excited."

"Lisa Penrose?"

Jeanie shook her head. "No, sir, I think it was Eliza Penrose."

"But she never ... well, all right. Hold my calls."

I opened the door slowly, sticking Reggie out in front of me with both hands, my arms fully extended. I wanted him to be the first thing Eliza Penrose saw. With luck, the sight might distract her, at least a little bit. Any edge is worth having when you're going face to face with someone smarter than you.

Let me say for the record that the only reason my company exists at all, not to mention thrives, is because of Dr. Elizabeth Penrose. Lawyer, psychologist, biologist, financier, and a fair field surgeon, not a day passed that I didn't thank whatever lucky star or guardian angel pushed us into one another's path. Even after five years as the sole Terran provider of buffalo dogs in Human Space, I still saw myself defined by my former livelihood. I'd been a professional hypnotist, an entertainer, and not a captain of industry. I'd learned to fake it, but with Elizabeth there I'd never had to do it for real. She made sure I didn't shoot myself in the foot, bankrupt the corporation, or cost our thousands of employees their own jobs. Given all her skills and assets, and her patience in putting up with my inexperience and ignorance, how could I not put up with her *minor* personality quirk?

That quirk was the reason Dr. Penrose could possess so many diverse skills and excel at them all. The short explanation was that she cheated. The more elaborate answer had to do with her being a terribly brilliant woman made even more effective thanks to a dissociative identity disorder. Prior to coming to work for me, she'd never shown more than a single personality to any employer. That changed when Elizabeth helped me start Buffalogic, Inc. Except, there really wasn't an *Elizabeth* Penrose at all. Each of her distinct personalities has her own name, her own style, her own likes and dislikes. Elizabeth existed just to keep things simple for the payroll department.

"Reggie!" Eliza cooed as I stepped into my office. She'd been standing by my desk sorting through a stack of report folders but immediately clomped across the room toward us on ridiculously heeled shoes. Reggie yipped, and squirmed to be put down. As soon as I obliged him, he scurried over toward Eliza Penrose, leaping into her waiting arms.

"How's my boy doing? How's my pretty boy?" She tugged on the chew toy that he still held, and they briefly engaged in mock battle. I used the opportunity to cross to my desk, settle in to the big chair, and prepare myself for the unbridled enthusiasm that I'd come to expect from the Eliza personality.

When hugs and scritches and cutsie talk had gone on long enough I cleared my throat and smiled up at her. "Do you have some preliminary numbers?" I said. We'd hit traffic coming back from Jersey, but even so it'd been less than two hours since I'd phoned.

"Preliminary, yes, but compelling all the same, Mr. Conroy." She clomped over to the corner and placed Reggie in his daybed. He made his trademark pouty expression—quite a trick with a tiny bison muzzle—and curled up to work on his chew toy. Eliza clomped back and stood in front of my desk. "It's elegant and brilliant, sir." She loomed over me from the front edge of the desk, radiating eagerness. Eliza always looms, it's the physical characteristic that sets her off from all her other personalities.

Objectively, Elizabeth is just over a meter and a half tall. She's a stunningly attractive and lithe woman in her late twenties, with a family tree that's half Japanese and half Scots/Irish. In fact, Elizabeth is so graceful and so small, that when she's quiet it's easy to forget she's in the room at all. Except when she's Eliza. Eliza is sixteen and has issues with being short. Eliza's shoes put the 'high' in high heels. Which would only go so far in and of themselves, but she has a real thing about her shoes; it's her Achilles heel, if you'll pardon the pun. Her high-heeled shoes are actually high heeled platform shoes. Despite the clomping, with her fluid grace she makes them work. Anyone else would look like a short girl walking around on stilts.

Of all the individuals that make up Dr. Elizabeth Penrose, only Eliza can loom over my desk. I'd only seen her do it a few times, mainly because she almost never comes to see me. She's the shyest of the Penrose personalities, and I still make her nervous somehow. She's a systems biologist and rarely leaves her lab, allowing her sister personalities to handle the legal and business ends of things when it's their turn to be in control. It would have taken something truly important to rouse her from her labs, rather than let one of the others bring me the initial projections.

"What's elegant and brilliant?"

"The solution to the waste problem." She beamed. I mean it, she absolutely glowed. I could have gotten a tan if I sat there long enough, that's how intense her presence felt, no slightest trace of shyness in her manner. Like all the Penrose identities, Eliza was brilliant. The same cannot be said of me. I had no idea what she meant so I nodded, and waited. She kept beaming. I made that vague circular gesture with one hand and she snapped back on track.

"The base idea was sound, so I extrapolated it out and then did some research on the globalink. We can do some demonstrations and pilot studies, but the big one is Mexico. That's where you should really start once we've worked out any kinks or bugs."

"Mexico? You want to take buffalo dogs to Mexico?"

She glanced down at one of her reports and read. "Mexico has a huge industrial waste problem. Massive. More industrial waste per capita than any other nation, while at the same time having one of the lowest levels of waste reclamation of any industrialized nation."

"Okay, I got that, they have loads of industrial waste. So?"

"The buffalo dogs can eat it. They can eat anything."

"Let me look at some numbers. How much waste are we talking about?"

"500,000 tons," she said.

I whistled. "That much in a year?"

"A day. 500,000 tons each and every day."

I tried to picture that much garbage, day in and day out. "That's insane," I said.

Eliza's head bobbed up and down at a frantic pace. "I agree completely. But there are complex historic and economic reasons that have led to—"

"No, no, I'm not talking about Mexico's waste problem," I said, interrupting her in mid-explanation. "I mean, yes, that's insane too, but I was referring to your suggestion we start there. There's no way a buffalo dog could eat that much."

"Not one buffalo dog, a couple dozen. That was the number you suggested on the phone."

"Well, yes, I did, but that's still not feasible. Do you have any idea how long it would take twenty-four buffalo dogs to devour that much raw material?"

"Just under eighteen months," she said. "Lisa ran the numbers."

I frowned as I shook my head. "That doesn't sound right." Even keeping in mind the magnitude jumps in hunger and consumption that I'd told the Mocker about, that kind of consumption would require years. But Eliza said Lisa had run the numbers, and Lisa was another of Elizabeth Penrose's personalities. She'd also been the first one I'd met, the reason any of them worked for me. As Lisa, she held doctoral degrees in behavioral psychology and xenoethology; she ranked as the greatest human expert on the nature and behavior of buffalo dogs. If she said it could be done, it probably could. Even so, the time frame seemed ludicrous and I said as much to Eliza.

"That's because you've never had them eat nonstop before. You know the theory, but you've never tried to apply it."

"We've had plenty of jobs where they've eaten their fill, eaten for days at a time."

"Sure, but Lisa says they always stop after no more than two weeks. Even last summer when they were eating through that collapsed mine. Their handlers never let one keep going."

"So?"

Her lower lip started to quiver and the enthusiasm drained from her face. She blinked rapidly. "So... I..." And she left. Just like that, she bolted, not from my office but from her own head. Her eyes rolled up showing all white for a moment. Her body twitched, once, twice, and then relaxed. Sighing, she kicked off her shoes and began tying her hair up off her neck. When she spoke it was in a light Irish trill, which meant she had become Lisa, the xenoethologist.

"Sorry. Where did she leave off?"

"The feasibility of two dozen buffalitos getting the job done," I said. After five years of working with one facet or another of Elizabeth Penrose, I'd learned to hide my surprise when she traded identities.

"Right. Okay, here's what we know. The more a buffalo dog eats, the hungrier it gets. The hungrier it gets, the more it can eat. You've seen how voracious they get after just a couple days on a job. Well, that's nothing compared to the consumption curve you get if you let them go continuously for a month. And the projections for the second month are even more amazing. And the third, oh lord, after three months, according to my analysis they'll be eating faster than anything that size can move on land." She opened a report folder to a brightly colored graph showing power utilization curves that rose geometrically.

"Lisa, even if you're right, how do you plan to stop them once they're going that fast? I've seen a normal buffalito get ravenously hungry, and it's not something you want to get in the way of. That kind of starvation/gluttony cycle could end up with one eating its way down to the molten core of the planet."

She smiled and closed her folder. "Please, Mr. Conroy, there's no need to exaggerate. I admit there're some logistical concerns, but I think I can knock them out quickly. I'm running simulations now. But that's not Eliza's point."

"Oh? What is the point?"

She took a deep breath, and set the proposal in front of me on the desk. "She's young and idealistic and wants to do her part to make the world a better place. She wants big results, inspirational results, and that's why she's glommed on to Mexico instead of something closer to home that would yield a more modest success. She's feeling under-appreciated, Mr. Conroy, and under-utilized. This is her big chance to contribute. She wants to use the resources of this company to single-handedly end one of the greatest ecological hazards of the modern world. She knows she's idealistic, but on the other hand she's afraid you might be too cynical to really do anything worth doing."

"Do you believe that?"

"What I believe isn't the issue," said Lisa. "This isn't something that she's just cooked up in the last two hours. It's been building up for some time, and it's what Eliza believes."

"And yet, you're speaking for her."

"Only because she lost her nerve, but that doesn't invalidate her opinion."

"No," I said, "you're right. It doesn't." I took a few minutes to glance through her report. "Do you think I could talk to Eliza?"

Lisa shrugged. "I'll try to get her. Hold on."

And just like that she rolled up her eyes while a tremor ran up and down her body. A moment later she blushed and stared at her feet as she fumbled and climbed back into her shoes.

"Sorry," she murmured, having traded the accent away for a touch of her earlier enthusiasm.

"Don't worry about it." I couldn't think what else to say to put her at ease. I looked at the report again. "Mexico. This is a fascinating idea, but I don't think it's that simple, Eliza."

"Why not? I told you, it's elegant."

"It's also unrealistic. Mexico is one of the most repressive nations when it comes to the use of non-Terran technology. They don't legally recognize the existence of most of the sentient races we've met. I don't think they'll allow us to just walk in with a couple dozen alien creatures and stay for a year and a half. Not to mention, as twisted as this may sound, there are probably hundreds of thousands of people kept employed by the very waste problem you want us to eliminate. What will happen when they suddenly lose their jobs because the problem has vanished? And what happens to the government when all those people stop paying taxes because they're out of work? Elegance aside, I don't think the president of Mexico is going to go for your solution."

Her face reddened. Her lip started to quiver again. I thought she would bolt, but instead she shoved her lip out and challenged me. "You don't know that, for sure. You're just theorizing. You don't really know."

"No, I admit I don't."

"Well, can we go ask him?"

"Ask him? You want me to have Jeanie pick up the phone, get the president of Mexico on the line, and just ask him?"

She bit her lip, and although I couldn't see it because of the desk between us I had the impression she was shuffling her feet a bit with embarrassment, which considering her monster shoes would have been well worth seeing. "No, ... not on the phone. I had something else in mind."

I waited. Regardless of which instantiation of Elizabeth Penrose was speaking, I'd learned not to rush one.

"I was thinking we could invite him here."

"Invite the president of Mexico?"

"Yes. We could meet up with President Ortiz, and give him a small demonstration, a scaled down demonstration."

"How scaled down?"

"20,000 tons. I've already located a site that will suit our needs. We need to do some trial runs anyway, and this can be part of the trials. If we schedule it toward the back end we'll have all the kinks worked out and we can put on a good show for President Ortiz."

I thought about that. It could actually work. A proposal on paper could be ignored, argued against, beaten back by special interest groups, lobbyists, and political maneuvering. But if the president of Mexico saw the thing happen first hand...

"Okay," I said.

"Okay?"

"You convinced me. Draw up a schedule and have Lisa select our most experienced handlers. Start working up the necessary training techniques for them. Do you suppose you can begin by the end of next week? I mean, it's industrial waste, right? How hard can it be to figure out the best way to devour canisters and drums? Within six months we should be able to field a team of two dozen buffalitos ready for the worst Mexico has to offer."

"Sir? You don't currently have two dozen unallocated buffalo dogs."

"No, but we can work around that, pull them in off of other jobs a few at a time. Besides, two dozen aren't going to be enough."

"They're not?"

"If we're going to do this thing, I want us to do it right. That means preparing an initial work force of twenty-four buffalo dogs, and having a second fully trained team for back up or replacement if anything goes wrong."

Eliza didn't say anything. She stopped biting her lip and just stood there beaming for a moment. Then she scooped up her papers and rushed out the door on her impossible shoes.

Mexico. In six months I was going to take my alien inventory to Mexico and transform the world, and all because I'd visited a friend for lunch. I shook my head and began drafting the first of several inter-office memos warning some of the department heads to expect jumbled and confused events over the next few weeks as one manifestation or another of Elizabeth Penrose pursued this latest project. That was the extent of my competence as CEO; I could write a clear and concise memo. It made me consider how much simpler my life had been when my only concern was entertaining a lounge of people for one hour, three times a night.

Chapter Two: The Snowman of Pompeii

BEING THE BOSS MEANS you're the end of the line. Sure, you delegate, but eventually someone's got to make the important decisions. Since starting Buffalogic, Inc., I'd happily let Betsy handle that task. Betsy is that portion of Elizabeth Penrose with the legal training that keeps my company running smoothly. Except, Betsy wasn't around. Lisa and Eliza were taking up most of the time normally allocated to her, forcing me to try and run things for a change. I was woefully unprepared for the responsibility. Late night paperwork is not my idea of fun.

For the third day in a row I'd been bound to my desk, working a twenty-hour marathon of departmental reports, bureaucratic teleconferencing, and media interviews. All the naggingly bureaucratic things that Betsy normally shielded me from were now mine to handle. This in addition to an increase in requests from various Arcon government officials and thinly disguised Arconi-staffed agencies, all eager for a chance to look me in the eye and confirm that single act of smuggling that had broken their buffalo dog monopoly. My sources informed me that several background checks had been performed on champion bowler Vladimir Valeeva, and Arconi diners were showing up nightly at my favorite restaurants. The joke was on them though, as I'd been too busy to go out to eat for weeks.

We were three months into *Project: Coprophage*. Buffalitos had been used for some time to handle minor disposal issues, but never whole sites. We had unleashed something new. Four demonstrations of the waste management power of my buffalo dogs had come and gone without a hitch. My company had become the media darling of nearly every news outlet, vid distributor, and ecological group in the U.S. and beyond. What had begun as a pro bono effort, giving a little something back to the planet, had turned into a bidding war as governments and private corporations began requesting similar clean-ups of their respective sites.

There'd been only a single dissenting voice, a group of Earth-First style ecological fanatics who denounced the use of alien creatures to clean up our world. Calling themselves GAEA—the Green Aggression for Earth's Assurance—their members had picketed the second clean-up test, demanding all buffalo dogs be removed from Earth. At the third, several dozen had chained themselves to barrels and drums of effluvia, halting the proceedings until the police charged them with trespassing and carted them away. They'd detonated small explosive charges during the last test run, breaching half a dozen canisters of toxic solvents and making an even bigger mess for the buffalo dogs to clean up. Ultimately, it added to the event as the team lapped up every last drop in record time and then chowed down on the canisters themselves.

It didn't end there. Since the last demo, every day brought a tub of hate mail from Green Aggression. Many of the letters accused me of being an alien dupe or a self-loathing human. Others ranted on and on about keeping the Earth pure by eliminating all alien life from the planet. The postmarks came from all over the world, but a majority had originated in Mexico. Even I could appreciate the irony there. With its xenophobic policies, Mexico was the obvious place for Green Aggression to use as its home base. Per Betsy's instructions, a three-person detail from building security pored through the mail each day. They forwarded a summary to me for review.

I'd just finished reading the latest summary when the door of my office burst open and the scowling figure of Elizabeth Penrose stomped in. I let the report's pages slip from my fingers and reached into my desk drawer for an aspirin tab and slipped it under my tongue. I knew from past experience that I was about to have a headache, just as I knew without looking which of her personalities had control of her body at the moment. Only one of them ever came into my office without knocking. I expected she'd begin shouting before I could count to ten. I didn't get past two.

"Conroy! You miserable excuse for a human being, what megalomaniacal trip are you on now?"

"Hi, Elly," I said, "nice to see you too."

"Cut the crap, Conroy. Why are you wasting everyone's time on this industrial clean-up project? Good god, how much false acclaim do you need for that ego of yours anyway?"

I might not know how to run a corporate empire, but working as a stage hypnotist had taught me a thing or two about dealing with people, even multiple people in one body. I pushed back from my desk and stepped around it to stand in front of her. On a symbolic level it should have been the same as giving up any pretense of authority and meeting her as an equal. Under the right circumstances, it's a great way to remove the chip off someone's shoulder and cut through all the posturing.

"Elly, you know as well as I do that both Eliza and Lisa back this project one hundred percent. You and I have never gotten along, but are you going to start fighting internally now?"

"Don't you even pretend that you know a thing about my relationship with either Eliza or Lisa. You don't have a clue what goes on in my head."

I put up my hands in a gesture of mock surrender. "Are you just looking to argue with me, Elly, or is something really bothering you?"

"You're what's bothering me, Conroy. You and this whole stupid company."

It was all I could do not to roll my eyes. I got along with every other personality inside Elizabeth Penrose, but from my first meeting with Elly—six months after Betsy—we'd grated on each other, and it only worsened over time. "Can you narrow that down for me, Elly? Is there something specific?"

"Ever since we met you, you've monopolized our time."

"How do you mean?"

"Are you completely clueless? It's always about you! Lisa runs the training and research of the buffalo dogs. Betsy manages the day to day financial and corporate decisions, as well as charting the long range plan. And now you've put Eliza to work for you too, on your stupid waste disposal project. Well, I don't work for you, Conroy, and I resent that you've got the others working for you. We were fine before you came along. I don't want to be waking up in a lab or a boardroom or any other space in your building. I want a life of my own, one that you're not any part of."

"What do you want me to do, Elly? Fire Lisa? Give Betsy a golden parachute and send her on her way? Break Eliza's heart by ending what she sees as a simple opportunity to give something back to the world for a change? All that will do is to make each of them as unhappy as you claim to be. If you're unhappy, offer me a solution that works for all of you and I'll do it."

She scowled, and even seemed to come close to hissing at me. "You're so glib. You act like you have it all figured out. You're so wrapped up playing your little games, Conroy the CEO, Conroy the philanthropist. It's all a lie. You don't know anything. Not about us, not about how your own company runs, and most certainly not about me."

I sighed. "Elly, I'm not going to stand here and have you ramble and rant at me. Give me a workable solution and I'll back it. But coming in here to bitch and moan at me isn't going to accomplish anything. If you like, I'll discuss it with Bess for you, and maybe she'll have a suggestion."

"That bitch! She's almost as bad as you are. I can't do anything about her, but mark my words, I'll find a way to get out from under your thumb."

"You're not under my thumb. The only time I ever see you is when you storm in here to complain."

"We're all under your thumb. Do you think I'm blind?"

There's a time to talk and a time to just shut up, and I'd long since passed the shut up point. I walked back to my desk, sat down, and picked up the security summary I'd been reading, in effect dismissing Elly. I heard rather than saw Elly make one final grunt of exasperation and then stomp out of my office. I glanced up in time to see the door slam shut, wincing as the promised headache materialized. Reggie, snug and snoring in his daybed, had slept through it all.

Caffeine can only push a body so far, but I soldiered on. The latest report from the security team listed seven letters containing toxic substances that day. None had been deadly, but even the mildest could have put someone in the hospital for days. I'd reached the end of it, and when I read that four of the toxins had originated offworld, the irony finally got to me. I put my head down on the desk with every intention of leaving it there for only a minute. That was all it took. Between the dullness of paperwork, my own very real fatigue, and the emotional drain of being shouted at by Elly Penrose, I fell asleep at my desk.

I think I'm like most people when it comes to dreams. I'm too caught up in whatever is happening in them to have the presence of mind to realize that they are dreams. That wasn't the case this time. I *knew* I was dreaming. There was a phantasmagoric feeling to it, with a whirlwind kaleidoscope of images more overburdened with symbolism than Indonesian shadow puppetry. Emergency klaxons blared in my unconscious, alerting me that Toto and I were not in Kansas anymore, much less Jakarta. That feeling receded. I still knew I was dreaming, but the frenetic pace and the barrage of images fell away. I had a moment to catch my breath, and then, in a very different way, all hell broke loose and I was face to face with a snowman.

We were sitting across from one another in a cable car, one of those tiny trams suspended by thin wires that carry people up and down mountains. The only passengers in this tram were the snowman and me. The air had a kind of crispness, a nonsensical non-scent free of pollutants, deodorants, and artificial fragrances: just fresh air, a rarity on Earth. Out the windows on either side of the car I could see plenty of bright blue sky behind me. A mass of fluffy white clouds surrounded the mountain, obscuring its top from view as it rose before us. I was trying to figure out what mountain it might be when the snowman smacked me with its hat.

"Pay attention," said Frosty, though that probably wasn't its real name.

"What am I supposed to pay attention to?"

Its hat was a faded, silk topper, the kind that you could still see in old black and white art films. It plopped it back onto its head at a rakish angle, and began waving its hands at me. The movement struck me as ludicrous, the way the fragile twigs of its fingers flailed inarticulately from the sticks of its arms.

"You are running out of time," the snowman said, moving the five bits of coal that formed its mouth into a downward arc. Frosty was frowning at me. No, not at me, I realized, but at something behind me. I turned and looked. The sky behind us had gone grey, and the clouds had thickened and darkened. A low rumbling began, like thunder heard from far away, but deeper and with a plaintive edge to it. The sound intensified rapidly, until an explosion hit us with a force so loud I thought I'd been struck deaf even as my head rang with an unending roar. The tram shook from side to side on the wire that had looked too thin to me in the best of circumstances, which we'd clearly left far behind.

"What's happening?" I screamed over the din. "What's going on?"

The day turned to night; it sounds trite, but that's what happens when a volcano erupts. I couldn't breathe. Ash was everywhere. It filled our tram car. The ash clung to the snowman like paint, and for a moment all I could think of was the ludicrous image of a snowman in Hell.

"It doesn't have to be this way," said Frosty; the twin anthracite lumps of its eyes implored me. "You can prevent this. Let me help you."

I was burning up. The ash was hot, too hot. I should have been vaporized. Our little tram should have burst into flames and been consumed. The snowman should have been reduced to a puddle and a few lumps of coal and sticks, and those should have ignited too. But it was a dream. Instead of vaporizing, the snowman began beeping. Frosty looked surprised, and it plucked at its belly with its twiggy fingers but, lacking elbows, couldn't quite reach the spot. I leaned forward to help, brushing off ash, and then a layer of snow, to reveal a telephone console that was the source of the beeping. I pressed a button.

"Yes?" I said.

"Mr. Conroy, Dr. Penrose is here. I told her you were indisposed, but she says she needs to see you at once, and you said—"

"Jeanie? What are you doing inside this snowman?"

"Excuse me?"

"Oh, wait," I said, as the realization hit home. "I'm dreaming. Just a second."

"No, stop," said the snowman, but it was too late. Knowing it was a dream, and having a reason to leave it, was all my unconscious mind needed to let go of the cable car ride through this version of Pompeii. I opened my eyes and slapped at the console on my desk.

"Jeanie?" My face was wet. I sat up and dragged a hand across my cheek, wiping away the drool. I had a crick in my neck and a throbbing in my forehead. I needed some real sleep in a real bed.

"Are you all right, Mr. Conroy?" Jeanie's voice sounded as tired as I felt. I glanced at the time glowing on my desk and frowned. It was a bit past six o'clock in the morning.

"Jeanie, I thought we'd agreed you were going to take the morning off. What are you doing here?"

"I checked in with security from home. They told me you never left last night. I looked in on you when I got in and you were sleeping. I'm sorry to wake you, but—"

"That's okay, Jeanie, really. Send Dr. Penrose in, and then take some time off, okay? One of us should get some rest."

I sat up straight, laced my fingers and raised them as far above my head as I could, stretching and trying to wake up completely. I was just bringing my arms down when the door opened and Bess Penrose walked in. Crap. I'd been expecting Lisa, or maybe Eliza, but not Bess. But I should have known; Bess only came to see me at dawn.

I stood up and stepped to the window. Bess was already headed there, slow and steady, a thin white cane sweeping from side to side in front of her as she moved. She liked things just so, patterns of behavior that she could depend upon, even if she imposed them on reality. Dawn. The window. Similarly, I knew she wouldn't speak until I did. I didn't, so she just faced the window. I did the same, gazing out through the polarized glass at the Delaware River and the first glow of dawn. First Elly and now Bess? Bess showing up meant bad news, and coming on top of my recent, weird dream, I didn't know if I could handle her. Still, something had stirred her to come see me, and she wasn't going away until she said her piece, whatever it might be.

"Nice to see you, Penrose," I said. Bess didn't use her first name, nor any titles. "Are you here about Elly?"

Her shoulders relaxed a bit. Still facing the window she said, "Elly? No, I don't have time for her foolishness. We have a real problem, Conroy."

Which only made sense. Unless something was going horribly wrong, Bess Penrose simply did not surface. She preferred to let the other personalities manage their respective lives, and as none of them liked her and at least two of them were openly afraid of her, that suited everyone just fine. But she had an indispensable role; she was the troubleshooter, the problem solver. In the five years since I'd first met Lisa Penrose I'd had maybe four dawn encounters with Bess. She always spoke simply and quickly, never

43

employed subtlety or posturing, just brutally pragmatic; Bess was as amoral and effective as a surgeon's blade. All of the other personalities were brilliant, but from my initial meeting with her, Bess had revealed herself to be a genius. During that first encounter, I'd seen her cajole a hostile circuit court judge that she'd roused from his bed, confuse him, elicit a compromising admission, and then blackmail him with it, all inside of ten minutes. I've never met anyone with more raw cunning. She scared the crap out of me.

"When have we ever talked when there wasn't a problem?"

The corners of her mouth lifted and she turned slightly, still not facing me. "If I didn't know better, I might think you don't like me," she said, staring into the distance without blinking. Bess was eighty-three and had lost her sight to cataracts decades before her other personas had been born.

"What's the problem?"

"Ortiz."

"The president of Mexico? What about him? His representative was at the last test site, and I spoke by phone with the president myself the day before yesterday. Everything is moving into position. Lisa's narrowed it down to one of three sites, in either Veracruz, Durango, or Oaxaca. Ortiz seemed quite eager; he's going to be a hero for this."

"It's not going to happen," she said.

"Why not? What's changed?"

"Green Aggression for Earth's Assurance."

"The eco group? They're nothing. Harmless, just an inconvenience."

"They are far from harmless, Conroy. Two years ago they were harmless. Two months ago they were an inconvenience. But as a consequence of your project they've evolved into something more. Their actions have escalated from mere irksome destructions of property. People have been injured. Are you aware we had a bomb threat here yesterday?"

"What? When? Was anyone hurt?"

"No. There was no damage to people or property. This time."

"Thank God." I relaxed. "Okay, so we'll step up security here. But what does this have to do with Ortiz? He wants us to come to Mexico. I can't believe he'd let Green Aggression change his mind on this. Surely they don't have that much influence."

"Not directly, no. But they have influence with many of the other members of the Mexican government. And they are in Mexico while we are here." She paused and turned to face me. Her eyes locked onto mine, saw nothing, but held me all the same. The effect chilled me to my core. "Unless we act, and soon, any proposed clean-up at a Mexican site will be mysteriously postponed, again and again, until it is ultimately abandoned."

"Damn! Green Aggression is feeding Mexico's xenophobia. How do we combat that? "

"We need an ally in the president's government, someone who can back him up and deflect some of the political heat. As of this moment, Ortiz stands alone in support of our project."

"Then we're screwed," I said. "We've already tried to build political support in Mexico. Neither promises of campaign contributions nor discounted government contracts on buffalitos has done any good."

Bess turned away from me and back to the window. She pressed one cheek to the pane and exhaled, fogging the glass. With her index finger she drew a dollar sign. "Those in power don't believe your agenda could be altruistic."

"It's not *my* agenda. This whole thing is Eliza's idea."

She only shrugged her shoulders in reply. No help there. I sighed.

"I've tried contacting the alien embassies in Mexico City, but no one even returned my calls."

"They don't trust you." She turned from the window and locked her blind eyes on mine again. "You stole from the Arconi. They don't understand how, but they know you did it. This entire company is based on that theft. They're wary of you and won't risk their own fragile status in Mexico to come to your aid."

"I'm not talking about the Arconi," I said.

She shrugged. "It doesn't matter. No alien trusts you at this point."

"Then, like I said, we're screwed."

"Not necessarily. There are other means, if you're willing to employ them."

I swallowed. I could almost feel the room grow colder. "What kinds of 'other means'?"

The rising sun illuminated her face as she said three simple words. "Blackmail Senator Cortez."

"The Senate Majority leader? Bess, that's crazy. What are we supposed to do? Set him up with an underage, vegetarian dominatrix?"

"I am thinking of something less carnal and more intimate."

"More intimate?"

"He has a son—"

"You want to set up his son with the vegetarian?"

She shook her head impatiently. "The son has a problem. He gambles. Poorly."

"How do you know this?"

Bess inclined her head slightly and gave me a faint smile. "Sources," she said, and paused before going on. "The son is a fool and a grave disappointment to his father. The senator provides a generous allowance but this son, Alejandro, has a fondness for no-limit games."

"Sounds like every father's dream."

Bess continued. "He likes to bluff, to bet extravagant amounts, intimidating his opponents and forcing them out of the game. Your friend called his bluff."

"My friend?" There could have only been one friend she was talking about. "The Mocker?"

"Yes. And brash Alejandro lacked sufficient funds to cover his bet." She smiled, and I shivered.

"And?"

"He gave your friend a marker for the amount. In so doing, he has also given us the opening we need. The marker has not been called in yet."

"You're saying Left-John Mocker has the marker of the son of the senate majority leader of Mexico?"

"Buy the marker, Conroy. Use it to persuade the senator to support President Ortiz. That will allow your project to proceed."

"There's just one problem with your scenario. What am I supposed to use to buy the marker?"

"You're one of the wealthiest men—"

"The Mocker doesn't care about money; it's just something that gaming chips convert to as far as he's concerned. I don't think he'll cooperate."

"He has to cooperate. There is no other alternative."

"But there are always alternatives," I said.

"There are many acceptable to me," she agreed. "But none that you would find palatable."

I didn't ask her about any of those other alternatives. Like I said, Bess scares me. "And you think using a son's weakness against his father is something I'll support?"

She shrugged and turned to face me again. Even through the polarized window the morning sun gave her face a washed out, almost corpse-like appearance. "You didn't cause the son to disappoint his father, he already has. You didn't conjure up the marker; it already exists. I don't believe in coincidence, Conroy. You're in the right place at the right time with the right acquaintance to make this happen."

"You talk like this is my destiny. If we don't take the project to Mexico we'll still have other chances down the road."

"No, Conroy, you won't. If you lose your moment here, Green

Aggression and the Earth-First groups will gain supporters and grow in strength. They'll keep you from ever using your buffalo dogs to benefit the world. You can prevent this. Let me help you."

Maybe it was just fatigue, or low blood sugar; a wave of vertigo washed over me. I staggered, and would have fallen but my hand came up against the window and steadied me. Bess continued talking, but her voice faded in my awareness as I remembered the rumbling cacophony from my dream and the final words of the snowman that Bess had just echoed. I'm not superstitious, and I don't normally believe in omens, but I'd just been whacked in the head by one, and even a professional skeptic knows when to surrender to the inexplicable.

"Fine," I said, interrupting her in the midst of an unheard sentence.

"Fine?"

"Yeah, you convinced me. I'll go talk to Left-John today." I glanced across the office to Reggie's daybed. The buffalo dog lay curled up, his shaggy head hanging over the edge as he slept. The sight reminded me of how tired I felt. "Besides," I said, "it's been months since Reggie had any Chinese food."

Chapter Three: Digestion of Fortunes Unknown

AFTER BESS PENROSE LEFT, I sacked out on my couch. Around noon I woke to the sensation of something alternately tugging at my neck and licking my face. I opened my eyes to find Reggie chewing morosely on my shirt collar. He hadn't actually bitten through the fabric, just wet it down with his spit. He clearly expected praise for mastering the distinction of not eating my clothing, or at least, not while I was wearing it. The previous week he'd consumed half the contents of my office closet.

I reached for him with both hands, muttered "good boy." I put Reggie down on the carpet and stepped into the bathroom to freshen up. There are certain perks to being the CEO of a hugely successful company, and one of them is having a fully equipped bathroom with shower and sauna attached to my office. I dumped my clothes on the Italian marble floor, and indulged in a lengthy, hot shower. Some of my best ideas come to me while in the shower; whatever hydro-creative gift I possess kicked in again. By the time I'd begun toweling off, I had the basics of a plan guaranteed to get the Mocker on board.

I scooped up my clothes, only to discover my shirt was missing. A trail of buttons and one cuff led to Reggie's daybed. He looked up with enormous, chocolate brown eyes, the way a four-year-old child gazes at his father the first time he tosses a ball and breaks a window. Hand tailoring may come and go, but a look like that lasts forever. Sighing, I went to the dresser for a fresh shirt.

Soaking my head in hot water had also helped me sort out my own motivations. During my career as a hypnotist I'd traveled to a lot of planets, and always met people I liked, though most of them weren't what you would call 'human.' I'm a xenophile. I like new places, new things, and new faces, even when those faces look more like talus piles or drip with other worldly goo. The people of Mexico had lost that kind of joy, had it stripped from them by their isolationist government. I wanted to give it back.

After the great Texas Temporal Disaster, Mexico had closed its borders and outlawed all aliens. My aunt Fiona had been there, and in those first days she'd seen nonhuman friends attacked by frightened mobs. Others had been carried off by soldiers, never to be seen again. The rampant xenophobia had faded over time, but fear and distrust of all things alien remained at the political level. Rigid isolationism had become governmental policy. Of the eighty-seven different alien races that have made contact with Earth, Mexico's government had only relaxed enough to grant "amigo" status to four. Any other nonhumans foolish enough to visit Mexico, or humans harboring them, were summarily rounded up and carted off to prison.

I had the opportunity to change that, to make them so beholden to my company's buffalo dogs, that they'd have to start widening their policy. And with a little help from Left-John Mocker I could make it happen.

I buzzed Jeanie.

"Yes, Mr. Conroy?"

"Jeanie, call the Golden Turtle Palace in Newer Jersey. Ask to speak with Left-John Mocker. When you get him on the phone tell him I'm on my way over to ask him for a favor."

"Yes, sir. A favor. And if he wants to speak to you directly?"

"Tell him Reggie ate my phone again, and that I've already left. Thanks, Jeanie." I slapped the intercom off, grabbed my coat, and scooped up Reggie. He bleated, made an unsuccessful lunge for my lapel, and then settled in comfortably under my arm as I hurried out the door.

"Get out, Conroy," Left-John grunted, "I'm not doing you any favors. People who show up asking for favors aren't welcome here."

"Mocker, c'mon, we have a pact. We're always welcome in each other's home." Rain was pouring down, as it had every day for the past twenty years in Newer Jersey. I'd stepped out of my cab in front of the Golden Turtle Palace to find Left-John Mocker blocking the door. He stood with his arms folded across his chest like some kind of cigar store Indian. Water trickled down through the collar of my coat, and Reggie squirmed within, trying to keep dry. I turned to the cabbie.

"Keep the meter running," I said. "I'll be right back. I'm just going to talk with my friend." But I knew he wouldn't. I'd already paid, and before leaving the cab I'd handed him a tip that would have choked most of your larger land mammals, while instructing him to ignore anything I said after I got out, and to drive off in a hurry within a minute.

I stepped away from the cab and walked up to Left-John, holding out my hand. He stared at it for a full beat before taking it with a grimace.

"That's all well and good," he said, "but you don't have a home. You live in a hotel. And, while we're on the subject, this isn't a home either, it's a restaurant. You don't show up at someone's restaurant asking for favors. Get back in your cab and go, and we'll forget this happened."

On cue, the driver threw the vehicle into gear. He splashed both the Mocker and me, and drove off, fishtailing away at high speed. Some of the water got through to Reggie and he bleated in protest. Trying my best to look chagrined, I waved ineffectually at the cab's retreating bulk before turning back to the Mocker. "Well, there goes my ride. You're stuck with me now."

He snorted. "Let's go inside. I'll call you a new cab."

Once inside the restaurant I set Reggie on the carpet and hung my dripping coat on a hook by the door.

"You can keep it on," said Left-John Mocker, squatting down to scritch the base of Reggie's neck. "I'll have a new cab here for you in less than two minutes."

"I'm soaked to the bone here," I said, "and Reggie needs a bit more than two minutes to dry off. The least you can do is offer me a cup of hot tea, maybe a dry towel for the pup. You and I have been through a lot together. Don't get all huffy over my asking for a favor."

"The last time I did you a favor, you nearly burned out my eye."

"Oh please, don't exaggerate. What I burned out was a prosthetic eye. I've already apologized a dozen times over, and I paid for the replacement."

"Fine," he said, stomping away and leaving me to follow or not. I paused only long enough to scoop Reggie up and wormed my way past waiters and busboys and tables of customers—it was a busy afternoon at the Golden Turtle Palace—to the Mocker's private table. We sat. A waiter appeared with a booster seat and piled a pillow on top of that, which Reggie immediately put to use. He curled up comfortably, high enough that he could look out over the table. A second waiter arrived with menus and tea. I poured a cup for Left-John, then myself, and then emptied the rest of the pot in a soup bowl for Reggie. I picked up a menu.

"What do you recommend today? Has your chef come up with anything new since I was here last?"

Left-John seethed. "I thought you only wanted tea?"

"What I want is to talk with you, but as long as I'm here I might as well order some food. I haven't eaten yet. Do you mind?"

"What is it that you want, Conroy?"

I glanced down at my menu. "Well, I'm leaning toward the 'Duck of Hidden Destiny.' It's not too spicy, is it?"

"I won't ask you again."

I nodded to the waiter, pointed at a line on the menu, waved two fingers, one at me and one at Reggie, and set the menu aside. "Fine, no build up, straight to the point. You got it. Here it is. I want to buy your marker."

"Excuse me?"

"Well, not your marker. Someone else's marker that you're holding."

"Oh, well, that's simple enough. I thought this was going to be complicated. The answer is 'no.'"

"Hold on, this isn't just anyone's marker. It's a specific marker."

"A specific marker?"

"Yes, exactly."

"Well, that's different then," said Left-John. "In that case, the answer is still 'no.'"

"Why are you so cranky today?" I sipped at my tea. "It's a marker, it has a monetary value. I'm willing to buy it from you. What's the big deal?"

"No big deal. It's just not for sale. I've never sold a maker in my life, and I'm not starting now. I'll either redeem it personally, eventually, or I'll tear it up. As far as I'm concerned, those are the only two options."

"Don't you even want to know whose marker I'm interested in?"

The Mocker finally picked up his teacup. "Honestly, I could not care less."

"Alejandro Cortez," I said.

That stopped him. "Why do you want Cortez? He's a punk."

"I don't want him, I want his father."

He didn't reply, just sat holding his cup without drinking. Several minutes passed, and the only sound was Reggie lapping up tea. "You want to use Alejandro's marker to get to his father? Have you graduated to extortion, Conroy?"

"Okay, first, it's not extortion. I'm not going to ask him for any money, so technically, it's blackmail. But it's not even really blackmail. It's, well, it's an incentive."

"An incentive? To do what?"

"To support his president."

"What, do you have advance notice of a coup in the Mexican government?"

"John, leave the sarcasm to someone less stoic."

He snorted at that and finally took a sip of tea. I had him listening, which was the proverbial foot in the door.

"Here's the thing," I said. "I'm scheduled to go to Mexico in two months. To bring four dozen buffalo dogs down there and clean up an industrial waste site that's been sitting in Veracruz for decades. President Ortiz wants this to happen, but he's getting pressure from the congress to keep out alien technology, and that includes buffalo dogs."

"And Cortez?"

"If Cortez sides with him, which is the right thing to do, he'll have enough political clout to withstand the outside pressure, and we'll be able to go in and do our clean-up."

He frowned at that. The Mocker never frowns. He's the poster child for poker faces. I'd only ever seen him visibly angry twice, and shed a tear once. This was his first frown for me.

"It's a marker, Conroy. Do you understand that? It's a gambling debt, nothing more. It's certainly not a tool for you to manipulate the father of an idiot."

I shook my head. "It can be whatever you choose to make it. Why not make it a tool, one which benefits everyone in Mexico?"

He didn't answer, and I realized that I'd been so wrapped up in my own concerns that maybe, just maybe, Left-John had problems of his own.

"Okay, what's going on? This isn't about the marker. You were in an ugly mood before I arrived. What's really bothering you?"

"Right now? How about your irritating approach to life?"

"What are you talking about?" I said. "How did this get to be about me?"

"I'm a student of human behavior, Conroy. When I'm playing cards I'm playing the people at the table with me. There are patterns, ways of thinking, that's part of everyone's mindset. Some take me longer than others, but before the end of the game I can always figure out how the other person thinks. Everyone but you."

I laughed. "Oh, please, I'm not so complex."

"Don't flatter yourself. It's not a matter of complexity. You're just . . . erratic. You don't have a pattern. You just do things, like pursuing improbable solutions to situations instead of admitting that no answer exists."

"So I'm more creative than you. Get over it and get on with your life."

"Unlike some people, I can't use bribery and blackmail to solve my problems."

"Problems? What kind of problems do you have? You're a professional gambler."

"My profession *is* the problem."

I waited. Even Reggie looked up and gave Left-John an inquiring stare.

"Fine. If you must know, the Probability Guild is considering restructuring its ranking system by species."

"So?"

"The game doesn't care whether or not you're human. When I sit at a table to play, I don't worry if the others have comparable DNA or not. And when I win, I want my ranking to reflect it. I have jazz master status, a double Coltrane rating. I don't want an 'among humans' to be tacked on to the end of it."

"Jazz master? Coltrane?"

"The guild uses various sets and subsets of musical classification for its ranking. Jazz is the highest class. Double Coltrane refers to my having ranked among the top ten players in the guild, twice. Now the guild is pushing for species identification as part of membership." He pulled a bit of pasteboard out of his vest and flipped it to me like I'd seen him flip playing cards into a hat across a room hundreds of times.

One side showed the ace of spades. The other was a membership form, the kind of thing used to update or change records. The Probability Guild didn't believe in online tools, and the limited size of the card kept things to the point. Left-John had marked most of the entries to be left as they were. A new item at the bottom of the very bottom of the card contained a series of check boxes with the names of the more familiar intelligent species by each, as well as a blank line to fill in as necessary.

I handed it back to him. "Don't check *Human*, check *Other* and write in Comanche. By definition, if they're asking you your species they need you to tell them. So tell them that."

"Last time I checked, the Comanche were still a subset of humanity."

"Now, sure, but not originally. What's the Comanche term for the Comanche?"

"Nʉʉmʉ. Why?"

"How would you translate it?"

"It means... Oh. I see. It means 'people.'"

"Right, and who gets to define what 'people' means?"

He stared at me in silence. I watched his eyes, watched him work it out."

"The guild's completely autonomous; you know that."

I nodded. "Which means they'd have to query all their Comanche members to achieve consensus as to what the word means."

"You're not making any sense, Conroy. I'm the only Comanche in the guild."

"Right, so it means whatever you tell them it means. Tell them it means anyone who can sit at the table and play cards. Problem solved.

The Mocker slapped his hand on the table, startling Reggie who bleated and took a break from his tea to glare at him. "Yes," said the Mocker. "Do you see? It irritates me that you can think like that, though a bit less when I'm on the receiving end of it."

I made a slight bow and waved one hand. "The honor is to serve. What are friends for if not helping one another out of a jam now and then?"

"Ah. So, we are back to the matter of your marker? I won't give you the marker, Conroy."

"But—"

"You don't need the marker, you only need me."

"Need you? But you're—"

"—coming with you. I was on the fence before, but the casual way you just resolved something that's been aggravating me for days convinces me I need to see you in action. Besides, the idea of using buffalo dogs to clean environmental waste on that kind of scale was mine. I said it right here at this table, or did you forget?"

The waiter arrived with a plate containing my lunch and a chafing dish with more of the same for Reggie. He had a second plate that he set down in front of the Mocker, though I hadn't seen him order anything.

The Mocker continued, "I'm hurt, Conroy, hurt that you haven't given me credit or invited me to one of your demonstrations to see first hand what you'd done with my suggestion."

"My apologies." I winced. "It's just when you're trying to impress political leaders it sounds better to credit the idea to my company's research department than to a friend from my less than savory past. But you're right. I'll tell President Ortiz that you inspired the whole venture. But you don't have to come with me."

"I do. I need to be there when you finally wake up and stop wasting your time with this corporate nonsense and return to your unsavory past."

I paused with a mouthful of spicy duck and met his gaze to see if he was kidding. I couldn't read a thing in his eyes. I finished chewing, swallowed, and said, "I think you remember it differently than I do. Before I started Buffalogic, I was routinely broke, frequently in trouble with the local authorities, and never certain where my job was going to take me."

"Exactly. Your life was an adventure, full of uncertain opportunities, chance encounters, and exotic locales. Now look at you. You're a businessman. Worse, you're an executive."

"You're giving me grief because I've finally grown up and I'm acting like a mature adult?"

"No, I'm reminding you that it's only an act. You've got thousands of employees depending on you, which strokes your ego in ways that an audience never did, but it's all a dream. It's only a matter of time before you wake up, and I'm betting the excitement of the cleanup in Mexico will remind you how much you miss that kind of action, and wake you up. So, do we have a deal?

"A deal?"

"You let me come along and watch your performance in front of the Mexican president, and I let you use my marker to leverage Senator Cortez to support him. Well?"

"If that's what it will take, okay, we've got a deal. But damn, when did you get to be so smarmy?"

"I'm not, I'm inspired. You're lucky to have around, Conroy, but you've gotten boring. I'm just trying to save you from yourself."

A waiter refilled our tea and deposited a small tray of fortune cookies. The Mocker picked up a cookie and held it at arm's length above his head. "Reggie! I've got a treat for you."

Reggie lifted his head out of his food in time to see the gambler toss the cookie high into the air. He tracked the cookie's arc and as it started to descend he pushed off from his booster seat, knocking it off the chair as he clattered up onto the table. I reached for the teapot and cups as my buffalo dog careened toward them, unaware of potential obstacles, his gaze fixed on the airborne cookie. I snatched the tea service out of harm's way as Reggie skidded past. He caught the cookie in his mouth, chewed for all of two seconds, and swallowed it, fortune and all.

"Good reflexes," said the Mocker, chuckling, a rarity in itself.

"It would serve you right if I'd let him break the crockery."

"Oh come on, one of you should be trained, and Reggie takes to it so much better than you do."

Reggie made a whuffing sound as if in agreement, and eyed Left-John Mocker with an eloquent expression that spoke of simple pleasures and the certainty that everything would work out fine. From Reggie's point of view that was probably true.

I finished the last of my duck and reached for a cookie, snapping it open and popping the pieces into my mouth while I read my fortune.

TRAVEL IS IN YOUR FUTURE;
YOU WON'T HAVE TIME TO PACK

Ominous stuff, these cookie fortunes, if you give them the proper spin. But I had a cab ride back to Philadelphia ahead of me, and the only thing I'd be packing was a buffalo dog stuffed full with spicy 'Duck of Hidden Destiny' and an unread fortunate cookie. I didn't give my own fortune much thought, but I wondered what had been written on the slip of paper Reggie had just eaten, as well as the philosophical implications of consuming one's fortune unseen. Not that Reggie could have read the fortune if he'd looked at it first.

Chapter Four: Kudzu for the Earth Monster

WHILE LEFT-JOHN CALLED A CAB I took Reggie to the restroom and dunked his face in the sink to clean him up. He squirmed in my hands and yipped with pleasure while I held him under the hot-air hand-drier. Left-John knocked on the door and called "cab's here," before Reggie's beard was fully dry, but considering we had a dash through the rain to get into the taxi anyway, I let it slide.

The Mocker stood waiting with my coat. Behind him one of the restaurant's managers glowered at Reggie and me, impotent and unhappy.

"I'll call you with the details tomorrow after I've talked to the guild. That will give you plenty of time to handle my accommodations and travel arrangements. Don't go cheap on me, Conroy, I expect first class all the way."

I laughed, "I've got a company aeroshuttle. You can have your choice of seats. And I've already reserved an entire floor at the El Presidente, the best hotel in Veracruz."

"That's what I'm talking about," said the Mocker. "Being rich is going to make you soft, not to mention predictable." He opened the door and ushered me to the waiting cab. I tumbled in, rain pouring all around. Reggie struggled out of my coat before we were inside, drenching us both in the process. We departed the endless rain of Newer Jersey and headed south and west back to the offices of Buffalogic, Inc. and some late afternoon sunshine.

The soaking had soured Reggie's disposition. Most times he's an enthusiastic and happy companion, but on the rare occasions when Reggie gets moody he's likely to take a bite out of nearly anything, just because he can. Traffic was light and I expected to make great time back to Philadelphia, but I knew that look in Reggie's eyes. Without some intervention he'd be looking for something to chomp on before we arrived, and at the moment that was limited to just me and the cab.

I took off my coat and wrapped him in it. It's a game that he usually likes, but not something we play too often because in the course of the game he tends to eat his way through the coat. But better my coat than to have to deal with an irate cabdriver because my pet tore up and consumed the upholstery or a piece of the door.

Reggie barked, a sound somewhere between annoyance and begrudged pleasure. I tied the arms of the coat in a knot and then knotted them again making a handle of sorts to carry it by, so that I wouldn't run the risk of losing a finger if Reggie happened to bite through the part of the coat I was holding. Midway through our game my cell phone rang. I'd left it in the coat. I started fumbling and flipping the coat around, trying to find the pocket with the phone. Reggie took it as some variation on our game and struggled within the folds in hot pursuit. He got to the phone first and bit into it. The ringing ceased. I could already imagine having to explain it to Lisa when I saw her tomorrow. It wouldn't be the first time she'd scolded me for allowing Reggie to eat a phone.

We crossed the river from Newer Jersey into Pennsylvania and soon after entered an older, industrial part of Philadelphia, heading for the street containing the office building of Buffalogic, Inc. The surrounding neighborhood left a lot to be desired, an aging collection of dilapidated four-story warehouses dating back to the middle of the twentieth century, all red brick under decades of multi-colored graffiti that some future social scientist might one day peel back, layer after runic layer.

I was doing my part to revitalize this section of the city. It didn't hurt that I'd gotten a full city block of gutted warehouse space for next to nothing. Rather than simply tear it down, construction crews had detached the brick outer surface before razing the building. Then they built a new facility from scratch, with all the space I'd need for the next fifty years of expansion. The result was an office complex that included some alien tech that wasn't widely available but made me feel a lot more secure. Having started Buffalogic, Inc. by smuggling a fertile buffalo dog out from under the noses of the Arconi, I wanted to make quite sure that the same wasn't done to me. So instead of fancy, I'd gone for secure. Once the major construction was finished, the construction crew restored the original brick façade, and it all blended back with the neighborhood.

Walking up to the dilapidated brick entrance and passing within, visitors encountered state of the art fixtures and furnishings, all the accoutrements and luxuries of a cutting edge corporation. The contrast of it always put me in a good mood. But today I wouldn't be smiling. Several police cruisers had parked in front of the building and two emergency vehicles were speeding away as we arrived. I grabbed my coat by its improvised handle, paid the fare, and climbed out of the cab. There were two cops standing by the entrance, and through the opened door I could make out at least ten people milling around the security screening portal.

"Sorry, sir, this building is temporary closed," said one of the cops as I approached. He reached out and shut the door. I stared from one cop to the other. They were anonymous, their identities lost behind mirrored faceplates and heavy helmets that matched their black, armor padded uniforms. Even for Philadelphia that wasn't normal police dress. Whatever was happening here involved something major.

"What's going on? This is my building," I said. "My company is in here. Is anyone hurt?"

The other cop flinched and backed up a step. "What do you have in the coat?" And suddenly I was looking down the barrel of a pressure weapon. I glanced down at my hand, and then lower. The bundle of my jacket was squirming.

"Easy, easy," I said. The cop's hand had a slight quiver which probably mirrored my own trembling. I held up my free hand as I began lowering the coat to the pavement, slowly squatting to do so. Before it got there, Reggie bit through to the outside and stuck his head out, bleating happily. "See? No problem here. This is just a buffalo dog. You've probably seen them on the news? Or like the big statue in the lobby? This one is named Reggie. He's harmless, really, just a bit frisky because he's hungry."

"Yeah, I've seen 'em," said cop number two, but all of my attention was on his partner, the one with the gun.

"That's what they do here, right?" he said.

"That's right," I said. "This is Buffalogic, Inc. I'm the CEO. Now can you tell me what's going on? I saw ambulances. Is anyone hurt?"

The first cop nodded but otherwise ignored my question. He did lower his weapon though, which was almost as good. The burst from a pressure gun isn't usually lethal, even at close range, but a sudden case of the bends can make you wish you were dead. I picked up Reggie and left the remains of my coat on the ground. Cop number two demanded some identification, which I promptly provided; silently grateful I put my wallet in my pants and not next to my half-eaten phone. Cop number two handed it to number one who looked it over and pressed a stud on his wrist. He seemed to speak to empty air. "I've got a fellow out here claiming to be the company's CEO. Says his name is Conroy." He stiffened. "Yes, sir. We'll ask him to stay until you get here."

"Until who gets here?" I asked. But neither cop offered more than apologies for making me wait and assurances that everything would be explained to me in just a few moments. From the angle of their helmets it seemed they were staring at Reggie, either because he kept trying to squirm out of my arms or just because they'd never seen a buffalo dog up close before. Several minutes went by in uncomfortable silence. I've been arrested, detained, held for questioning, and charged by security, military, and police officers on more than two dozen worlds—misunderstandings all, I assure you—and I've never found anything more unnerving than not being able to see the eyes of the law. When the door to the building opened, I felt genuine relief that the fellow standing there did not wear a uniform or a mirrored helmet, but was instead garbed in a comfortable looking mohair sports coat and wool slacks.

"Mr. Conroy? I'm Special Agent Arlen Montgomery; I'm with the Federal Bureau of Investigation." He flashed a badge, unfolding it as he raised his arm, and folding it back once his hand reached its apex and began its descent, until the badge was hidden away once more in a pocket.

"Agent Montgomery, was anyone hurt? Can you tell me what's going on?"

"First, let me assure you that none of your employees were seriously injured, mostly just cuts and scrapes. And your offices are relatively unharmed as well. All of the damage appears to be cosmetic rather than structural—"

"Injured? Damage? What are you talking about?"

He waved away the two cops and escorted me into the building. "We believe there were two separate bombs. Each delivered by messenger a little over an hour ago. Both made it up to your main floor; one all the way to your personal office."

I stopped half way across the lobby. My mouth hung open and I stared at the FBI man. "Bombs? You're saying bombs went off? Explosions?"

"No, not explosions, not the way you mean. Come on, I'll show you."

I shifted Reggie around, tucking him under my left arm, and followed. The lobby was a flurry of activity, men and women in various uniforms and protective gear huddled in groups of three or four, as still more people came and went. I recognized a few of them, employees who handled building security; one had her arm in a sling and was being interrogated by a man and a woman. I caught a glimpse of something green and flaky spattered in splotches but Montgomery hurried me past all of it, through the unmanned security portal, and to the elevator. An investigative technician wearing transparent plastic gloves pressed the call button at a nod from Montgomery. To my surprise and annoyance the elevator door opened without requiring a voiceprint or keycode. We stepped inside and rode up to the second floor, home of the offices of Buffalogic, Inc.

The elevator opened onto a crowded, chaotic scene. Nearly one hundred and fifty people worked on this floor, and although most had gone home for the day, the two dozen alter-shift employees were there, just fidgeting in place. I had the impression they had been roused from their workspaces and labs and offices, and for good reason. A few hours earlier, the foyer had been a sedate combination of polished wood and smoked glass; hidden light sources shone almost magically upon one wall which featured an original and notoriously expensive Gotherman triptych of a herd of buffalo dogs roaming the plains of Mars. That splendor presumably remained, but only miniscule bits and patches were visible, peering out from under what looked to be several layers of some kind of ground cover.

"What the hell is that, some kind of fungus?"

"It's kudzu, Mr. Conroy."

"Kudzu? In Philadelphia? In my building? On my walls?"

"Technically it's kudzu-nine. A genetically manipulated variant, engineered for its phenomenal growth rate. Researchers developed it for restabilizing hillsides after flashfloods or mudslides. A scattering of seedlings will take root and multiply in minutes."

The whole situation struck me as ludicrous. Maybe it was just relief that no one had been seriously hurt by whatever had happened. "Last time I checked, our walls were pretty stable and not particularly prone to mudslides."

Either Montgomery had no sense of humor or he'd been trained to treat everything as serious. "We believe this kudzu-nine was stolen from a locked facility by terrorists."

"Okay, but again, last time I checked, we had no more terrorists here than we had mudslides.

"I'm afraid that's where you're wrong, sir. They signed their work. I'll show you."

I followed the FBI man down the foliage-filled corridor to my office. Our feet made rustling and crunching sounds as we walked through the vines and leaves. We passed dozens of government personnel and a few of my employees, some of the former interviewing the latter, while technicians scraped samples of genetically altered kudzu from the walls. The undergrowth tapered off the deeper we went into the building, and by the time we reached Jeanie's desk we had left it behind. Jeanie wasn't there. In fact, no one was there. Montgomery stepped past my secretary's desk, opened my office door, and gestured for me to step through.

The room was dark, despite the far wall of glass that presented my much loved view of the river. It was warmer than it should have been, warmer and more humid. I reached to the wall to trigger the lights, and I pulled my hand back sharply as I touched something leafy. Reggie gave a little bark.

Montgomery wasn't as squeamish, but then he presumably already knew what was on the walls and in the room. He reached past me and slapped at the switch. A dim glow came from the radiance panels in the ceiling, most of the illumination lost behind the creepers and vines and hanging moss that coated almost every bit of surface area. It was more than just the kudzu that we'd passed on the way in. There were other varieties of vegetation here; even I could tell that, even in the dim light.

"Who did this," I said, "and why?"

"From what we've reconstructed, a package was delivered while you were out. Your assistant left it for you on the desk. Some time later it 'went off' and seeded your office. The remains of the package included a calling card."

I picked my way across the floor, a queasy feeling in my gut as something crunched or compressed underneath my feet with every step. Some kind of moss or fungus coated the surface of my desk, providing a cushion for the large chunk of burl wood that had been dropped upon it. Gouged into the wood was a message.

BUFFALO DOGS ARE AN ABOMINATION
IN THE EYES OF THE EARTH
—GAEA

I must have stood there, just staring at the words for several minutes. The whole situation felt too surreal. Behind me, Special Agent Montgomery had kept on talking, probably for a good while, before I realized.

"I'm sorry, what?"

"Mr. Conroy, the Bureau is aware that Green Aggression has been directing its members to flood your company with hate mail, as well as staging rallies at your various practice runs." He let the statement hang in the air. When I turned to respond I saw that Montgomery had remained at the door. In the gloom of my office he appeared almost featureless, silhouetted by the light pouring in behind him.

"They're unhappy with me," I said. "They don't approve of the methods I've proposed for cleaning up toxic and industrial waste." I ran a hand over the burl, tracing the letters with the tip of a finger. "I hired a PR firm to handle it. They focus the message on what we're accomplishing, rather than that we're using an alien lifeform to accomplish it." I recalled the public statements the publicity flacks had produced and let them tumble from my lips like well rehearsed patter from a stage show. "Green Aggression is entitled to their opinion, but we're trying to do something for the greater good of the planet." I closed my eyes against a sudden lightheadedness. How could this be real? "It was just a couple groups of malcontents with picket signs; it was just some hate mail.

"This goes significantly beyond hate mail. They're trying to send you a message, Mr. Conroy. Whatever the next stage of your operation, they clearly don't want you to proceed with it."

"Mexico," I said. "We're negotiating a major clean-up in Mexico. Everything else has just been a warm up to it."

"Green Aggression is based in Mexico, though neither the Ortiz government nor our own has been able to learn precisely where they're headquartered. This is not the work of malcontents. These are dangerous and organized individuals who likely see this next clean-up of yours as all the justification they need to change their tactics."

I shook my head and held Reggie more firmly. "I know they blew up the Clarkeson embassy in Istanbul last year, but emptied the place out first. They've never actually attacked anyone before. This is insane. No rational person can expect us to break off all contact with the rest of the galaxy."

He came forward and grabbed my arm in his hand, his grip incredibly strong. He hauled me back out into the light of the corridor. "That's not quite right," he said. "They don't expect humanity to turn its back on all the goodies and wonders that have come our way since first contact decades ago. That genie's long since left its bottle. But they want it off Earth. They're eco-terrorists, Mr. Conroy. What they want is our species's home planet, to be free of alien interference. No alien ambassadors, no alien tourists, no aliens of any kind on earth."

"No alien lifeforms at all?"

Montgomery just shrugged. "I can't pretend to speak for an eco-terrorist group, Mr. Conroy, but it seems they've decided you're a major threat. In their internal literature they've given you a code name."

"A code name? You're serious?"

"They call you the *Earth Monster*. You're a despoiler of the world in their eyes."

Words failed me. I turned and looked back into my office. Something of my mood must have been communicated to Reggie. He nuzzled his head against my side and offered up a low yowl, as forlorn as I've ever heard him.

"So, what happens next? What am I supposed to do? "

"That's not for me to say, sir. But if I were you, I might consider another line of work." He gestured down the corridor back to my office. "This was just a warning shot."

Chapter Five: Reggie Visits the Troops

DESPITE AGENT MONTGOMERY'S ASSURANCES that he had all the information he needed, specialists and technicians, representing a dozen different agencies, continued to pour in. They busied themselves with sampling, scanning, photographing, and otherwise collecting anything that might be evidence. Montgomery shuttled back and forth among them, collating whatever they could tell him. Meanwhile, I found Jeanie and had her gather the staff. She signaled me when they were assembled and I headed up to tell them what had happened. Montgomery appeared right behind me as I opened the door to the stairwell.

"Where are we going?" he asked me.

"Third floor." The kudzu hadn't reached there. We climbed to the next level. "The ground floor is all lobby, security, and an enclosed parking structure, and the second floor is where most of the nine to five clerical and paperwork gets done." I pulled open the door and Reggie barked once as a sudden breeze hit us all in the face. Montgomery stopped in mid stride and again he gripped my arm, pulling me to a halt.

"Where's the air coming from?"

I gestured for him to precede me. "This is our general training area. There are currently just over one hundred buffalitos living and learning on this floor. The air flow you're feeling is caused by a complicated series of fans that circulate the air and maintain the proper ratio of gases."

"Gases?"

"Buffalo dogs fart oxygen. Quite a lot of oxygen, actually. We release the excess to the outside through several thousand vents. The whole thing has triple backups, just in case."

"In case of what?"

"In case the system were to break down. Too much oxygen and the risk of fire becomes very high."

We'd emerged from the stairwell into a corridor that ran the perimeter of the entire floor, opening onto the middle area through a series of doors every ten meters or so. The carpet beneath our feet alternated in lanes of light and dark that curved away in both directions. At least twice a week the handlers used the corridor to race the buffalo dogs, both as part their training and as a source of friendly in-office competition and wagering. I led Montgomery to the nearest inner door and we stepped through into a brightly lit pit of sand with seven semicircular rows of stone benches rising up from it like a miniature amphitheatre. Jeanie stood just beyond the door, looking annoyed. Behind her, employees filled the benches, many of them holding buffalo dogs on their laps or under an arm. No sooner had we entered than all the animals began to yap and bark excitedly. As far the buffalitos were concerned it was a moment of extreme excitement. Reggie had come to visit.

It had something to do with a dominance thing that I didn't quite understand, though not for Lisa Penrose's lack of trying to explain. Basically, every other buffalo dog on Earth acted as though Reggie had been anointed King of the buffalitos and placed upon some alien omnivore's throne. His loyal subjects wanted nothing more than to cheer him and emulate his every move. Chaos always erupted when Reggie visited the training levels on the upper floors of the office building, and of late it had gotten so bad that Reggie and I trained elsewhere. Otherwise, all other training stopped, and instead the other buffalitos mimicked whatever he did. Right then he was squirming in my grasp and I needed both hands to hold him.

Like any good monarch, Reggie wanted to visit his adoring subjects. He craned his head and gazed back at me with pitiful eyes, but quickly gave up when I just held on tighter. "First things first," I said to him. There'd be time to indulge my buffalo dog later, but just now I needed to address the troops. I made a few throat clearing noises, but they didn't carry over the steady clamoring of the excited buffalitos. I raised two fingers to my lips and let out with a shrill whistle that brought everyone, handlers and their charges, to attention.

"Good evening. Those of you who are trainers, would you please attempt to calm down your respective pups? Thank you. By now I'm sure you've all heard one version or another of what's happened. Tonight's episode appears to be the work of Green Aggression. They have been a source of annoyance in the past, and though this incident marks a significant escalation, there's no cause for alarm. I'll be meeting tomorrow with Dr. Penrose and reviewing our security options. But let me stress again, no one has been seriously injured, and the only damage appears to be an infestation of some kind of extremely aggressive ivy that has taken over a few rooms downstairs.

"With your help we're going to fix that right now. I'd like all handlers and trainers to follow me with their buffalo dogs. If we all work together, we can have everything looking good as new long before the morning shift arrives, and maybe teach your buffalitos some new tricks."

I led them back down the stairs and out into the main corridor. The experts from the various government agencies were just packing up, but they all stopped in the middle of their tasks to watch the parade of buffalo dogs and handlers that marched past them. When we reached the anteroom I formed them up in a semi-circle and approached the wall containing the Gotherman triptych. Kudzu-nine coated it. I held Reggie in one arm, tucked him against my torso like a fuzzy football, and with my free hand tore off a few leaves from the wall. Then I turned back to all the people I'd brought down with me. Each of them held a squirming, writhing buffalito eager to pay its respect to Reggie. They'd have their chance.

"Okay, Reggie, try this for me." Careful of my fingertips, I fed several leaves to the buffalo dog. He chewed them thoughtfully, swallowed, and a moment later farted a little puff of oxygen. "You want some more?"

Reggie barked softly and I set him down on the floor. Immediately the other buffalo dogs began to yip. Reggie dashed to the wall and began tearing away strips of kudzu. He took his time, delicately eating away only the vegetation and leaving the wall behind completely intact.

"The rest of you, pick out a spot and carry your buffalito there. Give them a taste of the kudzu, and then let them get to work."

A low whoosh rustled through the anteroom and I felt a light breeze on my face. On most days, Reggie was the only buffalito down here, and he wasn't a working animal. Now, however, one hundred and seven buffalo dogs were cleaning up the place. They were swiftly and diligently ingesting every bit of kudzu-nine, their handlers having to raise them above their heads to reach the highest spots on the walls and ceiling. I took Reggie down the hall, and a few handlers followed. We repeated the same demonstration with the other vegetation in my office and the buffalitos went to work there as well. After a few hours, the entire task was done and the staff went back upstairs to put their buffalitos in their pens.

"Impressive work," said Montgomery as he walked me to the elevator. He looked pensive, one of those I-can-almost-see-the-gears-turning kind of moments. It flickered and fled when he noticed me staring.

We stepped into the elevator and I slumped against the back wall. Midnight had come and gone. I'd already been through a long day before the threats from Green Aggression had hit. All I wanted was to get to my hotel suite and fall into bed. I would have called a cab, but Montgomery had kindly offered to drive me.

"Yeah, impressive enough to attract eco-terrorists." I yawned as the elevator doors closed. I rubbed my palms down my face in an attempt to stay awake. We traveled down to the ground floor, which, without the teams of technicians, police, and agents, looked clean and airy. The company security team on duty nodded to us as we passed through the scanning arc and then on to the main entrance. One of Montgomery's agents held the door open for us and we stepped out of the building into the cool night air. Montgomery gestured to a black car parked askew upon the sidewalk and I headed toward it. I had Reggie tucked under my arm as usual, and before we had walked ten paces he began to howl.

Reggie never howls.

Montgomery had dropped back, presumably alarmed at the sudden ruckus. I stopped and swung Reggie around in front of me, holding him with both hands so I could get a better look at him. "What is it, boy? What's wrong?"

The howl turned to a rapid barking, and he squirmed in my hands, as if trying to leap at something behind me. This wasn't like earlier when he wanted to frolic with the other buffalitos. With a sudden lurch, Reggie wrenched himself from my grasp, bounded onto my chest and over my shoulder. I started to turn and call after him, when something struck me in the neck. It stung like the granddaddy of all mosquitoes.

My head swam, and without intending to I sank to my knees. I raised one hand to feel at whatever was sticking out of my neck, but I'd lost all feeling in my fingers. I heard ferocious barking, a vicious sound that I'd never heard from any buffalo dog, least of all Reggie. Then I was lying on my back with no idea how I'd gotten there. I saw Montgomery looking down at me. He was shouting something at someone but I couldn't make it out. I heard the clatter of footfalls and suddenly thought about my old high school marching band. What were they doing here? Reggie had come back and climbed onto my chest, barking and growling. I tried to say something, anything, but my mouth wouldn't work.

About then I finally realized I'd been drugged. The thing in my neck was some kind of tranquilizing dart. A still bigger wave of dizziness hit me. I thought I smelled burnt toast and my eyelids felt like anchors tugging downward. The last thing I saw seemed to be in slow motion. Two men ran up and reached menacingly for Reggie. And then everything went black and silent as a tomb.

Chapter Six: A Deep Subject

I WOKE IN DARKNESS, on a hard irregular surface, wet and cold. My head ached and my sinuses throbbed. I had a weight on my chest. I took a deep breath and tried to use my disorientation to beat back the growing sense of panic. I remembered the pain in my neck, followed by the realization that I'd been shot. Panic gave way to fear and I was on the edge of hyperventilating. I would have cried out, but I didn't know where I was or who might hear me, and my imagination happily painted answers that only increased my terror. Instead, I tried to steady my breathing and began an inventory. I flexed my fingers, which I've always found to be the most reassuring way to start. Proprioception immediately told me where my hands and arms were. I reached up slowly to remove whatever was sitting on me. My fingers encountered something shaggy, and then it jolted and rushed toward my head. An instant later Reggie rubbed his face against mine, whimpering with what I took to be relief. I knew exactly how he felt.

"Shh, shh, boy, it's okay," I whispered. My fingers combed through the ringlets of Reggie's fur and held him close as I slowly sat up. Water, or what I hoped was only water, ran down my back. I'd been lying in several centimeters of liquid, and it had soaked through the back of my clothes. Someone had taken my shoes but left me my socks. My belt was missing, and my pockets were empty. I wondered briefly about my coat and then remembered Reggie eating through it and that I'd tossed its remains back at my office.

Cradling Reggie in my arms, I got to my feet and began feeling around in the dark. I moved slowly forward, my squishy socks making faint splashy sounds, until my hands touched a wall. I followed it, walking in a steep arc, my feet splashing echoes. The wall felt like stone, or rather many stones with mortar in the grooves. I walked the wall until I'd gone a tight, full circle. I spent the next half hour feeling every bit of every stone as my anxiety expanded to fill the darkness around me, and discovered neither handholds, nor ladder rungs, nor any kind of opening at all. I tucked Reggie under one arm and jumped, flailed my free hand high in the emptiness above me, and touched nothing. Someone had put me put me here, in a damp room with round walls made of stone and mortar.

67

Lawrence M. Schoen

"Well, well, well," I said to Reggie; he whined in reply, not getting the joke but picking up on my own fear. I leaned against the wall and brought him close to my face. I still couldn't see him, but I could feel his breath. "I don't suppose you were taking any notes during my abduction, eh?"

Reggie again shoved his face against mine. He didn't lick me. Reggie always licks me. The oddity of it was a welcome distraction. I shifted slightly, held him against me with one arm, and brought my other hand up to his face. I tickled the tuft of beard under his chin, and as I did so I could feel him opening his mouth. Something dropped into my hand. Two somethings.

I juggled him a bit, pinning him against my chest with the crook of my elbow while using both hands to explore what he'd given me. They felt like spongy cylinders, several centimeters in length, much less than that in diameter, ragged at one end, probably where Reggie had bitten through. The other end had a curved chitinous edge to it, flat across its surface, which was the only part that didn't feel fleshy. I brought the things closer to my nose; I could smell blood. They were fingers.

Naturally I dropped them. They fell into the darkness with a pair of soft 'plops' and vanished as if they'd never been. In a day of one impossible thing after another, this one shook me most of all. While I knew that buffalo dogs *could* it eat anything, I'd never known one to sink its teeth into a living creature before.

"Reggie, did you bite off someone's fingers?" He squirmed against me until he achieved a comfortable position to lick my face. I slumped against the wall and let him while I considered my circumstances. On the negative side, I'd obviously been abducted and imprisoned. I was cold, wet, barely on the right side of panic, and likely I'd be adding hungry and thirsty to my list as well. I didn't want to test the potability of the puddle at my feet, but I knew it might come to that. On the plus side, whoever had done this apparently needed me alive. I clung to that fact; other than my frightened buffalo dog, it seemed to be all I had.

Judging the passage of time while sitting purposeless at the bottom of a dark well involves talents and skills that I don't possess. I passed the hours mentally reviewing the number of clubs I'd performed and trying to determine if there was an underlying pattern to those I'd been thrown out of. I didn't expect to reach any real insights, but it helped to calm me and keep me focused on something other than the fact that I'd been thrown into a dark well. I'd broken it down into three main causes: hecklers, drunk audience members, and crooked club owners. I still hadn't come to any solid conclusions when my solitude was interrupted by a scraping sound, like wood dragged across stone.

68

"Are you awake, Earth Monster?" said a voice from on high.

A heckler if ever there was one, I thought to myself. "Who wants to know?" I said, attempting a bravado that I didn't feel, but that's how you have to deal with hecklers. Reggie added an inquiring yip of his own.

"I rather hoped your beast had drowned. He nearly killed two of my men."

I looked up. In the blackness overhead I could see a faintly lighter circle of darkness and a twinkle or two that might have been stars, some six, maybe seven meters above. The acoustics of the well played with the voice. Despite a slight Spanish accent, I could tell from its flatness it emerged from a device and not a human throat. The speaker could have been foreign or alien, someone who needed a translator appliance, or just wanted to disguise his true voice.

"Are these 'men' the guys in suits who attacked Montgomery and me?"

"Our doctor has stitched up their other injuries, but we'd feared your beast had swallowed the fingers."

"He wouldn't," I said. "Buffalo dogs don't eat meat. There are so many tastier treats in the world."

"So the fingers are down there? Would you mind tossing them up? We still have time to reattach them, if we hurry."

"I would if I could, but I've dropped them. Why don't you come down here and we can look for them together."

"I'm sorry, but I can't do that." He sighed. "We'll just have to arrange for regrowth treatments."

My fear slipped a little, giving way to a growing anger. "That's alien technology. Isn't it a bit hypocritical for members of Green Aggression to take advantage of it when it suits your needs?"

"Not at all. Until our enemies are vanquished, we allow ourselves the full range of their creations, the better for us to know them and what they are capable of. Or did you think that Kudzu-nine was developed without alien assistance?"

"I can't say that I've given it much thought. You'll pardon me, but I'm a bit preoccupied at the moment."

"Such a cool head you have, Mr. Conroy. Aren't you afraid for your life?"

"You're mistaking logic for calm," I said. "If you wanted me dead, you've already had plenty of time to kill me. You clearly have other plans. And seeing as you've left Reggie with me, you appear to want me as kindly disposed to you as possible."

"You're right on the first point, but not the second. We tried to leave the beast behind, but he climbed on top of you and started snarling and snapping at anyone who came near. That's how Jimmy lost those fingers and Carl had his arm lacerated. Finally, we just threw a net on both of you and dragged you off. It was easier than risking any more injuries."

In all likelihood they'd done more than just attempt to leave Reggie behind. I didn't for a moment doubt that they'd tried to tranquilize him, or even shoot him with something more lethal, and had only been prevented by his nearly impenetrable hide. "Sorry we've been such a bother for you."

"More than you realize. We had planned for the kudzu to keep you and your company disorganized for days, maybe weeks. When you cleaned it up in a single night, you forced us to change our plans."

I laughed. It made a weird sound from the bottom of a well. "There I go, inconveniencing you again. So, how do you know the kudzu's all gone? Did you have a spy among the agents on the scene today? One of Montgomery's teams?"

"You're quick, Mr. Conroy, but we're quicker. We're fighting a war, even if you don't see it that way. We intended the kudzu as another warning, but your unwillingness to listen to reason, combined with the surprising adaptability of your creatures, convinced me to move up our timetable accordingly."

"So, what happens now?"

"Now? Now you sit and wait. When your company meets our demand to stop using your animals at the waste sites, and pays us the ransom, you'll get to go free and Green Aggression will have solved its financing problems for years to come."

It wasn't a bad plan. Despite its worth, Buffalogic was a tiny company, and my employees were fiercely loyal. They'd do anything Green Aggression demanded to get me back. "Sounds like you've got it all figured out."

"What, did you think we were novices? We often improvise, but we're not naïve; we're dedicated to our cause. But I wouldn't expect the Earth Monster to understand that."

"Earth Monster, right. Say, I don't suppose you could toss down a few towels for the ol' Earth Monster? It's more than a trifle damp down here."

"I'm letting you live, Mr. Conroy. I'm not inclined to offer you any amenities. But don't worry, I'll stop in now and then to keep you informed and fed. But, if you'll excuse me, I need to go leak word of our demands back to your friend Montgomery."

"You didn't kidnap him as well?"

"Better for us to have him running around trying to find you than persecuting us."

"What will you do if they don't pay the ransom?"

"The same thing we'd eventually do even if they did pay. Your buffalo dogs are an abomination on this planet. We won't be content until they are shipped offworld or destroyed. But we're not the insane fringe group you make us out to be. We're not out to ruin your business, just get it off our planet. If your people are smart and meet our demands that will be the end of it. Otherwise, we'll be forced to take more drastic actions."

"What does that mean?"

"Nothing complicated. If you or your company insists on being uncooperative, we'll blow up your building and kill your inventory. That should discourage anyone wishing to bring buffalo dogs to Earth."

"That's insane. You'd be murdering innocent people."

"They had their warning."

"What, the kudzu?" I asked. "The ransom demands?"

"We only tell you once. If your people are still working there after our little warning, well, they've made their own choice. Think of it as evolution in action. They're obviously too enamored of alien technology to be allowed to live in an Earth-based society."

Before I could work up any kind of reply, he slid the lid over the opening until even that suggestion of light was gone. Damn. I slumped against the wall and petted Reggie. "I don't suppose things can get much worse, do you?" Reggie licked my face again. Then he farted.

Chapter Seven: Drinking from Rhea's Daughter

Physiology is a funny thing. No matter how stressful or threatening a situation, the human body can only maintain that classic flight-or-flight mode for so long. Eventually your body demands some down time to recharge. That's when, willing or not, you crash into sleep. And sleep brings dreams.

A year had passed since my last trip to Titan—where they never quite get the artificial gravity right and you pay for the spectacular views of Jupiter with a queasy stomach every seventeen hours. I didn't have the slightest urge to return to that geologically quirky moon, but my subconscious crafted a dream putting me there, having conveniently forgotten I was really lying at the bottom of a well.

I was in Rhea's café, seated at a slab of local wood bio-engineered to grow into the perfect coffee shop table, neatly bypassing that bothersome tree stage. I was drinking out of one of the six special mugs known as 'Rhea's children' which the owner held in reserve for use only at this corner table. At different times of the Titan year one or another of the six mugs leaked, just a little bit. If you were using that mug at that time, you'd end up leaving a ring on the table. Over the years a lot of famous people had sat there, and sometimes they ended up with the right mug at the right time and left a ring. The custom was to sign your name and print the date alongside the ring, and then the table would receive another layer of a megaurethane varnish to preserve the event. The custom had a long history, as evidenced by the two-centimeter thick coating on the table.

My mug—Demeter, to be precise—contained an exquisite iced coffee made from blended Arabica beans with a taste of hazelnut and just the barest hint of mint. There's something about the gravity or the atmospheric pressure or both that just makes coffee taste better on Titan. Maybe it's just the *frisson* of drinking something so obscenely expensive as real coffee shipped in from Earth. While I sat reading the names and dates of previous occupants a server brought over a large cup of hot rococoa and set it in front of me.

"Excuse me," I said, "that's not mine. There's been a mistake." The top of the cup overflowed with the ornate flourish of sculpted whipping cream that gave the beverage its name.

"No mistake," said a lip-like pair of folds made of cream, as it expanded in volume and oozed over the limits of its cup. While I watched, it flowed over the table and onto an opposite chair. Twin tributaries of delicate white fluff sprang from the main river of whipping cream and took on definition and shape. They became arms, bright, white, cloudlike arms of creamy fluff that extended from what had grown to become a whipped cream torso. In the end, the last of the froth separated from the cup leaving behind only cocoa. The result looked like a man raising his head after sipping from a mug. A soft mushy man, one made entirely of white foam. A different server passed by, and placed a dark green fedora on the creature's head. It sank in several centimeters before settling.

"Oh, sorry," I said, "I thought you were just a regular cup of rococoa."

"Focus, you fool! You're running out of time."

As if to punctuate the dark foreboding of my bright white prophet, large cracks began forming in the window wall of Café Rhea. That got my attention in a way that my fantastical tablemate hadn't. Part of the allure of the café was its location on the perimeter of one of Titan's domed resorts. Its windows looked out upon the raw stuff of the moon's atmosphere, half again as dense as Earth's, and utterly unbreathable.

"What's happening?" I said, rising from my seat, and stopping only when I realized I was already backed into the corner. "That glass is built to withstand any impact. How can it be cracking?"

"Don't ask how," said the whipped cream creature. "Get it clear in your head; this is an allegory for what's coming. It's real but not inevitable. You've got to be ready to stop things before they get so far."

The cracks in the glass expanded and multiplied. The wall began to bow inward, as the greater external pressure exerted itself. All around me other patrons began panicking. I was ready to join in.

"Before what things get that far?" I shouted, trying to be heard over the din of the café.

"I can help you," it said, its voice soft and clear despite the cacophony around us. "If you'd just slow down I could mesh with you, guide you more effectively. I only need you to give me a little—"

"Whatever it is you want to sell, I'm not buying," I said, cutting it off and climbing up onto the table. "Either you're a just a fluffy figment of my own imagination—in which case you don't really need me to give you anything—or you're something else with no business in my head, and I'm certainly not going to trust you."

"Stubborn human! I am trying to help you so that you in turn can help me. Your enemies will attack your very foundation. They will explode it out from under you. Can you understand that? Let us mesh and—"

The window wall chose that moment to shatter in an orchestra of tiny sounds that drowned out whatever else my fluffy oracle had to say. Shards of nearly indestructible glass exploded into the room, a million jagged pieces, like runners in a marathon each with its own definition of the finish line. They sliced through everything they struck, propelled by the dense nitrogen fog of Titan's atmosphere. They passed harmlessly through my companion, slowing only long enough to acquire a slight coating of white foam. Some of these, and some which hadn't gone through him, pierced me in a double hundred places. I screamed, knocking *me* back into my chair.

"Time," said the whipped cream man, reaching up with one foamy hand to remove his hat, slicing away the top layer of his head in the process. "You need to let me in. Just a bit more. While there's still time."

And then I woke up, flailing my arms. I'd carried my scream into the waking world, feeling the slivers cutting me. Only, they weren't. I was in darkness, which at first was even more terrifying. And then I remembered where I was, and realized I'd been dreaming. I slapped my hands out around me and confirmed I was sitting in the same few centimeters of water, leaning back against the inner wall of a well, with my buffalo dog on my lap. Reggie snorted in his sleep at my unnecessary movement but did not awaken.

"Too real," I told myself. That dream, like the last one, had ended in disaster. And like the last one, it had contained some kind of cryptic warning. Once might have been a fluke, but twice? And first a snowman and this time a . . . what? a whipped cream sculpture? My years as a hypnotist had brought me into contact with a variety of telepathic phenomena; I didn't recognize this particular style, but someone was trying to communicate to me. But what was I supposed to stop? And what was that bit about my enemies attacking my foundation? Telepathy is supposed to be clearer than traditional, linguistic communication. A pity no one had explained this to whatever was poking its way into my dreams.

None of which changed the fact that I was still stuck at the bottom of a well. And yet, dreaming of sudden death had worked as a catharsis for my earlier anxiety. For the first time since waking up in the well I felt a kind of calm. Maybe the best thing to do was to wait for my captors' next move. They hadn't actually harmed me yet. I was their bargaining chip, and they needed me hale and whole. And yet, the same couldn't be said about my employees. Were they at risk? Was that the 'foundation' mentioned by the whipped cream man? No, I couldn't just sit passively in the bottom of a well with a soggy backside.

"Reggie, wake up. Time for us to get out of here."

My buffalo dog awoke with a confused shake of his head. I stood up and held Reggie at waist height, pressing his face to the wall, right up against one of the stones.

"Go ahead, boy, take a bite. You'll like it."

Squirming slightly, Reggie licked at the stone, his tongue making a faint rasping sound. He licked again, and then pressed his teeth in, cutting through the dense rock like so much soft cheese. I let him keep at it for a bit, until he'd chewed through enough to create a good-sized handhold. Then I lifted him up a bit higher and had him start in again. Reggie liked the game, and began chewing through the stone more rapidly. After only a few seconds the farting began, a very audible and steady stream of gas. Somewhere inside him, Reggie's remarkable digestive system had begun converting dense rock to pure oxygen.

I shoved a soggy, socked foot into the first opening, and balanced Reggie on my shoulder. Reaching my hand into the second slot I hauled myself up, leaving the water below. I positioned Reggie to eat the next rung in our ladder. His perch was precarious at best, but bite by bite we crept upwards, accompanied by the twin sounds of Reggie's flatulence and chewing, and with me hanging on for dear life. Long minutes later we reached the very top, where tentative probing with my head confirmed the well had been covered over with a wooden cap. Covered and tightly bolted. I hadn't expected that. I clung to the wall and teetered on the brink of exhaustion. The adrenaline that had taken me up the inside of the shaft, deserted me. A part of me wanted to just let go, push off from the wall and fall. I let that thought slip away. The way my luck had been running I'd probably break my legs. Instead, I set my mind to finding something a bit more productive.

I simply didn't have the purchase or the balance to hold Reggie above me, much as I wanted to let him eat through that lid. But maybe I didn't have to. This high up and close to the mouth of the well, we were surely above ground. With words of encouragement I directed Reggie to keep eating at the level of the last handhold. I rarely let him eat so much dense matter in so short a time. The little guy reacted like he was on holiday and dove in. He'd gotten his second wind and bumped up to the next level of buffalo dog satiety, if not the one beyond it. Listening in the dark to the horrible noises he made as he bit into the stone, chewed, swallowed, I envisioned a much more fearsome creature than my innocent looking buffalo dog. The release of oxygen from his back end became a steady breeze.

Once he'd eaten enough to create a tiny shelf I set Reggie in place and he was able to really tear into the wall. The shelf widened and deepened, and

I pulled myself in behind him, squeezing to fit the shallow height of it. Never had Reggie eaten this much, this quickly, and in an enclosed space. It felt like being in a wind tunnel and I had to duck my head to avoid hyperventilating.

Reggie barked when he bit through into daylight, and a wave of relief hit me, reminding me of just of how scared I'd been. I wasn't out of the woods yet, or more accurately, out of the well, but I was no longer lost in darkness. I gave Reggie a reassuring pat on his rump and he continued his feast, exhuming us in the process.

Reggie jumped through and I wriggled out right behind him, executed a forward roll and landed on my head in an open field. Soggy, sweaty, and dirty, I was content to just lie there and soak in the basic pleasure of sunshine on my skin. That, and I needed a few minutes before the trembling in my hands stopped. It looked and felt like late morning. Reggie dashed back and forth across the field, his mouth to the ground as he tore furrows like a living plow, caught up in the need to eat and eat and eat. I'd seen that same frenzy in other buffalitos during our waste disposal demonstrations. Those animals had been trained to go back and forth in orderly rows, but Reggie looked to be dancing in circles without a care, ravenous but happy. I doubted he had any real recollection of protecting me a day earlier, or biting off a couple fingers.

Thinking of those fingers, I brought a couple of my own to my lips and gave a whistle. Reggie swung around and frantically ate his way over to me, capering about my feet in ever widening circles as he consumed wild grass and dirt. I crouched, spread my arms wide, and lunged for him as I had in countless games before. This time though it wasn't a game.

"Easy, boy, easy. I know this seems like a big adventure to you, but feeding time is over. You've got to calm down."

Reggie squirmed in my grasp, genuinely unhappy and confused by the change. I rolled into a sitting position, braced my elbows against my knees, and just held him away from my body. He writhed and wriggled, desperate to get free, to bring his muzzle in range of something he could devour. His jaws kept working for several minutes, chewing the air. The roar of his flatulence diminished and finally faded completely. Reggie stopped squirming. His little blue tongue darted out one last time to lick his lips, and he barked as if to let me know it was safe to set him down and move on to our next game.

He had the right idea. If I believed my dream, the game was some kind of reverse sort of hide and seek. We'd been hidden, and now I had to seek a way back, before Green Aggression discovered we'd escaped, and definitely before they started blowing up my people, my buffalitos, and my building.

There were no paths leading away from the well. Judging by the size and shape of a depression in the grass, my kidnappers had brought me here in a floater or similar skimmer, leaving no trail that I could follow back to civilization. All I could see around me was empty field. One direction was as good as any other; I set my buffalo dog on the ground, stood up, and based on the position of the sun started walking toward what I thought was eastward. Reggie trotted along beside me.

I'm about as good at judging distance as I am at judging time, so I'm uncertain how long or how far we walked. My feet ached, but that was more due to my lack of shoes than the distance traveled. Eventually the empty fields gave way to cultivated fields, and beyond these I encountered a paved roadway. Reggie and I changed direction slightly and kept walking down the road. I flagged down the first vehicle to come along, a battered pick-up truck that had to be older than I was. Its driver couldn't have been more than seventeen. He pulled the truck over to the side of the road and flung the passenger door open.

"You lost, mister?"

"A little bit. Where am I?"

"That's the edge of the Dorrance farm there behind you, and the start of the Burke combine on the other side of this road."

"No, I mean what city? What state? This is the U.S., isn't it?"

He looked at me like I was from another planet, then glanced at Reggie which seemed to confirm it. "This is Bittersville, in Lancaster County. You're in Pennsylvania, mister."

So I wasn't that far from home after all. I had no identification, no money, and no means to get back to my office, but all of those had a common solution.

I climbed into the cab of the truck, settled Reggie on my lap and offered my hand. "My name's Conroy. What's yours?"

"Everett."

"Well, Everett, this is going to sound pretty strange, but tell me, what would you think about selling me this truck for a thousand creds in cash, and a registered bank note for another forty thousand?"

"Are you crazy?"

"Crazy in a hurry. I need to get to Philadelphia, and I need to get there fast. If you can drive me to the nearest bank, I'll buy this truck then and there."

That was all the argument it took. Everett pushed the old truck to its limits and twenty minutes later, according to the dashboard clock, we'd arrived at a Lancaster First National Savings hut. I scooped up Reggie, jumped out of the pick-up, and rushed to the bank kiosk. It was a standard design and within seconds of tapping on its wall terminal, I'd linked up to my own bank. I fed in responses to a dozen identification questions and code requests, until I convinced both smart systems that I very probably was who I claimed to be. That confirmation activated scramble software at my bank which began backtracking to the beginning of the transaction. By the time I finished, there'd be no way to trace where I'd accessed my accounts from. Maybe I was being overly paranoid, but when you're running scared it's hard to be certain. I'd made the mistake of underestimating Green Aggression more than once already.

I maxed out the kiosk's allowable cash withdraw, and then had to go through another series of questions and codes before my bank could convince it to generate a bank note for the extra forty grand I'd promised Everett. It was ten or twenty times the worth of the truck, but the number had popped into my head and it wasn't like I couldn't afford it.

Five minutes later, having traded some cash and the check for a set of car keys and a rabbit's foot keyring, I waved goodbye to a stunned but richer teenager. Reggie settled himself on the passenger side of the bench seat and gave me what I took to be a reassuring nod.

I drove to the nearest service station and acquired a map, a full tank of gas, and a meatloaf sandwich made more tasty than it should have been by my appetite. Unlike Reggie, I hadn't eaten since lunch the day before. I washed it down with a bottle of root beer and set off on the road to Philadelphia. With a good wind we'd be back home in less than two hours. I had just that much time to come up with a plan.

Chapter Eight: Crashing the Buffalitos

THE TRUCK SMELLED LIKE IT HAD BEEN hauling manure but other than a slight vibration at higher speeds it handled pretty well. Reggie found the buzz pleasant enough to be lulled to sleep. I drove with the windows down and tried to distract myself from the stink. The events of the previous day bounced around in my head, ricocheting off possible courses of action. The eco-terrorists had probably already delivered their ransom demands. Given the kind of money they wanted, they'd have to give my people at least a day to gather it. Anything I came up with had to happen soon.

As the truck barreled down the road, I realized that thwarting the eco-terrorists had become a goal unto itself. Oh sure, I agreed with the basic humanistic goals of the clean-up project, but they didn't motivate me the way they moved Eliza. Nor did the potential money and business opportunities that had started to come in as a consequence of it; that kind of thing worked for Betsy, not me. No, Left-John had been right, I was attracted to the game of it. It had the same thrill that I used to get on stage. I'd hypnotize someone, and for a brief time I'd get to play with the rules of their reality. Was this all that different? Being a CEO was just a means to let me change the rules for a lot of people all at once.

I'd been fooling myself since the day I started the company, and it took the bastards at Green Aggression messing with my game to make me realize the truth. And because it was *my* game, their attacks and threats on the project were personal. Maybe I couldn't fight back against a faceless opponent, but I didn't have to. To beat them I only had to keep the clean-up project online. My success would be their failure, and my motivation wasn't altruistic or capitalistic, it was simple revenge. They'd gotten this far because I'd been operating in the public eye, playing the role of the CEO. That was going to change. This was a different game, with other players to consider than just myself. It required different rules. For the welfare of my employees and my alien livestock, it was time to take things in a new direction.

I didn't bother to park when I got to my building; I just pulled the truck up onto the sidewalk where Montgomery's car had been the night before. Reggie yawned in his sleep when I snatched him up. As I strode into the lobby, I noted that everything had been restored; there was no sign of the previous day's attack. The usual two-person security team snapped to attention as I approached their scanning arc.

"Mr. Conroy? We heard—"

"Sir? The FBI said you had been—"

I interrupted their questions with a wave of my hand. "They did, and I was, and now I'm here," I said. "But don't worry about that just now. We're bugging out. I want every man, woman, and buffalito out of here. Go to full evacuation mode. Now."

They gaped for a few seconds, but by the time I'd passed through the scan and walked on to the elevator they had moved into action. As the doors closed, Reggie yawned again, squirmed, and came fully awake. I set him down as I stepped into the foyer of the second floor. Standing under the Gotherman triptych, each of them framed by a panel, were my assistant Jeanie, some incarnation of Dr. Elizabeth Penrose, and Special Agent Arlen Montgomery. Jeanie saw me first.

"Mr. Conroy! You're supposed to be kidnapped. I mean—"

"Been there, done that," I said, and turned to Montgomery. "Good to see you're all right."

He nodded and blushed slightly. "They took us out with trank darts. One of my own men was working the other side. I saw you go down, and then I was hit."

"I take it you've gotten ransom demands from my abductors?"

He nodded, glanced briefly down at my shoeless feet, and pulled a flimsie from an inside breast pocket. "Your COO here received it this morning, along with your wallet. My people confirmed its authenticity. I've got a team on it, hoping for a lucky break, but meanwhile Dr. Penrose has gone ahead and authorized full payment. We were about to go over the directions for the drop off."

Chief of Operations. That answered the Penrose question. "Fine, well, we don't need to worry about that now." I turned my attention to Betsy. "I want you to crash the office. Do you understand me? Crash everything."

She blinked once, twice, and let out her breath. She understood. "How soon?"

I'd thought about that on the drive in. Part of me wanted to march everyone out of the building immediately, but it just wasn't practical. That would have left too many loose ends for Green Aggression to tug on. "Two hours. First, put out the word that every buffalito we have ready to sell is available for immediate acquisition at half price for the next hour. That should free up at least a third of the handlers and trainers. Double people up on the remaining buffalo dogs. If you've got any personnel left over, triple up any teams with fertile buffalitos. Then, scatter all the groups. There are hard-coded travel vouchers and a box of dedicated securephones in my office safe. Show them to no one, just hand them out to each team, everybody gets a voucher and a phone. Give the gold tickets to the handlers with the breeding pups, okay?"

"Yes, sir, I understand. Anything else?"

"How many buffalitos do we currently have out on leased assignment, Earth only?"

She didn't hesitate. "Twenty-seven."

"Recall them all, now, before you do anything else. Rescramble the phone for each call and keep them short. Don't explain the orders to the handler, you don't have time and they don't need to know. Do an emergency recall for all twenty-seven buffalo dogs and their handlers. When they come in, give them vouchers and phones and send them right back out again."

"What about Mexico?" she said, and I knew she was trying not to have it sound like a plea, asking more for Lisa and Eliza than for herself.

"We are very much still on for Mexico. Once everyone here has gone, once you've handled the recalls, give the list for the phones to Lisa. You're going ahead with the project."

"I can't endorse this choice of action." Montgomery's hand was on my shoulder. "Moreover, where are you going to be?"

I smiled. This was my game. "I'll be calling in a favor or two. No offense, Montgomery, but I have some old contacts that play by very different rules and can probably turn up information on Green Aggression that your Bureau can't. I'm not going to sit by and let anyone, eco-terrorists or not, take shots at me or my people. Better to keep them off balance."

Montgomery's frown of disapproval was almost touching. "You're not going to Mexico with your clean-up team?"

I shook my head and turned back to Betsy. "Make sure Lisa understands that she's to go ahead with the project whether she hears from me before the target date or not."

"She's not going to like that."

"Maybe not, but solving Mexico's pollution nightmare will cut Green Aggression off at the knees. Okay, are we clear?"

Betsy held up a hand and ticked off assignments on her fingers. "Call in all active teams current onworld, discount the stock on hand for immediate sale, reallocate personnel, distribute travel and communication, brief Lisa, and crash everything."

"Perfect." I turned to Jeanie. "I need you to find all the other employees, from janitors to accountants to lawyers. Send them home."

"You can't just send people home," said Montgomery. "You'll start a panic in your company." Jeanie nodded in agreement.

I smiled. "Tell them we're going on hiatus for a couple weeks. Call it a paid vacation, until a security team can sweep the entire building. They all know what happened yesterday. Blame it on that kudzu, and tell them we're just being cautious. Bottom line, I want everyone out of here in two hours."

"Yes, sir!"

Montgomery said, "I can help you there. I've got a five-man team in the building, and they can help with the evacuation."

"Thanks, I appreciate the assistance."

Montgomery nodded, stepped to one side, and whispered a few curt instructions into his sleeve. A moment later he was back. "I need to talk to you," he said. "I need you to tell me what happened after last night. Where they took you, what they did to you, how you got away."

"Not a problem, but can we walk while we talk? I need to spend the next hour or so upstairs with Reggie. No matter how well we do this, the anxiety level will peak, and the buffalitos are going to sense that. If they see Reggie they'll know everything's fine, and we'll have an orderly evacuation."

"And after that?"

"After that, I'll be heading to Texas."

"Texas? You can't be serious! It's too dangerous."

"That's where my contacts are. I've been there before, and it's not the kind of place that Green Aggression is likely to be. Plus, it minimizes the time I'll be at risk. The way I figure it, there's not a better place to hide out than the lost state of Texas."

I turned back to Jeanie and Betsy and the look in their eyes bolstered my confidence. This was going to work. "Let's go. The sooner we start this, the sooner we'll all be out of here. I promise I'll see you both again real soon."

They scattered to their respective tasks leaving me alone with Agent Montgomery. I whistled for Reggie and headed back to my office. Montgomery followed me.

"Why are you doing all this, Conroy?"

Instead of answering him, I went straight to the safe in the wall behind my desk. Betsy would be dig through it later for the travel vouchers and phones. I helped myself to one of the phones and all the loose cash that I kept there. Agent Montgomery's people had left my wallet on my desk and I took and filled it. Then I headed to the closet for a change of clothes and some shoes. I'd have liked a shower, but I didn't feel I could spare the time. I glanced back at Montgomery.

"I woke up in the bottom of a well last night. I didn't get a look at him, but I had a chat with someone from Green Aggression. He threatened to blow up this building, threatened to kill everyone here, until they got their way. Well, they can't do that if no one is here."

Montgomery said nothing while I finished dressing, presumably processing everything I'd told him. I picked up Reggie and then, for the second time in two days, I led the FBI agent to the stairwell and up to the next floor. I stuck my head into the amphitheater first, just to confirm that it was empty. Then with Montgomery following a step or two behind me, Reggie and I made our rounds of the floor. I opened every office door we passed and offered reassuring nods to each trainer and handler I saw. Reggie yapped to their charges. There was a feeling of nervous anticipation in the air; everyone seemed to be waiting for the other shoe to drop. I intended to get everyone out before that happened.

Montgomery had pulled out a padd and as we made our rounds I went back to the beginning and told him everything I remembered, from the fingertips of someone named Jimmy to the truck I'd bought from Everett. Talking through it was oddly soothing, like it had happened to someone else. It was an illusory calm. In half an hour, the buffalo dog market would be in an uproar. An hour after that, almost everyone who worked for me would be on his way somewhere else. By the time the Green Aggression whackos found out they'd be too late. My people would be safe, and the company's critical resources, the buffalo dogs themselves, would be distributed throughout the country awaiting their call to action weeks down the road. I knew Lisa Penrose would see to that.

When we finished the loop of the third floor Reggie and I headed back to my office. Montgomery went off to meet with his people and do whatever FBI agents do. My next task had two parts. Before I could mount a successful offensive I had to find out what was really going on. Why had Green Aggression escalated their tactics from costly but essentially bothersome attacks to assault, abduction, and threats of outright murder. At the same time, I had to avoid being caught by the eco-terrorists. I'd just made that part a bit trickier by cutting myself off from my main source of information, and their loyal zealots might be anywhere. But I could manage a good deal of both pieces by getting myself into the remains of Texas, where legality was just a word in the dictionary and information worked better than currency.

I reached for my phone and I dialed the number of the Golden Turtle Palace. Texas was a big place, and while the various personae of Elizabeth Penrose could organize and execute the Mexico clean-up without my

83

assistance, I'm smart enough to know when I need help. Who better to invite along than a professional gambler, particularly since the place held a bit of history for both me and Left-John Mocker? There's no other man in any world that I'd rather have at my back in a fight, and I had no illusions; I was in for a fight. Besides, hadn't he been the one to say I needed adventure?

It took about ten minutes on the phone with the manager at the Golden Turtle Palace before I understood that Left-John Mocker hadn't been to the restaurant since our meeting the day before, and that I had no hope of leaving a message that would be passed along with any degree of coherence.

"Mr. Conroy?"

The words startled me. Jeanie stood in front of my desk, looking embarrassed at having surprised me. She held Reggie in her arms. "Jeanie? Why are you still here?"

"I leave when you leave, sir. Everyone else has gone."

"Really? Dr. Penrose too?"

She nodded, hesitated, and then added, "She said something about needing to take care of the fertile pups. It was odd; she sounded almost gleeful."

I shrugged it off. Even under the current circumstances, I knew there was no place that Lisa Penrose would rather be than with our breeding stock. "Did the FBI leave too?"

"Yes, sir. Special agent Montgomery and all his people left about five minutes ago. He asked me to give you this." She handed me a card with Montgomery's name, phone number, and globalink address. I slipped it into a pocket.

"Let's go, then." She gave Reggie to me, and we headed to the elevator and took it down to the lobby. Security was waiting for us. I took a moment and reviewed the log, confirming that everyone who had come in had indeed already left. Then we activated the building's internal security measures, floor by floor. If Green Aggression tried to get in here they'd find themselves stunned, tranked, and trussed up like Thanksgiving turkeys, with a complete video record transmitted to four different law enforcement agencies. I hoped that would be enough.

"Okay, folks. That's everything. The doors will lock themselves when the last of us exit, right?"

One security guard nodded. The other said, "Yes, sir."

"Great. One last thing then. Would the two of you mind escorting Jeanie to wherever she's headed? I'd appreciate it."

"No problem, sir. Ma'am?"

Jeanie frowned at me. "What about you, Mr. Conroy?"

"I'll be leaving soon after," I said, probably sounding more wistful than I'd have liked. "I just want to sit here a minute. I've never been here when the place was so empty. Don't worry, I'll be fine, and I'll check in when I get to Texas. Now scoot."

Jeanie traded her frown for a furrowed brow but let the security team lead her away. The door sealed behind them, locking the world out. I set Reggie on the floor and began a slow circuit of the lobby. Unlike the historic brick of the building's façade, I'd had the lobby designed with more modern decor. A vaulted ceiling invited visitors to look up as they entered, and a ten-meter tall bronze statue of a buffalo dog greeted their gaze. It stood upon a green marble base of the northern hemisphere, an alien colossus bestride the world. Radiating outward from that base, large black floor panels gleamed; flecks of light contained in their depths twinkled with the night sky as seen from worlds throughout human space. Walking across the floor set the constellations in motion. It was an effect that Reggie especially enjoyed, and he capered after me, barking at the stars dancing beneath his hooves.

A phone rang. Reggie skidded to a stop and we both turned toward the sound. Behind us, at the security desk's console, a small light flickered and a handset rang again. The timing of it reminded me of a bad vid.

"I don't believe it," I said. "Betsy checking up on me already?" I crossed the lobby to the desk and answered the call.

"Mr. Conroy?"

The voice was familiar, flat and artificial, with a Spanish accent. "Yeah?"

"Ah, good, I feared I might have missed you. I wanted to apologize."

"I don't think that will satisfy the FBI. An apology doesn't quite balance a kidnapping charge."

"Oh, I'm not apologizing for your abduction, just for underestimating you. I had the impression that you were just a corporate figurehead, but having seen you in action today, I know better."

"You were here today?"

"Of course. I left with the rest of the FBI."

"So Montgomery had more than one spy among his people. I'll be sure to let him know."

"I don't think you'll have the chance."

"Why's that?"

"While you were evacuating your employees I was checking on the charges I'd secreted throughout your building over the last twenty-four hours."

"Charges? You've rigged my building with explosive charges?" The hubris and efficiency of this particular eco-terrorist impressed me, but I wasn't worried. My building had been designed by a team of Glomarkan engineers, saurian aliens for whom architecture came as naturally as breathing. A spaceship could strike the place and it wouldn't budge. In fact, much of the same technology that allowed vessels to traverse the galaxy had gone into its design. If I ever wanted to expand, I'd need another group of Glomarkans to dismantle the place first.

"We tried to reason with you. We tried to take you out without injury. But you've left us no other choice. It would have been better for us to have broken you and your company before the eyes of the world, but we can make the death of the Earth Monster serve nearly as well."

A high pitched ringing started, inducing an instant case of tintinitus. It came from the entrance. I looked up and saw a flash of light encompass the doors. The light faded and took the doors with it, leaving behind a barrier of melted metal and poly-ceramo. Then the sound deepened and grew louder. It mimicked an oncoming freight train, as if a tornado was touching down just outside. Reggie began howling. The lobby shook as if in the grip of an eight point earthquake. And from the phone in my hand an artificial voice shouted at me over the din.

"Not explosive charges, Mr. Conroy, infra-spatial vibrational charges, courtesy of a Glomarkan demolition firm."

The phone tumbled from my hand and I ran for Reggie. Stars whirled beneath my feet in alien patterns. I stumbled, slid along the floor and reached for him as four floors of nearly indestructible alien architecture imploded above us. Reggie galloped into my arms, the safest haven he'd ever known. I hugged him against my chest as I rolled, and then cried out in pain when I stopped with a meaty thud against the base of the giant buffalo dog statue.

The roar had become a physical force; it drowned out everything else. Reggie squirmed in my arms until he could lick my nose, whether in reassurance or hope I didn't know. I looked upward and saw the lobby's vaulted ceiling started to crack, break free, and come crashing towards me with the weight and debris of three additional floors behind it.

Chapter Nine: A Chariot of Modern Egypt

Sometimes in moments of profound stress or instances of imminent death, time seems to change and your senses open wide. It's like the air around you has taken on the density of over-cooked oatmeal, and your awareness has grown to encompass your surroundings down to the tiniest grain of sand. Everything slows except you. Armed with new insights and a disregard for temporal laws it's trivially easy to step out of the way of an oncoming car, dodge that haymaker, or leap from the burning bridge. And then, once you're safe, the oatmeal turns back to air and you're left gasping to catch your breath, but alive.

This *wasn't* one of those moments.

I lay sprawled against the base of an immense, bronze statue with my office building falling down on top of my head. Neither time nor my senses had expanded. What happened next went by too quickly to allow me so much as the luxury of pissing myself in terror. I kicked the base of the statue where an artfully disguised maintenance hatch gave way. Amidst the clamor of collapsing Glomarkan architecture I rolled through the hatch and into darkness beyond. Reggie whimpered against my neck and I held him tightly.

While I'd missed out on the cliché of time slowing down, I did experience a sudden flood of memory, the highs and lows of my life's travels and relationships and experiences. All in all, it looked like a pretty good life, and something my great aunt Fiona had told me popped up center stage in my mind. "Regrets are for people who forgot to live the first time around."

The statue had been made in two pieces. The bronze buffalo dog contained a poly-carbon support frame, or it would have collapsed under its own weight. Four stems spread from the body of the statue down, the bones to its bronze legs. These in turn passed like giant bolts through the second piece, the base upon which the buffalo dog stood. Reggie and I occupied the crawl space inside that base where those bolts were fastened, locking the statue securely in place.

The base had been designed to support the weight mounted above it, and likely considerably more, but not the entire rest of the building. But it might hold it back long enough for me to squeeze through a security gate in the floor that opened onto an emergency escape route. That's why the statue had been placed in that spot. When the Glomarkans had built my corporate headquarters, they didn't just design their structures to be solid, they built them to be thorough too. Safety waited just beyond a simple gateway. All I had to do was remember the security code to open the damn thing.

It didn't use a physical key. When I'd talked it over with the architects, it made sense that, in an emergency, forgetting to bring along a key might defeat the whole point of getting out quickly. Instead, the gate had a series of five sliding ceramo plates that had to be quickly moved in the right order, like a child's puzzle box.

I hadn't done it since they'd built the place and I was having trouble remembering the sequence.

Security routinely checked it, tested it, and inspected the escape route itself, from under the giant buffalito statue down to the disguised one-way gate into a city maintenance alcove two blocks away. As I began working the panels for the third time the ceiling struck the statue and a pounding vibration rattled through to the base. The floor moved under me and I felt rather than heard Reggie squeal in the dark. With one arm I held him against my chest and with the other I slid the fifth panel into place and prayed that I'd finally gotten the sequence right.

The floor moved as the gate opened inward and fell away. Up became down, metal screamed around us, and a terrible vibration gripped everything and shook it hard. Tons of debris rained down on the statue, crushing it and wrenching the base it stood upon.

By which time Reggie and I had already tumbled through the open emergency gate and bounced down an air-cushioned slide tube at high speed. Emergency lighting in the escape tube illuminated our way, but as we hurtled downward like Olympic luge contenders, those lights went out. The nigh indestructible, self-contained emergency escape system guaranteed by my Glomarkan designers had succumbed to what I suspected was an equally impressive Glomarkan demolition warrantee.

We plunged on, in darkness if not silence, as the din echoed along every unseen centimeter of our route. And then, just as suddenly, it all stopped. My ears still rang, but it was different now. I could hear my own heart. I could hear Reggie whimpering against my chest. We were still sliding, racing blindly downward with little friction, but we'd left the chaos and devastation behind us. The silence felt as numbing as the noise.

I couldn't tell how fast we were going, but as we began to level out we slowed down. Then the escape slide vanished from beneath me and I was flying through black emptiness with Reggie clutched to my chest. I don't remember screaming, but I'm sure I did.

Whatever destruction had disrupted the slide's emergency lighting hadn't reached to every system. Sensors detected our hurtling bodies and a pressor field kicked in and caught us like a puffy pillow the size of an elephant. We landed gently and rolled to a halt. The pressor beams disengaged and we settled lightly on the floor. I flexed my fingers and toes and took an inventory, and thought back to waking up in a well not all that many hours ago. Amazingly, I still hadn't pissed myself.

"Reggie, either we somehow survived, or they're letting alien pets into the afterlife."

I crept forward until I reached a wall, and began running my hands over it until I found the supply cabinet I knew had to be there somewhere. It opened inward at a touch, and radiance poured out as a battery powered lamp came on.

Reggie climbed up until he could stick his face in the open cabinet. There were several rechargeable flashlights inside, as well as pico-fiber jumpsuits in the style of the city's maintenance workers. The cabinet also had an assortment of small firearms and a hundred rounds of ammo for each. My security chief had insisted on the weaponry on the grounds that they might well be needed if an 'emergency escape' was ever called for, but I'd never handled a gun in my life and wasn't going to start now. I needed more than fire power to defeat Green Aggression.

Ignoring the guns, I juggled Reggie long enough to pull on one of the jumpsuits and then helped myself to a flashlight. I studied the map printed on the inside of the cabinet, and when I knew where I was going I flicked on my light, set Reggie back on the ground, and started walking

We didn't have to go far. The escape route had been designed to allow access to a pre-existing tunnel via a door that couldn't be detected from the other side. A peep hole allowed anyone on this side to make sure the tunnel was empty before passing into it, and the door's mechanism opened with just a light touch and no call for coded slide panels, magnetic keys, or ancient Sumerian passwords.

I peeped and peeked, pressed, and passed through, with Reggie tucked lightly under my left arm. The door closed silently behind us and a swirling breeze of slightly fresher air brought the distant wail of emergency sirens. I waved the flashlight up and down the tunnel, and headed for the exit that, according to the map, lay about a hundred meters away.

When we emerged a few minutes later, I stood at the dead end of a long alley smelling of decaying fish and less pleasant things, about fifteen blocks from the location of my former corporate headquarters. Even here, dust filled the air like lightly falling snow. The wail of the sirens came closer now. I followed the alley to an adjacent street and kept walking in the opposite direction from the sirens. Several blocks later I came to a public globalink screen. I tapped for transportation access and requested a connection to the nearest available vendor.

The screen came to life with a burst of light that resolved itself into a star field. "Universal Cab Company."

"Hi, I'd like—"

"One moment please."

On the screen, one tiny bit of the star field expanded and coalesced into a spiraling galaxy. A cartoon arrow pointed at the mid section and the words 'you are here' appeared, followed by 'please hold.' The sounds of some Coptic-babble pop hit screeched from the speaker, and then just as abruptly, it ended. "Universal Cab, how may I help you?" The voice was young, female, and bored. Somewhere amidst her Newer Jersey twang I distinctly heard the pop of chewing gum.

"Tracking back to this location, how quickly can you get a cab to me?" I asked.

"We can have a vehicle for you in fifteen minutes, sir."

"Tell the driver I want to book him for the day. If he gets here in five minutes I'll not only cover any fines he incurs for speeding but I'll double his fee."

"Just a sec." And I was back on hold, listening to the sounds of bad covers of worse music, but only for an instant. "Bertram's on his way. He says he'll be there in three minutes, four at the outside, and that you'd better not be standing near anything combustible because he'll be coming in hot."

"Bertram sounds like just the kind of driver I need. Thanks a lot."

"Thank you for driving with Universal Cab."

I tapped off from the globalink. The sirens continued their wailing. As I waited, two fire engines roared through the intersection down the street, followed by a third vehicle that spun around the corner at high speed, and hurtled through the few blocks separating us. With little regard for inertia it stopped half a meter in front of me. Universal Cab had arrived; Bertram had beaten his own best time.

The cab looked like crap. It was a late model aerosled, retrofitted with conventional tires to allow it to both cruise on its own cushion of air or conserve fuel and roll along on roads as needed. The body had more dings and dents than the lunar surface, without any of the charm or historic significance. At one time, years earlier, it had been shaped for aerodynamic maneuvers and speed. Now the cracks rippling the length of its organo-ceramo shell marked it as having endured at least one high velocity collision.

The shell had grown back, maintaining or reestablishing its original lines, but never quite the same. The bright red paint job and black lightning bolts along the sides didn't help.

I studied the driver as he exited the cab and stepped toward me. I put him at seventeen, tall and gangly. Judging by the Egyptian style beard and the kohl tattoos around both eyes young Bertram either fancied himself a reincarnation of the ancient pharaohs, or more likely was an adherent of the current Coptic babble craze. That explained the musical selection while I'd been on hold; for all I knew Universal Cab might have been part of the mayor's youth business initiative. The driver wore a multi-pocketed jumpsuit of some coarsely woven, waxed fiber that had been dyed puke green. His shoes looked like gym socks if the gym socks had been dipped repeatedly in wax and allowed to cool. A large bronze ankh hung from a leather thong around his neck. His eyes had that intense focus that accompanies regular use of attentional agonists, a popular drug among Coptics which helped them to make sense out of the musical babble. It probably also explained why he could drive so quickly.

I nodded at him and asked, "Are you Bertram?"

"Yup. You the dude called for a ride?" He opened the rear door and cocked an eyebrow at me. I hadn't thought about it before, but I must have looked like a vagrant. Crawling after Reggie through the dust and debris had torn my clothes and left me filthy. Reggie didn't look much better. Before the driver had second thoughts I reached for my wallet and showed him a wad of bills. He relaxed at once.

"I am. Call me Conroy. So, what's your range on this thing?"

"How far you need to go, Captain?"

I flinched. The other annoying thing about the Coptic lifestyle was the preference to answer all questions with other questions. I wasn't even in his cab yet and I knew that Bertram was going to be a pain. But the meter was running, or would be soon, and I had to get out of town, so I climbed into the cab.

"Far," I said. I tried to decide just what that meant as I strapped myself in. I knew I had to get the hell out of Dodge, but where? I could head back to Newer Jersey and try to connect with Left-John, but I didn't know where he was or when he'd be back. Here and now Green Aggression assumed I was dead, buried under the debris that had so recently been Buffalogic, Inc. There had to be an advantage in that for me, one that would evaporate if too many people saw me.

Reggie chose that moment to fart, long and loud. I looked up into the cab's rearview mirror and Bertram's eyes locked on mine and then shifted to focus on my buffalo dog.

91

"I don't usually allow no pets in my ride," he said.

"Well, considering I'm paying double your normal rate, I hope you'll make an exception."

The driver looked about to reply but stopped as Reggie did an elaborate yawn and stretch, shook his head out from side to side, bleated, and tasted the air with his tiny blue tongue.

"Captain, is that some kind of mutant Llhasa mop dog? I've heard those genemod pets are getting popular, but I didn't ever have one in my cab before."

"His name's Reggie. Don't give him another thought, he's completely house broken."

"That's warp and wicker, Captain. But if he starts blowing chunks or piddling, I'll have to add it to the bill. Speaking of which, the meter started when you sat down. You got a goal state in mind, location-wise, or you just want to sit? Both are same to me, balance of Fahrfegneugen and fuel savings, you scan me?"

I'd followed maybe every other word, and taken my inspiration from the lack. Like most of the general public, Bertram didn't recognize a buffalo dog when one was sitting right inside his own cab. I doubted that would be the case tomorrow after the destruction of my building hit the local news. I had to be sure that 'far' was really 'far enough,' which meant going forward with what I'd planned all along. Even if Green Aggression's mole knew my destination, I had to hope that if they thought I was dead they wouldn't bother looking for me.

"Is there a log made of where your cab goes?"

"There doesn't have to be," he said.

Flexible reality. The favorite philosophy of modern American youth that insisted every aspect of life had to be lived like you were Schroedinger's cat. Listening to Bertram made me wonder if I'd been half so annoying to my parents. Probably.

"Pick a state. Log? No log?"

"Oh, is it like that, Captain? Hey, you don't need to get all Ozymandias on me. You want to go somewhere without anyone but you and me knowing we went, and me getting all forgetful like, then that's how it is. Costs extra, though."

And as quick as that I was on solid ground again. Flexible reality, but with a capitalistic core.

"Triple rate," I said. "Cash. And we go where I say and never went. Deal?"

"Captain, for a triple rate in cash I'd borrow Osiris's carriage and tour the underworld, you know?"

"I'm not planning quite so dramatic a destination. How do you feel about a trip outside the country?"

"Canada? No problem, Captain. I got map plug-ins for every province."

"Not Canada," I said. "Texas."

"Mud," was his reply, which from what I knew about Coptics could mean almost anything from an exclamation of wonder and delight to a protest over the essential foulness of some aspects of life.

I sat back and gave Reggie a pat. "The meter's running, and if you won't do it, that's fine, but I'll have to find someone else who will."

"Captain, why you want to go there?"

"Don't you think that's the one question you really shouldn't ask?" Hah! Two could play that annoying questions game.

He stared at me in the mirror. Then he turned full around, resting his arm on the back of the front seat as he looked at me face to face. I looked back, and so did Reggie.

"It's like this, Captain. This ain't no company cab; my medallion's paid for free and clear, mine, all mine. I'm an independent and I do subcontracting for Universal is all, when the private chauffer gigs are sparse. I can't go bopping across federal borders where my insurance doesn't sway, you follow?"

My nod told him I did. "I can respect pragmatics, but concern over insurance won't change if I told you why I'm going there."

"Yeah, that's fair, Captain. But tell me this then: where in Texas do you want to go? It was a big state back before."

"El Paso," I said.

"Mud. El Paso?"

"El Paso."

"Pardon my asking, Captain, but what's the differential there? I've heard stories you know, but, well, they're stories and it can't all be that bad."

"What have you heard?" I asked him.

"I heard that centuries pass like days in Waco. Is El Paso bad as Waco? I can't be driving into the twenty-second century, Captain, you can understand that."

"I wouldn't ask you to, Bertram, and I've got no intention of going to any place like that myself. El Paso runs slow but not that slow, only about seven to one. And I'll pay you for the full outside time, not just the subjective time. In any case, it's a one way. You'll just be dropping me off, not hanging around yourself. So, you driving me or not?"

He turned back around, put his hands on the steering wheel and then lowered his head to the top of it as well. "It's like this, Captain. If I don't drive you, I'm always going to wonder what might have been. But . . . Texas? Aw, mud!"

He started the cab and put it into gear. We were on our way.

"How long will it take?" I said, steeling myself for a responding question.

"Eight to ten hours, depending."

"Depending on what?"

"On how many times we get stopped once we get near Texas. They patrol the border you know."

"Yes, but poorly. It's not like they've got a raging tourist trade down there. Tens of thousands of people aren't trying to get into Texas every day."

"You are, Captain."

"Point taken," I said. Reggie was making snuffling noises, pressing his face against my stomach, which reminded me that while he'd eaten fairly recently, my last meal had been some time ago. I flashed back to my earlier thoughts of the Golden Turtle Palace, and the pity that they didn't do takeout.

"Bertram, you hungry?"

"Are you buying?" he asked.

I chuckled. Annoying and mercenary at the same time. "Find us something we can drive through and snag on route. Quality place, not a grease bar, okay? I'm guessing you don't mind eating while you drive."

"You ever been to the Anubis Deli, Captain? They're just south of Harrisburg and on our way. Best Egyptian food you can get in five hundred klicks. They make a sambusak turnover that will make you weep. I can call ahead and they'll have it ready for us on a fly by."

Visions of kosheri and hummus danced in my head. My stomach growled, casting its vote and startling Reggie. "Order three full meals. My treat of course. And see if you can get some kitchen towels from them, and maybe some soap and hot water. I'd like to wash up a bit before I eat."

"You got it, Captain. But, uh, *three* dinners?"

"You, me, and my faithful companion," I said.

"You're going to feed good Egyptian food to a dog?"

"Well, you wouldn't want me to feed him bad Egyptian food, would you?"

Silence filled the cab. I settled back in my seat with Reggie on my lap. Green Aggression thought they'd killed me. There was something oddly liberating in that.

Chapter Ten: Two Shows Nightly

HAVING AN OFFICE BUILDING DEMOLISHED around you can prove quite exhausting. At least that's what I told myself when I awoke with a start to the cacophonous blare of Coptic babble. The noise poured from speakers in the rear of the cab, speakers which until now had remained silent and unnoticed. "Would you turn that down?"

The music cut off at once. "Sorry, Captain, you wouldn't wake up. I don't think you could hear me over your own snoring. You were out and down deep in the sleep."

Reggie lay on my chest, curled up nose to paws and sound asleep himself. I eased him onto my lap and sat up. My mouth was dry but otherwise I felt well rested. "Why were you trying to wake me? How long have I been sleeping?"

"About nine hours."

"Nine hours? Where are we?"

"We're just about there. That's the border over there. That's why I woke you."

At my direction Bertram had driven west to Colorado and then cut south deep across New Mexico, taking advantage of the aerosled's ability to travel without the need for roads. The plan was to slip into Texas near the U.S./Mexican border just north of El Paso. I rubbed my eyes and peered out the window at the brightly illuminated line that marked the northern boundary of Mexico.

"Take us east," I said, and Bertram applied some speed and swung us around until we merged with a highway. As expected, we found no U.S. border patrols this far south. We did pass several warning signs alerting us to the imminent edge of the chrono-schism that extended slightly over the Texas border and had claimed a sliver of New Mexico.

"You sure about this, Captain?"

"We'll be fine," I said. "Keep it steady. You'll be on your way back out in under an hour."

We continued east, and without any more flourish than there'd been back when it was just another state, we crossed into the great nation of Texas. I allowed myself to wonder just what I would find waiting for me.

Bertram ignored the posted speed limit. No one challenged us. The highway was empty.

I leaned forward, peering over the headrest of the passenger seat at the signs along the road. Mere minutes after leaving the United States Bertram took an exit, leaving the highway beyond as we entered El Paso. I navigated us from memory, up and down El Paso's wide city streets, finally instructing Bertram to park in front of a night club in what was once the flourishing center of downtown El Paso.

"Why here, Captain?"

I stared out at the desolation of the city's entertainment district. Fifteen years had passed since my last visit, and I saw nothing that hadn't been here then. No new clubs had opened. No changes in signage or decoration, not so much as a new coat of paint. Arguably there hadn't been a pressing need; less than two years had gone by from the local perspective.

Time had begun breaking down in Texas back in 2042, moving at different rates than the rest of the world, trickling briskly back up to speed as people came and went, but always winding back down within hours or minutes. Central Texas had the worst of it. In Waco, even with the constant flow of scientists and social workers, less than a month had passed in nearly fifty years. Here near the western edge of the state the temporal dilation was negligible by comparison. At worst, days here would be weeks to the rest of the world. For a little while though, we still carried our old flow of time with us, giving the good citizens of El Paso a brief, temporal shot in the arm.

"I worked here once," I said, still staring at the Aztec Hotel, Lounge, and Casino across the street. "Fifteen years ago, I did a show there every night for two weeks. Well, to me it was two weeks, as far as the rest of the world knew, I'd been gone for three months."

"It's not very big."

"Most of it's underground," I said. "It's actually shaped like a big pyramid. Cheaper to build down than up, and safer too. I did my hypnosis act on a stage twelve floors down."

"You got an awful big bankroll for a hypnotist, Captain."

I had to laugh at that. "I'm in a different line of work nowadays. But back then the Aztec had been my big break. I was doing cowboy bars and frat parties when I first got home and started as a professional, but it was at the Aztec that I'd signed with an agent who was able to get me bookings back off Earth."

"From this dump?"

"The gigs off world were still dives, but they were off world dives. Anyway, it's all ancient history, even here. But if you don't want to get caught up in the chrono-schism you should be heading back out, and sooner rather than later. We dragged a little normal time in with us, but it's fading fast."

I took the towels Bertram had acquired from the Anubis Deli and fashioned a tiny hammock and eased my sleeping buffalo dog into it as I slid out of the cab. Reggie chuffed. Bertram retracted the driver's window and I leaned into it as I counted out cash for services rendered.

"You're staying here, Captain? I thought you was just passing through."

"Nope. I've got someone I expect to be meeting here. I'm sure he'll get here by and by, especially once the time flow reverts. I appreciate all the driving you did. When I get back to Philadelphia, I promise I'll be a dedicated customer of the Universal Cab company. Tell your boss you've made a customer for life. But remember, this trip never happened."

"Trip? I didn't take no trip, Captain. The fare I picked up was some joker who had me driving back and forth from Philly to Pittsburgh all night long. Something about trying to catch his wife and her lover but he kept getting the hotel wrong."

"That's just foolish enough to be believable," I said. "Nice."

Bertram winked at me. He tossed the money in a small glove box safe and popped his window back up. Seconds later he was revving the engine and driving back to the U.S. and its faster time flow. I waved, but I doubt he saw me.

I imagined I could feel Texas pulling at me, slowing me down relative to the outside world, but it was all in my head. Human senses couldn't perceive a chrono-schism directly. It was the kind of relativistic effect that would have made Einstein proud, and while not actually dangerous in itself, the social side effects could easily get a person killed.

The underfunded border patrol around Texas existed to keep track of the various elements that saw it as the perfect place to lay low. Criminals had discovered Dallas to be an ideal spot to hide out. Deposed warlords and exiled monarchs bided their time in San Antonio while their successors made a mess of their home countries. Vid stars lounged in Lubbock between projects, reading scripts and staying younger than the masses who idolized them. As a result, the entirety of Texas had developed a thriving sub-culture that supported an endless stream of bounty hunters, diplomatic flunkies, and Hollywoodville flacks.

I peeked into my makeshift hammock; Reggie still slept peacefully. I folded the ends over the top to conceal him and crossed the street. A warm breeze brought me the aroma of fried chicken from a nearby diner as I stepped into the alcove of the Aztec Hotel, Lounge, and Casino. Faux iconography of ancient Mexico surrounded me, intricate wall patterns and panoramic scenes rendered in gold depicted a blur of Aztec history and happy tourists. Bas reliefs showed blood sport and blackjack, and enthusiastic audiences for both.

A brief stop in the hotel's gift shop bought me a tacky vinyl gym bag emblazoned with the Aztec's logo. The nation of Texas still accepted American currency. In a men's room just off the lobby I transferred Reggie from the towels to the bag. I was about to toss the towels, but instead stuffed them in with Reggie in case he was hungry when he woke up. I cleaned up at the sink as best I could, but you can only do so much with grimy and abraded clothes that you've slept in. At least my hair was combed and my hands and face were clean.

I descended a glittering escalator and entered the casino proper. The muted buzz of hopeful gamblers enveloped me as the interior of the vast underground pyramid opened up, revealing row upon row of computerized games of chance. Holographic projections vied with one another, like sirens upon the rocks, singing longingly to lure passing sailors or anyone else with a little cash. They succeeded admirably; most of the devices had a dedicated supplicant standing or sitting before it, patiently feeding coins or chits or bills into their respective maws like some holy offering. A faint breeze of perfumed air circulated, removing or masking the stale odor of age and decay. Texas had become the perfect home for the pensioner with a gambling addiction. Let time pass rapidly outside, so long as arrangements had been made to deliver the monthly funds from an American bank to a Texas casino. The worst cases were of course deeper in the state, where the time distortion was much greater. There a year's retirement income routinely vanished in a day of playing the slots.

Diffused lightning cast a subdued warmth on the Aztec's main room. Every surface gleamed with a burnished façade that promised good times and a chance at fortune. Time stood still here in a way that had nothing to do with the Texas chrono-schism and everything to do with the nature of casinos the world over. I walked by the rows of slot machines and digital poker booths. I nodded as I wandered past the bored-looking cocktail waitresses and helpful currency exchangers, both dressed in colorful Aztec costumes. As I made my way deeper into the casino and entered the arena, an array of manned tables offered blackjack and craps, roulette and keno, spindola and castleblack. Few of these had many customers. Despite the frozen time of the casino, it was nonetheless just before dawn outside and the activity here was at low tide. Dealers and croupiers, handlers and pit bosses performed or lounged at their respective stations, all garbed like ceremonial warriors and priests with much gold finery and colorful plumage.

I spent a few moments just soaking it all in and getting my bearings before I approached a boss. Judging by the splendor of his uniform I assumed he held a certain amount of seniority; surely they didn't let just anyone go around dressed as a hierophant. The outfit looked ridiculous on him. Although short enough for authenticity, he was also pale, fat, and balding, clearly not a man able to rip out someone's heart and offer it up as a sacrifice to his gods. Just as well for me.

"I'm looking for Charlemagne," I said. "Is he in?"

The pit boss eyed me up and down. His gaze lingered on my ruined clothing and stuck on the gym bag in my left hand.

"Who should I say is asking for him?"

"Conroy."

"Just Conroy?"

I shrugged and attempted a sheepish smile. "The Amazing Conroy."

If this impressed or amused the pit boss he didn't let it show. He remained apathetic and signaled two burly and bare-chested Aztec ball players to escort me. I assumed they were taking me to see Charlemagne Thomas, the man who had managed the place when I'd last been through. In this I was somewhat mistaken.

They took me to a small but comfortable room decorated with antique furnishings from the end of the last century, all black leather and polished chrome. The carpet was an immaculate white shag and the mirrored bar stocked with both terrestrial and alien liquors and glassware. One of the ball players offered me a drink. I asked for some soda water and as he stepped to the bar to get me a glass, the other politely ran a detection wand past my torso and limbs, checking me for weapons and chemical agents. I checked out fine once I emptied my pocket of the flashlight I'd taken from that cabinet back in Philadelphia. The gym bag fared less well. Getting through security is one of the biggest drawbacks of traveling with a pet buffalo dog. When the pseudo Aztec swiped his security device over the gym bag it began to beep in alarm.

"Delta," said the man with the wand and a moment later his partner had decided he had something more important to do than fetch me a drink. With the speed and reflexes that would have done an Aztec ball player proud, he pinned me face first against the wall, and proceeded to twist my arms behind me. Something cold and hard pressed against my neck. I was too busy studying the grain of the simulated wood paneling to see if it was the business end of a gun or a beamer, though I guessed the latter. Guns tended to make more noise, and noise could potentially distract the customers in the arena.

"What's in the bag, sir?" said the fellow with the beeping detection wand while his cohort kept me pinned.

"You won't believe me even if I tell you."

The pressure against my neck increased slightly.

"Try me. I'm getting a density reading that's off the scale unless you're walking around with a bag of fissionables."

"He's got what?" The fellow holding me to the wall jerked back briefly and then slammed me back into place.

"Quiet, Ben. Keep hold of him. There's no radiation, just density. So, I'm asking you one final time. What's in the bag?"

"A buffalo dog," I said.

"What?"

"An Arconi buffalo dog. A buffalito."

"What's he talking about, Scott?" said the one holding me, once again easing up a bit. This time he didn't shove me back, and I could feel my face returning to its preferred shape.

"Shut up, Ben. He's got to be shitting us."

"I told you you wouldn't believe me," I said. "But look in the gym bag. See for yourself."

"Mister, I got a cousin who does terraforming with one of the big multinationals. I know what a buffalito is, and I got an idea that they ain't cheap. There's nobody going to be walking around with one in a souvenir gym bag, not in a casino, and not in the great nation of Texas. So, tell me what's really in the bag."

Reggie chose to answer for me at that moment. He's got quite a knack of timing, though usually it would be better for me if he didn't. From inside the bag came the sound of his frantic barking. The sound so startled Scott that he dropped the bag. It hit the carpet with a soft thud and Reggie's barking changed to an abrupt yelp. This was followed by a muted chomping noise. Moments later a hole appeared near the top of the bag and the buffalo dog's tiny teeth and delicate blue tongue could be seen expanding the hole.

"Make it stop," said Scott, and to my surprise I heard fear in his voice. How could someone be afraid of something as cute as Reggie? "Make it stop, or I'll shoot it. I'm not telling you again." His partner pulled me away from the wall, spun me around so I was facing the gym bag. He let go of my arms.

"Shhh, Reggie, it's okay, boy." I knelt next to the bag and fumbled with the zipper until I had it open and could reassuringly stroke Reggie's curly head. "He didn't mean to drop you, it's all fine."

"That's a buffalo dog," said Scott.

"That's a buffalo dog?" said Ben.

"That's *the* buffalo dog," said a new voice and we all looked up. The man with the definite article had delivered it with a rich Texas drawl. He stood nearly two meters in height, and thin as the proverbial rail. His big, hawkish nose, heavy forehead, and deep set eyes combined to give him a sepulchral look. His choice in clothing only added to the effect; a white linen shirt with a bolo tie, black dress coat and matching pants completed the image of a nineteenth century Texas undertaker fresh from the untamed West. A smile broke across my face and I stood up, lifting the gym bag and Reggie with me.

"Chuck!" I said. "How you doing?"

"Mr. Thomas, we were just—"

"Mr. Thomas, sir, he has—"

He waved them to silence with one long fingered hand. "That's all right, boys, Mr. Conroy here is an old friend. A much more prosperous friend than when I last saw him, if my reports from the states can be believed. Is it true, Connie? Have you joined the galaxy's Fortune Five Hundred since you graced my stage?"

I winced at the name. No one called me 'Connie,' no one but Charlemagne 'Big Chuck' Thomas. It's just one of those unstated laws; when you've got a moniker you can't shake, you're allowed to make up nicknames for everyone else. I shrugged it off; there really wasn't anything else I could do. "It's a different world out there," I said. "I've just been doing my part to leave a distinctive mark on it."

"Son, there's marks, and there's marks. You upended an Arconi monopoly. I always knew you were a rogue, Conroy, but I didn't have you pegged for a pirate."

"Well, there's pirates, and there's pirates," I said.

"True enough, but you never struck me as having the business savvy to go corporate. I would have thought you more likely to cash in quickly, blow all the money on gourmet food, or invest in a fancy restaurant and mismanage that until it went bankrupt."

I placed a hand over my heart and effected an injured and sorrowful expression. "Oh, Chuck, you wound me."

He snorted, clapped me on the shoulder and led me to the bar. "Not hardly," he said. "I wouldn't be where I am if I didn't have an exact eye for character. At worst you were an occasional con man, but never an empire builder. You've had help."

Scott and Ben both moved behind the bar and without a word began preparing the elaborate cocktail that I recalled was Charlemagne Thomas's beverage of choice. The man could hold his liquor better than anyone I'd ever met, and had created a concoction to take advantage of his talent. He'd named it *Death Warmed Over*. Its merits included a vile flavor, certain inebriation for lesser mortals, and a built-in hangover cure. I'd made the mistake of trying it once. Believe me when I tell you it's an acquired taste.

I returned my full attention to Charlemagne. "You know me too well. I had the great good fortune to fall in with some people of singular talent and fierce loyalty."

"To good fortune," he said, accepting an effervescing glass from Scott and raising it in a toast.

Ben handed me a somewhat tardy glass of soda water, and I clinked it against Big Chuck's. "To good fortune," I repeated and took a sip. "So, Chuck, what have you been up to, still collecting vintage cars?"

He grinned over the rim of his smoking glass. "Oh yes. Just last week in fact I added a '37 Mustang convertible to my collection. It's down in my garage right now, being detailed. Been here in Texas all along. Fellow just drove it in from Austin; took him about eight years to do it."

"What's the ratio in Austin?"

"About three thousand to one."

I whistled, low and long. "On a single tank of gas no less?"

Charlemagne laughed at that, tossed back the rest of his drink and slapped the empty glass firmly onto the table. The horrid potion hadn't fazed him one bit.

"Tell you what, why don't we cut through the pleasantries that we might return to them all the sooner? The last I saw of you, you had vowed never to come to Texas again, let alone my humble house. So, what's changed your mind? Why are you here, Connie? And why now?"

"I needed a place to wait for a friend," I said. "And as I didn't know how long it would take for him to get here, I thought I'd put time to my side and come visit." He knew about my company, but it was possible he didn't know about Green Aggression, and given the time differential highly unlikely he'd heard of the destruction of my building or my presumed death.

Charlemagne nodded, and I could tell from his expression that he wasn't satisfied with my answer but wouldn't press me for more details, at least not yet. Instead he turned to look at Reggie who had stuck his head up out of the gym bag. The buffalo dog sniffed the air, likely intrigued by the odd mixture of scents erupting from my host's drink. Charlemagne wrinkled his nose and stared back.

"Tell me then," he said, locking eyes with Reggie. "What do you plan to do while you wait for your friend?"

That stopped me. What little problem-solving my brain had managed on the trip from Philadelphia had focused on second guessing Green Aggression's next move, going over the plan for Betsy and Lisa to pull off the clean-up in Mexico, and plotting a counter attack to bring down the terrorists. I hoped to take advantage of some of Big Chuck's connections, but I hadn't given any thought to what to do while waiting to hear from them. I was as surprised as Charlemagne when I heard the answer that popped out of my mouth.

"I was hoping I'd perform," I said. "Two shows nightly, just like old times."

Chapter Eleven: The Undertaker's Undertaking

BIG CHUCK COMPED ME A SUITE and Scott and Ben escorted me to it. Along the way I inquired of the specialties of the hotel kitchen and asked them to have two large breakfasts sent up. Ben started to ask me why I needed *two* breakfasts, but Scott stopped him with a nod toward Reggie and assured me he'd put in the order.

One or both of them may have remained on sentry duty outside my door for all I know. I didn't care. I dragged Reggie into the bathroom, and tossed him into the shower amidst much bleating, then shrugged out of my clothes and climbed in after him. Twenty minutes of hot water, three tiny bottles of shampoo, and two miniature bars of soap later, we emerged. I dried off quickly and slipped into a complimentary robe I found hanging on the back of the bathroom door. Reggie usually enjoys being a brisk toweling down, but this time he seemed determined to sulk. "Cheer up, boy! We're both clean and dry. Soon we'll be well fed as well." He glared at me, so I dropped to one knee and spent a few minutes tickling him with one hand while I subjected him to the merciless ravages of the hair dryer. He yipped with pleasure through all of it and by the end was beaming at me with unconditional love.

The Aztec was truly a full service hotel. Although cut off from the globalink because of the chrono-schism, my room included localink access. In just a few minutes I'd used it to order some fresh clothes, to be billed and delivered to my room, no names needed, just the room number.

Next on my agenda, and already too long delayed, I needed to communicate with the outside world. Phones didn't work right in the chrono-schism, but old style telegraphy had made a grand comeback. Telegrams required a two step process, first to get the message out of Texas and the slower time flow, and next to pass it on by more conventional means to its final destination.

Given the seven to one ratio here in El Paso, I wrote quickly and kept my notes succinct. I addressed the first to the Mocker in care of the Golden Turtle Palace.

L-J, REPORTS OF MY DEATH EXAGGERATED. THERE'S A MOLE IN THE F.B.I. I'VE CRASHED THE

SHOP, SCATTERED THE PUPS, AND GONE UNDERGROUND. WE'RE STILL ON FOR VERAZCRUZ IF YOU CAN FIND ME SOON ENOUGH. I'M IN THE PLACE WE SWORE WE'D NEVER RETURN TO. DON'T FORGET TO BRING YOUR OWN CARDS. –C

I used my personal encryption key, scrambling the message into something unintelligible to anyone who I hadn't trusted with the other half of the key. The second telegram I aimed at Elizabeth Penrose. With all I'd dropped in her lap, I imagined that either Lisa or Betsy would be the one to read it.

DR. P, I'M NOT DEAD. REGGIE AND I GOT OUT AND WE'RE FINE. LET G.A.E.A. AND THE WORLD THINK OTHERWISE, BUT CONTACT ORTIZ AND TELL HIM THE TRUTH SO YOU CAN GO AHEAD WITH THE PROJECT. DON'T LOOK FOR ME, I'LL CONTACT YOU. –C

I considered sending a third telegram, this one to Agent Montgomery, but with an eco-terrorist hiding among his people I couldn't chance it. Besides, he'd be more zealous pursuing Green Aggression with a fresh murder charge than just the destruction of my building.

As things now stood, the clean-up in Veracruz was a lock. Betsy's organizational skills would see to it that all the scattered handlers converged at the right time and place, and Lisa Penrose would oversee the actual operation. My presence was purely ceremonial. If I managed to get there, I could pose with President Ortiz for the press. But short of taking on the Mexican government itself, I didn't see how Green Aggression could stop things.

I had a short-lived advantage for as long as they believed me to be dead, and to make full use of it I needed more information. Under Betsy's tutelage I'd learned two things since becoming a CEO. First, to recognize what you don't know, and second, to find someone who does. It followed that I needed someone with intimate knowledge of Green Aggression. They'd slipped a spy into Montgomery's group, and now I wanted an informant in theirs. Which is why I'd come to the Aztec. I had no doubt that Big Chuck's contacts within the greater sphere of semi-legitimate gambling and entertainment included people who knew what I needed to know. I just had to get him to help.

Someone knocked on the door, and before I could cross the room to answer, Ben was swinging it open and pushing a cart inside. "Compliments of Mr. Thomas," he said. He rolled the cart to the middle of the room, nodded to both me and Reggie, excused himself and left.

The next few minutes involved assorted clanging and barking as I uncovered various covered dishes while an impatient buffalo dog demanded I lift him up so he could get a taste of all the things he smelled. I portioned out the offerings into two plates and set Reggie's on the floor. He attacked it with his accustomed gusto, leaving me free to enjoy my own breakfast at a more leisurely pace.

Over Belgian waffles, fresh strawberries, turkey sausage, and French roasted coffee I began to lay plans for my next encounter with Big Chuck. In his own dark way, he considered himself a gentleman. That meant Chuck would allow me freshen up, chow down, and put on clean clothes—in short, to get comfortable and relaxed—before his interrogation began. The trick for me was to enlist him as an ally while he did it. I had no intention of throwing anyone in a well or blowing up any buildings, but if Big Chuck's contacts had information that could help me disrupt Green Aggression's operations, I'd certainly sleep better at nights.

I'd finished off breakfast and was enjoying my second cup of coffee when Ben knocked and let himself in again. He carried a suit bag over his shoulder and a well-stuffed brown paper bag under his other arm. Reggie barked at him once, which seemed to be all he deemed necessary to lay claim to his new territory, and then trotted into the closet where he'd earlier dragged a towel. He curled up in it like a baby in a blanket.

Ben stepped into the inner room and laid the bag on the bed before moving over to the dresser. I could see him through the doorway as he tore open the bag and put the contents into the top drawer. He finished and came back into the parlor. "You've got three shirts and two pairs of pants here. Also some clean underwear, socks, walking shoes, and a shaving kit with your basic toiletries. If you need anything else, just ask. Mr. Thomas will cover anything reasonable."

"That's very generous, and quick too," I said. "What's in the suit bag?"

"Your tux."

"My tux?"

Ben nodded. "Along with shirt, tie, cummerbund, and dress shoes."

"Why do I need a tux?"

"For your act."

"Oh, yeah, about that. See, there's a prob—"

Ben put a hand, cutting me off. "You'll have to discuss that with Mr. Thomas." He looked down at the plate I'd set on the floor for Reggie. I looked too. Reggie had devoured every morsel of food that had been on it, and to his credit he'd left the plate intact. Well, almost intact. He'd managed to lick off both the glaze and the patterned border.

"Was breakfast to your liking, Mr. Conroy?" Ben asked as he retrieved the plate from the floor.

"Just what I needed. Thanks."

"I'll pass along your appreciation to Mr. Thomas. He'll be dropping by shortly." He began moving things around on the cart. "I'll leave the coffee service for the two of you and take the rest if you're done."

I nodded and moments later Ben and the room service cart had removed themselves to the hall. I peeked in on Reggie in the closet but he was sound asleep. Big Chuck would be 'dropping by,' and it wouldn't do to greet him wearing only a hotel robe. I checked out the clothes Ben had put away, and dressed. Then I returned to the parlor, freshened up my coffee cup, and sat down to wait for my host's arrival.

Big Chuck knocked twice and then let himself in, leaving me to wonder if anyone in this hotel ever waited for someone to answer the door.

"Connie, you're looking much better," he said and settled himself on the sofa.

"Thanks. I'm feeling much better."

"Especially for a dead man," he said.

I shrugged. "Anything I might say about that has already been done by Sam Clemens."

Big Chuck didn't even smile. "You're not a nickel and dime lounge act any more, Connie. The people you piss off now won't settle for breaking your leg to teach you a lesson. And don't even think about staying here to hide. They've blown up one building you were in; I'm not risking the Aztec."

"The Aztec's not at risk. You said it yourself, the world thinks I'm dead."

He shook his head. "Your demise is not yet public knowledge, nor has anyone stepped forward to claim responsibility for the demolition. The authorities are currently saying you're unavailable for comment. It's only the FBI that thinks you're dead."

Big Chuck was being gracious, letting me know what he knew, and probably knowing I hadn't known it as well. "And the FBI told you?"

He shrugged. "Indirectly. They also informed me that Green Aggression had been harassing you, and had abducted you the day before. Presumably, they think you're dead now too."

"See? You have nothing to worry about. No one knows I'm here."

"I'd be more inclined to believe that if you hadn't sent two encrypted telegrams."

I waved that away. "C'mon, Chuck, you said it yourself, I'm running a corporation now. I had to let my people know what really happened."

He sat back on the sofa, raised one hand, and pretended to study his fingernails. "What happened," he said, "is that you've turned up at my door. Why is that, Connie? I never expected to see you again. So, I realize you've been shaken up a bit, but now you've had a chance to clean up, eat a good meal, put on some clean clothes. You look like your old self again. Now, tell me why you're really here. I'll give you one more opportunity to level with me before I throw you out."

There's a time to lie, and I'd already done that. There's a time to tell the truth, but with someone like Big Chuck truth can be cost you dearly and I couldn't afford to spend all of my coin yet. I was ready to invest a little of it though and with a nod and a tight smile I ventured into the grey area between.

"It's like this, Chuck. I'm here because of you."

"Me?"

"Your connections. You're right; I've got Green Aggression on my ass. I want to get them off, and I want to keep them off. I need information, inside stuff, that I can use to hurt them badly, maybe even bring them down altogether. I don't have the contacts to get me that kind of thing. Even when I was working the lounge I kept my nose pretty clean."

Chuck snorted and lowered his hand. "No one ever mistook you for a player, Connie."

"Exactly. But you are. You know where all the pieces are, or if not you can call in favors to find out whatever you're missing. That's why I'm here. That's what I need."

He didn't react. He just sat there, looking at me with that calm gaze that I remembered from years ago. Like he was sizing me up for a coffin. It was his own version of the Arconi truth glance, based entirely on psychology and raw instinct rather than alien telepathy, but nearly as effective. I'd told him the truth, just not the whole truth.

"That explains why you're here, and what you want from me. So, the next question. Why should I help you? What's in it for me?"

I shrugged. "I won't try to guess the price of your assistance. Why don't you save us both a lot of time and just tell me? What's it going to cost me?"

"Not money," he said. "That's too easy. I've followed your success, Connie, your meteoric rise. I don't want cash from you. I want something more valuable."

"That's not like you. More than anyone else, you taught me the value of a dollar. What's more valuable?"

"Power. You've become wealthy, but more importantly you've become powerful. You just don't realize it and don't know how to use it. But I do. I want you to owe me. I want your marker for one favor, deliverable upon demand. Offer me that, and I'll set my full resources to learning what you need to know."

I smiled. "Where do I sign?"

Chuck left a few minutes later with my name on a handwritten note. My marker. Before the hour expired he'd have reached out to dozens of contacts beyond the range of the Texas chrono-schism. The time distortion would work to my advantage, and within two days local time he'd have a full report for me.

I filled the rest of the day catching a nap followed by a light lunch from room service. Then I put on my new tux and, escorted by Ben, made my way to the Aztec's dressing rooms behind the lounge's stage.

After taking my marker, Big Chuck had reminded me of my offer to perform. I had time to kill, and doing my act would certainly distract me, provided I could do it incognito. I didn't want Green Aggression to know I was alive and well any sooner than I could help.

I looked forward to performing. There's something magical about being on stage, having a room full of strangers hang on your every word, dazzling them with the power of suggestion. Not that the life of a traveling hypnotist was really that glamorous, but it's funny how you don't realize you miss a thing until you get it back. I'd started doing a hypnosis stage act almost twenty years earlier, bouncing from one lounge to another, high class joints and sleazy dives, all over the Earth and in lonely little cabarets and nightclubs throughout the galaxy. I'd taken bookings beyond Human Space, places that had never seen an Earther before. I'd been in jail more times than I could remember, talked my way out of almost as many fights as I'd been caught up in, and been scared out of my wits by bouncers, unforgiving expert systems, and aliens with no sense of humor.

When fortune fell into my lap, I'd shed that life like a ratty old coat. Buffalogic started to take off and my future soared beyond even my wildest imaginings. But standing up on stage now, with a crisp white bow tie and an even crisper tuxedo, I realized I'd never worn anything so comfortable before in my life.

The name on the marquee established me as "the Mysterious Mezmerazzo." Don't blame me, I didn't pick it. By way of disguise I'd added a red silk turban to my wardrobe, which nicely matched my cummerbund. A pair of rose tinted pince nez masked my eyes and a pointy, reddish goatee and some spirit gum further obscured my true identity. It wasn't much, but I didn't expect to need much. Besides, I wasn't going to be the focus of the show. That honor went to the volunteers on stage with me.

For reasons known only to themselves, the San Diego chapter of the loyal order of the brothers of the Quartz of Saint Didace, some forty-six strong, had opted to have their annual retreat at the Aztec Hotel. Their five days of fraternal frolicking would cost them a month's time back in southern California. To a man they were middle-aged, overweight, balding, near-sighted, and pale. Each wore a plum-colored ulster and a matching fez. They comprised fully a fifth of my audience during my first show, and I pulled three of them up on stage to the wild cheering of the remaining forty-three. I can't tell you why, but during my career as a hypnotist I'd discovered that the kind of men who join lodges and fraternal orders make great hypnotic subjects. They go under with barely an effort. The quartz lovers of Saint Whoever proved no exception.

"You sir," I said to the first of three men I had perched upon stools on the stage of the Aztec Lounge. "You don't know how it happened, but you're in Lubbock. Do you understand?"

"I'm in Lubbock," he said.

"And you my friend," I said to the man next to him, "you're right here in El Paso, but you've got a terrible stammer."

"I st-st-st-st-stammer," said the second man.

There were a few chuckles from the audience as some of them got a glimmering of where I might be going.

"Which leaves just you, our third contestant tonight. It's your birthday today. And your two friends here want to help you celebrate it, so they're going to sing. Now the good news is that I'm sure they're both excellent singers, always on key. The bad news is that Lubbock's a bit deeper in the chrono-schism than we are here, but I'm sure it will balance out just fine. Everyone ready? Let's begin."

"Hap-p-p-p-p-py B-b-b-b-b-birth-d-d-d-d-d-day t-t-t-to y. . ."

"Haaaaaaaaaaaaaaaaaappyyyyyyyyyyyy Biiiiiiiirrtthhhhhdaaaaaaaaay tooooooo youuuuuuuuuuuuuu. . ."

The audience fell out of their chairs, and quite literally rolled in the aisles with laughter. And with that, the show was off and running.

After the performance Big Chuck himself came back to my dressing room, a personal touch that I'd never known him to do. I sat back on the couch, removing my goatee to let my chin breath, and enjoying one of the frosty bottles of raspberry root beer that had been thoughtfully stocked in my fridge.

"You're still amazing, Connie. Why did I ever let you slip away last time?" Big Chuck was dressed as before, but the gleam in his eye, which in another man would have denoted happiness, made him look greedy. Believe me when I say, a man who looks like a greedy undertaker does not inspire trust or confidence.

"Well, Chuck," I said, offering him a seat and a cold one, "as I recall it had something to do with you not wanting to pay me for the six bonus shows you begged me to perform for those conventioneers."

He settled into the dressing room's second chair and put his feet up on the coffee table between us. "You were younger then, a kid. You needed to pay your dues. I was looking out for you though, giving you some much needed exposure."

I gave him the eye and took a swig from my bottle, saying nothing.

"Okay, okay, you're not buying it. Did you ever consider that maybe I was sparing you from the kind of scandal that could have ended your career before it had even begun. Or have you forgotten your involvement with that ambassador's kid?"

I did my best not to choke on my drink. I knew I had nothing to feel guilty about, but even years after the fact there was nothing I could say to Chuck to prove my innocence. "So, what? You're saying I should be grateful to you?"

He waved my sarcasm away. "What's past is past. But look at you. You've done all right for yourself and you've come back to grace my stage once more, so the memory of those days you spent here can't be too painful for you. In fact, Connie, I think this place holds a soft spot in your heart. I think I do too. Go on, admit it."

I bit back the retort that burst into my mind. In the best of times it wouldn't have been healthy to offend Charlemagne Thomas. Moreover, he was calling in some of those favors at my request. I needed diplomacy, not righteousness

"Chuck, it's certainly true that I'll never forget the work I did here at the Aztec, and even to my dying day I'll never forget you."

He smiled at that, the smile of an undertaker who's learned that there are two bodies to tend to, not just one. I thought of the marker I'd given him, and wondered just how badly it might come back to haunt me down the line.

He leaned forward, one lanky arm reaching out to hand me a newspaper clipping. "I thought you'd want to see this article. It came out three days after you left Philadelphia, world time."

The clipping consisted of an old photo of me, and the caption *CEO missing from destroyed building*. "That didn't take long," I said. "When will you hear back from your sources?"

"You'll have some answers the day after tomorrow, local time. Guaranteed."

"Good. I appreciate that. Now, if you'll excuse me, I need to get some air and stretch my legs a bit before the second show."

Charlemagne nodded, appreciating the need to stretch one's legs more than most. I stood and moved to the makeup table to reattach my goatee, while studying him in the mirror. Watching him stand was like watching a man unfold himself. He set his bottle of root beer on the makeup table; he hadn't drunk from it. As he opened the door he paused and turned back to me. "You've changed, Conroy, you know that?"

I laughed. "Not so green anymore?"

"That, sure, but not just that. You were idealistic when I met you fifteen years ago. I don't see that in you so much now. Now I just see cynicism. And that's healthy, given both your business and mine. But cynicism isn't enough. You're still not a player. And in this game, if you're not a player, you're a victim. You understand me?"

"Better than I want to," I said. He nodded and closed the door behind as he left. I sighed, and scooped up Reggie from where he was snoozing on some cushions in the corner. He opened his eyes, yawned, and licked my nose. I stared into those liquid brown eyes, endless in their depths and innocent as any animal's. "C'mon, pal. Let's take a walk. You've never had a taste of El Paso before. I'm sure we'll find something that suits your palate. And if anybody asks, you're just the genemod pet of some spoiled gambler with more dollars than sense."

Reggie gave an appreciative yip when I set him down and he trotted along beside me as I left my dressing room and headed upstairs into the slow Texas air.

Chapter Twelve: The Ambassador's Daughter

THE NEXT DAY, HALFWAY THROUGH MY SECOND SHOW, Left-John Mocker stormed into the lounge and started making a fuss. My volunteers that night included a retired sponge salesman from Seattle, a Michigan housewife turned blackjack wizard, and a blue skinned culinary student from one of the Arcturan colonies. The retiree was pushing seventy, all but bald, and stout. I made him think he was a vid celeb, young and dashing and eager to stay that way, hence his need to slip over the border into Texas. The housewife clearly wanted a more exciting life, so I made her a French jewel thief who had just completed the heist of her career and needed to cross over the border from the States to let time slide by. Except in the most bizarre circumstances, Arcturans tend to emanate peacefulness and ease; that's handy when you want a mediator, but not much fun on stage. Instead, I wanted the Arcturan volunteer to be a source of conflict. With a few terse instructions I convinced it that it was a Texas Ranger working the immigration border, but with authority to admit only one of the other two into the chrono-schism. The audience ate it up, as the Arcturan's trilled falsetto acquired a heavy Texan accent while the housewife tried to bribe her way in and the sponge salesman alternated between charismatic fawning and brash entitlement to get his way.

"What the hell's going on?"

I looked up from refereeing my three volunteers and gazed out at the audience. With the stage lights glaring I couldn't actually see who was making such a ruckus, but I didn't need to. I recognized the voice. It was the Mocker.

"What iz zis interuptcíon?" asked the Michigan housewife. "Monsieur Ranger, do we have zee deal or no?"

The sponge salesman wanted none of it. "Oh please, you want to talk deals talk to my agent. And as for you, Mr. Whomever you are, take a number. Or better yet, come back next week. My good friend, Tex the Ranger here was just about to let me through, and not a moment too soon. Barry is expecting me for lunch. We're looking over some scripts, and you know, Tex, I just remembered he mentioned something about there being a part for a strong silent lawman type. I bet you'd be perfect for it. Let me set that up for you."

"Now hold it right there, kemo sabe. It's like I've been telling these two folks here, I ain't got clearance to let but one of you across the border today."

Left-John's silhouette had forced its way through the audience to hover at the foot of the stage. "You'd better have a—"

"Monsieur Ranger, really, I must insist—"

"Tex, be a good fellow and—"

"Now y'all just hold on one min—"

"SLEEP!"

Three of the four voices fell silent. None of them was the Mocker's.

"—damn good reason to have dragged me all the way to this hole of bottled time."

"Ladies and gentleman, guests and visitors," I said, signaling to the technical crew for a follow spot, "please join me in welcoming a true celebrity to the Aztec Hotel, gambler extraordinaire and winner of the 2090 Extra-Solar Poker Classic Tournament, the one, the only, Left-John Mocker!"

The spotlight snapped on, the drummer in the far corner managed a quick riff on the snare drum and a clash of cymbals, and there was the Mocker, dressed in a rumpled blue work shirt, black denims, and dusty snakeskin boots. His expression was stoic as ever, but his eyes burned with an anger that was only partially intended for me. Give him credit though, he turned to the audience, waved, and produced a handful of chips from somewhere and threw them into the crowd.

Left-John mounted the stage, illuminated all the way. He leaned in, placed one hand on my shoulder, and whispered in my ear. "You finish what you're doing here, and then you and I are going to have a chat. I'll ask questions, and the answers better suit me. You know I wanted to never return here."

"Left-John Mocker, folks," I said, improvising the way any good stage performer would. "Because here at the Aztec Lounge and Casino the best and the brightest come to play."

Still gripping my shoulder, the Mocker punched me, hard, just above my right kidney, blocking the action from the audience's view with his body. "A cheap shot for that last cheap shot," he said, then faced the audience once more, waved, and exited into the wings, stage left. I did my best not to double over in pain, and instead resumed my border act where it had been interrupted while I leaned upon a stool and caught my breath.

I put my volunteers through a few more improbable and humorous demonstrations, culminating in a game of imaginary blackjack. The dealer announced each card as dealt, and I made one fellow believe he had precognitive powers and could tell what card was coming next. This allowed him to stand pat when taking a card would otherwise bust him, but it infuriated the player on his left who got stuck with it as his card instead. It's funnier to see than to describe, and it's funniest when you see it in a casino. In any case, I wound down, took the hypnotic whammy off each of my volunteers and encouraged the audience to give them a round of applause. Then I took my own bows, and headed backstage to my dressing room.

A hallway ran behind the stage, a wide arc that went from one wing to the other, bulging enough in-between to make room for half a dozen large dressing rooms and a dozen smaller ones all on the same side of the hall. The hall smelled of showgirls' perfume, a heavy musky odor from some long gone animal act, and the disinfectant overlay someone had employed to eliminate both and failed. Less than half of the rooms were in use; the Aztec Lounge rarely had more than six acts running at a time nowadays. That might have been the justification for only powering every other light in the hall. As I walked toward my dressing room at the apex of the arc, I passed through alternating pools of radiance and darkness to the twilight that surrounded my door. I reached for the knob and started to turn it before I remembered that I'd locked my door. The knob turned easily under my hand.

Not only had I locked the door when I'd left, I'd used both the obvious deadbolt and the more sophisticated magnetic seal that should have made it easier to go through the wall. Apparently not. I pushed into the dressing room and found the Mocker sitting in my make-up chair, his feet up on the counter and my buffalo dog napping contentedly on his lap.

"Make yourself at home," I said as I closed the door behind me and began removing my bowtie.

"Home? More like 'make yourself at hovel.' What are you doing here, Conroy. I'm glad to see you're not dead and buried under the rubble of your company, and I can understand the need to go underground, but why here? Of all places, why did you come here?"

I went to the fridge, helped myself to an Uncle Waldo's™ raspberry root beer, and collapsed onto the couch. My feet hurt. The shoes Big Chuck had found for me nicely complimented my tux, but my toes had been squinched the whole time I was on stage. I kicked off the shoes, sighed, popped the cap on my bottle, and then took a long swig.

"You know that my office building was demolished. What you don't know is who blew it up."

"Tell me."

"Green Aggression. They also kidnapped Reggie and me the day before and threw us in a well. We got out."

"A well and a demolished building? Are you adding escape artist to your resume?"

"Better that than a corpse. More importantly, I need to stop being a victim in this. For that, I needed information, and the means to get it without being noticed. The Texas chrono-schism was ideal for the second, and Big Chuck certainly qualifies as someone who can handle the first."

Left-John said nothing for several moments. I took another sip and watched him stroke Reggie's fur as he mulled things over before asking more questions. "What are you planning on doing?"

"First, follow through on the clean-up project, which is what seems to have set GAEA on my trail in the first place. To succeed with that, I'm going to have to shut Green Aggression down. Hard."

"That's not a plan, that's a wish. You're not dealing with a rational opponent, Conroy. These people see no contradiction in using alien technology to achieve their goal of eliminating alien tech."

"That's where Mexico figures in. We've already won Ortiz over. If Big Chuck can get me something I can use, something the president will believe and see as a real threat, then I think I have a real chance to enlist his help in crushing Green Aggression."

"Putting aside your reliance on Charlemagne Thomas, why should the president of Mexico help you at all?"

"He wouldn't just be helping me, he'd be helping himself. Ortiz's own views on Mexico's alien issues are liberal; he sees the advantages of it but he can't fight decades of political policy. But I'm handing him the solution to his country's biggest pollution problem, showcasing an alien creature along the way. He'll be a national hero and he can ride the tide of public opinion to reverse some of those archaic policies. And crushing a group of reactionary eco-terrorists fits nicely into that."

Left-John lifted Reggie off his lap. He sat up straight and set my pet on the floor. "Which still doesn't answer the question of why I'm here."

"For your own protection," I said. "It's not like I have so many friends I can afford to have some of them picked off by eco-terrorists. I didn't just crash my company to protect the clean-up project. I did it to protect my employees."

"I'm not one of your employees, Conroy." The Mocker growled the words.

"No, of course not. But you're listed in the files as a participant, and you're occupying one of the 'employee slots' authorized by the Mexican government. The FBI has been all over those files, and the double agent could well have seen your name listed. That put you at risk. I tried phoning you before I crashed everything. When that didn't work, I sent you a telegram after I arrived here.

Left-John sat quietly for a few moments, his poker face giving nothing away. I watched and wondered if he'd ever taken as long to consider whether to raise or fold.

"You're aware I never wanted to come back here. I know that. You made a tough call, my word versus my life. A guild member wouldn't have made the choice, but I understand why you did it, and I should probably be grateful."

That was as close to a 'thank you' as I was going to get. I shrugged, and we both put the matter behind us.

"So the only person you've talked to since the crash was a cab driver and Big Chuck? What about your secretary or that mixed up Penrose girl? What about your account reps, your sales force, your training staff? Anyone else at your company at all?"

I shook my head and stared at the now empty bottle I'd been cradling in my hands. "There wasn't any need. Crashing the company sent most of them off on a company sponsored vacation, everyone except the trainers and handlers working on the project. Once I got here I sent a telegram to Lisa. She has a coded list to bring everyone together in Mexico as scheduled."

"Leaving you free to neutralize Green Aggression?"

"Well. . . Seeing as how you're here, with time on your hands and nothing to do, I was hoping you'd help me out with that."

I've rarely managed to make Left-John smile, and never as broadly as he did now.

"Your audacity is a wonder to behold. You may not know a thing about running a company, but you were always an impressive hypnotist. You have me sitting here against every bit of sense I possess, and now I'm about to jump through fire with you. And I never even saw you swing a pocket watch in front of my face."

"I don't use a watch, you know that."

"A figure of speech. So, when do you expect Charlemagne Thomas to come through with your information?"

"Tomorrow, at the latest," I said.

"In that case, you'd better grab some rest while you can. I want to be able to leave this place as soon as you have what you came for."

"I've got a suite. You're more than welcome to sack out there too, or I can ask Big Chuck for a room for you—"

"Are you kidding? I'm not going to sleep here. And I'm certainly not going to partake of Thomas's hospitality. Does he even know you brought me here?"

"Nope. He wouldn't have allowed it. Easier to apologize after the fact than get permission before." I pushed off the couch and stood. A moment later and I was scooping Reggie up and hoisting him under one arm. He whuffled once but didn't wake up. "Okay, I'll be in my room. Do me a favor, keep out of Big Chuck's way?"

"I never touched that ambassador's daughter. I was busy playing cards."

I shook my head. "I'm not going to have this argument with you. I'm too tired. I believe you, but it's your word against four surveillance cams, two waiters, and an accountant who claims to have been in the elevator with you both. It's in the past. Don't dig it up again. I'm going to bed, just like you suggested."

"I didn't—"

"Bed! I'll see you in the morning."

"I didn't do it," he said, softly and to my back. And, in truth, Left-John probably didn't shtup that girl, probably never touched her. Despite all the evidence, I believed him. But Big Chuck didn't. As I took the service elevator down to my floor, I muttered a prayer that their paths didn't cross. The world didn't need a meeting between an irresistible force and an unmovable object.

Chapter Thirteen: A Cotton Trail to Uxmal

I PUSHED OPEN THE DOOR to my suite, and my vision started to swim. I blamed my watery gaze on fatigue, staggered inside, and let my buffalo dog scamper free. The room had decided to go swimming too. It shimmered, and sort of split into two simultaneous rooms, one overlaid upon the other. I could see my room, with my few possessions and recent acquisitions. But I also saw another room, one with a lot more stuff strewn hither and yon, over hill and under dell. My version of the room looked pretty solid, but the other, the pieces of that phantom room, seemed vaguely transparent and wispy. "Reggie, I'm dead on my feet," I said. Reggie bleated in response and trotted deeper into the suite.

I stumbled after him, from the parlor into the bedroom, stripping off my coat and shirt along the way. The same double image overlay effect was hard at work in the bedroom too. Then I saw who was lying there in the insubstantial second bed. "I'm hypnogogic," I said to myself, "I've been walking in my sleep and didn't even known it." If the illusory figure of the daughter of the U.S. Ambassador to Texas could hear me, she gave no sign.

She looked like an angel, lying on top of the covers, clad only in a thin sheath of silk, some kind of undergarment that had been hidden beneath the vintage 2010 dress that now lay draped over a chair. I'd hypnotized her, that night fifteen years before. She'd been cute and spunky, and even though she was only seventeen I'd have probably made a play for her if I hadn't known her old man was the ambassador. Instead I gave her a few harmless suggestions that caused her to do various adorable things and made the audience fall in love with her even more than they already had. And later that night, while I was doing my second show, she'd slipped off to a room with someone that wasn't me, and probably wasn't the Mocker either. Regardless of whom though, it was one someone more than her daddy wanted her in bed with, and things had gotten quite ugly the next morning.

"So, is this the before or after picture?" I said as I walked closer to the bed.

"It doesn't matter, the details are irrelevant," said a voice behind me. I turned around, and saw a large figure, man-shaped but huge and indistinct. It stood silhouetted by the light coming from the bathroom.

"I know that voice," I said, slurring the words. "You're the snowman. Yeah, and the whipped cream guy in my dreams." I looked around. I didn't see Reggie anywhere. There was only the one suite now, and it wasn't mine. "So I'm dreaming."

"Not quite. But you have slowed down enough for me to speak to you more directly."

The light from the bathroom faded, or possibly the light in the rest of the room grew while the room itself faded away. I stood upon a sandy beach, some twenty meters from the water. The muted roar of the ocean soothed me a bit. The sun dipped down, setting out over the water, and its light painted the handful of distant clouds orange and pink. In the other direction the sand gave way to sparse patches of pale yellow grass. I watched as the blades rippled, showing the effect of a wind I didn't feel. Standing there with me, no longer hidden by backlighting was what I can only describe as a cotton golem. Absurd, but what else would you call someone who was big and bulky and looked to be made entirely out of wads of fluffy white cotton? Where its eyes should have been it had only empty cottony sockets, and its mouth gaped, a toothless maw. Stranger still, upon its billowing head it wore a lavender fez with a matching tassel.

"Who are you?" I said, giving in to the obvious question.

"No time for that. There are two things I must communicate. First, you must leave El Paso in the morning. Gather such information as has arrived, but do not tarry. Take the gambler with you."

"Oh? Just like that? On your say so? I have a better idea. Why don't you stop plaguing my dreams and save your commands for someone who enjoys visitations from fluffy apparitions."

The golem wrung the mittens of its hands. "Assert your independence another time. You must depart in the morning."

"And just where is it you'd like me to go? "

"I can't tell precisely. The probabilities have not yet converged. Perhaps Edzná, or Xpuhil, or Calakmul."

The names meant nothing to me. I waited for him to say more, but he simply stood and stared at me out of a vacant face. That was fine. Just because Mr. Fluffy wanted me to go there did not mean I was obliged to.

"What's the second thing you need to tell me?"

"Your purpose."

"My purpose?"

"You stand at a pivotal point for your world. You must take command of your purpose."

I rolled my eyes and shrugged. "I think I liked you better when you were foam or snow. Either way, I'm getting tired of having dreams of doom and gloom and heavy portents. Save them for someone a little more gullible. I prefer to make my own destiny, thank you very much. "

The sound of the ocean grew louder, moving from background roar to a thunderous noise. I turned from the cottony creature and gazed out across the water, seeing that something was different but not sure what.

"You need to know what will happen if you don't stop Green Aggression."

"Stop them from what?"

"From bringing about disaster. I perceive the probable, almost certain outcomes, and down those avenues that lead to the greatest disaster you are the key, the point of decision."

I was still staring out at the ocean. It seemed higher, somehow, but that had to be a trick of the horizon or the sunset. I shook my head. "This is just a bad dream. I'd like to wake up now."

"Your struggle with Green Aggression will inadvertently unleash great devastation."

I ignored Fluffy and continued to study the ocean. The height of the water really had risen out toward the horizon. The cotton golem kept talking but its voice sounded faint and far away and easy to ignore. Or so it seemed.

In the logic and motion of a dream it was suddenly directly in front of me. Its hands reached for my head and forced me to look directly into its face. Oven mitts gripped my skull.

"I cannot communicate at this speed. You need to slow down for a complete transfer if you are to understand me. You must move deeper into the schism."

I laughed in its face. "Deeper into Texas? Deeper into the temporal leakage? Trust me, that is *not* going to happen."

"There is not time for your resistance. A partial transfer will lack coherence, but you leave me no choice." It let go of my head and raised both hands above its own, rotated its fez all the way around as if unscrewing it. "You must go deeper into the schism."

I shook my head. "Even in dreams I'm not that crazy. El Paso is as far as I go. Much further in and the distortion differential really climbs. Days become months, or even years."

"Very well," the golem said, though by this time I could barely hear it, the roar of the ocean had grown so loud. I spared a glance past it and gasped. A wall of water climbed into the sky, right to left as far as I could see. It was drawing closer.

I turned back to my pessimistic companion. It gripped its fez with both hands. Then, acting quicker than any fluffy cotton dream golem has a right to move, it lifted the fez off its own head and set it upon mine.

I screamed.

Imagine termites climbing into your brain and deciding it's wood. Imagine every cell in your body turning into peanut butter and finding yourself in a sewer full of rats. Agony is too singular and discrete to describe it. Take a single unbearable misery and duplicate it over and over again and experience them all simultaneously. The human nervous system doesn't work that way. It can't. Unless of course it happens in a dream.

I collapsed onto the beach, pawing at the fez, clutching at my head. The cotton creature towered above me, and behind it, through a miasma of pain, the tidal wave arrived. The intensity of the pain from the fez doubled, then trebled, and I managed a truly remarkable feat: I fainted in the middle of a dream.

I awoke to the sound of water splashing and found myself sprawled out on my bed, wearing only my underwear and the lampshade from the room's desk lamp. The sound of splashing persisted and I rolled over, off the bed and onto my knees. From there it wasn't quite so impossible to lift my head up. I slowly staggered to a fully upright position. My head throbbed worse than it had the first time I'd drunk myself stupid. Recalling that incident I realized I had no memory how the lampshade had gotten there. I took it off. *Uxmal.* Just like that, the word popped into my brain. A shiver ran up and down my spine and the odd word vanished from me entirely. I had forgotten something, something important, but instead of having any anxiety over it I had a calm certainty that it would all come back to me in time. I became aware of the water noise again. It was coming from the bathroom. I opened the door to investigate, unsure of what I'd discover.

I found Reggie. He bleated plaintively as he saw me, and I had to laugh. He had gotten into the bathtub but had then been unable to climb back out. In his attempt to solve the problem he'd taken several large bites out of both the fixtures and the tub itself. He had eaten into the wall and chewed open one of the water pipes. The resulting geyser sprayed straight up into the air, and arced across the bathroom. It fell like a heavy rain. Most of the deluge had been hitting the sink and draining away, but enough had missed to soak the floor.

"*Dzilbichaltún,*" I said to myself, wondered why I'd said it, but dropped that line of inquiry to focus on the current problem. It took me several minutes in my muddled state to find the water shut-off valve, and several more to use all the available towels to sop up the floor. Reggie maintained a constant vocal accompaniment, and would not be mollified by word or deed until I actually picked him up and carried him into the bedroom. I draped a blanket around him and used it to give him a vigorous, drying rub. "*Aké*," I said, and Reggie gave me a funny look. "Okay, what's going on? Why did I just say that?"

Reggie did not answer, but then it's not as if I had been expecting him to. I carried him out into the parlor and set him on the sofa while I activated the room's localink access and called up a search for the words I'd been speaking, Uxmal, Dzilbichaltún, Aké. They popped up instantly, the names of cities, all of them long dead, and all located on Mexico's Yucatan peninsula. Which is about the time I remembered my dream and the cotton ball golem with the purple fez. The purple fez! I brought my hands up to my head and remembered the multitudes of agony I'd felt in the dream.

"It wasn't a dream," I said. "Or at least, it wasn't my dream. I've never heard of those places before. Fluffy put them in my head when it put its hat on me." I looked at Reggie who stared back at me. That was fine, I needed him as a sounding board while I talked myself through the pieces.

"It couldn't be using telepathy. Almost all projective telepaths need either past contact or a line of sight, and those that don't have a limited range. The cotton golem wasn't in the room last night. It couldn't have been anywhere near my office when I dreamed of the snowman, or in the well when I dreamed it up as whipped cream. This shouldn't be possible. And yet, it's clearly happening."

I began pacing across the parlor. Reggie watched me with the concentration of a tennis fan in the stands at Wimbledon. "Logically now, what do I know? First, someone is trying to mess with my head. It's not anyone working for Green Aggression, either. Next, there's an ecological theme to all the dreams, but Fluffy made it clear that they're going to muck something up. That's right, it said my destiny was to stop them. And . . . something else. I know I'm not remembering all of it. There were two things. Stop Green Aggression and. . ."

And that's when I remembered. Not something it had said, something its damn hat had leaked into my brain along with the strange names. The reason I had to leave, immediately if not sooner. *Green Aggression knew where I was.* I knew it with the same certainty that I knew my name or that gravity would kick my ass every time I jumped off a roof. And I knew something more, I knew they were en route to the Aztec!

I left Reggie on the sofa while I plunged back into the bedroom and threw on some clothes. Then I scooped up my few possessions, and stuffed them into my buffalo dog's gym bag. I could ponder ecological catastrophes and fluffy, dream oracles later. Right now I had to find Left-John and get out of here.

Reggie sensed my urgency. He stood in the doorway from the parlor and barked twice. I sealed the bag, juggled it to my right hand, and called him over. I tucked him tightly under my left arm and headed out. I didn't need an ocean to fall on me. It was time to be moving on.

Chapter Fourteen: Fifty-Two Missing Winters

I CAME BUSTLING INTO THE MAIN CASINO and caught sight of Big Chuck at once. His back was to me, but recognizable all the same, his bony shoulders and head rising up above the intervening patrons and employees. I couldn't hear him over the general noise of the casino, but as I drew near, I could see he was yelling at someone. My heart sank. The object of his tirade was none other than Left-John Mocker. I put on some speed, and caught the tail end of Chuck's latest remark.

"—got the camera feed, Mocker. Deny it all you like, but the cams don't lie."

"Are you saying that I am?" Unlike Big Chuck, the Mocker didn't shout. His voice was calm, too calm. "I want to be clear. Are you calling me a liar?"

Oh crap, I thought. *Please, please, please.* I knew things had gone ugly for Big Chuck the day after Left-John and I had left the Aztec fifteen or two years ago. There'd been accusations and scandal and a quick cover up to help the ambassador save face, but with the prime suspect conveniently vanished, the heat and the blame and the retribution had all fallen squarely on Charlemagne Thomas, owner and operator of the Aztec Hotel, Lounge, and Casino.

Big Chuck of course knew it better than anyone, and the source of what must have surely been more aggravation than any ten men deserved was standing right there in front of him. He had the security vids, and the sworn testimony of three employees, to convince him of the Mocker's guilt, to say nothing of the gambler's convenient departure hours before the deflowered daughter had been found in his suite. A suite which, it should be noted, the Mocker had never had his luggage in, let alone entered himself.

Something in Left-John's flat tone reminded Chuck of the gambler's deposition, delivered weeks later by courier. A deposition taken not in some lawyer's office, but in the Probability Guild's main hall, signed and witnessed by a trio of master gamesmen. Few people take certainty more seriously than those who have dedicated their lives to chance.

"I'm not calling you a liar," said Chuck, his volume dropping from a roar to little more than a gravelly whisper that I was now close enough to hear.

"And yet, that's what it sounds like you're doing."

"I can't call you a liar," Chuck grumbled. "Your guild would judge that to be the same as calling you a cheat."

"Charlemagne Thomas, are you calling me a cheat?" The formality of including Chuck's full name added weight to the question though Left-John's tone hadn't changed. He stepped closer, so close that he had to tilt his head back to look Chuck in the eye."

"Gentlemen," I said, putting down both my bag and Reggie right there in the middle of the casino and resting one hand on each man's shoulder. "We've got bigger problems. Current problems."

"What are you talking about?" both of them said, almost in unison. Comical, if the situation wasn't so dire.

"Chuck, one of your contacts must have leaked info instead of slurping it up. Green Aggression knows I'm here."

"How do you know that?"

"I've got . . . sources, of my own. There are eco-terrorists on their way, and they are not the kind of people you want here."

"Don't be melodramatic, Connie. You're not on stage here. Even if your information is correct, they want you, not me. I've done nothing to thwart their plans or compromise their ideals. When people spend their money at the Aztec, I don't ask them how they came by it."

"We're not talking about some underworld cartel coming in for a holiday. Have you forgotten? These people are fanatics. They blew up an entire building, with me in it. A Glomarkan designed building."

"Glomarkan design? That wasn't in any of the reports I read," said Big Chuck.

"It's not something that was widely known," I said. "The point is, regardless of your differences with the Mocker, I don't think you want to keep arguing with him if it means we'll still be here when Green Aggression comes looking for me. You got a nice place here, and I don't want to be the cause of it becoming a debris-filled pit. We need to leave, and we need to leave now."

Big Chuck hesitated, his gaze flitting back and forth from Left-John to me.

"Don't even think about holding us here," said Left-John. "I have three words that would spoil any attempt you might make to sell us to them to save yourself."

Big Chuck's jaw dropped. Left-John had nailed it. "Three words? What are you talking about?"

"Aid and comfort," said the Mocker, and the corner of his mouth lifted in a faint smile. "Conroy is their enemy. You took him in, gave him food, shelter, access to your resources, the benefits of your patronage. Don't try and bluff here. Fold."

Give Big Chuck some credit, in that instant he made a decision and never looked back. "I want both of you out of here. Right now."

"That's what I've been saying," I said. "Do you have the information you promised me?"

He scowled. "A bit late for that, isn't it?"

"Not once we're away from here. Do you have it, or not?"

"Of course." He slid a hand inside his suit and withdrew a datapadd. "Names, codenames, addresses, and daily routines of the members of GAEA's command structure inside Mexico. This cost me big, Connie, very big."

I snatched the datapadd from Big Chuck. "Then we'd better not waste it. Now, I need one more favor and I don't have time to argue or haggle."

"Fine, fine, what do you need?"

"A car. Something with a good sized tank and decent mileage."

"You want one of my cars? Are you insane, Connie?"

"Chuck, they're not going to do you any good if they get blown up or you get dead."

He frowned, bit his lip, and said, "There's a Yugo you can have. One of my people just drove back from New Mexico in it. It's just been washed and refueled."

"Fine. Let's go. The sooner I get behind the wheel the sooner we're gone."

"Do you even know how to drive?" Chuck frowned, but he turned and started toward a private elevator at the back of the casino. I picked up both Reggie and my bag and followed after.

"Chuck," I said, jerking my head at the Mocker to follow along. "Those cars are classics, they practically drive themselves."

"All the more reason for me to drive," said Left-John as he followed us out of the casino.

Big Chuck's private elevator connected to a private garage which in turn had its own private access to the street above. I had gotten the tour years before, tagging along with a small party from the Ambassador's entourage the day before everything hit the fan. I've never been bitten by the collector bug, but I know plenty of folks who have, and then as now I could appreciate Big Chuck's desire to show off his collection of vintage automobiles. That last time I'd visited the garage had been dark; motion detectors had activated track lighting on each car as we drew near, revealing spotless chrome and lovingly restored paint, and eliciting the appropriate oohs and ahhs from members of the group. Big Chuck had beamed like a proud father. This time, as we stepped out of the elevator there was plenty of light. The car nearest the elevator was the Yugo that Big Chuck intended for us. I started toward it but stopped as Big Chuck blocked me with his arm.

"Something's wrong," he said. "The lights shouldn't be on." He gestured us back into the elevator and as we entered its light went dim. Big Chuck tapped the alarm button. Nothing happened.

Left-John bristled. "What's going on?"

By way of answer, Big Chuck slipped some kind of remote control out of his pocket and peered around the edge of the elevator, only to jerk his head back quickly at the sound of gunfire.

"Bastards!" Chuck shouted. "If you so much as ding the paint I'll feed you your livers!"

A woman's voice echoed from somewhere in the garage. "Come out, Earth Monster! You can't escape us this time."

Big Chuck turned to me. "It's over," he said.

"What's that mean? Get us out of here." I pressed the close button on the panel. The doors didn't close.

"The elevator's without power," said Left-John. "We can't go back to the casino."

"Well, we can't go out there," I said. "They've got guns, and I don't think they have any qualms about using them."

I hate being right, but my guess was confirmed by a sudden burst of automatic weapons fire, shattering glass, and ricocheting bullets bouncing off of waxed sheet metal. The body of Big Chuck's Yugo looked like a sieve.

"Damn you, Connie. This is your fault." He began pressing buttons on the remote. A short high-pitched squeal reverberated through the garage, followed by horrific screaming and more gunfire. Reggie started to yowl and squirm.

Left-John grabbed Big Chuck's arm, yanking the remote out from under his other hand. "What did you do?"

"Neuro weapons. Hidden in the walls for security." His eyes all but bulged from his head, and his face had lost all color. "The beams scramble impulses from the brain but bounce off anything denser than bone, so the cars are safe."

"You maniac, they're going to want blood now."

I shook my head. "They weren't going to let me walk out of here anyway. You two, maybe, but—"

A new voice called to us, a man's voice. "More alien tech, Earth

Monster? Why are we not surprised." Another volley of weapons fire began, tearing into several more cars.

"No!!!" Big Chuck jerked free of the Mocker's hand and slapped at a hidden panel in the elevator. He took a ceramo shield from within and passed it to Left-John. Then he pulled out a stun rifle and several small pear-shaped objects.

"Get out of here, Connie. Five seconds after I throw the first flash bang you run like hell for any car that hasn't been shot up. The keys will be under the floor mat on the passenger's side. I'll lay down cover fire until you're in and rolling. Then more grenades and neuro beams to slow them down and give you a chance to get away." He bent down and retrieved the remote control.

"What about you?" I said.

He glanced up at the elevator's ceiling a hand's breadth above his head. "I'll climb up top and call security to come get me. But I doubt they'll even look in here, not once you drive out. Now get out of here, before they start shooting up more of my cars!"

Without further discussion, Big Chuck twisted a tab off one of the flash bangs, swung around the edge of the elevator's open door, lobbed it in the direction of the eco-terrorists, and swung back. "Go!" he yelled. He dropped to one knee and raised the stun rifle to his shoulder, and lunged back out of the elevator as thunder and lightning exploded in the garage.

Reggie's yowls increased in volume. I clutched him like a wooly football and dashed into the garage with Left-John right behind me. Big Chuck had nearly twenty vintage cars in that garage; more than half of them lay in ruins. I aimed myself at one a bit apart from the others and recognized it as Big Chuck's recent acquisition, a '37 Mustang convertible. The doors were unlocked and we threw ourselves inside. Left-John came up with the keys, jammed them in place, and slammed the gas pedal. The car roared to life. I looked up, saw the curve of the exit ramp twenty meters away. I also saw six or seven figures with guns aimed back in the direction of the elevator.

"What are you waiting for," I said to Left-John. "Get this thing moving!"

"Not yet. Wait for it," he said and closed his eyes.

"What? Wait for—" Flash. Bang. Lightning. Thunder. Left-John opened his eyes, put the car into gear, and charged up the exit ramp, banking hard to the right as we began the long spiral to the surface.

Let me say this about the '37 Mustang, they sure don't build 'em like that anymore. We roared out of the Aztec's underground garage and onto the streets of El Paso, much to the alarm of a handful of other motorists.

After a brief flurry of honking, traffic lights, and artful swerving, Left-John drove us onto the same highway Bertram's taxi had departed just a few days before.

"Nice driving," I said as I buckled up. I started to pet and soothe my trusty buffalo dog, holding him firmly in my lap with both hands as the Mocker floored the accelerator sending us racing away from El Paso on the former interstate. "You think he'll be all right back there?"

"Either way, I'm not going to lose much sleep over him. He'd have handed us both over, if he could have gotten away with it. The only reason he helped is because they started shooting up his precious cars."

I couldn't argue with that, but I didn't quite see it the same way. You don't blame a scorpion for wanting to sting you; that's just who Big Chuck was. And yet . . . I took out the datapadd he'd given me and started flipping through the information. He'd come through with the goods. Somewhere behind us was a marker with my name on it that I knew I'd have to honor one day.

Left-John kept the pedal pressed to the floor; the digital readout of the speedometer ticked upward alarmingly as we headed southeast, paralleling the border dipping ever so slightly deeper into the chrono-schism. We reached the Mustang's top speed and continued like that for a good twenty minutes before the Mocker decided that Green Aggression hadn't followed us.

"So, where are we going? And if you say Dallas, or even Houston, I'm stopping the car and walking back, because even on foot I'll get out of Texas before you do, eco-terrorists or no." His eyes gazed fixedly forward, and though his ponytail remained tied back by a leather thong, some few strands of black hair had pulled free and whipped about his face as the wind blew over us. He eased up on the accelerator and dropped us down to a slightly less unlawful speed.

"Not to worry, we'll skirt the worst of the distortion. We'll keep following the Rio Grande until we have to cross over the border."

"So, where are we going then?"

"The Yucatan," I said.

"Why? What's there?"

"Uxmal, Dzilbichaltún, and Aké."

"You just named three dead Mayan cities. Hell, until a hundred and fifty years ago at least one of them had been lost completely."

"Really? How do you know so much about them?"

He shrugged, but still didn't take his eyes from the road. "It's an Indian thing."

"Come on, you're a Comanche. What do you know about the Maya?"

Reggie reared his head, barked once, and thumped on my leg with his right front hoof. Almost without thinking, I dug in my pocket for a treat to keep him happy. He had me well trained. That particular bark was to let me know that he was a bit put out, and would only be mollified with a great deal of personal attention or something dense to eat. I fed him a few silver dollars.

"There aren't all that many Comanche left in the world. When I was growing up, I made it my business to learn about all the native peoples in the Americas. The Maya had a thriving civilization, far outstripping anything else on the continent. They abandoned their cities centuries before the Europeans arrived. No one knows why.

"Come on, that's bullshit."

"Have you seen the ruins of Uxmal? Xlapac? Oxkintoc? Sayil?"

"No."

"Then shut the hell up about it until you do, because I have. I know you, Conroy. There's nothing there to interest you, so why do you want to go to any of those places?

"I doubt you'll believe me."

"I doubt I will too. Look, I can understand if all this running from Green Aggression has made you squirrelly, but rabbiting to some Mayan ruins makes no sense. You've got the data from the Undertaker, let's get out of Texas, find a working globalink, and pass it along to the Mexican authorities and be done."

I sighed and fed Reggie another dollar. "It's not that simple. Sure, I want to do all of that, but we still need to go to the Yucatan."

"You still haven't said why."

"Because an alien told me."

"When, back at the Aztec?"

I nodded. "Right before I came down to the casino."

"What alien? I didn't see any alien there."

"He wasn't exactly in the Aztec, not directly."

That prompted a slight head turn from the Mocker. He looked at me for several beats and then turned back to face the open highway.

"He was in my head," I said. This wasn't going well. "In a dream."

"So, we're on the road because you had a bad dream?"

"It was real. Or, actually, it was a dream of what would become real. That's how I know Green Aggression had learned I was in El Paso. From the dream."

Left-John snorted. "So your unknown alien is a precognitive telepath?

That's a little too convenient to be believable. You and I both know that telepathy doesn't work that way. There's not an alien race that both does precog that good and can share it."

"This wasn't like any alien I've ever seen. And you know I've been out there, all around Human Space and beyond. I've met, spoken with, and even hypnotized more alien races than most people ever meet."

"So what's your point?"

"Just that this is an unknown. There's something else going on here, more than just the clean-up and Green Aggression. Don't look at me like that; I was skeptical too, but being shot at in Big Chuck's garage has convinced me to at least try to learn more."

"And you can only do that in the Yucatan?"

"Not exactly. There's one other thing I want to try. It's on the way, and if it doesn't pan out then we can bail on the Yucatan."

I opened the Mustang's glove box. Big Chuck had said it had been in Texas all along so I wasn't surprised to find a digital highway map of Texas. I ran my finger along the lines and markers until I found what I needed. "We've got plenty of time, but when we get to Eagle Pass, we'll be making a slight detour, cutting straight east to San Antonio."

The Mocker sat up straight. "San Antonio is significantly inside the chrono-schism."

"I know. The ratio is about a hundred and twenty to one," I said. "It'll be all right, though. We'll drag some of the current time flow in with us, and that should linger for a bit. I only need an hour there."

"What do you expect to do with an hour?"

"I'm going to take a nap."

On a sunny December morning in 2042, Gilman and Ryne, two physicists at a Waco university, made history. Having run hundreds of computer simulations that convinced them they could successfully bend other dimensions to their will, they decided to conquer time. In their laboratory on the second floor of Petrini Hall, they powered up a device to open a chronal portal into the past. Instead it redefined the laws of temporal physics throughout most of Texas, mucking up the state more than Pancho Villa ever had, and creating the world's first and only sustained chrono-schism. Now, fifty-two years later, Gilman and Ryne's little problem had become my problem. It was a question of cartographic validity. The map showed bands of differential time and listed the relativistic ratios one could expect, but they were only estimates. Not surprisingly, no cartographer had ever walked all of Texas's time bands. That kind of dedicated empiricism just didn't exist.

None of this mattered to the remaining residents of Texas. If you stayed in one place the distortion made no difference. It was a relativistic phenomenon, and one that everyone in Texas—with the exception of the millions of souls in Waco who were still living just a day after the effect began—had grown to accept, along with their removal from the United States. But for travelers like Left-John and myself, the accuracy of the distortion map held more interest. Every hour we spent in San Antonio could translate to five days in the rest of the world. Dawdling was not an option.

We entered the outskirts of town, and cruised the suburbs until we found a public park. It was late afternoon, barely an hour left until sunset. The park looked empty, everyone presumably gone off to their respective homes for family dinners, homework, and a few hours of vid. Much of San Antonio's population had evacuated in the first days after Waco; those that remained had adapted and established a normal, albeit relatively isolated, existence. Similar instances of civil equilibrium had happened throughout Texas. How long any of them would last had been the subject of more than a few dissertations. For the good folks of San Antonio, fewer than six months have passed since that lab blew up in Waco.

Left-John stopped the car in a shady spot of an otherwise empty parking lot, and I reclined the passenger seat.

"You're just going to sack out and wait for your alien friend to show up?"

"Can you think of a better plan?" I said.

"I think you're taking profound liberties with the meaning of the word 'plan.' You're following a hunch, at best."

"Look, give it an hour, then wake me. If I've got nothing, we'll head south toward the border and cross over as we travel down the gulf coast. Even at this level of distortion we'll only have lost a week or two."

That's what I don't understand about this," said Left-John.

"What?"

"It's coming on sundown, right?"

"Sure."

"How? The days here are still twenty-four hours, same as the rest of the world, same as deeper in the distortion. So how can there be a sunset every day?"

"What do you mean?"

"We're all *rotating* around on the same planet, but in the time it takes for San Antonio to experience day and night, my grandparents in Tulsa get four months of sunsets."

133

"Your grandparents are still alive and living in Tulsa?" I asked.

"Conroy, I'm serious."

"Sorry. I never thought about it that way before. I don't know, maybe Hamlet said it best. 'There's more between heaven and earth than is dreamt of in your philosophies.'"

Left-John looked to be considering this for a minute, then nodded curtly and said, "Go to sleep. I'm not missing any more sunsets than I have to because of you."

Reggie was already napping as I reclined my seat and half rolled so I was on my side. I bent my knees and tucked them up a bit, my back to the Mocker. Reggie had a good snugged-in spot against my stomach. I rested my head on my right arm and closed my eyes hoping to follow him quickly into sleep, thinking thoughts of melancholy Danes, to sleep, per chance to dream.

Chapter Fifteen: Twenty Questions and a Ghost

NEVER TAKE A NAP WHILE THINKING ABOUT SHAKESPEARE. I fell into a dream of a dark and stormy night. I stood upon the battlements of a castle, wet and shivering in the dark. Men in arms and armor ignored me as they walked their rounds, and in the distance I could hear them challenge one another. I caught the name 'Bernardo' through the noise of the storm, but I couldn't be certain I heard clearly.

Nearer to hand I spotted a ghost-like figure, human in shape but insubstantial as if made of roiling smoke. A jeweled crown, solid and opaque as the stones of the castle, sat lightly upon the figure's smoky head. It wore clothing made of indistinct vapor. Its features flowed as I watched, one moment a hawk nose, now a button. High cheek bones and a prominent jaw appeared, only to be replaced seconds later by a flat round face. If it had eyes, I never saw them, yet from the angle of its head it gave every impression that it saw me well enough.

It came toward me, limbs moving, knees bending, as it stepped closer. Something about the movement made me think of a man walking in place while standing on a platform rolling forward upon dozens of wheels. I frowned at the creature. It waved at me and opened its mouth. Dense rings of smoke emerged, the kind you only associate with a champion cigar smoker showing off. Its voice broke through the rain with a recent familiarity.

> "Well done, my human friend, you've done the best,
> more than I'd hoped when I made my request.
> This pace it suits me well and we can speak
> without the strain that left my words so bleak."

I grimaced, as memories of the world's worst freshman lit class flashed through my head. "What the . . . are you speaking in rhyming iambic pentameter?"

> It replied, "And if I am is that a cause for fright?
> Wouldst thou object my choice upon this night?
> From your own mind I've drawn this place and time
> To share with you some words to halt a crime."

I rushed forward, closing the distance between us. "Okay, just stop that. You're giving me a headache. I got it, it's my dream you're shaping so you use things in my mind. Can you just please use something a bit less obnoxious? I'm not ready for alien Shakespeare."

The world shimmered, and the rain and the castle faded away, replaced by an indoor scene. I recognized our new surroundings as the penthouse suite at the Brunizibar Star, a hotel more than fifty light years from Earth. During my stay there a couple years ago I'd been accused of murder, fallen in love, been exonerated, and had my heart broken. But that's another story. The décor in the penthouse was expensive and modern, with touches here and there that reflected a Terran anglophilia that had been all the rage when I'd been on Brunzibar. I felt a light breeze coming in from a door that opened unto a garden terrace. The air smelled of springtime and a recent light shower that bore no resemblance to the downpour I'd just come from. The only carry over from the castle was the crown worn by my smoky alien host.

"Better?" it said.

Instead of answering I walked over to the bar, opulent and fully stocked as I remembered it and found a bottle of Blusharie. I poured myself two fingers, and took a slow sip. Even in whacky dreams it doesn't do to gulp Blusharie. Glass in hand, I turned back to face my host.

"So, is this your true form then? You're some kind of ghost?"

"Ghost? Is that how you see me? No, I am no spirit of the dead. Quite the opposite, I am nearly new born and bursting with the possibility of life. That is why I have been drawn to you."

"Why me? Why are you plaguing my dreams? What am I to you?"

"Am I a plague on your house then?"

"Stop with the stupid Shakespeare bits and just say what you have to say. And keep it brief; I don't plan to stick around here."

"Succinctly then. The probabilities are falling closer."

"Okay, not so brief as to make no sense. What does that mean? And what crime were you talking about before?"

"What would you call the destruction of your world?"

"'Hyperbole,' I hope. Tell me what's going on, and what it has to do with me."

"Your consciousness is different from those of most other humans, and even nonhumans. You've been touched by other minds, vastly different from your own, and they have left their marks. To my particular kind of perception, you stand out, like a flare amid the muted background of this planet. That drew me to you. I saw you as the confluence of events. I saw your possible and probable futures."

I shook my head and took another sip. "Human beings have a rich literature describing the futility of knowing your own future. We're big on free will. Keep it to yourself, okay?"

"I cannot. You have something I need, some knowledge that I must have."

"Yeah? What's that?"

"I don't know. I only know we will speak at some point in your future."

"Not if I have anything to say about it. I don't like aliens who show up in my head uninvited." I stepped closer and tried to look into the thing's eyes, but it had none. "Get lost," I said.

"I cannot. I must protect your immediate and near present so that our future conversation remains a possibility."

The dream Blusharie had gone to my head, but I didn't care. "Oh great. You're back to vague warnings of doom and gloom."

"In this time flow I can communicate more specifically. I perceive an escapable future in which the organization you call Green Aggression induces a volcanic eruption. This in turn will put profound stress on several fault lines. The sudden shifting of land mass will in turn result in tidal waves battering your shorelines, causing still greater geologic stress and setting off a cascade of destruction, killing more than a billion humans."

I sobered up at once. A billion people? If there was even a chance this creature was right... "Do you also see how I can stop it from happening?"

"I don't know. I see the initial state and probable outcome, but not the proximate cause. I only know that you are involved, that the Green Aggression for Earth's Assurance is involved, and that the event occurs in Mexico."

"Hold on, you can't just say that I have a part in the way the world's going to end and then not tell me what to do."

"I have already done so, to the extent that I can. In your last dream I shared my perceptions of probabilistic precursors with you.

"What are you talking about?"

"I placed knowledge of possible futures into your subconscious. Coupled with your own cognitions they may give you insights that I am unable to perceive."

I flashed on the names of Mayan cities that I'd known without knowing I'd known. "That's in my head now? How do I tap into that knowledge?"

It paused then and folded its arms across its chest. The smoky limbs slowly merged with the torso until they vanished entirely leaving only bumps to show where its elbows had been until they too vanished. New arms sprouted from its shoulders and hands grew from the ends of the arms. It reached up and took the crown from its head and held it out for my inspection. The crown's substance shimmered and shifted from metal to some kind of fabric.

"This will be your key."

"You want me to wear a hat? That's going to help me?"

"That is my hope. I need you to survive."

"Yeah, I kind of need me to survive as well," I said and put my drink down on the bar.

It returned the crown to its smoky head, restoring it to precious metal in the process. "Then heed my warning. Use the gift I have shared with you. Only in this way will you be poised to act when the probable futures converge. Go to Mexico and you can avert disaster for yourself and your people."

"So that's it? You're giving me some vague fortune teller prediction of death and destruction and you're done?"

"Go to Mexico," it repeated. "Among its ancient cities, you'll find your choice point."

It dismissed me then, ending its audience with an imperial gesture. Its crown glinted in the penthouse's light, which in turn faded to black.

I opened my eyes to find myself curled up on the passenger seat of Big Chuck's '37 Mustang, with Reggie snoring softly against my abdomen. Left-John Mocker sat in the driver's seat, softly tapping his fingers against the steering wheel.

"I'm awake," I said. "How long was I out for?"

The Mocker checked the dashboard clock. "Not quite an hour. You have your little visit?"

"Yeah, after a fashion." I sat up, juggling Reggie a bit as I resituated myself. "I'll fill you in on the way. Let's get going."

Left-John started the car and moments later we left suburban San Antonio behind. "Where are we going?"

"Mexico," I said. "We've got to save the world."

"Oh yeah? And just how are we going to do that?"

"I haven't the faintest idea. You think that will be a problem?"

He gave me a long, hard look, but he didn't answer. Then he turned his attention back to the road in front of us and just drove.

We were maybe twenty minutes past the city limits when the Mocker's curiosity got the better of him, and he asked me about the dream. I'd been mulling it over in my head since we'd left the park, all the while combing my fingers through the tight ringlets on Reggie's head and shoulders, a treatment he's quite fond of, but I hadn't come to any conclusions. I described the dream, from the castle battlements to the offworld penthouse.

The Mocker said nothing, and continued driving in silence for several kilometers. Then without any preamble he asked, "Why did it pick you?"

"I explained that," I said. "It said my consciousness was different, that I'd been touched and marked."

"What's that supposed to mean?"

I had a hunch. "Kwarum," I said. Years ago, I'd told Left-John the story of the Svenkali and how I'd gotten my start as a hypnotist. Since that beginning I'd had a few other experiences with telepathic aliens, but nothing as profound as hosting my great aunt's consciousness for a short while.

"And you think that's what your dream alien meant when it said you'd been marked?" asked Left-John.

"Maybe," I said. "Kwarum Sivtinzi Lapalla, the only Svenkali ever to be hypnotized. If he was right, then I've just brought his consciousness back from whatever collective awareness or afterlife it had been hanging out in, and he's now sitting in the car with us, listening through my ears, and seeing through my eyes."

"You seriously believe he's here now? Present at our conversation?"

"I don't know. I suppose it's possible. I got word that he died not long after I left Hesnarj. And every year since I've kept my word, shared his name, and told his story, and encouraged others to do the same. Maybe one time I'll see him peeking back at me from your eyes."

The Mocker shook his head. "Oh right, like I'm ever going to say that name in my life?"

We drove on in silence for about another ten kilometers when without warning Left-John pulled the car to the side of the road. "My turn to nap," he said. He opened the car door and got out, walking around to my side where he shooed me over. I managed the transition without waking Reggie, put the car into gear, and pulled us back out onto the highway. Left-John reclined his seat and a few minutes later he began to snore.

Chapter Sixteen: The Saint of Sandwiches

SINCE LEAVING SAN ANTONIO we'd passed or been passed by fewer than a dozen other vehicles. We skirted around Brownsville in the empty hours just before dawn and came to the border crossing of the southernmost portion of Texas. This had been a thriving area once, tourists wanting a quick taste of Mexico, and business interests visiting and eager to partake of the advantages of the maquiladoras. Waco had changed all of that.

The lone border guard didn't challenge us as I slowed the Mustang at the crossing. He sat inside a small kiosk, his beret pulled down low. His head had dipped forward so that his chin pressed against his breastbone.

I stopped the car at the gate and waited. Left-John yawned, stretched, and sat up. Reggie jumped into his lap and demanded attention, which was soon granted in the form of neck scratching. We continued to wait. After a solid ten minutes, with no cars coming up behind us, no cars driving up from the south, and no sign of the guard waking up, Left-John reached a hand over and beeped the car's horn. The effect was instantaneous. The guard jerked awake, nearly fell off his chair and out of his kiosk. And he drew a gun. We sat very still. The guard pointed the gun at us and started shouting in rapid Spanish. Seconds later he stopped, apparently realizing where he was and what had happened. He holstered his gun and returned to his kiosk, emerging moments later with a clipboard in hand as he feigned indignation.

He was an elderly man, short and frail. He wore a uniform of faded green and blue, and the matching beret sat upon a head full of wiry grey hair. I put him at seventy years old, at least. He may well have been working border patrol back when Texas had still been a state.

Reggie eyed the guard warily and ambled back over to sit in my lap, while the guard walked a slow circle around the car. Then he leaned on the passenger's side door and stuck out his hand in that universal gesture of border officials on any world that indicates the time to present one's papers.

His mood appeared to brighten as he inspected Left-John's passport, and not just because of the cash he pulled from it and slipped casually into one pocket. The gambler's passport was a gaudy affair. In addition to leather and paper, ceramo and ink, it had been imprinted with specialty chemo-glyphs that stimulated the brain's olfactory bulb and evoked archetypal associations. One glyph stirred feelings of nobility and a lost history; he had that because of his position as member at large of the Bureau of Indian Activities. A second glyph brought to mind a breathtaking sense of risk with undertones of mastery, which was his mark as a rated member of the Probability Guild. The third and final glyph evoked a sense of the exotic, travelers from foreign lands. My own passport bore that one, an artifact awarded after filling a standard passport with stamps from more than a dozen worlds beyond Human Space. Apparently the border guard had never seen a passport with three chemo-glyphs before, and it seemed like he'd be willing to let us slide right through—with the appropriate bribe of course. That changed when he gestured for my passport.

It was one of those stomach tightening moments and I silently began cursing myself for a fool. My passport was sitting safe and secure inside an allegedly indestructible wall safe buried amidst the rubble of what had once been my office. Between escaping Green Aggression's ambush back at Big Chuck's garage and trying to get answers out of an alien in my dreams, I'd overlooked the obvious need for documentation to legally enter Mexico.

The guard stared at the buffalo dog curled up on my lap. Reggie looked back, though quite a bit more politely. Neither of us said a word for several tense moments, and then the guard looked me in the eye.

"¿Qué es esto?"

Despite Mexico's rigidly xenophobic policies, I had to hope that genemod pets had made some inroads. I gave the guard my best smile and said, "Esto es mi perro. This is my dog."

That seemed to satisfy the guard, at least with respect to Reggie. Moments later though he was glaring at me after I again shrugged and spread my empty hands in response to his repeated gesture for me to hand over my papers. He stormed back into his kiosk. Left-John was even less sympathetic.

"You're the Amazing Conroy, right? Why don't you just hypnotize him and make him think you've got a passport?"

"I can't," I said. Even assuming I could manage a flash trance, I had pretty much exhausted my store of Spanish with that one exchange. How could I do an induction if I didn't speak the language?

"Well, bribe him then."

"You already bribed him," I said.

"That was for me. And I had a proper passport. Throw more money at him, it's a language I'm sure you can both communicate in without problem."

I read people pretty well; it's a handy knack for a hypnotist. Still, five days out of six I'm likely to concede that Left-John's vocation as a gambler has made him several times my superior. When the border guard returned he handed me a fresh clipboard overflowing with forms and paperwork, all in Spanish. I clipped a stack of currency under the first page and returned the board. The guard frowned, counted the money, frowned again, and walked back to his kiosk. Left-John and I looked at one another, and again we waited. And waited. Eventually the guard returned; he handed me a plain and battered looking passport. The photograph inside was blurry and nondescript. It could have been almost anybody, though according to the name in the passport it was Santiago MacLeod.

I showed it to the Mocker who glanced at it, handed it back to me, and said, "Welcome to Mexico, Mr. MacLeod."

On cue, the guard raised the crossing bar and waved us through. As we drove forward I watched in the mirror as the old man climbed back into his kiosk, considerably wealthier for twenty minutes' work. Moments later we passed a billboard:

WELCOME TO MEXICO
LAND OF MAGIC AND ENCHANTMENT

"Congratulations, Conroy, you've done it again," said the Mocker.

"Done what again?"

"Smuggled a buffalo dog. This time, you've smuggled it in, instead of out. I wonder if the Mexican government would count you as a repeat offender or not. What do you think?"

"I think you should shut up and let me drive," I said. Welcome to Mexico indeed.

From the border crossing it was a short drive to Matamoros, which according to the guidebook lay safely outside the effects of the Texas chrono-schism. The city had history. Last century it had been the site of the first maquiladora. The population had dropped from its peak of half a million people to barely two hundred thousand. Although the southern edge of Texas suffered almost no effects of the chrono-schism, the pallor of the entire former state had been painted with a single brush and had shattered the economy of the Mexican border towns. The once vast cotton industry had dwindled, and the maquiladoras had been crushed. But Matamoros, despite its beaten down economy, still had one thing that I wanted: an airport. The city was just starting to wake up when I pulled the Mustang into an empty lot and parked in front of the municipal terminal building.

"What makes you think anyone's here yet?" said Left-John.

"If they're not, then we wait a few hours. Or would you rather drive all the way to the Yucatan?"

"No, but I do like the idea of putting as much distance between Charlemagne Thomas and his precious car as possible." Left-John smiled as he said it.

"Actually, I was hoping we could hire someone willing to drive it back to the Aztec for us."

Reggie did not want to go back into the gym bag, but we looked conspicuous enough. With a combination of coaxing and bribery (would Big Chuck really miss the car's cigarette lighter?) I had my buffalito safely hidden from view before the Mocker and I got out of the car and entered the terminal.

A single clerk was on duty behind a broad counter bearing signs for several different regional airlines. He wore a jumpsuit with patches on the shoulders that matched one of the signs, and a ball cap with the same logo. He had his head down staring at a disposable bookpad, his nose practically touching the screen and the brim of his cap casting it in shadow. The book must have been engrossing; we walked right up, stopped in front of him, and even then he gave no sign of noticing us until I knocked on the counter.

"Buenos dias. ¿Que quieren señores?" He turned the bookpad face down and set it on the counter.

"I don't suppose you speak English," I said. I looked into his eyes and held his gaze. It's a hypnosis trick that with some people predisposes them to you. The clerk's eyes were like a forest of endless brown bark.

"Sí. What do you gentlemen want?"

Left-John looked at me. Clearly this was all my play. "My name is Santiago MacLeod. We've just driven over from Brownsville and would like to fly to the Yucatan." I tried to reestablish my eye contact, but the clerk was a head shorter than me and dropped his gaze so all I saw was the top of his employee cap. A beat passed, than another, and he looked back up, nervously I thought. His face was flat, a long chin with a wide nose and broad forehead. He had a pencil thin moustache that could have been painted over his lip, and when he smiled as he did when he next spoke I saw one of his front teeth was capped with gold. His skin color was as almost as red as Left-John Mocker's, just a shade muddier. I wondered if his ancestors were Aztec or Mayan or some other group of people native to the region and dating back centuries before Europeans had arrived to these shores.

"You don't got no luggage, señor. When it is you wish to fly? Tomorrow? The next day?"

"Today. This morning, in fact."

"I am sorry, señor, but we have no scheduled flights to the Yucatan. Most of our pilots just fly back and forth from Monterrey. I can put you on a shuttle to Monterrey at ten o'clock, and from there you will easy find flights throughout the Yucatan."

I turned to Left-John. "Okay, so we go find a coffee shop, have some breakfast, and come back in a few hours." Inside the gym bag Reggie began making whuffling noises. I patted it reassuringly and he stopped, at least for the moment.

As I turned away from the counter, Left-John grabbed my arm and pulled me up short.

"Look, you've got me following you all over the place, to El Paso, to San Antonio, and now into Mexico. I got it, you're on some quest, but can we at least not dawdle?"

He stepped back to the counter and said to the clerk. "What about a charter?"

"That is not a cheap proposition."

"So there are pilots available?"

"Sí, I could fly you there myself."

"You're a pilot? What's your name?"

"I am Miguel Garcia Delgado, owner and pilot of a sweet plane that knows the Gulf like the curves of a woman. I am also mechanic and counterman, and I make the sandwiches you eat on the plane."

"So, you can take us there this morning?"

"I can fly you, señor, but not this morning. I cannot fly you to Merida without a day for the paperwork. They love the paperwork in Merida. It is where the touristas all go."

"No," said the Mocker, "We don't want to wait, and we don't love paperwork or tourists. There's got to be somewhere else you can land in the Yucatan."

"I take you to Champoton, it is just south of Campeche. Six hundred new pesos."

"Six hundred? A moment, please," I said, stepping back up to the counter long enough to pull Left-John away from it for a hurried consultation. "How are you fixed for cash?"

"Me? You're the industrial tycoon."

"Yes, well, I'm sorry, but that border guard took the last of my money."

"So find a bank kiosk."

"Won't work," I said. "I crashed the company, remember? All the assets are probably still frozen. But more importantly, they're probably being watched by Green Aggression. How much cash do you have on hand?"

"Don't worry about it, I've got a better idea."

Before I could ask what he meant, Reggie started kicking up a fuss again, shaking the gym bag. He was trying to anchor himself so he could start eating his way out. I turned my back to the counter and put the bag down on the floor. I unzipped it quickly and was rewarded with Reggie practicing his most sheepish expression, the buffalo dog equivalent of a four-year old caught with his hand in the cookie jar.

"Will you just calm down for a bit?" I didn't expect him to understand the words, but I'd hoped the tone might get through. I needn't have bothered. Reggie expression flowed from sheepish to petulant. Clearly he considered himself the wounded party.

"Six hundred new pesos to get us to the Yucatan," said the Mocker, back at the counter. "How soon can we go?"

"Oh, you misunderstand me, señor. It is six hundred for each."

"I see. Tell me, what kind of car do you drive?"

"Car?"

"Every pilot I've ever met also had a fine appreciation for cars. We have a classic parked just outside. Why don't you come take a look at it?"

"You want I should look at your car, señor?"

"Please. And then ask yourself what such a car might be worth to you. Perhaps we can come to an arrangement."

"What are you doing?" I said, hastily pulling the bag closed, eliciting a squawk from Reggie as I scrambled up behind the Mocker. "You can't do that with Big Chuck's car."

"Oh please. You have a problem with me selling his car? What happened to your mission to save the world from your alien's cataclysm of doom?"

My pang of conscience fizzled quickly, and not because of the Mocker's obvious attempt at manipulation. "You're right, but that car's worth fifty times the cost of the plane charter."

"Your point?"

"Trade him the car," I said, "but get him to go to the bank and throw in some cash too. No sense giving the thing away."

Left-John nodded. "Good point. Nice to see that the corporate life hasn't cost you your sensibility. Leave him to me, Mr. MacLeod. You go find a means to mollify your friend in the bag, before he eats his way out of it."

The Mocker was as good as his word. He walked our potential pilot all around Big Chuck's prized vintage car, pointing out the low odometer reading and the advantage of the car having spent most of its time in Austin. The lack of a pink chit didn't bother Miguel Garcia Delgado; Texas property laws had no bearing in Mexico since the Waco disaster. Within half an hour the two had gone off to a bank for cash, as well as to see to whatever preparations were necessary before our flight. With Reggie clamoring for my attention, I went looking for a public globalink.

I found a small booth at the end of the room, and the complete lack of other travelers or employees provided adequate privacy. I punched in a private number President Ortiz had given me for emergency use only. The screen lit instantly, and I was looking at a serious faced woman of middle years and jet black hair.

She said something in Spanish that sounded terribly official. I shrugged at her. "Sorry. Do you speak English?"

"I do. Calls to this address are not authorized from your location."

"Oh? Sorry, President Ortiz didn't mention that when he gave me this code."

She scowled at me, seemed to be studying something outside my field of view, and then turned back. "Señor Conroy?"

"That's me."

She shook her head, an incredibly economical gesture that she limited to just her chin. "You are not dead?"

"Right. But I am in a bit of a hurry. Is the president available? I have information that he'll want."

"One moment, señor." Her image dissolved and the screen filled with a stirring representation of the presidential seal.

Reggie had been watching the exchange intently, and seemed to decide that it was time once more for me to play with him. He began to bark. As soon as I tried to shush him the screen went active and I found myself under the gaze of Mexican President Ortiz.

"Mr. Conroy! You are alive. I had received reports that you had been killed in the destruction of your building by Green Aggression."

"We escaped," I said. "And everything is still on for the clean-up project. Dr. Lisa Penrose should be contacting you soon, if she hasn't already."

"Yes, yes, I spoke with her yesterday morning. But my advisors are recommending that we cancel the project, and I am inclined to agree. Green Aggression poses too great a threat to public safety for us to proceed."

"That's why I'm calling," I said and took out the datapadd Big Chuck had provided; I readied the files for transmission. "I'm sending you data on the names and whereabouts of every eco-terrorism leader and major operative in your country. Your security agency should be able to remove their threat quickly and completely." I initiated the data transfer and watched as the datapadd poured everything it knew through the globalink and into President Ortiz's receiving station.

"I will have my people test the validity of your information at once. If it checks out, then yes, I believe we can proceed as planned. Thank you, Mr. Conroy, I don't pretend to understand the motivation that makes you stick with this project, but you have the thanks of my country."

"No problem," I said. "When you've confirmed the data and defused the situation with Green Aggression, please contact Dr. Penrose and let her know you're back on schedule."

"You will not be involved yourself?"

"I'm in the middle of something else at the moment, Mr. President. I promise to be in touch with you as soon as I can. Thank you, sir." And I terminated the connection. I had no doubt that Ortiz would wonder why I was in Matamoros, but I also knew he'd be too busy surprising the leaders of every Green Aggression cell throughout Mexico to spare it more than idle speculation.

I turned to Reggie. "Okay, boy, you've got my full attention now." Moments later I was outside on the tiny runway behind the terminal throwing the now useless datapadd down the tarmac as Reggie chased after it in an improvised game of fetch.

Eventually Left-John Mocker returned. The pilot led us to one of the planes and motioned for us to enter. The tiny craft had seating for six passengers, three rows of two seats, with a narrow aisle running between. Left-John took the left seat in the front row. I moved past him and set Reggie and his tattered gym bag on the seat behind him and sat across from it.

"Here, put this in your pocket or your wallet or wherever." Left-John handed me a stack of new pesos, keeping a similar wad for himself.

I rippled one corner of my stack for a quick count and came up at about twenty thousand new pesos. If the other stack was comparable, even with the cost of the tickets, the car had been a steal. Still, it wasn't like the Mocker to cut himself such a poor deal.

"That's all you got for the car?" I said as I secured Reggie to the seat via his bag and then buckled myself in for take-off.

"Hmm? Oh, no, that's just the cash. I also got us these." He reached back over the seat and across the aisle to hand me a paper bag. Inside were half a dozen sandwiches wrapped in waxed paper. I looked up, and Left-John was strapping a small ice chest into the seat across from him. When he was done he opened it and withdrew a bottle of beer.

"Beer and sandwiches?" I said. "You traded the car for beer and sandwiches? Was he out of magic beans?"

"I doubt Charlemagne Thomas would appreciate you comparing his vintage automobile to a cow."

I squeezed my eyes shut and rubbed them, feeling a sharp pain coming on. I silently counted to ten. Then counted to ten again. When I spoke it was with manufactured calm. "John, the car was worth a small fortune. And all you got for it was a few thousand new pesos, a pair of plane tickets, and some beer and sandwiches."

"Not just that," said Left-John, "I also wrote up a bill of sale so it'd be nice and legal. I mailed a copy to Thomas via a courier in Albuquerque. He should get it within six months."

The pain behind my eyes jumped up a notch or two, from sharp stick to red hot poker. Left-John's reaction to my expression was to hand me a bottle of beer.

"Cervezas! It's your adventure, Conroy. I'm just along for the ride, or flight as it happens. Try one of the sandwiches. Our pilot made them himself."

I sighed, unwrapped a sandwich and took a small bite, getting only bread. The crust was thick and chewy, dark and a little bitter. It reminded me of a traditional black bread or pumpernickel, and not at all the sort of thing I'd expect to encounter in Mexico where, if even half of the vids I'd grown up watching could be believed, everything should have been wrapped in flour or corn tortillas. With the next bite I tasted some kind of meat, finely chopped and heavily seasoned. The spices made my eyes water, but they meshed perfectly with the thick brown bread. I took another bite and another and before I realized it, I'd eaten the entire sandwich.

"Good huh? If he's half as good a pilot, we'll be in the Yucatan seconds after we lift." He handed me a bottle opener and I popped the cap on my beer.

"My god, that was the best sandwich I've ever had in my life."

The Mocker nodded vigorously around a beer bottle as he took a long swig. "I know. I had one while we were getting everything. Had I known beforehand, I might have traded him the car just for the sandwiches."

I was about to agree, at least in principle, when the miracle maker of sandwiches, Miguel Garcia Delgado himself, climbed into the plane. He hauled the steps in behind him, folded them away and secured the hatch. With a wave and a wink he pushed aside a pleated blue curtain at the front of the plane, stepped through, and disappeared into the cockpit. Seconds later the engines turned over and the entire plane began shaking violently. Reggie began to howl.

"Forget the sandwiches, this plane is a deathtrap," I said. "Didn't he claim to be a mechanic?"

The Mocker looked thoughtful. "He's a pilot and a hell of a chef. I'm sure his mechanical skills are on an equal footing."

"How do you know how well he can fly?" I said. "He only told us he was a pilot. Maybe as a pilot and mechanic he's just a really good sandwich maker?"

The paper bag fell from my hands as I began fumbling to unfasten my belt. Before I could finish, let alone open the hatch and escape, the plane rolled forward. It lurched, spun around, lurched again, and then started picking up speed, all the while shaking so hard that every bolt holding it together should have worked its way loose. As we reached the end of the short runway, the plane's nose pulled up, its wheels left the asphalt, and the trembling ended. We were airborne.

Left-John Mocker's expression was as stoic as ever, though his face had drained of color.

"You know, it's a pity," he said.

"What is?"

"That we didn't just die."

"What's that supposed to mean?"

He gestured at the bag I'd dropped which had slid under my seat. "Well, it would have been a hell of a last meal."

The plane dropped suddenly. My stomach, a great believer in the laws of inertia, assured me it wanted to stay at our previous height and rejected the notion that it should follow the rest of me.

"Then again, maybe I should just try to keep that last meal down," said the Mocker.

The plane wobbled from side to side as it struggled to gain altitude again. Reggie whimpered piteously and looked to me for reassurance.

I leaned forward and reached a hand under the seat, grasping blindly until my fingers found the paper bag. I pulled out a sandwich and fed it to the buffalo dog, waxed paper and all. The plane leveled off and settled down to a comfortable flight.

"Give me another beer," I said. "If our landing is anything like the take-off, I'm going to need it."

Chapter Seventeen: A Philadelphia-Sized Puzzle

SEVERAL SANDWICHES, TWO BOTTLES OF BEER, and one perilous landing later, we arrived at what must have once been a thriving municipal airport. The remains of more than a dozen hangers and outbuildings skirted a trio of runways. Only the farthest of these was useable, the encroaching jungle having begun to reclaim the other two.

"Welcome to the Yucatan," said the Mocker. "Now what?"

It was a fair question. The alien from my dream had directed me to the Yucatan but provided no advice as to what to do once I arrived.

"I need to find a hat," I said. I didn't really believe it, but that was all I had.

"You dragged me down here so you could buy a hat?"

I put on my best enigmatic stage face, letting my eyes go dead and my expression completely lax, knowing that it wouldn't count for much with the Mocker even as I did it. "All will be revealed in time," I intoned with resonant solemnity. Our pilot chose that moment to pull back the curtain and join us in the plane's tiny main cabin, sparing me further explanation or theatrics. He indicated the windows on the starboard side with an expansive gesture.

"Champoton Airfield, señores. Almost no international flights come here no more. No jets. No stacks of paperwork. No touristas. They are all north at Campeche or Merida." He flashed his gold tooth in a broad smile and then turned to undog the hatch and unfold the portable steps.

I tempted Reggie back into his gym bag by dangling a plastic lined air-sickness pouch under his nose. He chuffed once, and then lunged for it, knocking it from my hand and tumbling with it into the bag. I picked up the bag with one hand and followed the pilot out. As I set my foot on the first step I glanced back. "C'mon. I've got to find a hat. It's the only advice the alien gave me."

He glanced up at the cloudless sky. "He's worried about heat stroke?"

"Will you come on?"

"Just a moment." And with that the Mocker pushed his way past me to the pilot. "Miguel, por favor. Can my friend borrow your hat?"

"My hat? I do not think it will fit him. He has the big cabeza."

"Just for a moment," he said and held out a hand. The pilot shrugged, removed his cap, and passed it over. The Mocker turned back to me and offered the cap.

"Here's your hat. It's a loaner. Try it on."

It was a mechanic's cap, and had the grease stains to prove it. I closed my eyes and put it on.

And nothing happened.

I'm not sure what I'd expected. Maybe not some bodhi tree enlightenment, but at least a little insight. But, nothing. I took off the hat and stepped over to our pilot.

"Thanks, I, uh, always wanted to try on a pilot's hat."

"Well?" said the Mocker, at my elbow again.

"Nothing," I said. "I was hoping for something, but the cap's no good to me. I fold." As soon as the words were out of my mouth I knew something. A tiny piece of knowledge danced before me, spinning on that one word, *fold*. It was as if I could see a small part of the future, though for the life of me I couldn't tell you what it meant. I turned to the Mocker. "I know why we're here."

"You do?"

I nodded, and even so slight a gesture set my head spinning. I reached out a hand to steady myself and closed my eyes. I saw fragments. Shards. Bits and pieces of probability that varied in vividness, depending on how close they were to being actualized. And all of it seen from a perspective that had no understanding of the human condition.

Imagine a novel about life on Earth, written by an alien possessed of different senses and perceptions and who has never so much as met a human being. That's what I had in my head. I was tapping into the precognitive mappings of my dream alien, at least as much as my brain could manage. The future, *my* future, was like the pieces of a vast jigsaw puzzle that's just been emptied out of its box onto a table the size of Philadelphia and some of the pieces just naturally fit together. The mental cacophony hit me in that instant. Then, just as quickly, they slipped away, like some mercurial liquid decanted and then poured back, leaving the barest of perceptible traces. I'd had just the tiniest tease of a glance before my mortal brain recoiled and purged it from memory. But it was enough.

"I just figured it out," I said as I opened my eyes and straightened up. Left-John stared at me. The pilot stared at me. I realized I was grinning like an idiot, but I couldn't stop.

"In my suite at the Aztec, the names of cities I didn't know started popping out of my mouth. The same thing is happening now. New words and phrases are on the tip of my tongue. 'Fold,' 'button,' 'the river,' 'the turn,' 'the flop.' They're all part of something."

"That's poker jargon," Left-John said.

I nodded vigorously. The dizziness had left in me, and been replaced by a glorious sense of euphoria. "I know. And it ties into the next piece of highest probability to unravel all of this. I know why we're in the Yucatan, and what to do next."

"Okay, just so I'm clear . . . it's not buying a hat, right?"

"Nope, though we might want to pick one up on the way. The real reason we're here is to play some cards."

"We could have done that back in the States."

"No, playing cards is just a mean to an end."

He snorted at that.

"Maybe for some people—"

"That's not what I mean. It's because we'll be playing cards that I meet someone I'm supposed to meet."

"And who's that?"

"I don't know. How could I? I haven't met him yet. Or her. But I know, I *know*, it's somebody who is as much a part of this as I am. I have this sense of certainty that we'll meet over a game of Hold'em."

"Fine by me," said Left-John. "You don't look good in hats, anyway. Something about the size of your head."

One of the outbuildings adjacent to the runway served as immigration. A bored customs officer frowned when she saw Reggie. She spoke English and started to question me about the buffalito's origins. All too painfully aware of Mexico's xenophobic policies, I'd been preparing an explanation that would serve, one to go with the identity listed on my passport. I'd decided that Santiago MacLeod was a sales rep for a designer biologics firm, and that Reggie was a sample of our latest genemod product, miniature bison for Mexican ranchers.

As the customs agent listened, I unwound a long series of fanciful lies and business models, as if it were part of a hypnosis stage show. I started warm and friendly, humble and subservient, inducing a suggestive state in the agent through the modulation and rhythm of my voice, and used my narrative to create what people in the hypnosis biz call a *rapport*. This wasn't like the situation back at the border where shortness of time, a language barrier, and my utter lack of papers prevented me from working up a hypnotic solution. Here I had a conducive setting, a plausible story, and a civil servant with English fluency. I didn't need to make this woman believe that black had become white or day turned into night, just that my explanation was reasonable unto itself and not worth bothering over.

By the end, her frown had changed into a smile. She seemed pleased with her role in helping to make possible the exciting future of Mexico's ranchers. She waved me through. The Mocker showed his own passport, and the agent almost sneered at the assortment of fancy chemo-glyphs. Still, his documentation checked out and she cleared him after a moment's delay.

As we exited the building the Mocker put a hand on my shoulder and said, "Don't pretend to tell me you didn't find that more satisfying than sitting behind a desk and pushing papers around."

"A CEO's pay is better," I said, shrugging. "And the worst thing that ever happens to you is a paper cut."

"Unless you piss off an international group of eco-terrorists."

"You have a point." We rounded a corner and found a battered, white and green jitney parked in the shade by the curb. Several dents decorated the vehicle, and all of its tires were balding. The door was open, and through it we could see an elderly man slumped back in the driver's seat. From three meters away I could hear him snoring.

The Mocker asked, "You want to take this bus?"

"We're looking for a poker game. Games need locations. If there's a game for us to get into, it's likely to be found at a hotel. This jitney goes to all the hotels."

"Fair enough," said Left-John. He stepped through the open door and onto the bus, turning at the tiller and taking a seat in the front row directly behind the sleeping driver. I followed, and paused alongside the sleeping driver, considering the best way to wake him up.

"Let him sleep," said the Mocker. "He looks so frail that if you startle him he'll wake up only to have a heart attack and die. It's too early in the day for a poker game anyway."

With a nod I stepped past the driver and slid onto the faded and patched vinyl bench seat across the aisle from the Mocker. I set the bag with Reggie to my right, firmly against the side of the tiny bus. Reggie craned his head and peered out the window.

Left-John sat silently, gazing out through the window on his side. Whether he was studying the traffic on the main street that ran past the airport or merely ignoring me I couldn't say.

In my head pieces bumped into one another as they tried to fit together. This whole precognitive thing bothered me. The alien had spoken of probabilities, suggesting the future was still in flux. Was I going to deliberately avert the impending ecological disaster, or would my attempt to do so be what actually caused it to move from a probable to a definite future? I couldn't see it through to the end. All I knew with any certainty was that I had a poker game ahead of me, a game with people I couldn't quite see, but whom I knew I had to meet.

I sat there, lost in my own thoughts for several minutes, oblivious to everything until the sudden snorting, yawning, and stretching of the driver hauled me out of my wool gathering.

"Can you take us to the hotel," I said, moving one hand over to pat Reggie on the head and ease him down a bit and out of the range of the driver's line of sight.

"Sí, señor, I take you there now." He turned the ignition over and the jitney sputtered to life. A cough of cool air emerged from the vents overhead and moments later we were in motion and trundling forward at a leisurely rate away from the airport.

Ten minutes later, the jitney pulled up in front of a smallish tourist hotel. Large plastic letters hung from a plaster façade to proclaim the hotel's name, some complex bit of Spanish that I couldn't pronounce or keep in my brain. Behind these letters though, the faded outline of a hotel chain's well-known logo could be made out. Clearly this place had once been on the map. Just as clearly, it had left its glory days behind.

We disembarked and a porter materialized, determined to carry our bags. He was a middle-aged man with a slight paunch, made more noticeable by an ill-fitting red bellman's uniform complete with matching cap. I clutched Reggie's gym bag to my chest and Left-John shrugged to indicate we had no other luggage. The porter gave us a look of disdain that, while it expressed scorn, nonetheless made it clear he expected a tip, whether we had any need of his services or not.

The Mocker passed him by without a second glance and proceeded into the lobby. I followed, but only after pausing long enough to tip both the jitney driver and the fat, surly porter. What can I tell you? I always tip. I've worked too many bars and clubs, known too many people who depended on tips for their livelihood for me to do otherwise.

Despite the exterior's impression of faded glory, the inside looked fresh and modern. The lobby gleamed with light. Tropical plants and flowers lay scattered about in riotous profusion, suggesting enthusiasm and gaiety, and filling the air with a fragrant perfume. The broad counter of the front desk was dark wood, heavily oiled and carved with old world skill, contrasting with the organo-ceramic fresco mounted on the wall behind it. Left-John Mocker already stood at the desk, and as I approached he turned my way and handed me a room key.

"I've booked us a suite with the tour," he said.

"Tour?"

"You said there's someone you have to meet, and according to the clerk the only other guests here are part of a tour group going from city to city visiting Maya ruins. So I signed us up. They're all out at a site right now, but we'll join them for dinner. If they're not who you're looking for, we can opt out."

"That'll work," I said. "At dinner, when we introduce ourselves, remember I'm Santiago MacLeod, and I'm a sales rep for a designer biologics firm. And you introduce yourself as yourself. Then, after we've made everyone's acquaintance we can inquire if anyone's interested in a friendly poker game after dinner."

"That's your plan? You don't think it's too subtle, Conroy?" Neither irony nor sarcasm suited the Mocker. His level inflection masked his intended meaning.

"If you have a better suggestion you can be sarcastic, but otherwise, yes, given what little we know I'd prefer to keep things simple."

"You can't really expect me to play cards with . . . tourists! I have my professional reputation to consider."

"Fine, if you're that concerned we'll spin it differently. I'm a beginner, a rookie on the amateur circuit. We met up at a tournament, got along very well. So much so that you've agreed to mentor me in the finer points of gambling wherever I happen to be able to scare up a game. We'll make it clear that you're just going to watch me play, so you can break it all down for me afterwards as my 'poker coach.' Do you like that better?"

"I hope you can bluff better than you lie," said the Mocker. "That's got to be the dumbest plan I've heard out you."

"Do you have anything better?" I asked.

"No, but that doesn't make it any less dumb."

"But you'll do it?"

"If I don't, at the rate you're going you'll probably just come up with something even dumber."

"Thanks for your vote of confidence. When is the tour group due back?"

"Not until this evening. Why?"

"Well, we might want to use that time to go up to the room, get ourselves cleaned up, and do some quick shopping. I'm thinking maybe pick up some spare clothes, toiletries, maybe a suitcase. Reggie has almost eaten through this gym bag in at least three places."

"There may be hope for you yet, Conroy. That's an excellent plan. It will give us a chance to spend the money from Thomas's car."

I rolled my eyes. "Right, and afterwards maybe we can have our picture taken so you can send that back to him too."

"It's tempting," he said. "Yes, there's definitely hope for you."

The Mocker turned away and headed up to our room, just before I broke into a smile.

Chapter Eighteen: The Horns of Purpose and Precognition

THERE'S SOMETHING ABOUT the first hot shower in a foreign country after a marginally illicit plane flight and a day in a car wearing the same clothes that just makes you feel like a new man. Fresh duds helps too. The hotel clerk directed us to the Mexican equivalent of a haberdashery, barely a block from the hotel. We wasted no time, and outfitted ourselves in the local fashions, each to our own tastes.

When evening came, I left my hotel room carrying a handsome, alligator physician's bag. I'd removed the inside compartments and partitions, creating a more comfortable place for my buffalo dog to snooze. At the moment though Reggie was wide awake and his wooly head stuck out through the opening as he checked out the surroundings. I wore a white linen shirt, hand embroidered with an intricate Mayan glyph on the right breast and a comfortably fitting pair of pico-fiber slacks, as good as any I might have gotten back in Philadelphia. My hair was still damp and smelling of the tiny bottles of hotel shampoo and conditioner, and my skin had that fresh scrubbed look that thirty minutes in a hot shower produces.

Left-John was similarly refreshed and looking crisp and professional all in black, with a black on black patterned kerchief, folded and knotted into a headband, holding his long hair out of his eyes.

We stepped into the dining room and the tour leader, a tall, dark-haired woman, hurried over from a long table where the members of her group awaited dinner. She greeted us in English tinged with the barest hint of an accent that placed her origins somewhere in Maine.

"Gentlemen, welcome to MayaWorld Tours. My name is Angela St. Croix and I'm your tour leader. Today was our third stop, but you're joining us in plenty of time and we'll be seeing Edzná tomorrow and Hochob, Xpuhil, Dzibilnocac, and Chacmultun in the next few days."

She handed us both several brightly colored brochures and proceeded to outline the tour's itinerary. The schedule was pretty simple. Every morning we would travel by a chartered MayaWorld bus to a new site and spend the day in a guided walking tour, followed by an informal picnic lunch and two or three hours of private self-paced tours. Then, onward, again by bus, to one of the fabulous quality hotels listed in the brochures, which conveniently lay on our route. At that time we'd be free to go off to dinner on our own or join with other members of the tour group for a common meal in the hotel's restaurant or dining room. Thus far, the tour members had taken their evening meal as a group, as they were doing now.

"And after dinner?" I asked.

"As you choose," said the tour guide. "Enjoy the night life of the current city; a list of tourist-friendly locales is provided at each hotel. Or you can simply socialize with your fellow MayaTourists."

"That sounds fine," I said, and glanced back at the Mocker who nodded in agreement.

Ms. St. Croix then gestured at the other tour members, encompassing them all with the wave of her arm. She rattled off names, introducing them to us en masse. I was surprised to find that only two of them were human. The rest consisted of six Taurians, two Arcturans, and a Clarkeson, representing three of the four alien races Mexico allowed in the country. Seeing them together illustrated the simplicity of Mexico's policy; only aliens who were overtly and obviously nonhuman at a glance, were permitted. Any alien who looked enough like a human to pass among us unnoticed lacked any rights in Mexico. Appalling, but simple.

The Taurians met the requirements most obviously, though only from the neck up. They looked like the minotaur of Greek mythology, well-muscled, deeply tanned, human males with bull heads. I'd never encountered any during my time traveling as a hypnotist, but had met several dozen over the last few years working with a Taurian archaeological combine that needed buffalo dogs. The ones I'd dealt with had routinely dressed themselves in the traditional garb of Spanish bullfighters, usually showing up at my office in groups of three, one matador and two picadors. They found it an amusing conceit. The group touring the ruins of the Yucatan had no such agenda and simply clothed themselves in durable jumpsuits of a denim-like material not available on Earth.

The two Arcturans made up half of a mated quad, and while the presence of one in a group guaranteed a tour free from anxiety, a pair meant that everyone's spirits would be light and joyous. They have some kind of magnetic field of *rightness*, or release a pheromone of *fulfillment*, or something of that sort. No one's ever figured it out, and the first person who does is going to make a fortune.

Their skin tone ranged from deep navy blue around the eyes and fingers fading to robin's egg blue across most of the torso. They had their arms wrapped around each other's shoulder at the dining room table, the fingers of each melding into the other's skin, fusing phalanges and scapula every few seconds and then separating again, having transferred bits of themselves. Arcturans have four sexes, but the particulars of reproduction are entirely internal, and at least to a human glance there's no physical difference. Left to their druthers Arcturans eschew clothing, and they all look like sexless blue teens. There were of course stories, urban legends, of humans shaving away their body hair, dipping themselves in blue food dye, and masking their genitalia one way or another in a comical attempt to pass themselves off as Arcturans.

The Clarkeson most closely resemble a human, but in actual fact possessed the greatest biological differences. Clarkesons aren't living individuals. Rather, they're colonies constructed by a collection of millions and millions of intelligent cells that work out their appearance and actions through committees, working in concert to create the illusion of a solitary persona. They look like circus clowns. Their complexions are almost always a fishbelly white, and the hair on their heads often shows patterns of baldness, existing only in thick and pointed tufts, most typically in bright fluorescent colors. This one had more hair than any I'd ever met before, and every lurid green strand of it stood on end. Like the Taurians, the lone Clarkeson appeared to be dressed in a utilitarian jumpsuit, in this case patterned in a camouflage print that utilized seven different shades of purple. In fact though, its clothes were an organic construction created by a dermal subcommittee to generate a clothing-like façade.

The humans were an elderly but very distinguished looking Japanese couple. They spoke neither English nor Spanish, but wore real-time translation collars that whispered conversions of whatever was said around them into their native Japanese, and could likewise rebroadcast their own utterances, matching them to the languages of other speakers within earshot. They were dressed in the latest fashion of human travelers throughout the galaxy, bright green colored trousers with no less than ten pockets, matching utility vests, and pearly white oxford pinpoints. The entire outfit, even down to their reinforced fabric boots, was constructed from breather-ware, an organic weave that had hit the market barely two years earlier. Crowning their ensemble, they each wore replica antique pith helmets.

If the Mocker was surprised to see only two humans in the tour he didn't indicate it to me. Instead, once Ms. St. Croix completed her briefing, he began working his way down the table, politely introducing himself to each individual in turn, gesturing back to me where I remained talking to our tour guide.

Space was made for us at the table, smack in the middle so that we sat across from one another, each with three of our fellow tourists seated to our right and left and six more spread out evenly on the other side of the table. I set Reggie's new bag under my chair and after placing my napkin on my lap, put Reggie there as well. He spent a few moments peering in obvious curiosity at all the people seated around him, but soon lost interest and settled himself comfortably for a nap. Menus arrived, and after a quick glance we placed our orders. Following the Mocker's lead I introduced myself as Santiago MacLeod.

The six Taurians turned out to be classmates, architectural students on a holiday from their university. Only two of them, Efdar Yal and Kaljor Rus, had yet achieved sufficient distinction within the academic community to merit names. The others could only be addressed by pronouns or context specific references that rendered them temporarily distinct from one another.

The mated Arcturans sat to my left. They informed me that they had previously been named Lilbrittah and Hreshtil, but had merged that as well, and that I should feel free to address them both as Lilbrishtil. They were touring the ruins of one of Earth's vanished civilizations as part of a premarriage honeymoon while their second mated pair attended to some urban consultation work with the Mexican government. Lilbrishtil anticipated reuniting with the other pair before leaving Earth, at which time they would again merge names. All four would be one when they consecrated their union. I found the concept fascinating, but across from me the Mocker had donned his poker face, hiding any reaction. We'd been in enough exotic venues that I knew he hadn't a xenophobic bone in his body, but he was still a long way from my own fascination with all things alien. Likely, the mental image of four Arcturans entwined and merging their flesh made his own skin itch, even as their soothing presence kept him from having any anxiety over it.

The Clarkeson sat to Left-John's left, and insisted that we call it Yucatangelo, a name which it had selected for itself in honor of the tour we were all a part of. While all the others at the table had plates and typical meals laid out before them, the Clarkeson had only a tall glass and a very large bottle of single malt scotch in front of it. Not for the first time I found myself wondering what life was like for a colony being, though on this occasion I had to include the additional wonderment of life as both a colony being, and plastered beyond the effective remedy of detox pills, assuming the scotch brought its myriad cell collectives to inebriation at all.

Via their translation collars, the Japanese couple introduced themselves as Hiro and Chieko Tanaka. Hiro had recently retired as a vice president from the company he'd joined fresh out of school. Their three children had grown up, moved out, and had children of their own now. Having fulfilled their biological and societal requirements, the Tanakas found themselves elderly, healthy, and bored. They had no interest in traveling into space, but instead had decided to travel the Earth, top to bottom, and expected to spend the rest of their lives going from one tour package to the next.

Chieko Tanaka sat across from me on Left-John's right, with her husband to her right. She looked to be younger than her graying husband, or perhaps simply dyed her hair. They quickly engaged Left-John in conversation. Mrs. Tanaka did most of the actual talking; her husband contenting himself with the occasional comment and nod. Among other things, they discovered a mutual appreciation for Cuban cigars, specifically the Hermano Rojo. This worthy smokeable had become nearly impossible to obtain on Earth, the smart money in Cuba eagerly exported both fresh tobacco leaf and the finished cigars to the stars.

Despite this, the Tanakas seemed to have an endless supply of Hermanos and were quite willing to share them with the gambler. Within minutes of our menus vanishing all three of them had lit up and begun a smoke ring competition. The heavy fragrance of the tobacco roused Reggie from his nap. He craned his neck to track each ring as it floated delicately through the air to either dissipate or collide with one of its predecessors. His nose twitched, but either he didn't mind the aroma or was too captivated by the rings to care. In the background I noted the slight whine of the restaurant's air scrubbers kicking in, but part of the pride of smoking an Hermano Rojo was the certain knowledge that humanity hadn't yet built the filter that could entirely remove its potent presence from a room.

I turned away as much as I could and sighed with relief when the food arrived.

I like Mexican food, in all its many forms and flavors, from the ancient and simple recipes that met the arriving Europeans to the gustatory synthesis that resulted when old world traditions met new world fruits and vegetables, meats and grains. I'd ordered chille rellenos del pescador, a dish I'd had once before during a two week stint at a lounge in Acapulco. It had been exquisite then, the chilles blended perfectly with five progressively tastier types of fish, all of which lay wrapped in delicate blue corn tortillas. I raised my fork and took a tentative taste.

The aroma of Left-John's and the Tanakas' cigars had already worked their will upon my palate. Across the table from me they continued their friendly smoke ring competition, using one another's rings as targets for their own. They looked to be having a very fun time, and even Left-John's stony face seemed alight as he enjoyed the company. I was pleased for them, but not for my dinner. The heavy smoke, even with the intervention of the air system, colored the flavor and overwhelmed any subtlety that might have been in the meal. It was good, maybe even delicious, but short of grabbing my plate and racing for the exit there was no way I was ever going to find out if it had been truly exquisite.

Whatever insights or gifts my alien dream visitor might have given me, projective telepathy was not one of them. Neither the Mocker nor either of the Tanakas blanched, withered, or blushed at the unkind thoughts I aimed their way. In resignation I pushed back my plate. I signaled to the waitron for some brandy and turned my attention to the Clarkeson who was talking with one of the Taurians. Kaljor Rus was holding forth on some religious topic and Yucatangelo seemed to give its full attention to every word, though given the colonial nature of all Clarkesons this was probably not the case.

Discussions of religion and faith are typically divisive among members of the same sentient race (unless the proponents and believers of one path have had the great good fortune to completely exterminate all nonbelievers). However, the same is not true when aliens meet on neutral ground. In situations where neither side has the home advantage rabid fervor is set aside in favor of curiosity. Indeed, the three most common themes of conversation to be found when traveling between the stars are religion, politics, and technological loyalties.

I had grown up in an exceedingly religious household. My great aunt had been among the first human missionaries to venture into space, before transferring her zeal from religion to amateur xeno-sociology. In turn, I'd begun my education with a major in xeno-religious studies. I'd chucked it all when I took up the life of a traveling stage hypnotist, but I still retained a fascination for the belief systems of other races.

My brandy arrived. I twisted my fingers to form the Traveler hand sign of polite self-invitation. The Taurian noted the gesture and responded with the confirming two-fingered twist and swirl that indicated I was welcome to participate. I edged my chair closer, and put the aroma of the cigars out of my mind as I took a sip of fine Mexican liquor. On my lap, Reggie began chewing on a corner of my napkin and settled in for another nap.

"Then you are saying your people could never follow the path of Purpose. Do you not believe your people have Purpose? Has there never been a Precognitor among you?" said the Taurian to the Clarkeson, apparently coming to the end of some point. That one word, *precognitor*, had caught the attention of my subconscious and drawn me to the conversation.

"Not as you describe it, no, nor any need for one," said Yucatangelo. "Oh, perhaps it might be said we have purpose, but on a different scale. Your path is one that is embraced by a society, but I am a society embracing itself. To appear here before you as I do now requires a kind of determinism more restrictive than your own beliefs of purpose."

"Excuse me," I said, and the Clarkeson turned my way, giving me a broad clown smile. "What did you mean by a 'precognitor'?"

"It is one of the three positions one can occupy upon the path," said Kaljor Rus. "One is either a Bider, a Precognitor, or one of the Purposeful. Though, some sects hold that it is possible to be in more than one of these states at the same time, though only the Precognitors could be aware of it. That is their nature, after all."

"These precognitors . . . they glimpse the future?"

The Taurian nodded to me, and there was something in his posture and tone that made me wonder if back home Kaljor Rus put in some time teaching the Taur equivalent of Sunday school. "They can determine who among us have been given a Purpose, and the nature of that Purpose."

"Your pardon, singular Taurian," said Yucatangelo. "This is the piece I find both distressing and amusing."

"Do you scorn Purpose?"

"Only as you see it being enforced by the will of the Universe," said the Clarkeson.

Kaljor Rus grunted, which coming from a Taurian could mean anything. "When the universe imposes upon you some destiny to fulfill, that same universe ensures that you complete your role. It is simply a matter of physics. Our mathematicians, many of them Precognitors, have mapped it out as clearly as the rules describing inertia or momentum."

"What do the precognitors do," I asked, "once they've identified people with a purpose?"

"They guide them, moving them into position where they may complete their Purpose and fulfill destiny."

"Unless they adhere to the beliefs of Dark Purpose," said the Clarkeson with an odd twist to its tone. I couldn't tell if this last was meant as a joke, sarcasm or something else. The Taurian grunted again.

"I do not wish to speak of Dark Purpose. It is anathema to me and very offensive. I will not tell you again."

"Now, now, no taking offense," said Yucatangelo. "We are merely discussing philosophies, and if we are to educate our new friend here surely he must be given the whole picture."

Kaljor Rus said nothing. I stared into his large, bovine-like eyes, but couldn't read him. This was Mexico, after all, and no alien here was likely to have any kind of human expressions. I could no more tell what Kaljor Rus was thinking by studying his expression than I could second guess a bull in a field.

The Clarkeson took the silence as an indication to pick up and continue the lesson itself.

"The Path of Dark Purpose follows naturally from the notion that some singular beings are endowed by the universe with a purpose. A consequence of being so endowed means that the universe must keep you alive and well until such time as you make good on your destiny."

"Okay. . ." I said. "How is this different from the path Kaljor Rus was describing."

"There is only one true Path," said the Taurian.

"That may be," continued Yucatangelo, "but portions of it are dark. You see, singular Terran, some Precognitors are not content to identify those of Purpose and guide them to their appointments with destiny. Instead, they take these individuals and place them far from the circumstances they must eventually encounter for the sake of Destiny. They position them near others of more traditional forms of importance; political leaders, brilliant scientists, wealthy patrons."

"Why?"

"To keep those leaders, scientists, and patrons safe from the hazards of living," said the Clarkeson.

I shook my head, which of course is a gesture wasted on Taurians. A race with two large and pointed horns protruding from their heads, they'd never developed that kind of movement as a part of communication. "I don't understand," I said. "How does that keep them safe?"

"Let us suppose, that the universe has endowed you with Purpose, that you work some Precognitor's Path—"

"That seems unlikely," I said. "No offense intended, but I practice a different religious view."

"That's immaterial," said Yucantangelo. "Your own faith does not matter. If a Precognitor sees that you have Purpose, you automatically become a part of his religion. Is that not true?"

Kaljor Rus blinked. "I would not have phrased it so, but yes, you have it essentially correct. The Path does not belong to any one people or group, it is the Path of the universe and all who dwell within it, whether they choose to acknowledge it or no."

"Fine, well then, to continue. Let us suppose that you, Mr. MacLeod, have a Purpose. Do you see how I might find it useful to have you in our tour group? You have a destiny to fulfill, perhaps something as simple as being present on a bridge to witness a ship coming home from the sea halfway around this world. The universe will protect you, to ensure you live to complete your destiny. So, you are thus my good luck charm. If you are with me, I know our bus will not careen off a mountain killing us all. I know we need not fear harm from vigilantes or pirates because you cannot suffer any permanent harm. There could be explosives in this very room, but because of your presence they would not go off as planned and we are all spared. This is the Dark Path of Purpose.

"If you believe in the Purposeful and their appointments with destiny, and you believe that the Precognitors can identify both the person and his purpose, then you have to allow for the possibility of this insight being misused, perhaps for a short while or perhaps a long while, depending how far in the future the Purpose exists."

"Is it always so clear to them?"

"Who? The Purposeful?" said Yucatangelo.

"No, the precognitors. Is their vision of the future always clear?"

"It is not so much what you would call a matter of clarity, Friend MacLeod," said Kaljor Rus. "Perception can be cloudy while still being precise. They are as accurate as they need to be. If they misjudge and interpret their perceptions too broadly, it would not matter."

"Not matter?" I said, my head buzzed from alliteration and images of pickled peppers. "How can that be? Aren't these purposeful people depending on the precognitors?"

Kaljor Russ snorted, a surprisingly loud and disarming sound that made me flinch and awaken Reggie with a jerk. I moved one hand down to pet and reassure him as the Taurian explained.

"Oh, not at all, Friend MacLeod. The Precognitors help, but they are not essential to the success of the Purposeful. After all, the universe is looking out for them."

Yucatangelo and Kaljor Russ continued their discussion. I sat back in my chair and let their words wash over me as little more than abstract sounds. I sipped absently at my brandy. Dream images of volcanoes and tidal waves and fluffy white aliens in hats swirled through my brain. If the universe had a specific purpose in mind for me, I wasn't taking any comfort in it.

Chapter Nineteen: Visit To A Chapeau

WORN OUT WITH CONVERSATION and pleasantly aglow from the brandy, I staggered into my hotel room and aimed myself straight for the bed, not even bothering to turn on a light. Springs squeaked as I crashed and rolled onto my back, clutching the alligator bag with Reggie in it to my chest. My buffalo dog yipped happily at the game and scrambled to escape and lick my face. I kicked off my shoes, bouncing them off the wall in the process, and warned Reggie not to eat them. His soulful eyes spoke of innocence; I hoped I hadn't planted the idea in his brain. My head fell back against the pillow. With a disappointed whuff that play time had ended so soon Reggie settled in alongside me.

Despite being asleep, I realized there was someone else in the room. I opened my eyes and sat up. Bits of moonlight trickled in through the window, creating more shadow than illumination. I could smell jasmine, soft and faint. Someone was here. I stood up and turned back to look at the bed. The blanket and spread lay thrown back. The pillow on the left held a sleeping buffalo dog; the one on the right bore a depression that matched the back of my head but was otherwise empty. And then it began to change.

It expanded like something from a cartoon, growing by spurts. The fabric casing burst and white feathers filled the room in a soft explosion without sound. I backed away, but the feather storm had ceased before I reached the door. All the feathers had swirled back together and gathered to create a humanoid figure. It reached down and picked up the torn pillow case and wrapped it around its head, tying it into a do-rag.

"I thought I wasn't going to see you again," I said. "I'm not in the chrono-schism any longer."

"We are nearer to the moment when the probabilities converge. And I am much closer to you physically now as well. Both factors help."

"How much closer?"

"My vessel lies in a scrap of jungle less than two of your kilometers from here. Come to me." Having just finished putting it in place, it began unwrapping the do-rag from its head.

"Why would I do that?"

"Because you need to believe. There are too many competing factors in your mind. You are attempting to map other referents onto these dreams, these communications. You must come and see me directly."

"How will I find you?"

It moved closer, like some hideous feathered monster from slumberland. Its hand came up and bound the do-rag about my head. Images sliced into my brain, sharp edged and not at all like downy feathers.

"Wake up, and come to me."

I woke up to find myself on the floor, clutching the pillow tightly. Reggie lay where I'd seen him in the dream, asleep on the other pillow. I found my shoes in the dark and stopped myself with one hand on the door. Why was I doing this? Was it compulsion or my own curiosity? At some level, it didn't matter. If I had no choice, then I needed to simply get on with it. If there were no compulsion and I didn't go, like the Coptic Babble cabbie that had driven me to Texas, a part of me would always wonder what I'd missed out on, which is another way of saying that, really, I had no choice. Thinking back on futile discussions from college philosophy courses of long ago, I stepped out into the hall.

The attendant on duty at the front desk spoke a bit more English than I spoke Spanish. A fifty new peso bill spoke more eloquently than either of us and soon I had 'rented' his bicycle and found myself peddling through the starlit night. I didn't need to see, a map burned in my brain with an image of every centimeter between myself and my destination. Dawn was still three hours away. I rode the bicycle down the main street for less than a kilometer and turned off onto first one side street and then another and another. Large modern buildings gave way to more modest structures, bungalows, shacks, and finally empty fields. The paving became cracked and then cobbled and then little more than an intention of a road, and finally just dirt. The dirt became overgrown with jungle grass and then any semblance of a path vanished, though in my mind I still saw the route clearly. When I could peddle no further I abandoned the bike and continued on foot.

Despite the darkness the jungle opened for me. I walked without hesitation for perhaps fifteen minutes, climbing over and around more plants than I had names for. Behind me lay the twenty-first century, but the jungle, despite its proximity to the city, was timeless. I felt like I could walk forever and never emerge on the other side, but long before that point my map made me stop.

I didn't see it at first, but a spacecraft lay in front of me. It resembled a giant pie plate, like the classic UFOs of the last century. It was bigger than the personal yacht I had back at a Philadelphia spaceport, but smaller than most commercial vessels. Its surface shimmered as I stared at it, gleaming with a polished surface like ice, then a moment later seemingly lost in a riot of green shades, a part of the jungle all around.

The map in my head led up to a specific point on the ship's surface and when I reached it, the certainty of destination faded from my mind. A portal opened. Stepping within I could make out an illuminated, curving corridor. Somewhere at the other end of it I'd meet the alien that had been plaguing my dreams.

The portal closed behind me, but that didn't surprise me. The four whirling dust devils that roared down on me from around the curve of the corridor, however, more than made up for it. One moment I was standing just inside the ship, committed but still hesitant. The next I was borne aloft, jumbled and tumbled like lawn furniture in a tornado. I swept forward, carried down a series of arching corridors until the final passage opened onto a wide round room. My whirlwinds abandoned me, and I was unceremoniously dumped on my ass. I got to my feet, smoothing my clothing into place as I took a look around. Then I noticed my host.

And I stared. I stared in exactly the way you're not supposed to stare at aliens, with my eyes wide and my jaw slack and six different species of confusion running rampant through my brain. It was tacky and crass and the worst kind of rude parochial human behavior, but I couldn't help it. I couldn't make any sense of what I was seeing. You'd have stared too.

More than a century ago, Sigmund Freud said, "Analogies prove nothing, but they do make us feel at home." I'd always liked the quotation, but I never appreciated its subtlety until now. I couldn't force an understanding of what I was seeing, it just didn't map onto anything in my experience. Instead I had to settle for coming close, fold my perception of it onto something it was like. Or in this instance several things. Picture a mass of boiling, watery milk. But it wasn't quite boiling, it was roiling, turbulent and violent, alternating between a bubbling transparency and a frothing white like the rushing of river rapids. Then shape that into a torso; give it arms and legs and a head, make it humanoid. That was part of it. Another part was like vapor, delicate strands of mist drifting upward, and managing somehow to do so in a way that suggested that same humanoid shape by the way each white puff flowed over or around and even through the roiling liquidy part. But that wasn't it either. Any detail vanished if you looked at it directly.

That was the figure standing (hovering? floating?) in front of me. It had a head at the top of its torso, but if it possessed any sensory organs I couldn't recognize them. Mainly it was a figure of stirring action, lost between invisibility and pale pure reflected light.

And it wore a hat. Or, that's what it looked like. Upon the rounded protuberance that rose up from the creature's torso lay a grey, misshapen lump that resembled nothing so much as a battered flannel hat. It was by far the most solid, tangible, understandable thing about the alien.

Smaller versions of the creature were all around, moving through the vessel, conveying a certain ponderous motion by their gait while their own forms sped like internal tornadoes and water spouts and other things that had no name or clear representation. None of these wore hats.

"Ah, yes, that is as good a name for us in your language as any. Call us Roils." The alien's voice had an ethereal quality that I recognized immediately. "And if you will pardon the pun, I suppose I am the Royal Roil, though you might find it easier to simply call me The Hat."

"You're the one in my dreams." This was the snowman, the golem made of whipped cream, the ghost of Hamlet Sr.

"It was the only way I could communicate with you. I was trying to warn you."

"You haven't done a good job," I said. The familiarity of its voice balanced the fear and awe of its true appearance. "Green Aggression has already beaten me up pretty good."

"That is past and irrelevant. Focus on the future. You have to stop them."

"I've done that," I said. "Any time now, President Ortiz will round up their leaders and their organization will be crippled. Powerless."

"I see this. You have disabled many of the probabilities I foresaw. But Green Aggression will still attack you."

"And you were telling me this because. . . ?"

"Because you can prevent it from happening."

I shook my head. "The toxic clean-up notwithstanding, world-saving's not the sort of thing I do," I said.

"And yet, the potential is there."

"Oh? Right. And did you see how it is I do this thing?"

"No."

"That's not all that helpful, Hat."

"Please, The Hat. I am the only one. I am the sentience and consciousness that emerges when the Roils generate one of their kind of sufficient size and power."

"So, what, you're a fusion of their minds?"

"No, by themselves, they have no native intent or intelligence."

I looked around. "Aren't they running this ship?"

"Only because I am guiding them to do so."

"Is that what you call what you're doing to me? Guiding me?"

"It is your world that I am trying to save, human, not my own."

"So, you're doing me a favor?"

"One could look at the situation that way."

"But other than telling me who the threat is, you can't actually offer me anything else?"

"Yours is one of the few human minds I can even touch. And then, only because you and I share a destiny. If I am to achieve mine, I must ensure that you achieve yours."

I looked around the room and began edging toward the corridor I'd been carried through. One thing was clear, whatever it was that the Hat knew, it wasn't going to offer me anything solid or specific to use. "That's great. Look, I'm real happy for you. But that doesn't help me solve the problem.

"And yet you must, or your world will be destroyed and we will not have the meeting that I see in our future.

"Yeah, those don't exactly have equal weight for me. Okay, let me out of your ship. I'm certainly not going to save the world standing around talking with you all day."

"I am leaving," it said, ignoring my request. "It is unwise for my vessel and I to remain on your world when I cannot effectively communicate with your kind. I will remove myself to this system's asteroid belt, close enough for our relationship to continue."

I was about to snort at its use of 'relationship' but before I could several of the smaller Roils converged on me. I was suddenly airborne again, whirling back the way I'd come until they dumped me to the floor just inside the ship's entrance. The morning sun streamed into the ship, and I could smell the jungle outside. Not far away, I heard birds chirping. I rose to leave.

The Hat spoke to me, its words reverberating down the corridor. "I am only as far away as your dreams, Conroy. If you think of any way I might aid you, I will know and appear to you. It will be easier now that you have seen my true form."

"Maybe," I said as I dusted myself off and stepped into the jungle. "But I think I liked you better as a snowman."

Chapter Twenty: Aliens Amidst the Ruins

BREAKFAST AT THE HOTEL consisted of an assortment of light pastries, various fruit juices, and strong coffee. Left-John and I partook of each, as did most of the other members of the tour group. After eating, our guide had us assemble in the hotel lobby and then directed us to our bus. Moments later we were on the road, with Ms. St. Croix behind the wheel. We had gone fewer than ten kilometers north northeast toward the port of Campeche, when our driver took us off road and begin weaving her way along no apparent trail through the jungle.

Only Left-John and I reacted in the slightest, and he limited that to a significant look in my direction. None of the other passengers found the encroaching jungle or the unmappable route we were traveling the least bit remarkable. We continued in this way for the better part of an hour, bouncing and bulling our way along at a fraction of our highway speed, climbing higher as we zigzagged our way up a steep mountain. The jungle grew thornier, darker, denser, and then all at once it stopped. It didn't thin out, it simply ended, and our bus rolled out onto an open savannah. The massive ruins of an ancient Mayan city lay before us, sprawling stone structures, terraced stairs as wide as the entire façade of some of the buildings. One massive palace boasted five stories and my jaw dropped as I gazed upon it. I'd seen ancient ruins before, but only on other worlds. The stone buildings here had been erected by human beings; individuals not so different from myself had piled block upon block, more than two thousand years ago, and though the builders had departed their work remained.

The bus rolled to a halt. Ms. St. Croix stood and faced us. "Ladies and Gentlemen, Visitors to the Earth and native sons and daughters, welcome to Edzná!" And with that she unlatched the door and led us out onto the grounds of the city. I set Reggie down and he began to scamper and cavort. As long as I made sure he didn't take a bite out of any stellae or palace façades, I figured I'd be fine.

Over the next few hours we climbed the Great Acropolis, explored the Platform of Knives, humbly walked the length of the Ball Court, and clambered up and down the Nohochá Platform on the main plaza. Ms. St. Croix pointed out the intersection of Puuc and Petén styles, treating us to a litany

Lawrence M. Schoen

of facts and reconstructions about the daily routine the city's residents must have once lived. The other tourists paid little attention to the recitation, though in fairness they'd likely heard variations of the same thing on previous days of the tour. Instead they busied themselves in the manner tourists have long employed to ensure their memories of a visit; they recorded it.

Each of the unnamed Taurians had strapped portal vid studio cams to their forearms and spread out around Kaljor Rus and Efdar Yal, capturing their experience of the tour for posterity. Chieko Tanaka and the Clarkeson both used battered but working cams of Terran manufacture which they had leased from our tour guide. The Arcturans had brought along a sensorial cube, light weight, but at nearly half a meter on a side more than a little bulky. Staring into its depths I noted a tiny figure that was also me, standing idly in a ruined Mayan city and staring at a pair of Arcturans holding an even smaller cube. Even the Mocker seemed to have caught the photo bug; more than once I caught him staring intently at some stellae or ruin, one eye closed in concentration as his prosthetic recorded an image. Personally, I've never understood the mindset of someone who goes on holiday and spends the time recording the experience for later instead of simply living in it. Like my great Aunt Fiona, I preferred to bask in the moment rather than reminisce.

After several hours of guided tromping, from the Moon Temple to the Steambath, we broke for lunch. Three of the unnamed Taurians offered their assistance and together with Ms. St. Croix they retrieved several collapsible tables and portable coolers from the storage area under our bus. Large woolen blankets, brightly colored and patterned by local craftsmen, were spread out upon the ground, positioned to take advantage of what shade could be found as the Mexican sun had reached its zenith and begun beating down on the ruins of Edzná without mercy.

From the coolers Ms. St. Croix prepared a respectable picnic spread of cold cuts, cheese, fried chicken, three kinds of potato salad, sliced fruit, and honeyed ice cream. The Taurians were the first to descend upon the table, sampling everything and carrying away fully three quarters of the contents to a pair of blankets. Efdar Yal and Kaljor Rus had spent the day in the company of the Tanakas, when they could get away from their unnamed cohorts, and after filling their plates the four went off together to continue their conversation. The Arcturans took only potato salad and fruit, and seemed more than content to feed one another from their fingertips. Yucatangelo the Clarkeson probably couldn't usefully ingest any of it, but nonetheless helped itself to some ice cream and made its way over to join the unnamed Taurians. Ms. St. Croix, Left-John and myself, like the Taurians, took a bit of all of it, though in much more modest quantities, and we then settled together on one of the remaining blankets. Reggie gamboled nearby, playing with the ceramo bucket the ice cream had come in.

"How are the two of you enjoying the first day of your MayaTour?" said Ms. St. Croix as she delicately bit into a drumstick.

It's fascinating," I said. "The grandeur, the sheer size of everything. It's hard not to be overwhelmed."

"Most of our guests have that reaction, Mr. MacLeod. And have no fear, that sense of wonder will not diminish as you visit other sites upon the tour. I promise you, you will not become jaded."

"I'm surprised that aliens make up the majority of this group," said Left-John. "Is that commonplace?"

Ms. St. Croix nodded. "Actually, it's quite typical, and not unusual if you consider it from an extraterrestrially economic perspective."

I looked up, finished chewing the bit of brioche in my mouth. "How so?"

"We're the newcomers to the galactic party; most other races have been out among the stars for centuries. Beyond the rare exception, with respect to science and technology they're much further along than we are. In terms of trade that puts us at a serious disadvantage."

"We don't have anything they want," I said. "Anything we can do, they can already do better, is that it?"

"To an extent, yes. But there's one thing we can do better than any alien. We're much better at being human."

Left-John nodded, "Yeah, we have the market cornered on that."

"And it's a novelty to them. Just as they've all been out in space, and in each other's space, for centuries, they've had just as much time to grow accustomed to one another. But we're fresh. And so are our languages and our histories and our cultures. In fact, MayaTours was created specifically with alien tourists in mind. They're captivated by these sites, not just because they're human, but because they're a mystery even to us."

"Mystery?" I said.

"The people," said Left-John. "The Mayans. They had this incredible civilization, built these cities. Then, one day, they all just up and abandoned it all. No one knows why."

"And we probably never will," said Ms. St. Croix. "Perhaps it was simply their destiny."

I said nothing in response to that. Instead I tried to catch the Mocker's eye, but he appeared suddenly fascinated with some aspect of an apple he was eating and refused to meet my gaze.

* * *

It had been a very full day, and the drive to tomorrow's site promised to be a bit more involved, necessitating a slightly earlier departure. Pleasantries and good wishes for sound sleep and peaceful dreams flitted back and forth as everyone called it a night, and slipped away to their rooms.

Left-John and I had been assigned a suite at this hotel, and we'd checked it out briefly before dinner. I'd stayed in much better accommodations as a CEO and much much worse as a lounge act hypnotist; it would do. As we returned to it, my only thought was to kick off my shoes and sprawl out on my bed. I had the feeling that I could just close my eyes and fall blissfully asleep. Left-John had other plans.

"I think that Taurian is the one you're supposed to play poker with." He said this as I was all the way across the outer room and stepping into the adjoining bedroom.

"Which one?" I said over my shoulder as I sat on my bed and let Reggie out of his travel bag. He skittered across the room and then spun around and hurtled back, testing the limits of the room for game playing. I glanced up at Left-John as he came in. "Efdar Yal or Kaljor Rus?"

"Rus," he said. "Yal appears to be a serious student of terrestrial architecture. I spoke with him at length at dinner."

"And what do you think Kaljor Rus is then?"

"Some kind of prophet or near-prophet for his religion."

Reggie barked once for my attention. I opened the drawer in the bedside table and took out a fist sized chunk of obsidian laying atop the Spanish language version of the Gideon bible. The bible had come with the room, but I'd purchased several chucks of rock from the hotel's gift shop before we'd first checked in. I lobbed the glassy rock across the suite and through the open door into the next room. Reggie darted off in pursuit. Then I gave Left-John my full attention. "What? Where did you get the idea that he's a prophet?"

"Maybe not a prophet, but some kind of religious leader, maybe more like a bishop or cardinal. Only he claims to know something of the future. Sound familiar?"

"He told you this?"

"No, Mrs. Tanaka did. According to her, before we joined the tour Kaljor Rus made a point of asking her a range of questions over the course of several days. He apparently had done the same with the Arcturans, as well as that Clarkeson."

"We've all been asking questions. Strangers in a tour group do that. It's a form of socializing, Left-John, you should try it?"

174

"Don't be dense. It was the kind of questions. Mrs. Tanaka said he seemed to be looking for someone, someone he expected to find in this group. Someone with a purpose or a destiny to fulfill."

"Purpose? She used that word? She said he used that word?"

"Yes to both," said Left-John. I must have looked as stunned as I felt. "Why, is that significant?" he said.

Reggie chose that moment to come bounding back into the room. He dashed clockwise around my bed three times, diving under near the back and reemerging on the other side to complete each circuit. Then he halted directly in front of me and let the lump of obsidian drop from his mouth onto my left foot.

"Conroy?"

Reggie barked, reminding me of my part in the game.

"No, probably not. It's just something I've already heard. Sorry; chalk it up to déjà vu." I patted my thigh and Reggie jumped up and settled himself on my lap. From his silence I knew Left-John wasn't satisfied with my answer.

"He's not a priest or a prophet, he's a Precognitor," I said, and explained to Left-John everything I'd heard the night before about the Path and the Purposeful. I also brought him up-to-date on my late night meeting with the Hat. When I finished he frowned at me, proving that the muscles in his face truly worked like everyone else's.

"So, you now have two different aliens talking to you about precognition and destiny. I don't like this, Conroy."

"Why? So they both believe in being able to glimpse the future, so what? The Taurian was talking in purely philosophical and religious terms. Plenty of people have destinies. It's not like he mentioned me specifically."

The Mocker shook his head. "That's naïve. If there's some event coming up, something so significant that it's making ripples that anyone with a sensitivity to that sort of thing can perceive, wouldn't you expect them to come running?"

"Well, by that logic, the question would be, why aren't there more of them here?"

He didn't have an answer, but Left-John had started me thinking. The Hat indicated that the probabilities were still too large; dwindling, but still too numerous to make clear predictions. Maybe that was keeping other prescient humans and aliens away. Or maybe it was because we were in the middle of the Mexican jungle.

My thoughts must have shown on my face; Left-John snorted. "If you've got an appointment with destiny, it might just be that you're lit up like a Christmas tree on some kind of psychic radar scope."

"Any or all of that could all be true," I said, "but none of it matters. I know what I have to do."

"And what's that?"

"Same as before. We need to play cards." I reached down and picked up the chunk of obsidian from where I'd been balancing it on my shoe and waggled it in front of Reggie. He lunged for it, caught a portion of it with his teeth, and with no more effort than he'd need for a piece of cheese, bit it in half as I pulled it away. "Tomorrow, when we get back from the day's tour, let's see if we can't interest some of our fellow tour group members in a friendly game."

Chapter Twenty-One: The End of Coincidence

THE NEXT MORNING, AFTER A HURRIED BREAKFAST, Ms. St. Croix rustled us all back onto the tour bus and on our way. She drove down a fairly comfortable highway for most of an hour, and then turned the bus due south, leaving the road in favor of an overgrown jungle trail. Once more we trundled along, but unlike the previous day's trek, this time our bus did not emerge from the dense jungle onto an open savannah. Instead we went from the dense jungle to an only slightly less dense jungle, and stopped halfway up a hill.

"Welcome to Hochob," said Ms. St. Croix as she applied the parking brakes. "Unlike most of the other sites on our tour which were reclaimed from the jungle during the 19th and 20th centuries, most of the city of Hochob has never been thoroughly explored or documented."

The Clarkeson asked, "Then why are we here?"

"The Chenes style," said one of the unnamed Taurians, and the others grunted in support.

"Chenes?" I said. "I thought the Mayan architectural styles were called Puuc and Petén."

"Two of them are," said Ms. St. Croix. "But our Taur guest is correct. Even though only a small portion of it can be viewed, the palace façade here at Hochob is considered by many to be the most representative example of the Chenes style. If you'll all come with me, we can hike the rest of the way up the hill and get a first hand look at the Earth Monster gate."

I gasped and froze where I stood in the bus's center aisle. "Earth Monster?"

Kaljor Rus came up alongside me. "Be not afraid, Friend MacLeod. It is only a myth. There is no monster here."

"I didn't realize the Maya had monsters, that's all."

Ms. St. Croix waved us forward to the exit. "It's perhaps a misnomer. In many of the myths, the Earth Monster is the god Kankin, who brings abundance to the land."

We all exited the bus and Reggie began squirming in my arms, eager to get down and explore. This was very different from the open savannah of Edzná, and I was a bit reluctant to let him wander. But buffalo dogs are

177

pretty tough, and short of falling off a mountain I didn't know much that could hurt one. I held him out in front of me with both hands and stared into his face.

"You just remember to come when I call," I said. Reggie's response was to stick out his tongue and lick my nose. I interpreted that as agreement and set him down. He took off at a run, bounding through the undergrowth. The rest of us broke into groups of two and three and began struggling up the side of a very steep hill. There was something looming at the top, but the jungle growth was still too dense to make out anything clearly. I noticed the Mocker moving in the direction of the Clarkeson, likely intent on climbing with it, but I pulled him aside before he caught its attention.

"I think we have a problem," I said, as he fell in alongside me and we continued to climb.

"I'm sure we have several. Is there one in particular you're concerned with at the moment?"

"Back before they kidnapped me, I learned that the eco-extremists of Green Aggression had a name for me. They call me the Earth Monster."

The Mocker said nothing, and we climbed in silence for several moments. Eventually he grunted. "And you don't think it's a coincidence?"

"Normally, I might, but I've been thinking about what you said, and you're starting to win me over. Those future probabilities seem to be shrinking down to a handful, and pressing closer all the time. First the Hat goes on and on about me being critical to some event, and then Kaljor Rus turns out to be a Precognitor looking for someone with a Purpose. And now, we come across a reference to a mythological Earth Monster in the very country that Green Aggression is based in. Coincidence?"

Left-John shook his head. "I believe in luck, not coincidence. Luck can be good or bad and occasionally both at once. But none of this strikes me as luck." He paused and looked around; the other tour group members were all further up the hill. "I'm declaring this a coincidence-free zone. Anything that happens from here on out occurs as it does for a deliberate intention or reason, and likely a dire one at that."

"Is that supposed to be helpful?" I said.

"My point is that things aren't happening randomly. Whether it's your Hat, GAEA, one of the Taurians, or some combination, there's someone behind each piece. There's nothing random about any of this. That's what allows even us non-telepaths to predict the future."

I snorted at that. "I've had a secondhand glimpse of the future and I'm still in the dark. The only bits I saw were about playing cards."

"Fine. Then that's what we'll focus on. Relax, Conroy, if you're a pawn in some larger game that's being played, worrying about it is only going to make you crazy. And if you're not a pawn, well, that's all the more reason to keep your wits about you so you'll ready when your moment comes. Don't worry about the poker game. I'll set it up."

"Thanks, Left-John."

"Nothing to it. C'mon, let's go check out this Chinese architecture." And with that he pushed on, climbing ahead of me.

"That's Chenes, not Chinese," I said, and followed after.

The palace at the top of the hill was truly breathtaking, a sight which rivaled the gate of the Earth Monster at its center. Despite the intrusion of the jungle into the city, the many buildings were largely intact, yet they'd been abandoned more than a thousand years earlier. Movement from one structure to the next was much harder here than at Edzná. Our tour group had only begun to work its way outward across the plaza from the main palace when without warning thunder crashed through the air. Rain poured down in sheets, in buckets, in buckets of sheets. I'd never experienced rain more pounding and brutal.

Almost as one body we hurried back to the palace, briefly seeking some shelter within its gate. We didn't find it. The wind and rain were too intense. St. Croix began shouting, desperate to be heard over the downpour. We bolted from the city, and the jungle swallowed us at once, providing better protection from both the wind and the rain. Slowly, and with more than a few slips, we made our way down the steep hill and back to our bus. Reggie had beaten us there and sat shivering and miserable on a dwindling island of dryness under the bus.

We scrambled onboard, and once inside Ms. St. Croix did a quick head count to confirm no one had gone missing. All were present, but we were a bedraggled and sorry looking lot. Not only our clothing, but our spirits were sodden. The usually ebullient Tanakas appeared to have aged forty years and even the unclothed Arcturans looked beaten down.

"Well, unfortunately, we've all just had a taste of the unpredictable and occasionally violent weather that's possible here on Mexico's Yucatan peninsula, as described in your tour brochures. At this point I think our best option is to call this trip to an end and continue on to our next hotel stop. I'm sure I'm not the only one who would welcome some dry clothes and a hot lunch. We should arrive in plenty of time to allow you to take advantage of the local market area if you'd care to do some shopping for souvenirs."

And with that, Ms. St. Croix settled into the driver's seat and started up the bus. Moments later we were plowing slowly through the dripping jungle, sliding as much as driving. I glanced around at the others in the group, marveling to myself at the universal expression of numbed respect for nature that I saw not only on the human faces of the Tanakas, but on each bull-like Taurian, and even the huddled Arcturans, the downpour having strained even their normally uplifting influence. Only the Clarkeson, Yucatangelo, seemed unaffected by the sudden onset and sheer power of the storm. If anything, it appeared radiant and delighted to have been caught in such a thing. Odder still, it was completely dry.

As the bus descended the hill, the booming echo of thunder surrounded us. Eventually we emerged from the jungle and its limited protection from the downpour and reached the highway. The rain still fell in epic proportions, but Ms. St. Croix continued on, albeit at a greatly reduced speed than our trip out.

Disappointed and bedraggled, we slumped off the bus and into the lobby of the *Perrando Azul*, the latest in the string of hotels included in the MayaTours package. We had the place to ourselves, and while the actual sleeping rooms were a bit smaller, every pair of rooms shared a spacious parlor in-between.

Maybe Ms. St. Croix had called ahead without my noticing, or maybe they'd figured we'd arrive early because of the weather, but whatever the reason the hotel had a warm dining room waiting for us, complete with hot soup and an array of sandwiches on fresh baked bread. The wait staff, as if trying to atone for the inclement weather, doted on us. The Taurians reacted with sheepish embarrassment, our lone Clarkeson with undisguised amusement. The rest of us just appreciated the extra pampering after an unsatisfying afternoon.

Sometimes it's the simplest things that restore the human spirit, and they can work miracles on alien dispositions as well. After a quick change into dry clothes (or presumably a toweling off for the Arcturans) we all met up in the dining room and warmed ourselves inside and out. The collective mood soon improved. No longer were we simply travelers sharing a tour. An almost illusory bond of fellowship had formed among us, common survivors of the forces of nature and an unsuccessful assault on the gate of the Earth Monster of Hochob.

We consumed soup and ate sandwiches. We told jokes and shared stories. At some point, someone opened bottles of several different sweet wines. As we sampled the wines the conversation turned to the next day's trip. We were scheduled to explore the ruins of Xpuhil, a city to the south. One of the unnamed Taurians started talking very loudly, something about the temple there having three towers instead of the usual two, and appeared quite excited about this fact. I didn't see the significance, and attributed his enthusiasm to a low tolerance for terrestrial wines. His comrades had the good sense to calm him down though, and he continued his fascination among them in whispered tones.

At about that time the Mocker refilled his own wine glass and ventured a casual invitation for a game of skill and potential profit. This was the first reminder that they were in the presence of a professional gambler, an occupation that even in our modern starfaring world still bears a certain cachét. Several of our tour members immediately demurred, likely imagining their chances against Left-John would be akin to surviving a friendly bout of sparring with a heavyweight champion. This changed though once he explained that he would limit his role to that of dealer. The Arcturans whispered to one another, their eyes widening in what may have been excitement. Hiro Tanaka gave Left-John a huge grin then, and his wife responded with a vigorous nod of her head. The Clarkeson inquired as to the nature of the buy-in and the likely stakes, and the unnamed Taurians, almost as one body, leaned in to hear the answer.

Left-John specified the finances, ten thousand new pesos, an amount which surprised me. It wasn't an unusual buy-in for a professional's game, but pretty steep for a friendly game among strangers on a rainy night. Names were not the only thing that group of Taurians lacked; their initial interest drained away at once and they returned to their hushed architectural discussion and the occasional remark about student stipends.

Left-John turned his attention to the remaining Taurians, Efdar Yal and Kaljor Rus. They conferred, and then the former opened a wallet and counted out the buy-in and passed it to the Mocker.

"I will play," said Efdar Yal.

"But not you?" said Left-John to the other Taurian.

"I regret, no, I cannot," said Kaljor Rus. I must meditate upon certain religious matters, but I expect a full accounting tomorrow."

"We'd like to play," said one of the Arcturans, with a gesture that included both beings now named Lilbrishtil, "if we may be permitted to play together as one player.

Yucatangelo and both the Tanakas also produced the buy-in amount, and I dug through my own wallet to do the same. Through all of this Reggie had been sitting quietly on the table, making the small stack of sandwiches between his paws considerably smaller.

"Well, now we are six," I said, "or seven, depending on how you choose to count it."

"I count by the number of hands I'll be dealing each turn," said the Mocker.

"That is probably a useful distinction," said Yucatangelo with a wide clown grin, "as unlike such singular individuals as yourselves, I alone am far more than six."

"Why don't we move this to the parlor next to my room," said Left-John Mocker. "I have several decks of cards and a sufficient number of chips to accommodate us in my luggage."

"You travel with such things?" said Efdar Yal.

"Tools of the trade," said the Mocker, who I imagined had bought them during our first day when we'd picked up our clothes. "One never knows when the opportunity for a friendly game will turn up."

Don't get me wrong, but generally speaking I don't like to play cards with aliens. It's not that I have anything against aliens, quite the opposite. I'll happily chat, hypnotize, or do business with anyone regardless of race, creed, or planet of origin. But playing poker is different. In my opinion, there's something intrinsically human about the game, from the psychology of betting to the body language that often belies bluffing. Alien players just throw everything off. Left-John Mocker doesn't share my view, but then he's a professional. He's happy to take money from anyone, and he's probably worked through the relevant kinesics and chronemics of dozens of alien races.

Our little game of six quickly settled in to the parlor between the Mocker's room and my own. Room service obligingly sent up several more trays of sandwiches, thus allowing us to play through dinner, which seemed a likely thing. Efdar Yal made a point of inspecting both decks of cards as well as the Mocker's chips, more out of curiosity than from anything else, and then spent the next two hours meticulously drawing variations of cardbacks on paper napkins whenever he dropped out of a hand.

The parlor had a full bar, and after everyone helped themselves to their respective beverage of choice we sat down to play us some old-fashioned Texas Hold'em. It's worth noting that of all of human culture, our card games have been received by the other races of the galaxy with the most enthusiasm, second only to the confusion caused by the many many flavors and brands of chewing gum we produce. Go figure.

The buy-ins were set aside, chips were doled out, and we drew cards to determine where the dealer's button would start. Chieko Tanaka lit up one of her cigars, offered it to the Mocker and then lit up another for herself. Left-John shuffled and dealt, and for the next several hours we surrendered ourselves to four suits and fifty-two cards.

*   *   *

"Fifteen hundred to you, MacLeod. You in?" said the Mocker, waking me from my reverie. Three of the others had folded. The Arcturans had raised. I had already contributed the small blind to the pot, but they had just raised over and above the blinds, in a clear attempt to force my hand.

The room's air conditioning labored in the background, attempting to purge the room of cigar smoke and whiskey fumes. I wasn't smoking and I wasn't drinking, and judging by the short stack of chips in front of me, I might as well have been doing either or both because I most certainly wasn't winning.

I picked up my cards. In another game, with other players, they might have been worth seeing the fifteen hundred, but not here. I dropped them to the table face down. "With this hand?" I said. "Not on your life." During the years of my association with Left-John Mocker I've managed to learn a few things about gambling. For one thing, winning at cards is almost never in the cards themselves, though knowing when to throw away a lousy hand is certainly useful. But the real secret is being able to read your opponent, and the best way to do that is to watch your opponent's eyes. It's a trick familiar to every great diplomat and salesman since time immemorial.

Those 'windows to the soul' give away our lies. It's part of the cognitive process, at least in humans. Our eyes dart in one direction or another, a guilty twitch perhaps, right when we make up our minds to deceive or dissemble. As if we're reaching off to the side to grab at some untruth. I became very good at noticing it back in my days on the stage, and it's a useful talent to have when playing cards. After a few hands I can usually work out the baseline pattern of an opponent's eye movements and see when he's decided to bluff by the sudden jerk up and to the left or a dart down and to the right. It's not full proof, but knowing how to read those unconscious glances gives me an edge.

Except it doesn't work with aliens, at least not reliably. Every species is wired differently, and even a xenophile like me hasn't spent enough time with enough members of enough species to have it all worked out. The trick also doesn't work on Left-John Mocker; he's just that good.

So given that I held a pair of fours I took the better part of valor, folded, and used the opportunity to devote my full attention to the other players at our table. Yucatangelo the Clarkeson sat to my left. I'd never seen one of its kind play cards before, and there's probably a doctoral dissertation waiting to be done on how the tens of thousands of proto-sentient cells that make up its committees of intelligent thought reach consensus on whether to bet or fold in a fast paced game of Hold'em. Somewhere between the dining room and the current parlor its committees had decided to wear dull reddish skin and a matching dermal one piece, making it look as naked as the Arcturans, but nearly the same hue as Left-John Mocker. You never know with a Clarkeson; Yucatangelo could have been doing it as an homage, or, just as likely, as an attempt to irritate the gambler.

Hiro Tanaka sat to the Clarkeson's left, looking weathered in body but clearly still vibrant, as his aggressive poker style revealed. To my annoyance, he'd put on sunglasses before sitting down to play.

Directly across the table from me, seemingly sitting in one another's lap, were Lilbrishtil. By some arrangement of their own one of the entwined Arcturans held their cards while the other placed their wagers and collected their winnings. How the second of them knew whether their hand was worth betting on I couldn't tell. In the face of that mystery, I didn't even try to find patterns in either Arcturan's eyes.

Beyond them sat Mrs. Tanaka. She'd been chain-smoking Cuban cigars from the moment she sat down, fastidiously passing her cards from one hand to the other whenever she needed to flick the ashes into the tray on her left. I'd been watching her eyes for cues without success. Clearly I was losing my touch.

Efdar Yal was situated between her and the Mocker. Contrasted against Chieko's small stature, the Taurian seemed to loom at the table. The effect was a bit unnerving, but would have been more so if he'd sat between her and her equally slight husband. I've played cards with Taurians before, including one who had a telepathic edge, and there's no white to their eyes. If they flicker in one direction or another when they think about their cards I've never been able to pick up any patterns. Efdar Yal did seem to have a nervous habit of tapping his drawing pen, but so far as I could determine it wasn't actually a tell, just tapping.

"I call," said the Clarkeson, throwing its chips into the pot. The Arcturans grinned at one another. The Mocker revealed the flop of three cards common to all remaining players, and another round of betting began. Not that it mattered to me; I'd folded.

I pushed away from the table. "Who needs a refill? Anyone?"

As long as I was up anyway, everyone was happy to let me refresh their drinks, mineral water for the Mocker and the Arcturans, a local beer for the Clarkeson and an imported rootbeer for me, high test lemonade for the Tanakas, and a water glass full of single malt scotch for the Taurian. One by one I brought the drinks over, and as I handed Efdar Yal his whiskey he turned his head and whispered faintly in my ear.

"Kaljor Rus was right about you. After hours at the table, I can almost see the destiny dripping from you."

There was nothing I could say in response, and the Taurian didn't expect a reply. He thanked me for the drink and turned his attention back to the action at the table. Stunned, I took my chair again; I twisted the cap off my rootbeer and took a long swig from the bottle. I tried to focus on the game, but the cards swam before my eyes. Despite feeling the Mocker's glare, I lost all my chips over the next hour.

Chapter Twenty-Two: The Death of Santiago MacLeod

I SLEPT BADLY THAT NIGHT, troubled by dreams of my own making for a change. It was one of those mechanistic nightmares, the kind where you find yourself repeating the same set of actions over and over like some helpless automaton. I sat playing cards, but instead of the assortment of players from the previous evening, all six Taurians sat there. Kaljor Rus loomed on my left and Efdar Yal loomed on my right. The remaining four unnamed students filled in the space between. Each of the unnamed sat shuffling a deck. One by one they dealt me cards and before I could pick them up either Kaljor Rus or Efdar Yal would predict the suite and rank with unerring accuracy. And even though I knew they would correctly call each card, I still had to turn them over. The cards kept coming. First standard playing cards, then an art deco tarot deck, followed by a Zener deck, and finally every American League baseball card from the 2067 series.

It might have gone on forever, but I was awakened by a stray shaft of sunlight streaming into the room through a gap in the curtains. Baseball stats swam in my head as I rubbed my eyes. I slapped at the headboard and looked up at the ceiling where it projected the time. Six o'clock. Morning had come and I felt more weary than when I'd gone to bed. With an effort worthy of at least two of Hercules's labors I pulled myself out of bed and staggered into the bathroom. I rubbed my fingers through my hair, splashed cold water in my face, and gargled something green and vile that had been included in the room's basket of complimentary toiletries.

In the midst of these ablutions I realized I'd neglected to undress past the stage of removing my shoes the night before, and had sweated through the previous day's clothes. I needed a shower, but I needed coffee more. I stumbled out of the bathroom, stripping as I went. I pulled on a lightweight sweatshirt, drawstring pants, and a pair of rope sandals that I just knew Reggie would be chewing on sooner or later. I wouldn't win any fashion awards, but I was dressed enough to get served by the hotel staff. My stomach grumbled as I unlatched my door, and I added food to my list, second only to the mind clearing need for hot coffee. I didn't expect to be gone all that long, so I left Reggie snoozing and posted the 'do not disturb' sign on my door.

At the *Perrando Azul* they did not serve breakfast in the hotel's restaurant. Instead, the bar (which I'd passed by the night before but not actually entered) had been transformed, with an assortment of traditional breakfast items laid out in serving trays set in still larger trays of hot water. Somehow it didn't occur to me to find a row of bay maries in Mexico, but there they were, forming an elaborate buffet for a typical hotel lounge, all dark and smoky. A bar took up one long side of the room; the wall behind contained a trio of mirrored shelves and about forty bottles of different kinds of alcohol. A pair of meter and a half vid screens gazed down from the ceiling at either corner, sound down but beamready to anyone with a tunable earbug. All in all, it was the kind of place where weary business travelers might loiter for a mug of brew and a chance to watch the latest sports highlights.

That made perfect sense to me. The oddity was seeing such a place by morning, with the lights cranked up full, and bright sunlight gleaming off brass railings and polished wood. I've seen such places before, particularly throughout Europe, but to me 'breakfast bar' will always be an oxymoron.

Few guests had yet arrived, and from our tour group only the Clarkeson had come in. He stood at a clear space at the bar, at the end of the buffet, gazing with what appeared to be only slight interest at the vid screen overhead. I grabbed a plate and utensils and began working my way through the range of options. The day promised to be unpredictable, and so I piled my plate high with scrambled eggs made with Mexican sausage and cheese, fried potatoes, and some bacon on the side. The plate went on a tray. I found the coffee, filled a cup, and took a sip. Caffeine bliss. Either you know what I mean or you can't appreciate the sensation. Let's just say the coffee was good and strong and fast acting. With that first sip I felt the fog begin to slip from my brain.

Tray in hand, I made my way over to the end of the bar and joined Yucatangelo. His tray overflowed with several plates, each with the partial remains of different breakfast selections that had been picked at and abandoned.

"Good morning," I said, setting down my tray and climbing onto a bar stool. "So, did you enjoy last night's card game?"

"Oh, yes, Mr. Conroy, thank you for inviting me. It was a truly interesting experience, although I confess more costly than I had intended. Not that I accuse the singular Taurian of . . . what is the term? *Hustling* me? Not at all. I have noted the expense in my journal as tuition, and the steepness of the fees merely reflect the caliber of my instructors. But enough of that, tell me, how do you fair this bright morning, and where is your furry companion, Reggie?"

And that's when it hit me, he'd called me *Mr. Conroy*, and not Mr. MacLeod.

"You called me Conroy," I said.

"Was I wrong to do so? That is your name, is it not?"

"I'm more interested in how you know that?" My paranoia flared and I looked around the breakfast bar for Taurian priests or aliens wearing hats.

"You don't really know much about Clarkesons, do you?"

"No, but how is that relevant?"

"It has every relevance. Most humans fail to understand my people. You focus on the collective aspects of our being, the colonial endeavor that makes each Clarkeson a concerted effort in and of itself. But you stop there. Your kind typically sees that as an end rather than a beginning. Your people never ask what the purpose of such beings might be in the universe."

A shiver ran down my spine at the word 'purpose.' Was it just weeks ago I was carefree and bouncing along with free will? "Okay," I said. "I'll bite. What purpose does the universe hold for all Clarkesons?"

Yucatangelo stuck two fingers into a bowl of oatmeal on his tray. The level of the bowl dropped slightly and he pulled his hand free. The fingers were clean. I had the sensation that someone was looking at me, even though its gaze remained on the breakfast tray. "As we interact among your kind, Clarkesons generally serve as catalysts."

"Catalysts?" I said.

"Just so. We spark reactions and trigger chains of events. And in doing so, we are not consumed by the reactions, nor typically an essential part of the resulting events." It laced its fingers together and looked directly at me.

"You are aware, Mr. Conroy, that one of the Taurians is a Precognitor. He has made no attempt to hide this fact, and indeed prior to you and Mr. Mocker joining the tour, he spoke of it quite freely. He feels he was drawn to our tour group, that here among us is an individual of great purpose that he perceives a need to shepherd."

"Yes, I know this. What of it?"

"He believes that individual to be you."

"Yeah, I worked that out on my own. I don't intend on being shepherded, by Kaljor Rus or anyone else."

"What you intend is irrelevant, because the Taurian is in error."

"He is?"

"You are not the individual of purpose that drew him here. This fact should have been obvious to him, as he felt the pull of the tour group even before you were a part of it."

"So if I'm not the person of purpose that he's drawn to, who is?"

"I stand before you," said the Clarkeson. "And I attribute the singular Taurian's confusion to whatever interaction the multiplicity of my nature must surely have on his precognitive sense. It seems unlikely he has ever been drawn to a Clarkeson as someone possessed of a critical destiny."

"And what is your destiny, Yucatangelo? To call me by my name and reveal my identity?"

"No, nothing as simplistic as that, though ultimately almost as simple. My destiny is to be the catalyst to your life at this place and time. I suppose that might be the flaw in Kaljor Rus's nearsighted precognition. You will have a destiny, but only as a consequence of my own. If I do not trigger the required sequence of events then your own life continues along its unremarkable path."

I tried hard not to smirk at the Clarkeson's innate arrogance; it truly believed in its superiority and specialness. And for all I knew it might have been right. "Well, assuming you choose to trigger my destiny, how would you go about doing that?" I glanced around the room again.

The Clarkeson smiled, the painfully happy smile of a clown with a painted grin. "Initially, by directing your attention to the news story playing on the vid behind your head. It has repeated several times this morning. I've been waiting for it to come around again so I could be sure you watched it."

I whirled around and there on the vid screen I saw a handsome, darkly groomed newscaster. A smaller window hung in the display just to the left of his ear. It showed some old footage of me announcing the IPO of Buffalogic, Inc. I was smiling and nodding, mugging for the cameras as I stood there with Reggie tucked under my arm. My name and title appeared on the bottom of the screen in vibrantly blue letters for five full beats. That image winked out, only to be immediately replaced by one showing the President of Mexico wearing a hard hat, standing with several engineers at an apparent dump site.

The display was silent in consideration of the bar but a stream of real time captioning ran in Spanish at the bottom of the image. I picked out one word in ten, and maybe a phrase or two I'd come to learn from preparing for the clean-up project. Pieces like 'Mexico' and 'industrial waste' and 'secret,' were more than enough for me to realize there'd been a leak. Green Aggression knew we were coming, but they hadn't known when. From the look of the vid screen, now everyone knew. Even if President Ortiz had managed to cripple GAEA with the information I'd sent him, he'd only have arrested the organization's leadership. Every individual member, every sympathetic, amateur, leaderless eco-terrorist might very well see this newsfeed as an invitation to show up at the clean-up site.

"Son of a bitch," I said, and then turned back to the Clarkeson. "How long has this been running?"

"All morning. Congratulations, you seem to be the 'big news' for the day here in Mexico. I believe your identity will shortly be a matter of common knowledge among our tour group. Santiago MacLeod and his charming sample from the designer biologics firm will have been replaced in their minds by Conroy, the environmental savior, and his faithful buffalo dog."

I stared at my tray of food, my appetite gone. I had to find a secure line and phone first President Ortiz and then Elizabeth Penrose. I looked up again and found the Clarkeson studying me intently.

"You seem less disturbed by this revelation that I would have expected," it said.

"Spilled milk."

"Then I understand. I hope you are not too inconvenienced by this. Though I may be the catalyst of these events, I do not take pleasure in causing anyone discomfort."

"What makes you think you're responsible for the news leak?"

It shrugged, a gesture that I happen to know is not native to Clarkesons, but rather a sign of how thoroughly Yucatangelo had been studying human behavior. "I was intrigued by Santiago MacLeod's biological sample. There is an acquaintance of mine in Xalapa, a human with whom I have been conducting business. He has a little girl who delights in small, domesticated animals. I had thought your creature might appeal to her and make an expensive but suitable gift. I inquired about it on the globalink."

"And you found no reference to Santiago MacLeod or anything remotely like a miniature bison among available designer genemods."

"Oh, I found many individuals bearing that name, but none led to you or a biologics firm. So I expanded my search parameters and found references to the Arconi buffalo dogs and from there I soon found you. I was astonished to read that you were presumed dead quite recently, and when I searched further, I found myself quite intrigued by your waste elimination plans, as I am here on your planet in the capacity of a seller of ecologically sensitive devices."

"I still don't see—"

"Allow me to finish, please. I was intrigued. Why were you traveling under an alias? Why were you in Mexico? I initiated a new search and learned of the destruction of your facility in the United States. I followed that back to threats you have received by the humans who call themselves the Green Aggression for Earth's Assurance, and why they have named you

'Earth Monster.' I did a final search, looking for environmental events in Mexico, which might explain your presence here, and found plans for the country's largest dump site to be closed for a year, a presidential mandate that had left several journalists confused and suspicious."

It fell into place. "GAEA no doubt left tracking spiders on the globalink," I said. "They followed your trail and came to the same conclusion."

"That would be my guess. As I said before, we Clarkesons are natural catalysts."

"Friend Conroy! A moment of your time, if you please!"

I turned at the sound of a new voice calling my name. Kaljor Rus, Efdar Yal and the four unnamed Taurians poured into the bar and aimed themselves my way. It was Kaljor Rus who had spoken.

"Ah, the misguided Precognitor comes," said Yucatangelo.

"Friend Conroy, you have been playing with us these past few days, yes?"

"Plays within plays," added Efdar Yal as he gave me what I assumed passed for a significant look among the Taur. "Your poker face reveals itself to be more formidable than Friend Lilbrishtil's."

The unnamed Taurians clamored with excitement as well. "We have all seen the morning news." "Is it true you successfully deceived the Arconi?" "Is it true these bisonary canines can eat anything?" "Are you really planning to cripple the Earth's autonomy?"

"What? What was that last?" I said.

One of the unnamed stepped forward, far bolder than I'd ever seen any of them. "One of the broadcasts suggested that you were intent on undermining your world's autonomy, that far from attempting to cleanse this planet of its wastes you were actually enslaving it to offworld technology."

"The news said that?"

Efdar Yal snorted at his unnamed companion and shoved him back into the ranks of the others. "No, Friend Conroy, not the news, not per se. Rather, a spokesman for a private group critical of your proposed actions."

"Yes, yes, that is what I meant," said the unnamed from among his peers, all of whom bobbed their heads in support. "He called you a traitor to humanity and the monster of the earth."

"Green Aggression," I said.

"That was the name, Friend Conroy, or part of it." Kaljor Rus paused and studied me for a beat. "He spoke with that way humans do when they have conviction and direct experience of a thing. He spoke as if he knew you, but that confused me."

"How so?" asked the Clarkeson who had been hovering just behind and to my right.

"The fellow passionately believed his words, this was clear. Yet surely if this Montgomery fellow knew Friend Conroy he would know him to be a man of good character—"

"Montgomery? Arlen Montgomery?!"

Kaljor Rus broke off, turned to Efdar Yal and said something in a language that sounded like birdsong, if birds sang like snare drums. Efdar Yal said something to the other Taurians, who responded with a brief chorus of bass chirping.

"Yes, that was the name," replied Efdar Yal. "So, you *do* know this man? And he knows you? Remarkable!"

"That bastard!" I said. "He kidnapped me in Pennsylvania."

"Are you sure, Friend Conroy?" said Kaljor Rus. "This Montgomery man was in Ecatepec, speaking at a university there. He had several hundred supporters behind him; they were holding some kind of rally."

"Agent Montgomery is in Mexico?" I sighed, wondering if things could get any worse.

"Earth Monster!!!"

Everyone turned to look to the entrance of the breakfast bar. The Tanakas had arrived, crisp as ever in their green breather-ware outfits which prior to this moment I'd failed to realize was the same shade of color favored by Green Aggression. And they'd seemed like such a nice, quiet, retired couple.

"Earth Monster!" they said again from just outside of spitting range, which they demonstrated by trying to spit on me and falling short, to the annoyance of a couple of the unnamed Taurians who became targets. Their voices were loud and incomprehensible, but their translation collars provided the meaning in calm even tones. "You betray our world and leave us at the mercy of alien technology. You are an abomination to all that is human and pure, and a traitor to your race."

"That's it, I'm out of here," I said and began to move forward. Efdar Yal and the unnamed Taurians gave way before me but Kaljor Rus stopped me with a heavy hand upon my shoulder as I tried to move past.

"Friend Conroy, I must go with you," he said.

"And why is that?"

"You are clearly a being of Purpose. You are why I was drawn here. I must work to ensure you are in the place you need to be at the time you need to be there."

"Not according to Yucatangelo," I said.

192

"I do not understand."

"Well, the two of you work it out. I'm going back to my room to pack up, and then Reggie and I are leaving." I turned to the Clarkeson. "When you did your globalink queries, did you use a private connection or one here at the hotel?"

"Ah, I see your concern. I simply connected via the hotel's service."

"Great. It's only a matter of time before some ambitious member of the media backtracks the trail of activation you created and shows up here. Assuming they're not already on their way. Excuse me, we're done."

"Earth Monster!" said the Tanakas' translation collars, and as I shoved my way past them this time they did succeed in spitting on me. I hurried across the lobby to the stairwell rather than wait for an elevator and climbed the stairs two at a time up to my floor.

The tour was definitely over for me. And I never got to eat my breakfast.

Chapter Twenty-Three: The Spud on the River Styx

I POUNDED MY FIST ON LEFT-JOHN'S DOOR in a way that reminded me of a similar door pounding years before. We'd been on a mixed world populated almost entirely by Flen, an alien race that had an intense religious aversion to hypnosis, gambling, spicy foods, and percussion instruments, but only during odd-numbered months. We'd managed to get off world, hidden inside a pair of kettle drums, barely an hour before midnight of the last day of the local calendar's second month. The current situation seemed just as dire.

The door opened only wide enough to reveal the Mocker's face. "You look like hell. What do you want?"

"Have you packed yet?"

"Yes, why?"

"We need to leave. Now."

"And again, why?"

We didn't have time for this. I pushed on the door and he stepped back, allowing me into the room. I closed the door behind me and leaned upon it. "There's another player in the game."

"One of the Taurians?"

"No, the Clarkeson. It's triggered some unwelcome publicity. I'm all over the news this morning. I don't know if President Ortiz was able to round up the leaders of Green Aggression, but at least one of them is still on the loose, and surprise, it's Arlen Montgomery."

"Your FBI agent?"

"Cute, isn't it? He knows the timing of the upcoming clean-up. The whole world knows, and it's a sure bet this hotel is going to be crawling with reporters and maybe even an eco-terrorist or two if we don't get out of here. Is that enough of a reason for you?"

"Don't get snippy," said Left-John. "I'm the one that's already packed."

"Point for you. Okay, grab your bag and let's go to my room. You can wake Reggie while I finish my own packing."

He grabbed his suitcase from the bed and opened the door to the common parlor our rooms shared. We stepped through, and across the site of last night's poker game. I swiped my keycard at the opposite end and held the door open to let the Mocker precede me into my room.

194

"Your life just keeps getting more complicated," said Left-John from inside my room.

"What are you talking abou—" I followed him in and saw what had prompted his remark. The two Arcturans named Lilbrishtil sat on my bed, one arm resting easily upon the other's shoulder, with Reggie positioned contentedly between them as he chewed on what looked to be a large leather sandal.

"How did you get in here?" I said.

"We broke the lock," said the Lilbrishtil on the right.

"You broke—why are you even here?"

"We know about the clean-up site in Veracruz," said the other Lilbrishtil. The first Arcturan nodded in support.

"You saw it on the news this morning?" said Left-John.

"Yes, but we knew the site before that. We just didn't know that you knew."

"How could you know prior to the news? It was a secret," I said.

"President Ortiz told us," they said together, and I noticed that they didn't simply have an arm around each other, but that each of those arms had melded into the shoulder of the other Arcturan.

"How do you know Ortiz?"

"The one formerly called Hreshtil is an expert in population design," said Lilbrishtil."

"And the one formerly known as Lilbrittah is an authority on sanitation and recycling in urban densities," said the other Lilbrishtil. "The other members of our impending quad have similarly complementary specialties. They are in Veracruz now, consulting with President Ortiz's staff. We are scheduled to join them after your buffalo dogs begin their work."

I should have been alarmed by the synchronicity, but the mere presence of the Arcturans prevented that. "So you knew about buffalo dogs? You knew what Reggie was all along?"

The first Arcturan shook its head. "No, neither of us had ever seen one before, but we immediately recognized the species when we viewed today's news broadcast."

"That is what caused us concern," said the second Arcturan. "Our only intent is to assist the Mexican people in restoring the lifeforce they have stripped from the soil. We do not wish a confrontation with Green Aggression, but they clearly seek one with you."

"Truer words were never said," said the Mocker.

Lilbrishtil nodded. "They will determine your current location, and

195

descend upon this hotel and our tour group. We believe they may have knowledge of our quad mates. A violent confrontation seems inevitable, so we have arranged to depart before that happens. It occurred to us that you might have similar reasons to avoid such conflict, and we came here to await you, and offer transportation.

During this exchange Left-John had stepped to the window and pulled back the curtains. "Leaving looks to be a problem," he said over his shoulder. "Two news vans just parked in front of the hotel. Camera crews are coming out and heading inside. No, wait, correct that. A bus and three more cars just pulled up. People are spilling out of them. With protest signs. Green Aggression is here, Conroy. I don't think you're getting out easily."

"We anticipated this problem," said Lilbrishtil. "We have a bakery van waiting at the hotel's loading dock." The Arcturan patted Reggie's head, causing him to look up from his task of devouring the sandal. "We must leave at once."

I glanced over at Left-John. He scowled, actually scowled, and said, "What are you waiting for? If you're going to try to make a break for it, let's do it now while they're still outside. Once they get into the building and learn your room number, they'll come surging up the corridor from both ends. We'll be penned in right here in the room. That might be proof against reporters, but it makes you a sitting duck if any of the Green Aggressors get it into their heads to stop their Earth Monster once and for all."

"That's what I was thinking too." I picked up Reggie and tucked him under my arm. "Let's find that getaway van."

Left-John picked up Reggie's travel bag. He opened the door to the hallway and peered out, first left then right.

It's still clear," he said. "Let's take the stairs, the first wave will probably come up the elevator"

"No," said Lilbrishtil. "Halfway down the corridor on the right is a service door. Inside is the staff elevator that goes to the kitchen in the basement. The loading dock is behind the kitchen."

Our fugitive conga line moved down the hallway with all deliberate speed. The service elevator was there as promised and Left-John pushed the call button. We listened for the hum of the approaching elevator and in seconds the door opened. Inside, looking as shocked as we must have looked to them, stood Mr. Tanaka and two young men dressed in jungle camouflage. All three had stun batons in their hands.

I had Reggie under my left arm. One of the Arcturans stood on my right. Lilbrishtil grabbed my arm and I gasped. Arcturans *never* touch other people, not skin to skin. Lilbrishtil had grasped my bare forearm, and reality changed in that instant. My entire arm went numb, and any interest I might have had in my surroundings disappeared. A sense of perfection and euphoria spread out from where Lilbrishtil's alien fingers had begun to meld into my arm. In that moment my will vanished, and along with it every negative emotion in my being. I loved Lilbrishtil, and Lilbrishtil too. I loved Left-John Mocker. I loved Hiro Tanaka and the two eco-terrorists that stood next to him in the elevator. Bliss filled me.

"I have him," the Arcturan said. "I have the Earth Monster. Quick, take him before he can break free."

Lilbrishtil gave my arm a yank and shoved me into the elevator; its fingers slipped free of my flesh as easily as they had merged with it. The intense sense of well-being all but fled and reality reasserted itself with enough cognitive dissonance to stop a truck. I nearly dropped Reggie as I stumbled forward into the waiting arms of the two young eco-terrorists. One dropped his baton as he reached to take hold of me. The other handed his baton to Lilbrishtil. Reggie began yowling.

The other Lilbrishtil rushed forward into the elevator and practically threw itself on Mr. Tanaka, hugging him close and sobbing. "Oh, Mr. Tanaka, I knew you would save us. Thank you!"

"Damnit, Conroy, they've set us up and now—"

The rest of whatever the Mocker said was drowned out by a sudden buzzing that filled the elevator. Tanaka and the other members of Green Aggression crumpled to the floor of the elevator. Both Lilbrishtil held glowing batons. The nearer Arcturan tossed it to the Mocker and reached down to reclaim the third baton from the floor of the elevator. Reggie stopped yowling.

"Would you push the button, Mr. Conroy? We really should be going."

I admit it, I half expected the two Arcturans to strip the unconscious pair of their clothes and don the uniforms themselves. Perhaps I've watched too many vids or read too many thrillers. In reality, they merely moved the inert bodies to the side so they wouldn't be immediately visible to anyone glancing into the service elevator. This turned out to be a useful precaution. When the door opened onto the basement kitchen, fully a dozen hotel employees turned to stare.

"Go forward and then to your right," said Lilbrishtil, pressing a hand in the small of my back to propel me. I flinched at the touch, but the fabric of my shirt was apparently enough to prevent a repeat of the earlier mindless euphoria.

"You'll see a pair of grey double doors. That's the loading dock. Push through the doors and our bakery van is just beyond."

I started forward but the other Lilbrishtil stepped in front of me. The Arcturan held a baton lengthwise along one arm, handy and nearly invisible. We proceeded out of the elevator and down the corridor, one Arcturan in front, and one bringing up the rear. We didn't encounter any more members of Green Aggression and seconds later one of the Lilbrishtil, Left-John, Reggie, and I had settled more or less comfortably in a narrow aisle on the floor of a large bakery van, between racks of fresh baked goods thick with warm smells. The other Lilbrishtil sat up front in the driver's seat and soon had the van pulling away from the hotel. We sped past an ever-expanding mob composed of the media, enthusiastic well-wishers, and eco-terrorists. For a moment, surrounded by the olfactory reminders of safety and serenity that fresh bread always evokes, I felt like I imagined one of Kaljor Rus's Purposeful must feel, comfortable in the notion that I had a destiny to fulfill and protected by the universe that needed me to fulfill it. The feeling only lasted a moment.

"I never did get to finish my coffee," I said.

The Mocker glared. "We're fleeing a hotel, hidden in a bakery van, and you're complaining about coffee?"

"I'm a bit groggy, that's all," I said. "Adrenaline only carries you so far, and then the payback hits. And I was groggy before the adrenaline rush, so I'm double groggy now. And the smell in here isn't helping. It's like a lullaby for the nose."

Lilbrishtil started to raise one hand noseward and paused. "We have several hours of driving before we stop, if you wish to nap. Perhaps you might find it a refreshing use of the time?"

Left-John surprised me by agreeing. "Don't mind if I do." And with that he grabbed several loaves of bread from one of the racks and propped them behind his head as an impromptu pillow. I shrugged, and prepared to follow suit, but I took more time and studied the racks around me, ultimately selecting a thick pumpernickel rye that probably had no business being in Mexico in the first place. Then I settled back and closed my eyes, and tried not to dream of coffee.

There was a rowboat, brownish grey in color and oddly delicate. I sat in it, clinging gingerly to the sides while a man-sized, well-scrubbed potato wearing a white sombrero with red embroidery pulled on the oars and propelled us through the dark water. Time passed, ten, maybe twenty minutes of utter silence except for the slapping of the oars against the water.

Darkness surrounded us. The only illumination came from a tiny candle affixed to the middle bench of the rowboat, midway between me and the potato.

"This is too incredibly stupid and bizarre," I said, and knew I must be dreaming. In acknowledgment, the potato opened several dozen of its eyes and fixed me with its vegetable gaze. "Do you know where we're going?" it asked.

I shook my head, wondering where its voice had come from. It was all eyes and no mouth, though it clearly had hands and arms with which to row. I couldn't quite tell how those arms connected with its potato body.

"Why don't you tell us?" said another voice, a woman's voice. There was something familiar about it, something that seemed so right. I looked around but there was no one else in the boat, just me and the giant potato.

"Lift up the candle," it said, almost before the woman had finished her sentence, as if it hadn't heard her. I leaned forward to comply, gripping the candle firmly at its base. The candle stuck fast. The potato narrowed some of its eyes and repeated itself. "Lift up the candle." I gripped it more tightly and yanked. The candle came free, sort of. I still hadn't managed to separate it from the bench, but rather I'd broken the plank it had rested upon. Crumbs fell away. I sniffed at a familiar scent.

"The boat is made of graham crackers?"

"That's original," said the woman's voice. "You were always so creative as a child."

I knew that voice, but I still couldn't put a name or face to it.

"Hold the candle up higher," instructed the potato. I did so, transferring it to my other hand and licking bits of cracker crumbs off my fingers. The light spread out in a growing circle, illuminating the water around us. It was dark red, seething and bubbling and thick, and not like water at all.

"What's in the water?" I said. "Why does it look like that?" I could see farther, but it was all the same. I looked back at the potato; it had removed its hat.

"Death," it said. It clutched the hat against what would have been its chest if giant dream potatoes had chests. It gasped, all of its many eyes opening wide in surprise as it pitched backwards over the prow of the little rowboat. It bobbed briefly, coated in oily redness, and then sank beneath the water.

"This is a stupid dream," I said and broke off a piece of the rowboat and began munching on it.

"That might be my fault," said the woman. "I'm distracting you from using your full cognitive function. I don't think the dream is supposed to go this way. Give your mind a moment to catch up and then everything will be clear."

"Do I know you?" I said.

"As well as anyone can know a blood relative a couple generations removed and several decades deceased."

"Aunt Fiona?"

"In the flesh," she said, and began to take form, translucent at first, but soon she was sitting opposite me in the boat.

"I'm having another of those dreams, aren't I?" I asked.

"Who are you talking to?" said a voice from beyond the boat's edge. I looked over the side, and there was the potato's sombrero, black now instead of white, but I knew it was the same hat. The potato itself was nowhere to be seen. I reached over and picked up the sombrero.

"You're not going to put it on, are you?" said Aunt Fiona.

"No, I don't think I'll ever wear a hat again."

"Well? To whom are you speaking, Conroy?" said the sombrero in the Hat's voice.

"My Aunt Fiona. Can't you see or hear her?"

"No," said the sombrero, "but that's to be expected. My ship is en route to this system's asteroid belt, and though our face to face meeting has brought us more closely in sync, your mind still creates distortion and allegorical imagery in our communication."

"What a smug sombrero," said Aunt Fiona.

"I'm not talking about the imagery," I said. "My aunt is here, and she's not distortion. She's deceased, but she's really here. I can tell; I spoke with her once before since her death, and I know how it feels."

"You are not making sense," said the sombrero. "Worse, the probabilities surrounding you are in flux. That is why I have come. It is essential that I effect another transfer to help you position yourself correctly. Put me on your head."

But I didn't. Instead, I let the oily sombrero slip from my fingers and fall to the bottom of the graham cracker boat. "What happened? I was just in the bakery van with Left-John and the Arcturans. Why am I in this dream?"

"Your brain shut down unessential bits for a while," said Aunt Fiona. "Consciousness is a luxury it couldn't afford. It's been busy restoring the neural pathways you used when you channeled me that time on Hesnarj."

"Transference and calibration," said the sombrero, still giving no sign of hearing my aunt. "Do it now. I cannot maintain this contact indefinitely."

Hearing the Hat use that word, 'contact,' brought it all into focus. Lilbrishtil had touched me. I remembered that brief euphoria and the feeling of rightness. "So, when I wake up? What then?"

"We'll still be able to talk," said my aunt. "Though you probably won't want to do it too often. I'm sure it's quite exhausting."

"Things are moving as they should," said the sombrero. A regular sized potato had appeared inside it, and was slowly growing larger. "Although I cannot perceive the particulars, I detect a significant shift. You have somehow reclaimed a part of your past. You need to bring it to your future. Even if you don't achieve another transference, you must heed me!"

"What now?"

"Your pet creature. Keep him with you at all times."

"I usually do that anyway. Tell me something useful. What about the Arcturans? What can you tell me about them? One of them touched me."

The potato had continued to grow, and had already reached the size of a young boy. It sprouted arms like a potato left in a dark cupboard would. It pulled the sombrero firmly upon its vegetable body but didn't otherwise respond.

"What about the Taurians? What about the eco-terrorists?"

"I don't think he's going to answer you, dear," said Aunt Fiona. And she was right. Instead, having at last grown to its previous size, the potato lunged at me and pushed me from the boat. I started to splash, and then to scream. The water wasn't water, it was lava. I flailed about, burning and drowning at the same time, while my great Aunt Fiona watched in silence. I dropped the candle stub and the tiny bit of light winked out, leaving only blackness and pain.

"He's coming around, give him some room. No, not like that. Hold him down so he doesn't hurt himself."

Gravity changed its orientation. Molten lava no longer seared my flesh or filled my lungs. I gulped cool air tinged with the scent of fresh baked bread. I opened my eyes and saw Reggie looking at me, his head tilted to one side like he was an art critic and I was an abstract painting hanging on the wall of a museum. Then he gave a small yip, and turned his attention elsewhere. I followed his gaze, took in racks of baked goods, Left-John Mocker and one of the Arcturans called Lilbrishtil. The fog cleared from my head.

"I just had the most amazing dream," I said.

"Was anyone wearing a hat?" asked Left-John, which produced a confused expression from the Arcturan.

"Yes, but that wasn't the amazing part. I saw my Aunt Fiona again. And not a memory of her, but like that time I channeled her. It felt so real, and so peaceful."

"Peaceful?" said Left-John. "I thought you were having some kind of seizure. Just a couple seconds after you shut your eyes you started thrashing around."

"I was out for at least half an hour."

"Uh, no, you weren't. Under a minute, Conroy. Besides, how could you know how long you were having a seizure for anyway?"

"It wasn't a seizure," I said.

"You were flailing about, waving your arms, while you whole body shook. What do you think you were doing?"

"I was drowning. Also being burned alive. It was a dream."

"You dreamed you were in boiling water?"

"No, lava. A lake of molten lava."

"Ah, that is propitious," said Lilbrishtil joining the conversation.

"How's that?" I asked.

"The hotel where my intended quad mates await us lies in the shadow of the Citlaltépetl."

"The Citywhat?"

"In Spanish it is called *el Pico de Orizaba*. Orizaba's Peak. It is the highest point in Mexico."

"What does that have to do with Conroy's dream?"

"The Citlaltépetl is a volcano," said Lilbrishtil.

I sat up quickly. "Okay, stop the van. With all the precognitive stuff floating around, if I'm having dreams of being consumed in lava, the last place I want to be is on a volcano."

"Please, Mr. Conroy, there is no danger. First, be advised that the Citlaltépetl has not erupted in more than four hundred years. And second, as I stated, we are not going to be on the volcano, merely near to it. The Citlaltépetl is located in the state of Veracruz. We are going to the city of Veracruz in the state of the same name where my quad mates are consulting with the Mexican government. At no time will we need to be on the actual site of the volcano."

Chapter Twenty-Four: Distraction and Dispossession

HOURS PASSED BEFORE LILBRISHTIL FINALLY STOPPED the bakery van. We emerged to find ourselves on the tiny airstrip at Champoton facing a familiar figure.

"Señor Delgado?!"

"Ah, Mister MacLeod! Mister Mocker! How fine to see you both again. Would you like a sandwich?"

Left-John stopped me before I answer and whispered, "Remember what I said about a coincidence-free zone? What are the odds that our blue friends would pick the same air field and the same pilot?"

I shrugged him off, "I got it," I said, "we're being pushed by destiny. But that still doesn't mean it's *my* destiny. Maybe it's yours, did you ever think of that? What if I'm the one who's just along for the ride?"

"I'm not the one with the buffalo dog," said Left-John, and turned to accept a sandwich from our pilot.

Meanwhile, both Arcturans stepped up to us and asked simultaneously, "You know the pilot?"

"Miguel Garcia Delgado is a man of many talents," said Left-John Mocker as he reached into the paper sack Delgado had given him. "Piloting a plane may well be the least of them. His true calling is sandwich making."

Further explanation was put on hold while we crossed the airstrip to the same plane that had brought Left-John and me to the Yucatan. The pilot unfolded the tiny set of steps and we boarded.

"How much is he charging for the flight?" asked the Mocker as he settled into one of the port side seats in the front row. I sat across from him, and the Arcturans took seats in the next row, and immediately entwined their arms across the aisle and fused. Reggie sat in his alligator travel bag which I held on my lap with both hands.

"Six hundred new pesos per person," said the Lilbrishtil who was mostly on the right.

"I throw in the beast for free," said Delgado as he climbed into the plane, pulling the steps up behind him and sealing the hatch. He pointed to a small ice chest wedged under Left-John's seat. "Help yourself to some refreshment, please. Then put on your safety belts. We will be airborne in dos minutos."

The sandwich had apparently improved Left-John's humor. He liberated the ice chest and passed out bottles of cold beer to the rest of us.

"Is there an opener in there?" said Lilbrishtil.

"There was on the flight out but I don't see it now."

"Not a problem," I said. "Let me show you the one trick I've managed to teach Reggie." I offered the buffalo dog the business end of my beer bottle. Reggie closed his mouth around the neck and then I slowly pulled it free. The cap was gone.

"That's disgusting, Conroy. It's got buffalo dog spit on it now." A vibration filled the plane as its engines turned over.

I shook my head. "Nope, dry as a bone. Not to mention perfectly clean. All part of the buffalo dog magic. Here, see for yourself." I handed the Mocker my beer in trade for his own and let Reggie repeat his trick.

Left-John took the bottle, dubious by action if not expression, and inspected it carefully. The Arcturans each handed me their bottles and Reggie opened them in turn.

"The utility of buffalo dogs is impressive," said Lilbrishtil, "but I believe this is a most uncommon usage." The plane lurched forward and began taxiing down the runway. We jerked and bounced as it swerved from side to side for reasons known only to our pilot. Reggie began yowling, but only for a moment, as with a final stomach-wrenching jolt we left the ground and rose steeply into the air. I swallowed hard, and considered my beer with some trepidation. Then I turned back to look at the Arcturans.

"So, what are your plans once we reach Veracruz?" I said.

"The other pair of our quad mates will not yet have completed their consultations with the president's assistants. Until they become available, we will make use of their suite at the El Presidente Hotel."

"You're kidding, right?" I said.

"Is something wrong?"

"Do you know why it's called the El Presidente?"

"I believe it is because, in the past, when the Mexican president was in Veracruz he stayed at that hotel."

"Right, right, and as such it's also the place where guests of the president are likely to stay."

"Yes, it has an impressive security force," said Lilbrishtil. "We noted that when we checked in, before our initial double pairing—"

"That's why my secretary booked it for me."

"Why would she book rooms in this hotel?"

"Not just rooms, an entire floor. And security guards along its length, and in the stairwells, and in the lobby. For the same reason I was all over the national news today. It was scheduled months and months ago. My company is bringing dozens of buffalo dogs to Mexico to clean up an industrial waste site."

"Oh good," said the Mocker. "Because we haven't had enough synchronicity yet on this trip."

We flew into a small municipal airport easily three times the size of the one in Matamoros. Our pilot undogged the hatch, unfolded the steps, and we staggered out onto the airfield. Lilbrishtil went off with Left-John to secure a taxi, while I waited with Reggie and the other Lilbrishtil.

Moments later we filled a cab. I sat in the back seat between the Arcturans and Left-John sat up front next to our driver who expressed no interest in having either aliens or even Reggie in his cab.

"When is your waste disposal clean-up to occur?" Said Lilbrishtil.

"Tomorrow, if everything is still on schedule. The first thing I need to do when we get to the hotel is to phone Dr. Penrose and check in with her."

"Were you planning on being present at the event?"

"Actually, no. The clean-up will take months, with the buffalo dogs eating nonstop and the handler teams working in shifts. My people all know their jobs; they've been preparing for months. If anything, I'd only get in the way. Originally, I wasn't going to arrive until the very end, when President Ortiz and I toured the site after it'd been scoured clean."

"You do not wish to even put in an appearance?" said the other Lilbrishtil. "Perhaps to witness the beginning of such an historic occurrence?"

"Sure, this is one of the few things we've done that I feel really involved in, and the outcome could change my world's pollution problems for all time. But I can't. It's one thing for me to sneak into the same hotel as my company is using, but quite another for me to be present at the clean-up operation itself. My presence there would only draw the attention of Green Aggression. Right now as far as they are concerned, I'm still somewhere in the Yucatan. And while they might think I'd come here, they know that I'll know they think that."

"I wouldn't assume they're clever enough to bet on a double-think," said Left-John. "Those people are fanatics, they're not strategists."

"That might be true of many of them, maybe even most of them, but even if President Ortiz was able to arrest the majority of those in charge, they only need one leader with any cunning to be dangerous. Based on the people we saw with stun batons, I think it's safe to say they're dangerous now. And we know they have at least one such leader."

"Montgomery?"

"That's the man," I said. "He'll probably think I'll come here, just because I think he thinks I won't. It's a mess, but the one thing he won't expect is for me to be here, but not check in with my people. So he'll be watching them, hoping they'll lead him to me. And that's not going to happen."

"You're overlooking another problem," said the Mocker. "Green Aggression knows what you look like, Conroy. So does all of Mexico by now. And even if they didn't, you're pretty conspicuous walking around with Reggie, and I know you're not going to leave him behind, not even with me."

I grinned at that and gave Reggie a reassuring pat, because sometimes it seems like he understands when people are talking about him. "That's a non-issue. We're at the same hotel where all the handlers are staying. In fact, it's about the only place in all of Mexico where it's legal to have a buffalo dog. President Ortiz granted the hotel a variance for the purpose of this trip. For the last few days they've probably seen dozens of foreigners walking around with buffalo dogs. Other than to go to the disposal site tomorrow, the buffalitos aren't allowed out of the hotel until the return trip home."

"There's still the problem of being recognized," said Left-John, "and not just by Green Aggression, but also any of your own people."

"Yes, particularly with all the security I've hired to keep an eye on the buffalitos and their handlers. That's why I need you to provide me with a distraction."

"What kind of distraction?"

I thought back on my dream in the bakery van. "Maybe something along the lines of an epileptic seizure."

"Not me," said the Mocker. "I had too many of those for real, back before the war."

"What war was that," asked Lilbrishtil, but Left-John ignored it.

"Get one of them to do it. I'm not reliving that, even in roleplay."

"Trust me on this," I said. "I promise you, you won't even know it's happening and you won't remember a thing."

"How's that?"

"Please, I'm still the Amazing Conroy. Now just sit back, make yourself comfortable, and focus on the sound of my voice. . ."

The cab pulled up in front of the El Presidente. Both Arcturans stepped out and headed to the lobby to get their room key. Left-John and I drove half a kilometer away to a shopping mall and while I waited in the cab he dashed in to acquire a few simple items for a disguise. It wasn't much, but

I didn't need much. While the meter ran and the cab driver watched, Left-John treated my hair to a swift rub-in color treatment leaving me grey. A few more dabs went to a thick, black moustache that looked a bit less comical rendered grey. I wouldn't fool anyone who actually knew me, nor anyone who came too close, but it would do.

We drove back to the El Presidente, taking a very slow and quiet route as I engaged the Mocker in a one-sided conversation in the back of the cab. We arrived, and Left-John and I headed for the lobby. Reggie, tucked under my arm, kept squirming, trying to turn his head around to look at my grey hair.

I passed Lilbrishtil in the lobby, and as he bumped into me the Arcturan dropped its room key into my cupped hand with the skill of a reverse pickpocket. As it circled away I aimed Left-John toward the lobby's large central couch.

"It looks well padded, perhaps even soft," I said. "You'll have ten seconds, which should be more than enough time to get within range so it can break your fall."

"Damn you, I don't want to do this. This is the last time I let you sucker me into one of your parlor tricks."

"Don't worry, you won't feel a thing."

"It's humiliating," he said through clenched lips.

"Maybe. But it's also necessary. See you on the other side."

He gave me a curt nod and a final glare. I murmured the two-word trigger I'd programmed into him in the back of the taxi. "Cayenne Gilgamesh."

Left-John hurried away from me then, walking with deliberate speed toward the couch. He arrived with time to spare but didn't sit down. It wouldn't be as dramatic if he simply slumped over from a seated position. Instead he positioned himself next to the couch, bracing one leg against the cushioned edge. I counted to ten, and right on schedule the delayed effect kicked in. Left-John Mocker's eyes rolled up into his head and his knees buckled out from under him. He fell forward, striking the couch at two places with his shoulder and hip, lightly bumping a man already seated there, and then slid down along both couch and man to the floor where he began thrashing violently.

Lilbrishtil by this time had made its way a third of the way around the lobby and began shouting and pointing.

"Oh! Help! That human is having a seizure."

All eyes immediately turned in one of two directions, either at the naked and blue Arcturan who was shouting and pointing, or to the Mocker who writhed upon the elaborately tiled floor. And that's what people would remember. I gave Reggie's head a rub for good luck and turned toward the elevators. The security guard there waited only long enough to usher me and my buffalo dog into an empty car before rushing off to help the Mocker.

My ride up went off without any complications. I stepped into a hallway free of security where the other Lilbrishtil waited for me. Moments later we entered the Arcturans' room, a deluxe suite which I felt sure was considerably better than the accommodations assigned to all the buffalo dog couriers and their charges. I closed and locked the door behind me, and only then set Reggie down upon the carpet. He scampered off to explore. I removed my fake moustache and called room service, asking to speak directly to the chef. When he came on the line I ordered the best meal he had in him. Not for myself, mind you, but for Left-John. It was the least I could do.

Chapter Twenty-Five: The End of the Beginning

WHILE WAITING FOR ROOM SERVICE I placed a second call to the front desk and asked to speak with Dr. Queen. That was the code name that Elizabeth Penrose was supposed to use while at the El Presidente, a minor attempt to throw off any media that might be looking for her. She wasn't in, but I left a message for her to phone Professor Mesmer in the hotel, and I left the Arcturans' room number. I didn't have a code name myself, but she'd figure it out.

As I hung up, Lilbrishtil knocked and let itself in; Left-John followed after. The gambler looked a bit rumpled and made a point of ignoring me entirely.

No sooner were they inside than another knock sounded at the door. We all froze.

"Room service!"

The more recently arrived Lilbrishtil glanced my way and I nodded. Left-John, and I hid ourselves in the next room as the Arcturans opened the door to admit the bellman and a heavily laden cart. The trio spoke briefly, and then we heard the door open and close again.

"You may come out now," said Lilbrishtil, who with Lilbrishtil was already laying out an assortment of plates and covered dishes.

Left-John inhaled audibly and finally acknowledged my presence. "My god, Conroy, what did you order? It smells incredible!"

"I've been here before," I said. "One of the perks of staying at the El Presidente is the caliber of the chef here. Jarocho cuisine is like nothing else in the world. In addition to the tradition of the pre-Columbian Indians, there are also influences from Arabian, French, and African foods. Here, try some of this soup. It will do wonders to improve your mood."

Left-John sat down and draped a napkin across his lap as I filled a cup from a small tureen and set a plate of lime wedges and chili strips along side it. He leaned over the steaming cup for a moment, eyes closed, savoring the aroma. Then he dipped his spoon and tasted. And then he delivered one of his rare smiles.

"This soup . . . I've never tasted soup like this."

"Caldo de Mariscos," I said. "Seafood soup. It's actually a fairly

209

common dish here, and local belief is that it will cure the worst of hangovers. I figure it might extend to helping you over your hypnotic experience."

The Mocker began eating with unrestrained enthusiasm. "Serving up the best meal of my life isn't going to get you off the hook for that," he said. "I don't share your obsessions, Conroy. How can you even be thinking about talking with the hotel's chef when you've got the clean-up project looming over you and Green Aggression breathing down your neck?"

"We must concur," said Lilbrishtil. "While we do not pretend to understand or appreciate all of the intricacies, it does seem as though your priorities are somewhat jumbled."

I nodded toward the Arcturans. "That would be true, if it was a case of one thing or another, but it's not. I've already set in motion a contact with Dr. Penrose, and until I see her there's really nothing else for me to do." I filled two more cups and handed them to the Arcturans. "After the soup, we have picaditas with black beans and shrimp, followed by cuaremeños, large chiles stuffed with spiced crab. And for dessert, a yam and pineapple campote that made me weep during my last visit here." As I spoke, I opened the various covered dishes, filled some plates, and passed them around.

"This is truly marvelous," said Lilbrishtil. "I did not realize you possessed such an interest in food, Mr. Conroy."

The excellent meal restored both Left-John and myself to good humor after a long day of too many surprises and too much frenetic travel. The Arcturans seemed to enjoy it too. Only Reggie was less than pleased with the meal; maybe the used plates did not crunch enough for his taste. Left-John finished his dessert, going so far as to scrape the last bits of pineapple and yam from the serving dish with his index finger and popping the digit in his mouth.

I wandered into the bedroom the Arcturans had graciously allocated to me, to check the latest bits from the media. I took my shoes off, sat on the edge of the bed, and turned on the room's globalink. There was a follow-up story to the morning's interview with Montgomery. He hadn't been alone, but rather speaking in front of a group of loyal members of Green Aggression staging a protest rally. The police had allowed the protest, content to just stand by, until one of the protestors set fire to a twice life-size effigy of a buffalo dog.

Chaos erupted, and the police moved in and with brutal swiftness, arresting more than one hundred protesters. I followed up, checking several different sources, and the public reaction overwhelmingly favored the police. President Ortiz had huge support for the clean-up project, and Green Aggression was considered nothing more than a loose group of generally harmless malcontents. I knew otherwise, but couldn't have asked for better public sentiment.

Before shutting off the globalink I tried, unsuccessfully, to reach Elizabeth Penrose again. Either she hadn't called in to check her messages or simply hadn't returned to the El Presidente yet. There's a time to plan and a time to rest. A good hypnotist and CEO knows which is which. I let myself fall face first onto the supremely soft mattress and surrendered myself to sleep, vaguely aware that my last conscious thought was a prayer that I be spared any more dreams of big white aliens wearing hats.

Left-John roused me from a dreamless sleep with a repeating tap tap tap of his index finger on my forehead. I sat up and opened my eyes, only to quickly shut them again. The Mocker had already pulled back the window curtain and bright morning light poured into the room. Nearby, I heard Reggie yawn.

"It's tomorrow," he said. "You've slept the afternoon and night away."

"Of all the faces I've awoken to, yours most definitely doesn't make the top twenty."

"The feeling's mutual. But you've got to get up anyway. Lisa Penrose just called. She was off at the clean-up site all day yesterday and just happened to check in and got your message. She'll be here in less than an hour."

"She called? Why didn't you wake me? Is she still on the phone? "

"There wasn't time. As soon as she confirmed you were here but asleep she said she was on her way and hung up. So, let's get moving. I've called down to room service for some fresh coffee; by the time you go and soak your head it will likely be here."

I nodded groggily, yawned and lay back down.

"I'm sorry, was I too polite? That wasn't a request or a suggestion."

Grumbling, I struggled out of bed, discovering along the way that Reggie, curled up on a pillow near my head, had gone back to sleep. Lucky him. I spared the buffalo dog an envious glance and staggered into the bathroom. The plumbing in the El Presidente was less sybaritic than many other places I've been, but still more than enough to make many a schoolgirl blush even this late in the twenty-first century. Certainly the heat, volume, and pressure in the shower had the potential for sin. In more traditional modes it was quite what I needed to invigorate myself and prepare to face the new day.

I emerged from the bathroom wearing a white fluffy robe and toweling my hair. Lilbrishtil stood waiting for me.

"Mr. Mocker explained to us a bit about the situation you find yourself in, Mr. Conroy."

"Oh?"

"He claimed that several non-human entities consider you to possess a great destiny, that you stand at a pivotal place in time and space, one which could affect themselves and many others. Do you believe this is so?"

I finished drying my hair and combed it a bit with my fingers before answering. "I believe that trying to second guess human motives is hard enough; I can't plan my life trying to figure out why an alien, or several different aliens, do what they do."

"You have not answered my question."

"No," I said. "I don't suppose I have."

The Arcturan nodded but made no move to leave. After a long silence it said, "I owe you an apology. Although it was my intent to touch you yesterday, as part of the ploy to confuse those who would attack you, I did not intend to meld my flesh with yours."

The memory of helpless euphoria and perfection sang in my mind. I shook my head to clear it. "Why did you?"

"An accident. Usually my people have great control over the experience; but Lilbrishtil and I are only recently made two, and soon to become four. A merge that would normally require deliberate effort to achieve can be accidental at this stage, particularly in moments of high emotion or stress. I hope you did not experience anything undesirable as a consequence."

"No, not at all. It was . . . unique. If anything, I felt revitalized by the experience."

"I am relieved and pleased. You are a curious individual, Mr. Conroy. I do not believe your outlook is a typical representation of human behavior."

"I'll pretend that's a compliment. Now, would you excuse me? I need to get dressed. I'll be out in a moment. Has the coffee arrived?"

"Yes, Mr. Mocker ordered breakfast for you as well."

"Great," I said as I ushered the Arcturan out of the bedroom and closed the door behind it. Alien or no, naked and possessed of a gender that eluded my understanding, I wanted to put on my pants in private.

Minutes later I joined everyone in the parlor around a table laden with a platter of scrambled eggs, an assortment of breakfast meats, pitchers with three kinds of juice, and a large pot of coffee. I pulled up a chair and began filling a plate.

"Have you seen the morning paper?" said the Mocker. "There's an article about American business owners assuaging their corporate guilt by performing ecological salvage work here in Mexico."

Both Arcturans looked up, surprise written across their bright blue faces. "It says that?" said Lilbrishtil.

"He wouldn't know," I said. "Or have you learned to read Spanish since our border crossing a few days ago?"

"I can look at the pictures and make up captions as well as the next man." He showed me the front page. "The photo has our own touring friends, the Tanakas, along with quite a few other well-meaning eco-terrorist types standing in front of our tour bus shaking hands with the local police."

"Don't show me that before my morning coffee," I said.

"Excuse me, how uncivilized of me."

A knock at the door interrupted further commentary or debate. "Professor Mesmer? Are you in there?"

I leapt to my feet and made it halfway to the door before she began knocking again.

"Wait," said Left-John, and the command in his voice caused me to pause with my hand on the doorknob. He operated a security panel and even from the oblique angle I could see the familiar features of Lisa Penrose on his screen, and no one else. She stood dressed in denim pico-fiber overalls, a white shirt, and work boots. I flung the door open, and Buffalogic, Inc.'s foremost authority on the care and training of buffalitos nearly knocked me over as she threw her arms around me and entered the room.

"Mr. Conroy! You had me *so* worried!"

The sound of his second favorite person's voice must have awakened him, and Reggie came bounding out of the bedroom, a one animal stampede straight for Lisa. Not wanting to be bowled over, Lisa detached herself from me and dropped to her knees in time to catch Reggie with both arms as he hurtled through the air for the final meter.

As Reggie served up an enthusiastic lingual face bath, I knelt next to Lisa and squeezed her shoulder to get her attention. "Lisa, it's a joy to see you again, it truly is, but I need you to bring me up to speed on the project. Is everything in place for tomorrow? Did President Ortiz make use of the list of GAEA's leadership I sent him? Did the breeders and their handlers all check in from the safehouses?"

Amidst Reggie's insistent licking Lisa had nodded eagerly to each question, but her face fell and her eyes squeezed tightly shut with tears at my final inquiry.

"Oh, Mr. Conroy, I'm so sorry. It was horrible, and it's all my fault."

"What's your fault? Lisa? What happened?" I said.

Left-John was suddenly towering above us. He gently but firmly took hold of Reggie and pulled him away from Lisa Penrose; settling himself on a chair, he kept Reggie on his lap and scritched my buffalito behind the ears.

"The breeders," said Lisa. "They're gone. All gone."

"Gone?"

"The Arconi have them." She pulled a handkerchief from a pocket, dabbed at her eyes, and blew her noise.

"That's impossible," I said. "The breeders and their handlers all went to separate locations when I crashed the company. No one knew where they would be. You're the only one who had the complete list."

"I know," she said, sobbing louder. "Elly took it. It must have been when I was asleep, just after I last saw you. Security walked me home and I was so tired and there was so much to do the next day, I didn't even make it to my bedroom. I just lay down on my sofa and fell right to sleep. I think Elly used the opportunity to wake up."

"You think? You don't know?" said Left-John Mocker from his seat behind us.

Lisa Penrose shook her head. "No, she blocked any memory of the event. That's why I think it must have happened then. I was supposed to be asleep. Any other time, one of us would notice a deliberate blank."

"I still don't understand," I said. "What did she do?"

"She must have contacted the Arconi embassy. They've been trying to meet with you since you started the company. . ."

"The Arconi want to meet with you, Conroy?" said Left-John. "After what you did to them?"

"No, *because* of what I did to them. They want to use their ability of telepathic veracity to confirm what the rest of the world knows, that I successfully smuggled a fertile buffalito from one of their worlds. If they could, it might give them a claim on my entire operation."

"But you just said the world knows you did it," said Left-John.

I nodded, "Yes, but their own records unequivocally and explicitly state that I did *not* smuggle one. They have to resolve that first. But never mind any of that. Lisa, what did Elly do?"

"She forged a series of transfer documents over the globalink, and handed over the arrival information for every breeding pup's handler. An Arcon and a federal marshal met each of them as they got off their planes. The marshals presented paperwork of ownership. At each airport Arconi took possession of the fertile buffalo dogs and paid the handler a courier's fee."

"All of them?" I asked, and Lisa nodded mutely, tears leaked from her eyes anew as she saw my face fall. The fertile buffalo dogs made up the core of our operation, the source of our renewable supply of furry, omnivorous, oxygen farters. That still left us with several dozen adult buffalitos, most of which were here in Mexico now, but there wouldn't be any more. The meteoric rise of Buffalogic, Inc. had come to an abrupt and premature end.

Chapter Twenty-Six: Old Zealots Never Die

I COULDN'T SPEAK. It's not that I had nothing to say, quite the contrary. There were too many things I needed to ask, possibilities to discuss, options to explore. The myriad ideas and issues I needed to express formed a logjam in my mouth. I had to talk not just with Lisa, but with Betsy and possibly even Eliza, and sooner or later with Bess. I began making a mental outline, sorting my thoughts for the best place to begin.

That's when Montgomery made his big entrance.

An explosion burst into the room from beyond the drawn curtains. The fabric shredded, admitting a shower of shattered glass and masonry into the hotel suite. The carpet smoldered in patches and the room's sprinkler system kicked in, dowsing everyone and further adding to the confusion.

"Earth Monster! Your time has come!"

Give him credit for distracting us from our other problems; even Lisa Penrose, guilt stricken and sobbing, turned to gape. Arlen Montgomery, Special Agent and possibly the only remaining member of the Green Aggression for Earth's Assurance's leadership still at large, stood in the crowded cargo hatch of an alien flittership hovering fifty meters above the street level and less than a meter from the outer wall of our hotel suite. He wore a jungle camouflage jumpsuit, super-traction boots, and a wraparound visor of black glass.

In his right hand he held a bright shiny blaster that looked like a children's toy, but clearly wasn't, the kind of lethal beam weapon that could be all too readily obtained from offworld contraband traders. Wisps of smoke came from the business end of the blaster, making it clear to everyone just what had obliterated the outer wall and window. Montgomery pointed it at us. In his left hand he held something small and round, like a dull red golf ball. He tossed it into the room and it flared. Everything went white. Reggie howled and tore free of Left-John's hold. He leaped into my arms, his tiny paws scrambling fiercely until I caught and held him tightly. I was snowblind. And then I felt hands gripping and hauling me away.

"You and I have an appointment with destiny," said Montgomery.

"I've already had one appointment with destiny today," I said, surprising myself at being able to speak. "And that one isn't going so well."

216

His hands grabbed my wrists and wrenched them free of the buffalo dog. I heard Reggie yelp, the sound moving away from me until it stopped abruptly with a thud. "Sorry, I'm just taking you this time. I learned my lesson at the well."

"Reggie!" I shouted.

"Conroy! What's happening?" The Mocker's shouts came closer.

"I recommend the rest of you stand perfectly still, while I leave with Conroy," said Montgomery. "You will all get your vision back in another ten minutes, with no ill effects if you don't do anything stupid. There's a rather large hole here that you don't want to step through."

"What did you do to Reggie?" I said.

Montgomery didn't bother to answer. Instead he jerked my hands behind my back and bound them with something sticky and tight. Then he dragged me across the room. I fell, but instead of finding the hotel room's carpet beneath me I felt cold metal. I struggled to my feet and heard the sound of a hatch closing followed by a thump.

"Sit back down on the floor," said Montgomery. "I won't tell you a second time."

I blinked, still lost in my own private blizzard. The ship changed direction, orientation, and speed. I lurched, tried to catch myself, and failed, my hands still glued behind my back. Instead I tumbled over, and slid across the floor until I crashed headfirst into something harder than my skull. As I passed out I felt a minor sense of triumph; my vision went from white to black. Yay for me.

"Now is not the time to take a nap," said the man in the barber's chair. His lips didn't move, but that was because of the thick layer of shaving cream coating the lower half of his face. The barber ignored me, and kept stropping his razor back and forth along a half-meter strip of leather.

"I'm not asleep," I said. "I'm waiting my turn for a shave."

Something was wrong here. The lather upon the man's face began to expand. It flowed down his chest as if it had a life of its own.

"Oh, it's you," I said.

The shaving cream billowed, formed a small torso upon the lap of the man in the barber's chair, grew arms, legs, and a head, all of white foam. Then it pushed off and stood on its own foamy feet. It looked like a kid of ten or eleven years of age made entirely of shaving cream.

"You have to stop him," said shaving cream kid.

"I wish I could." What could I do? I was unconscious and cuffed. Montgomery held all the cards.

217

"If you don't, a series of volcanic eruptions will destabilize a major fault line along the western edge of your North American continent."

"How?"

"I don't know. At this stage I can only see outcomes, not their proximal causes." It came closer. "Stop delaying and wake up!"

"But if you've already seen the outcome. . ."

"One outcome," said a new voice that I recognized as my great Aunt Fiona's. "I think I understand what your foamy friend means. You're at a choice point, dear. That outcome, or a different one, hangs on what you do next."

Before I could ask anything else, the barber shop faded to grey and I was on my way back to the waking world. I opened my eyes. My vision had returned. I lay on my side on the floor of Montgomery's flittership. It had stopped moving and hovered in mid air once more. The cargo hatch stood open and I had a magnificent view halfway up the side of a low mountain. And far below, in the shadow of the mountain, I recognized the waste site where Dr. Lisa Penrose had gathered every working buffalo dog I had left on Earth. I saw tiny specks of movement, and wondered if the buffalitos had started.

Inside the flitter, Montgomery puttered over two large pieces of equipment, gleaming metal and brightly colored bits of poly-ceramo, connected with cables. He briefly glanced my way.

"Welcome back, Mr. Conroy. I almost gave up hope for you, you've been unconscious for hours."

"What are you doing?"

"I'm saving the world," he said, still intent on his machines.

"How is any of this going to save the world?"

"I wouldn't expect you to understand. You're part of the problem."

"Me? I'm the one trying to help the planet, restore the ecology," I said.

"No, you're only making matters worse." Montgomery hadn't looked my way, but that didn't stop him from lecturing to me. "Humanity has to learn on its own to heal the wounds it caused. We have to take responsibility for our mistakes and fix them ourselves, without alien assistance, methodology, or technology."

I tried to sit up. Waves of nausea and dizziness convinced me this was a bad idea and I slumped back down.

"We have to solve our own problems on Earth," Montgomery said, "or we give up our very humanity, Earth Monster."

"Why do you call me that?"

He turned from his equipment and met my eyes. Working the

entertainment circuit of Human Space and beyond for all those ten years I'd seen every kind of person, from swindlers to fools, eternal optimists to self-fulfilling doomsayers. I'd met zealots too, individuals who had found not only their mission in life, and not just their life, but your life too. And every one of them shared that same burning look I saw in Montgomery's eyes. There'd be no reasoning with him. Nothing I could say would change his mind or alter his intent. I pressed my wrists back against the edge of a crate and tried slowly sawing through the glob of plastic that bound me.

"You're Tlaltecuhtli, the Earth Monster. A demon from ancient Mayan mythology."

"What does GAEA care about ancient Mayan mythology? This is the twenty-first century."

"It is a metaphor, Conroy. When the world was young, some believed that the Earth Monster brought abundance to the world. But that is a misperception. Tlaltecuhtli was indeed a monster, and young Quetzalcoatl and Tezcatlipoca sought his lair. They attacked him there, each taking hold, gripping with all their fierce strength, and together they tore Tlaltecuhtli in half. But they erred, and Tlaltecuhtli did not die. Worse still, as a salve for his pain, Tlaltecuhtli ever after demanded human hearts and blood in tribute. And so mankind bleeds and dies to restore the Earth. So it has always been."

"If I'm this Earth Monster, what tribute have I demanded? Whose heart? Whose blood? Your metaphor reeks."

"The tribute is the vitality of our world, a world that has forever bled because of men like you. You gaze out to the stars and turn your back on the world of your birth. That ends today, Conroy. I will stop your offworld servants by following the same path as Quetzalcoatl and Tezcatlipoca. That's what I've named my machines here. They will rip open the volcano below us, and though it has slept for centuries, now it will pour lava onto your alien creatures and drown them in righteous pyroclastic fury."

"That's insane! You'll kill tens of thousands of people, maybe more."

"The volcano will not erupt."

"But you just said—"

"Quetzalcoatl and Tezcatlipoca will produce a precise micro-eruption. There'll be only a brief venting of gases, and a few tons of molten rock spewing forth, all of it aimed at your experimental clean-up site."

"What about the toxic waste? The lava will superheat the containment vessels and create clouds of toxic gas right at ground level."

"That won't happen. My simulations show the lava enclosing the entire site. When it cools, all the waste and all your buffalo dogs will be sealed away as well." He paused and adjusted some control mechanism. "I'm just about ready. In fifteen minutes you'll have a bird's eye view as your precious buffalo dogs die by my hand, the hand of terrestrial justice."

"The hand of a raving loon more like it." Montgomery kept on with his tirade, but I tuned him out. I was running out of options. The 'sawing through the bonds' trick wasn't working. All I could think of that might succeed involved deliberately dislocating my shoulder to get the added range needed to slip my bound wrists in front of me. But I couldn't do it. Maybe with time and proper conditions and a bit of self hypnosis to convince myself there was no pain. Then again, maybe not.

The thought of wrenching my arm out of its socket reminded me of Lilbrishtil melding with me. Twice since then I'd been visited in dreams by the Hat. Each time I'd had my great Aunt Fiona in my head as well, as clear as that one time I'd channeled her back on Hesnarj. The Svenkali who had made the channeling possible had told me it would be a one time event, believing the experience burned out the facility in humans. Had Lilbrishtil's accidental melding brought it back?

I closed my eyes and tried to open my mind to whatever might be trying to enter it. I spoke my aunt's full name, "Fiona Katherine St. Vincent Wyndmoor," and a reel of images washed through me, scenes and scents and sounds I associated with the woman who had inspired my world-wandering career. And just that easy, growing slowly into mental focus, there she was.

"Hello, nephew. You're not asleep this time?"

"This is the living world," I said softly. I felt foolish for not knowing if she would hear me if I simply thought my reply instead of speaking it aloud. "But I may be joining you in the next all too soon."

"You're much too young to be dying just yet, boy. How can I help?"

I gave her a sotto voce summary of the situation including the righteous fanatic, my bound state, and the impending volcanism. She's already heard the Hat's prophecy.

"I'm sorry, dear, but I can't see any way to help. Perhaps your friend from Hesnarj will be more useful."

"Kwarum? How? I've never—"

"If you could channel me so easily, surely you can manage to do him; as I understand it, he anticipated the process his whole life. But hurry, dear. Megalomaniacs have a way of growing tired of their own ranting just when you've come to rely upon it."

I felt the mental equivalent of a kiss on the cheek, and she was gone. Maybe she'd never been. Maybe the Hat's constant intrusions into my brain had shattered whatever claim I had on sanity and Aunt Fiona was nothing more than a figment of my own making. Or maybe not.

Then I heard gunfire.

I looked up at once. Montgomery stood where he'd been, still fine-tuning his twin devices with the colorful Mayan deity names. A police flitter had arrived, visible through the open hatch. I could hear amplified Spanish, probably saying something about a 'warning shot,' but I couldn't be sure and didn't care. The Mexican police were getting ready to blow us out of the sky!

"Don't worry about them," said Montgomery without even looking my way. "Quetzalcoatl and Tezcatlipoca each generate a protective field as needed, larger than this ship. They can do so for more than an hour."

"More of that alien technology you want removed from the Earth?" I said.

"Mock me all you like, Earth Monster, it will not spare you my retribution."

"Retribution? You're completely nuts, you know that?" I stopped. Sometimes the only way to defeat lunacy is with the madness of desperation. I tried to picture the Svenkali who had died more than a decade ago. "Kwarum Sivtinzi Lapalla, the only Svenkali ever to be hypnotized."

I sensed nothing at first, then a sensation like a minty breeze whistling between the hemispheres of my brain. And then, with none of the gradualness with which Aunt Fiona had appeared, Kwarum suddenly existed in my mind.

"Oh, you *are* amazing, Conroy," said Kwarum. "Well done! You've ended the exile my own people imposed upon me. "

"You're really here? I'm not deluding myself?"

"Ah, an interesting philosophical dilemma, as surely if you were deluding yourself, how would you tell? But I suspect you haven't the time for sophistry. What has prompted this summoning that I never expected to experience?"

I gave him the quick summary I'd laid out for Aunt Fiona, adding in the Hat's dire warnings and the briefest of remarks about the creature itself.

"This Hat sounds fascinating. I'd love to discuss it with you at greater length, but first you need to get free and stop this Montgomery. As I see it, your only option is to injure yourself so that you can circumvent your bonds and then, taking advantage of the surprise, overpower your foe."

"And how do you propose I do that? I can't dislocate my own shoulder."

"Of course you can. Brace your body and throw your back against the edge of this crate."

"I tried," I said. "I held back at the last instance. I've got a nice bruise to show for the effort but nothing more."

"Don't hold back," said Kwarum.

"Do you know the expression 'easier said than done?'"

"Then give me control."

"Excuse me?"

"Give me motor control of your body," said Kwarum. "Do it now, before you can start thinking about it and freeze yourself out of even that action."

"I don't know how," I said.

"It's all mental," he said. "Use a metaphor. Imagine a control device, any kind, which you can hold in your hands. Then let it go."

I pictured the reins of a horse, the steering wheel of a groundcar, the yoke of a space yacht, and more. I imagined myself gripping them tightly, and then relaxing that grasp and letting them go. I was visualizing releasing the control rings of a Glomarkan powerchair when Montgomery called my name and distracted me.

"Watch this. I don't want you to miss what happens next."

He stood between his two devices, each of his hands lightly clutching a slender lever with a bright orange knob at the end. If not for the flittership, I'd have thought he resembled a man standing between two slot machines in Atlantic City. The ship filled with a teeth-grating whine. I realized that I couldn't move, not even my eyes. I could see Montgomery, and the open hatch of the flittership, and the mountain beyond. I couldn't feel my body at all.

Montgomery pulled down on both levers and beams of dark orange light lanced from his twin machines. Like bolts of Halloween lightning they leapt from the flittership and impaled the mountain. But that's all I saw, just orange light streaming across the open sky and touching the side of a mountain. Then nothing. Had Montgomery failed? For a moment I felt Kwarum in my mind, questioning what was happening. Me too.

But as any stage performer could tell you, timing is everything. No sooner had I begun to wonder then an explosion shook the mountainside. Rock flew in all directions, leaving a gaping hole on the mountain. And then the lava began to flow.

The police started shooting at us again, but just as Montgomery had promised none of it got through. He left his controls and stepped closer, looming above me. He turned toward the open cargo hatch and shook his fist at the police. "They cannot prevent me. I will heal our world. Your vile, alien beasts will be destroyed."

"Now," said Kwarum in a voice I alone heard.

I still couldn't feel my body, but my field of vision changed with violent speed, followed by a wet popping noise as I bounced off a crate. I was looking down at my feet. I saw my bound wrists shimmying down the backs of my calves, past my ankles, over my heels and then suddenly coming up in front of me.

"Hurry," said Kwarum, "manipulating your muscles was more taxing than I imagined. I've tweaked your nervous system slightly but the effect will be short lived. Our link is fading. I'll block the pain from you while I remain, but you need to take back physical control and seize the moment while you can."

I stood up too fast and my head spun. Pain flooded into me.

"You call that blocking?" I said even as I smiled at Montgomery's expression of astonishment. I laced my fingers together and brought my hands up with as much force as I could, courtesy of an abnormal burst of adrenaline. I connected with Montgomery's chin, making a very satisfying sound. His head flew back and I shrieked in agony as I felt the last bit of Kwarum vanish from my awareness. He'd actually been doing a phenomenal job blocking the pain. I staggered after Montgomery and as he fell backwards I tried to knee him in the groin. He twisted, and I scored only a glancing blow. Then we were both falling against the controls of the flittership.

With a gut-wrenching lurch the floor tilted more than fifty degrees. Montgomery had super-traction boots, and he tried to put them to good use. As I slid across the floor toward the open hatch I saw him spin in place and reach to reset the attitude control we'd jostled. Tried and missed. That was about the time I became airborne. Montgomery followed in the next instant, striking the controls of his machines along the way. The expression on his face was a mix of wonder and horror. And why not? We were falling to our deaths.

Chapter Twenty-Seven: The Final Mimicry

THE TWO OF US PLUMMETED five hundred meters or more, and I had every expectation we'd splatter across the mountainside. If by some impossible quirk of fate we survived the impact, our rejoicing would be cut short when the advancing lava flow engulfed us. But there was more. Montgomery's machines, Quetzalcoatl and Tezcatlipoca, had slid to the edge of the open cargo hatch after us, tipped, and followed us down. Montgomery's careful calibrations for their surgical strike of Orizaba's Peak was a thing of the past. Tumbling alongside them, I heard their distinctive whine as they cycled themselves to fire again and again. Orange force beams lanced out, most of them arcing harmlessly through empty air. Some punched holes in the mountain slope, producing explosions of rock, followed by expanding trickles of lava. One beam clipped the police cruiser and sent it rolling through the air. The machines fired upon one another as well, but to no effect. Their shields were proof against themselves.

We kept falling. There's a surreal beauty to it, and I might have enjoyed the sensation, if not for the excruciating pain from my dislocated shoulder, my lack of a parachute, the lava coursing below me, and the frequent, random beams of blistering, orange energy that threatened to slice me in half. I didn't actually produce such a list at the time; I was too busy falling to my death. Montgomery, though, kept yammering on and on about the righteousness of his actions. Fanaticism transcends the more trivial fear of being reduced to jelly upon impact. I tried to reconcile his ravings with the calm and professional façade he'd worn in his guise as an FBI special agent. I tried and failed, and we continued plunging to our deaths.

But it didn't happen. The same defense mechanism that kept the machines from blasting one another into bits of scrap included some alien widget with proximity detectors or velocity detectors or some such. Moments before what should have been a brutal and fatal collision a cushioning presser field kicked in. It slowed the machines' descent and absorbed their momentum. The field caught Montgomery and me as well, throwing us up above the machines. With a bounce that I will always prefer to liquefaction, we bobbled on the top edge of the field, nearly weightless, suspended two meters over the machines and twenty meters above the ground. Quetzalcoatl and Tezcatlipoca had stopped tumbling, coming to rest against the yielding surface of the presser field, their business ends aligned downward. Montgomery and I gawked at one another in amazement. It was short lived. The machines resumed firing. Their beams blasted into the mountain beneath them, digging our graves. With each burst the presser field recalculated where the ground was and we dropped another few meters into the growing crater. I didn't know how long Montgomery's machines could operate, nor if the field would keep lava from overflowing onto us. I didn't want to wait to find out.

Trusting to the invisible support, I performed something on the order of a shoulder roll against the energy field. I was facing downslope. Far below, at the base of the mountain, smoke rose from the edge of the waste site where the lava had breached and ignited sealed containers of toxic leftovers. Through the smoke a shadow advanced, crossing the ground to the afflicted area. When shadow reached the edge of the lava the plumes of smoke lessened and started to dissipate. Moments later the shadow spread out, forming a wide thin line, a demarcation against the progress of the lava flow. As I watched the line advanced and curved, pushing the lava backwards up the mountain.

"Would you look at that," I said. I doubted Montgomery heard me, but I just needed to say it out loud. "They're eating lava. My buffalo dogs are actually eating the lava. Who taught them how to do that?"

Quetzalcoatl and Tezcatlipoca discharged again, shattering the bottom of our crater beneath and dropping us deeper until the top edge of the presser field lay a scant meter above the crater's lip. I'd worked some questionable venues during my stage days, and I knew the value of getting the hell out when you can. I cradled my useless arm against my chest with my working one and threw myself forward, bouncing across the rippling flow of the presser field like a body surfer. I skidded to the field's edge, near enough to solid rock and scrub to reach over and down. I grabbed hold and pulled myself onto a spot of mountain proper that lay free of lava.

My knees didn't want to work, but on the third attempt I got to my feet. Down the mountain, the shadow line of my buffalo dogs continued to push upward, making progress against the lava. One lone speck of a buffalito separated itself from the slow progress of the line and rushed up hill. It darted this way and that, finding a safe passage through the lava. Where no route existed, it paused long enough to eat a clearing and then raced on. The rest of the pack held their formation for a while, continuing to advance on the lava. Then, by ones and twos, they broke off and followed, forming a sinuous line coming ever closer to my position. He was still too far away to see him clearly, but the first buffalito had to be Reggie, and the others were only following his lead.

That's when I realized I was far too calm and analytical. "I'm in shock," I said, and saying so only confirmed it. With that same sense of detachment I turned back to check on Montgomery. He still floated above his precious machines as they dug themselves lower and lower. From his expression it seemed he'd noticed the buffalo dogs spoiling his plans.

Quetzalcoatl and Tezcatlipoca cycled again and produced another blast. The presser field's upper edge dropped a meter below the edge of the crater.

"Get out of there, Montgomery, while there's still time." I dropped to the ground and extended my good arm over the edge. He was out of range. I couldn't reach him, and with only one working arm I couldn't hold onto the edge and stretch any lower.

He glanced up and his face bore an angelic expression. It could have been shock or fanatical zeal.

"Give me your arm," I said. Whatever his crimes, I didn't want his death on my conscience. Whether it was my words or just my voice, something got through. He bobbled his way across the top of the field, his hand stretched out to grasp mine.

Which is why, following some postulate to Murphy's Law that applies to emergency situations, the machines chose that moment to again cycle through their firing sequence. Orange blasts consumed more rock and the machines dropped another two meters. Montgomery had jumped. His fingers grazed mine but I couldn't grab him, and he fell beyond my reach, striking his head against the inside of the crater wall on his way down to the field's new level.

And he bounced.

The presser field took his momentum and pushed him back the way he'd come, giving him a second chance. He grabbed me with both hands. One locked around my wrist and the other just above it on my forearm. I curled fingers around the wrist of his lower hand, in a grip parallel to his own.

Quetzalcoatl and Tezcatlipoca completed another cycle with a din of explosive force, all of it projected downward into the mountain. I lay sprawled along the crater's edge, desperately gripping the man below me, the presser field dropped another few meters and lava bubbled up from below it.

I couldn't pull him up. It took all my strength just to lie flat and not be pulled over the edge. And I couldn't use my other arm to brace myself. Montgomery's grip weakened. He'd definitely slipped into shock. His complexion had gone all waxy, and his eyes were vacant.

226

My options appeared limited. I could let go of Montgomery, and likely no one would blame me. But then I'd have to watch him fall into the lava, and I couldn't do that. But the choice wasn't mine. Neither of us were likely to keep hold much longer. Where were the police? Had they gotten their cruiser under control? Had they called for back-up? The place should have been swarming with cops, and probably would have been if we had been anywhere other than halfway up the side of a volcano. No, the most likely help to arrive would be my buffalo dog, but I couldn't conceive of anything Reggie might do to get Montgomery out of the crater. He wasn't strong enough or large enough to drag both my weight and Montgomery's to safety. And it would take too long to eat a trench underneath me to support our weight—I'd be forced to let go long before that happened.

The machines in the pit cycled again. The sound was different this time, higher in pitch and of longer duration. It built and built, and when the machines fired again, the results differed. They dropped lower, but not the meter or two that each previous cycle had caused. This time they plunged more than twenty meters; the crater had become a pit. A sudden rush of heat burned my face. I saw a flash of brilliant light that must have been the presser field finally giving way because lava welled up and engulfed Quetzalcoatl and Tezcatlipoca, and then rose. Fast. Fast enough that it might reach Montgomery before my arm gave out, so rather than watch him fall to his death, I'd have to watch the lava cook him.

In the distance Reggie barked. I know the full repertoire of his barks. The sound reaching me now only occurred in dire situations, such as waking up from a nap to find himself alone in a room with the door closed, or on several occasions where he had bitten into some object expecting a substantial meal only to discover that his snack was actually hollow.

More barking followed, like an echo or an undercurrent. It wasn't just Reggie; I heard the combined noise of many buffalitos, yapping excitedly and drawing ever closer.

Montgomery's machines roared, drowning out all other sounds. They punched ever deeper and the surface of the lava pool dropped, splashing as it fell twenty meters, and began to refill.

The mountain vibrated like a great earthen bell. Every few seconds the lava level fell again, rose again as fresh lava rushed up from below, over and over like a deranged, pyroclastic perpetual motion machine. I thought of the warnings from the Hat. If ever there was a choice point for an environmental disaster, this had to be it. How deep would Montgomery's machines go, and what would be their ultimate effect? Would they trigger a full scale eruption of the dormant volcano? Could their digging and blasting destabilize the local tectonics?

If anything happened it would be my fault. Montgomery's machines might be the immediate cause, but he had used them in reaction to my buffalo dogs coming to Mexico. And he lost control because I'd knocked him into the flittership's controls. I had been the choice point all along, and I'd made the wrong choice again and again. There was nothing I could do now to turn off Montgomery's machines; even without their protective fields they were built of sterner stuff than lava. I wasn't, and I couldn't get through molten rock to shut them down, break them, or otherwise halt their progress. What choices remained to me?

Reggie arrived. His barking broke through the din from the pit and entered my awareness a bare instant before his hooves landed upon my buttocks. He didn't stop barking until he'd galloped up my back and over my shoulder. I gasped and almost let go of Montgomery, wincing as my arm jerked in response, and the pain I'd almost gotten used to stabbed at me in a new way. Reggie's warm breath fell against my right ear. He licked it and then shimmied carefully forward, his front legs clinging to my upper arm as he gazed past me into the pit, his furry head alongside mine. He saw Montgomery and gave a growl. Clearly, Reggie wanted nothing to do with the man, and though I shared his feelings, I still wasn't ready to just let go and have him fall into the lava below.

The decision was taken away by the arrival of the remaining buffalo dogs. Because of the Arconi monopoly, no company could field more than ten buffalo dogs in one place at one time. Never had a herd of buffalitos been seen on Earth before, and never in any records that Dr. Penrose could find had they ever been observed to stampede. Until now.

Even Reggie was caught by surprise. He had seen them mimic his every action, followers content to do whatever their leader did, without hesitation or debate. They had done so when they ate back the advancing lava. They had done so when they followed him up the mountainside. And they were doing so now as they drove their tiny hooves across my back to join Reggie in his precarious perch on my shoulders.

As the first of the herd landed upon my back Reggie barked at them but it was too late. I winced and cried out, and both Reggie and the front runner of the herd toppled off of me and tumbled into the depths of the crater. I didn't even have a chance to reach for him, it happened so fast. Reggie fell past me, his eyes wide in surprise, his legs working the hot air, his little blue tongue sticking out as he bleated. He struck Montgomery in the head as he fell, and the impact caused him to lose his grip. I couldn't hold on.

He slipped from my grasp and followed Reggie down.

But they didn't go alone. Like eager lemmings or merely loyal subjects, the rest of the herd thundered blindly into the pit, some taking the time to trample over me while others simply dove in from the edge. They barked as they sailed past. It happened in seconds. First Reggie, and then the others, struck the lava with little splashes. They sank beneath the molten surface, their tinny barks stilled for all time. Arlen Montgomery vanished as well, consumed alongside the creatures he so opposed.

After the last buffalito clambered over me and dove into the pit I just lay there, staring at the lava. For all their prodigious invulnerability, despite the fact that every buffalo dog comes into the world in a burst of thermogenesis that would flash fry any native Terran lifeform, I couldn't imagine any of them surviving immersion in lava. They were gone. My entire company had vanished. A man had died before my eyes. But none of it mattered. All I could think about was Reggie.

"Hey! Are you al—Holy spit, Mr. Conroy? Guys, it's Mr. Conroy."

Hands pulled at me. My own were numb. The pain in my shoulder couldn't compete with my heartache. I barely recognized my rescuers. The buffalo dogs' handlers had followed them up the mountain and arrived at last, a cavalry of my own employees.

"We've got you, Mr. Conroy, you're gonna be all right. Buck, get on the phone now and call for an ambulance. And get Jean up here."

Hands raised me to a sitting position. Jean, the paramedic among the handlers, braced my shoulder, asked me to look away, and wrenched my arm back into its socket. Someone eased me back from the lip. I had no feeling in my hands and arms, and a newly medicated ache in my shoulder. Several dozen Buffalogic, Inc. employees formed a protective circle around me, stared at me, stared at the pit, and glanced at each other. I could only blink at them. I knew their names, had met with each of them personally and at length. I'd taken their measure before entrusting them with a buffalito. They were like extended family, and I was too spent to meet their gaze and offer them hope.

A hospital flitter arrived. Emergency medical techs hustled me aboard. Quetzalcoatl and Tezcatlipoca had gone silent, and indeed Oriziba's own troubled rumblings had ceased. All was right with the world, just as Green Aggression wanted it.

A med tech knelt over me, tearing open foil packets and smearing goop on me. It felt cool, but smelled like spoiled cabbage. I tried to pull away.

"Hold still, Mr. Conroy. You've managed to burn yourself pretty badly all over your face and arms. This is going to sting at first, but it will quickly feel much better."

She continued applying the salve to my skin, awakening pain that I hadn't realized I felt. My eyes ached and tears streamed down my cheeks as a soothing coolness washed over my skin. The med tech said nothing, and I didn't tell her that my crying had nothing to do with my burns or her salve. I didn't have words for it.

Chapter Twenty-Eight: Balancing the Equation

IT IS A BLESSING TO BE ABLE TO MOVE THROUGH LIFE with certainty, to have every action a matter of assurance, every decision an instance of confidence. That used to be me, but it was all gone. The simple truth that Left-John Mocker had told me kept coming to mind: I was a hypnotist, and I didn't really know a thing about running a business, let alone a major company. I couldn't work up any concern that the Arconi had seized all of my breeding stock, or that Green Aggression had won and most of my company's assets had vanished into a volcano. I couldn't work up any interest in learning the status of that handful of buffalitos leased to projects offworld, or distress over the thousands of employees depending on Buffalogic, Inc. for their livelihood. None of that felt real. All I could think about was Reggie, and the look of surprise and shock on his face as he'd fallen and disappeared beneath the lava and the rain of falling buffalitos. He wasn't simply an animal, nor even a pet really. For the past five years Reggie had been my daily companion. Only his passing had any reality.

Running Buffalogic, Inc. had just been a game to me, like something I'd hypnotized myself into believing was serious. Conroy, the Amazing CEO. And now, counting backwards from three to one, I'd awoken to discover I didn't know what to do, didn't care that I didn't know, and felt helpless because I didn't care. I just wanted some clever trigger phrase that would make it all right again and bring back Reggie.

Further meditations of denial and self-loathing were interrupted by the arrival of Dr. Penrose.

"Boss? Why are you sitting in the dark?" She slapped a wall switch and my hospital room flared into existence around me. I'd expected Lisa Penrose. Lisa had been in charge of the project, had doubtlessly been on site when all hell had broken loose. But Lisa never called me 'boss'; of all the Penrose personalities, only Betsy ever called me 'boss.' In her own mind Betsy was 29, blonde, and on the board of Regents for the University of Washington. She had a tattoo of a poem by Edna St. Vincent Millay that circled her left wrist, and some psychosomatic quirk of multiple identities made it slowly become visible when she was in control and running Elizabeth Penrose. A bit headstrong and prone to rash action outside of her profession, when on the job Betsy was a professional's professional. She was a lawyer, senior counsel for Buffalogic, Inc. I hate lawyers.

"You look like a mannequin in that stuff. Does it itch?"

I shrugged, one of the few communicative gestures I could manage. I was sprawled out on my back in a hospital bed, with an assortment of wireless monitoring patches glued to my chest. My face and my entire right arm from fingers to shoulder had been painted with a flesh-toned, medical organo-ceramo designed to treat my burns in record time. I felt like I was wearing mud.

"I have good news and bad news."

A modified padd rested under my right hand and as I tapped with one encased finger a voder spoke with my voice. "Go ahead," I tapped.

"Okay, the good news is that before the buffalo dogs broke ranks, they had managed to consume over a million tons of industrial waste from the site. President Ortiz's popularity just shot through the roof, a record seventy-three percent, and any senate opposition has gone into hiding. The government is convinced of the efficacy of the project, and wants to resume it, if and when we have the resources to come back to it.

"The bad news is that because the buffalo dogs bolted in the middle of a planned sequence, more than twenty tons of toxic materials were left exposed and, as a consequence of the damage done by the lava, the waste site itself is now too contaminated for human workers and a whole host of new problems have been created. Despite statements of support from Ortiz, the Mexican senate is holding us responsible. They've filed a suit in the international courts and are requesting a freeze to be put on the company's assets pending the resolution of their suit."

"Not wasting any time."

"Nope, nor is anyone else."

"There's more?"

"A group calling themselves the Guardians of All Earth and Air is suing you for attempting to activate a volcano and trigger a geo-physical reaction, including manipulation of fault lines throughout North and Central America. They've also requested the courts to freeze all our assets, pending the outcome of their suit."

"Guardians of All Earth and Air? G.A.E.A.? Is that supposed to be a coincidence?" The voder asked the question without inflection. I hadn't figured out how to type sarcastically.

Betsy rolled her eyes all the same. "They insist they have no formal ties to Green Aggression, but they've been under investigation themselves for acting as their litigious front on numerous occasions."

"What else?"

"The insurance company that provides coverage for all our buffalo dogs has provisionally agreed to a payout on our policy, including our estimates of lost revenues incurred until such time as each and every buffalo dog can be replaced."

"Really? That is good news."

"Yes, but only provisionally. They also filed for bankruptcy before the end of the business day. The accounting and legal departments both agree that we'll be lucky if we manage to get a penny for every dollar owed."

"Is there more?"

"The FBI has released a statement that Special Agent Arlen Montgomery had been under internal investigation for months now, and they are reviewing his reports regarding Green Aggression's alleged—"

"Alleged?"

"—attacks on Buffalogic, Inc. They've also issued a warrant for your arrest, charging you with, among other things, treason, collusion with a renegade agent, environmental sabotage, and the murder of a federal agent. Lisa spoke to President Ortiz earlier today and explained the situation. Because of the surge in his popularity he's feeling magnanimous toward you and has temporarily suspended Mexico's extradition policy with the U.S."

"That's something anyway."

"Maybe, but it's short lived at best. The Mexican senate is already considering a resolution which would overrule the president."

"So when do I get out of here?"

"The doctors say you need to stay under your burn coating for a week. They want to keep you here for at least the next two days. Assuming you're not extradited or otherwise arrested, subpoenaed, or indicted."

A sudden calm fell over me. None of it would bring back Reggie, so none of it really mattered. Every bit of it was just pieces in a puzzle that Betsy had brought, something to poke at while I lay in my hospital bed.

"So, we've lost our breeding stock to the Arconi, and all our working animals here on Earth" The voder spoke with dispassion, a perfect mirror of my mood.

"Yes, sir."

"And the company's assets, all of our cash from the leases and services, and the recent discount sales after I ordered the crash, that's all locked up?"

"Tightly, as well as all real property and equipment, everything's been frozen and double frozen with court documents blocking our access."

"So the company is basically gone."

"Well, for now. But according to the final report filed by the Legal department—"

"Final report?"

"I let everyone go when you ordered the crash. Two week's suspension with pay, renewable as needed pending word from you. The payroll's completely automated through the bank, but that's likely frozen now too."

"Right, right," I tapped. "Back to what you we saying, what did the lawyers think?"

"They think the company will probably weather it, sir. The legal battles will eventually resolve themselves, one way or another. Buffalogic's assets will become liquid again, and you can rebuild."

"Without any buffalo dogs?"

"There are the remaining twenty-two buffalitos currently offworld, but some diversification would definitely be called for."

My head ached. All the responsibilities of my once and future business empire suddenly constricted more than the ceramo coating me. Somewhere near, a monitoring station blinked with telltales of my heart rate and blood pressure soaring. I was supposed to be resting, but I was closer to exploding. Having to tap on the padd didn't help my mood any either. I drummed my fingers on the padd, the manual equivalent of clearing my throat, and started again.

"How soon until Legal thinks this is an option?"

"Five to ten years, depending on your next course of action."

"Course of action?"

"I believe, and the majority of the legal division agrees, that you need a bold stroke and a scapegoat. If you can blame this entire fiasco on one person your own credibility will be retained. Toward that end, I've prepared a letter of resignation. It's only fair; if not for Elly you wouldn't be in this situation. And the entire clean-up procedure was my idea too."

"Technically, the clean-up was Eliza's idea," I said. "And I don't hold you responsible for what Elly did. How could I?"

"Sir, I've always respected the way you distinguished among us, but I doubt the business community will be so discriminating. This is another point on which we've reached consensus. Once you've accepted the resignation and tie it to the project, you'll be able to point to it as a well-intentioned piece of pro bono work gone horribly wrong. Between that, and the string of civil suits that Legal is preparing to bring against anyone even remotely involved with Green Aggression, you should be back on top quickly."

"I'm not going to let you resign; you, all of you, are the ones who built the company."

"At the moment, that doesn't amount to much, Mr. Conroy."

The door to my hospital room swung open, revealing the starched whites of Paloma, a no-nonsense security guard turned nurse. Literally. I'd managed to wheedle a bit of her life story from her earlier in the day while letting her spoon feed me soup. She'd seen combat during the Mexican border wars, and had the rare experience of breaking men's bones and then having to set them within the same hour. She was efficient, dependable, and didn't like me even the least little bit. Her expression made it clear that there was nothing in the room, nothing I could say or do, which would meet with her approval. She glared first at me and then at Betsy, as she advanced.

"The patient needs his rest. You'll have to leave. Now."

"She's right," I tapped. "Go. I'll think over all you've told me. But, tear up that letter. I'll fire myself before I let you go."

Betsy didn't get a chance to reply. Nurse Paloma escorted her bodily out the door. An instant later she was back alongside my bed and fiddling with my IV drip.

"Rest, means rest, Mr. Conroy. And one way or another, that's what you're going to get."

No nonsense. Right. My eyelids drooped and the world went blurry and faded to black.

I awoke to new visitors and a warm tingling feeling in my arms and face that was undeniably pleasurable, more than a little intoxicating, and a milder taste of something I'd felt before. I opened my eyes to find four bright blue, naked, sexless teenagers standing around my bed.

"Hey, Lilbrishtil. Nice to see you too, Lilbrishtil. Who are your friends?" I muttered through the painless haze. Only after I'd spoken did I remember I shouldn't have been able to speak; the healing ceramo had my face locked up tight. I started lifting my hands up to touch the ceramo mask but realized that an Arcturan had hold of each, their fingertips lightly melded with my own.

"We are Lilbrishtil no more, Mr. Conroy. These two are the other half of our quad. We have been fully mated now and are all Lilbrinthklortil."

"Lilbrin ... uh, I'm feeling kind of woozy. Can I just call you Lil?"

All four nodded, so I continued. "What are you doing here?"

"We are leaving shortly, returning to our home. We are merely finishing up what you would call a few loose ends, before we go. Your injuries are one such matter. You will recall the inadvertent effects of Lilbrinthklortil touching you when we were fleeing the Tanakas? Now that our bonding is complete, not only does each of us have full control once more, but as a functioning quad we have mastery. Lilbrinthklortil and Lilbrinthklortil are healing you."

A few moments later and the ripples of pleasure receded. The Arcturans pulled their fingers from mine, and stepped back.

"Be sure to drink extra fluids today," said Lilbrinthklortil.

"Oh, I will," I said numbly. "Am I—?"

"You are restored to perfect health." Lilbrinthklortil turned and nodded to the others. "And now we can leave."

"Oh? Where are you guys going?"

"To our ship." Lilbrinthklortil stepped away from the bed and opened the room's small closet. It pulled out some clothing. "Mr. Mocker left these for you."

"The Mocker was here?"

The Arcturan nodded as it brought my clothes to the bed. "He has been close at hand since your people brought you here. He only departed a few hours ago."

The Lilbrinthklortil closest to me nodded to its lifemate. "Given all that happened, our quad thought you might want to leave the hospital sooner rather than later, and without alerting the staff."

"Aren't they monitoring my vitals?" I said.

"Lilbrinthklortil and Lilbrinthklortil will shortly create a distraction at the nurses' station. They were intrigued by Mr. Mocker's simulation of a 'seizure' and wish to try it themselves," said Lilbrinthklortil. "While this occurs, Lilbrinthklortil and I will lead you to the stairwell and freedom."

"Thanks," I said. "I don't think I could take another of Nurse Paloma's sponge baths."

Lilbrinthklortil stared blankly in response. After a moment it shrugged and handed me my clothes. Left-John had seen fit to provide me with a set of cotton underclothes, a ruffled, maroon dress shirt, as well as a used but serviceable tuxedo. A paper box contained a black bowtie, and a pair of shiny, black slip-ons with built-in socks. There was a folded note in the tuxedo coat's right pocket, marked in the Mocker's tight printing "open when alone." I returned it to the pocket and checked the left. Cash. A quick rifling of the bills revealed about eight hundred new pesos, likely the last of the money Left-John had gotten for Big Chuck's car.

I took off my hospital gown and started to dress. As I did, Lilbrinthklortil conferred quietly with the two of its mates that had healed me. A moment later the newer pair headed off for the nurses' station. Lilbrinthklortil returned to my bedside and said, "You will remember the Taurians from our tour group?"

"Of course," I said. I put on the shirt but left it unbuttoned because of my chest monitor patches. "What of them?"

"I have discussed this with my quad, and we concluded that Kaljor Rus is indeed a Precognitor."

"I don't dispute this."

"Then you must also accept that his perception of you is real. You have a destiny to fulfill."

The memory of Reggie tumbling past me flared in my mind. "Maybe I did, but not anymore. It was completed when the plasma cannons stopped blasting their way to the fault line."

"We can see why you might believe that, Mr. Conroy, but that was not your destiny."

"What is that supposed to mean?"

"I melded with you before the events on the volcano. I felt it in you then. Lilbrinthklortil and Lilbrinthklortil melded with you to heal you, and I have just shared their experience. The same feeling is still there. It has not passed with these events. There is something else ahead of you. We do not have the Taurian's gift to see the specifics, only the general shape of the thing. It is huge and unique."

Then Lilbrinthklortil motioned to Lilbrinthklortil and the two of them headed out the door. I put on my shoes and waited. A moment later Lilbrinthklortil stuck its head back in.

"Let us go now," it said. "The hallway is clear."

"You don't have to tell me twice," I said. I tore the handful of monitor patches off my body, threw them on the bed, and followed the Arcturans down the hall to the stairwell and out of the hospital.

Chapter Twenty-Nine: Dialectic Dinner For Four

I STEPPED OUT OF HOSPITAL into late afternoon, with sunset fast approaching. Lilbrinthklortil hailed a cab for me as I hung back. The other Arcturans gathered close around, lessening the likelihood of my being recognized. They escorted me to the vehicle and gave me departing blessings of long life and tranquility.

I still didn't speak much Spanish and the cab driver didn't know much English. Between the two of us we arrived at an agreement to take me to the center of the city. I didn't have a particular destination in mind. It was enough to have the cab in motion.

Away from the soothing presence of the Arcturans, reality came flooding back. I filled the backseat of the cab with grief. Reggie was gone. By now Nurse Paloma or some other member of the hospital staff realized I had vanished. Orderlies would be scouring the hall and searching supply closets for a man with a ceramo mask on his face. I didn't care. Depending on the status of the suits filed against me, there might be a dozen lawyers looking for me now, in addition to the federal agents President Ortiz would feel compelled to set on me. Given his unwillingness to extradite me, there were now probably bounty hunters after me as well. None of it mattered.

I could return to the El Presidente, but the hotel seemed too obvious a place. I wasn't ready to be taken back into anyone's custody. But where to go? There was nothing left for me in Mexico, nothing to keep me here. I didn't have Santiago MacLeod's passport anymore, but there were plenty of places I might slip across the Texas border if I didn't mind losing some time. But to what end? Buffalogic, Inc. no longer existed physically or financially. I had a hotel room back in Philadelphia, but I'd spent little enough time there, and the odds were pretty good that Montgomery or some of his people had thoroughly ransacked it anyway. I had no place I had to be, and I couldn't expect the cabbie to drive all night.

I tapped on the intercom plate and the partition separating me from the driver grew transparent. "Sí, señor?"

"Take me to a restaurant," I said. "The best restaurant you know of. Do you understand? The number one restaurant? ¿El primero?"

"Bastante bien." The partition darkened again. I sat back, thought about eating in a restaurant without ordering a second meal for my buffalo dog. After the anesthetic presence of the Lilbrinthklortil, all I had was raw pain. For distraction I pulled Left-John's note from my pocket and unfolded it as night deepened across Veracruz.

> *C-, Sorry I'm not there, but I thought I'd be of more use drawing people off your tail and making a few false trails. The Arcturans insist they can fix you right up. I've left you what cash I had on me and some clothes to remind you where you come from. In a week's time I expect to be on Titan. There's no extradition there, and they're not fond of bounty hunters. Meet me if you can, or leave word where I can find you. –LJM*

Titan? How was I supposed to get to Titan with less than a thousand new pesos, no ID, and half of Mexico looking for me? And for what? To let Left-John say 'I told you so'? I couldn't think about my future; the absence of Reggie kept pulling me up short.

The cab slowed to a stop. I stared at the entrance to a sedate and clearly expensive venue with *La Opción* scrawled in gold across double doors of polished ebony. I didn't have a clue what the name meant, but something about it seemed perfect. I paid my fare, including an extra tip for his choice of restaurants, and then went inside.

The walls burned with a muted incandescence that provided ambiance but little light. As I waited for my eyes to adjust the maitre d' arrived. His expression conveyed disapproval, and I realized I'd never buttoned up my shirt, let alone tucked the ends into my pants or tied the tie. I reached into my pocket and palmed an absurd number of new peso bills. I pressed them into the maitre d's hand as I stepped forward and shook it and asked him where the men's room was so that I might clean up. He feigned a cough, brought his hand to his mouth to cover it, and inspected the bribe. He coughed again, nodded smartly, and escorted me around a corner and gestured down a hall.

Nurse Paloma's sponge baths notwithstanding, I required a bit more sprucing than just tying my bowtie. Maybe it was a side effect of the Arcturans' healing, but I was a little ripe. The restroom attendant discretely averted his eyes as I all but bathed in the bathroom sink and made generous use of cologne and hand towels. When I finally stepped back out the maitre d' looked upon me with more approval and nodded for me to follow him to a table. I had the last of Left-John's cash on me, and I couldn't imagine a better way to spend it than with the grandest meal Veracruz had to offer. It'd make a fitting memorial to Reggie to eat well in his name.

Lawrence M. Schoen

The maitre d' led me into the restaurant's main dining room. The evening had barely begun and diners occupied only a single table. Amazingly I recognized the trio seated at it.

"Ah, you see? I told you he would come," said the Clarkeson with a flamboyant wave of its left arm in my direction. His two Taurian companions silently lifted their bullish heads to look my way and then pushed their chairs back to stand.

"Greetings, Friend Conroy," said Kaljor Rus.

"Well met, Friend Conroy," added Efdar Yal.

The maitre d' paused, glanced at me, glanced at the aliens, glanced at me again and came to a conclusion all without breaking stride. He changed direction slightly, and went from leading me to the vacant table of his original trajectory to escorting me to the occupied table, acquiring a needed chair along the way and positioning it for me. *Destiny*, I thought, *takes many forms*. I nodded for the Taurians to sit back down and settled into my chair at their table. I regarded Yucatangelo.

"You were expecting me?"

"My companions persuaded me with your world's own dialectic."

"Come again?"

"As I told you before, they believe you are the point source of a destiny to happen. Consider that their thesis. My own interpretation, the antithesis, is that I, and not you, am the focus of their perception."

I nodded. "I remember that. And the synthesis?"

"Ingenuous, really. I am the catalyst by which they come to know you and bring you to your destiny. Thus, all egos and interests are served. Elegant, is it not?"

"And how are my interests served?"

"In any number of ways. First, you will be our guest at this fine meal, made all the finer by brisk and scintillating conversation. Second, I believe we have information that will correct some misperceptions you have and answer some questions. And third, my companions here will reveal to you the coordinates of your true destiny."

"Coordinates?"

"Yes," said Kaljor Rus. "We learned them by working together. Unfortunately as in quantum physics, once we determined the precise location, we relinquished the ability to know the time of the event."

I shook my head. "Taurian religious observances involve quantum physics?"

"We use whatever the Truth demands us to use," said Efdar Yal. "Would you like to look at a menu?"

240

* * *

The menu at La Opción, in addition to possessing a smartswitch with English translations, had the twin gifts of variety and rarity, forcing me to make hard choices. The chef daringly modified traditional continental cuisine through the use of local spices and preparations. All of which only made my choice that much harder.

Aliens anywhere in Mexico would have been uncommon, but in Veracruz, so far from the capital, finding three together and of two different races was like the circus slipping quietly into town at night while you slept. The simile came readily to mind given the florescent green tufts of Yucatangelo's hair, its bleached skin, and the riotous colors and polka dot patterns selected by its dermal subcommittee. As the restaurant filled with elegantly dressed and well-to-do patrons, a zone of quiet disinterest formed around our table. Back in the states the locals would have found excuses to repeatedly cruise by the table. In contrast, the clientele at La Opción studiously avoided betraying any interest in my companions. In its way, it was more distracting than gawkers.

After placing our orders I turned back to the Clarkeson and asked, "How did you know I'd be here?"

"No great mystery. I had observed your appreciation of food on several occasions. It seemed reasonable that you would seek out a fine meal at your earliest opportunity. Not knowing the city yourself you would rely upon recommendation. When I learned you had left your hospital bed I contacted these singular Taurians and we came here straight away."

"How did you know to come to *this* restaurant?"

"He paid the taxi cab dispatchers," said Efdar Yal as the waiter arrived with our first course. "They had their drivers recommend this place to any of their passengers who asked for a fine restaurant."

Kaljor Rus nodded in vigorous agreement. "An inspired strategy, truly."

"Please, you give me too much credit. You were dubious as to the plan's success when we first sat down here."

The Taurians both waggled their hands in the familiar Traveler gesture of denial and negation. They'd been in the company of humans too long, and their massive heads briefly paralleled their shaking wrists; they grazed the tips of their horns, and laughed. The whole thing probably seemed quite reasonable from the Clarkeson's perspective of constant group dynamics. I just rolled my eyes.

Never let it be said that Taurians are picky eaters. Far from sharing my problem of what to select and what to perforce leave untasted, they contented themselves with enormous bowls of mixed salad greens in a spicey vinaigrette. Yucatangelo, who being a Clarkeson used its mouth only for speech and never for consumption, ordered a tureen of creamed almond soup, garnished with shredded cactus and peppers. It discretely dipped its fingers into the soup, ingesting it slowly. As for myself, I ate rabbit in courgette and tomato sauce, a dessert of spiced partridges in dark chocolate, followed by strong coffee. I'm sure everything was exquisite, but I can't remember how any of it tasted. Each bite stirred a memory of a different meal in a different restaurant, with Reggie at my side begging for a lick or a nibble or, all too frequently, an entire plate. I couldn't enjoy the meal. I couldn't even wonder about the Purpose these two Taurians believed still awaited me, or what angle the Clarkeson saw in all of this. I kept imagining Reggie in those last moments before he slipped beneath the lava.

I wrenched my attention back and tried to follow the dinner conversation. The topics flowed and changed like water, ranging from opinions of the curious Earth customs and government positions to gossip about our former tour group. My three dinner companions told mutually inconsistent versions of what had happened since I had left the group. I sat and ate, and several times had to catch myself as I went to slip scraps under the tablecloth for a buffalo dog that wasn't there.

As our meal wound down the Clarkeson took its hand from its soup bowl for the last time and dried it on a napkin. "Are you ready for your destiny, singular Terran?"

I shrugged, trying to look calmer than I felt. I was tired of all the talk about destiny and purpose. "You make it sound so ominous. Was this my last meal?" I effected a smile.

"You are in no danger," said Kaljor Rus. "And as we indicated, your destiny's location is fixed." The Taurian handed me a locator chit, but the coordinates displayed on its face went beyond mere global positioning; this chit's transmitter was nearly two astronomical units off Earth.

"Where is this?" I said.

"Where you need to be, when you're ready," said Kaljor Rus.

"And what makes you so sure I'll go?"

"Curiosity," said Yucatangelo. "Do you know why I came to your world? How I came to be on the tour with the others?"

"You said you're a geology consultant."

"Just so. El Pico de Orizaba is expected to erupt soon, and I came to show officials how they could coordinate the time and manner of its eruption, tame the volcano and harness it to supply the nation's energy needs."

"Harness the energy of a volcano?" Suspicions formed in my mind.

"Yes. I made my presentation but they wanted time to think it over. So I went off to tour indigenous ruins. But while I explored Edzná with you, someone gained entry to my rented storage area and stole the very devices I used for my demonstration."

"Devices? The machines Montgomery used to pour lava down on the waste site—"

"—were my machines, yes. Crudely directed, but still my machines."

"How did you even get clearance to bring that kind of technology onto the planet? It almost triggered a tectonic cataclysm."

Yucatangelo seemed to glow in response, as if each member of his self-aware cells' committees was grinning from one side of their cytoplasm to the other. "Which is why I came directly to Mexico. This nation is not a signatory to the Terran compact that regulates offworld technology. This is one of the few places on your planet where I could show my wares and make a sale."

"Until Montgomery stole and ultimately destroyed them."

"Yes, and given the nature of my venture I had not been able to obtain insurance for them. Until this morning I expected to incur significant financial loss, perhaps so much as to require my dissolution as a consolidated entity. Luckily, a buyer came through and I remain solvent and whole."

"A buyer? Of what? Your machines are buried under tons of lava and buffalo dog corpses."

"Were buried," said the Clarkeson.

"This is true," said Efdar Yal. "Both Kaljor Rus and I witnessed the extraction earlier today."

Kaljor Rus nodded in agreement. "Never have I seen a more impressive spectacle. A vessel dropped from the sky without warning and cut into the mountainside. The military responded quickly, with many craft filling the air, but before they could fire on the vessel, it pulled free a massive chunk of rock and flew off, as swiftly as it had arrived."

Efdar Yal nodded this time. "Oh yes, quite astonishing. Its speed was particularly impressive. It must surely have been an uninhabited drone vessel though, no living being could withstand the acceleration forces."

"Why would anyone want your damaged machines?" I said.

"I'm sure I have no idea, and even less interest," said the Clarkeson. "My only concern was that the payment cleared. It was not until I encountered our former tour-mates here that I became curious and we reached our position of synthesis."

"What do you mean?"

"Ask yourself, why was Kaljor Rus also at el Pico de Orizaba? Do you think it coincidence?"

The Taurian bowed to me. "I was there because your destiny was there."

"On the mountain?"

"No, not on it, but rather above it," Said Kaljor Rus.

"Above it?"

"Yes, it made no sense to me either, until I saw the vessel appear and extract the machines from the mountain. That is when I realized your destiny awaits you aboard that ship."

I shrugged. "It's going to wait a long time."

Kaljor Rus started to rebuke me but the Clarkeson placed a hand on his arm. "We have served our purpose."

"How can you say so?" asked Efdar Yal. "He denies his role in the universe."

"For now, but that will change. There is nothing more for us to do."

And with that the Clarkeson pushed back in his chair and stood. "It has been an education knowing you, Mr. Conroy. For a singular Terran I find you to be surprisingly multiplicitous. You have the unanimous respect of my parliament. Fare well."

The Taurians waited for him to leave before speaking again. Kaljor Rus said simply, "You have a Purpose, friend Conroy, and Purpose can not be set aside." He stood then, glanced at Efdar Yal who still sat there, drawing upon the cloth of his napkin. He waited for a beat, and when his companion did not look up he whuffed once and stomped out.

I watched, curious, as Efdar Yal kept drawing. After several minutes he stopped, put his stylus away, and handed me the napkin. "This is the ship you seek, friend Conroy. When you are ready to seek it." Without another word he walked out.

I sat there, utterly dumbfounded. The image on Efdar Yal's napkin was unlike any ship I'd ever seen, save one.

"Son of a . . . it's the Hat's ship!"

"Señor, are your dinner companions returning?"

I looked up to see the waiter standing over me.

"Huh? Oh, uh, no, no, I guess they're not."

"Very good, señor, then I will leave this with you." He set a slim leather bifold on the table next to my right hand and departed. Not only had the aliens set me up for a destined second meeting with the Hat, they'd also stiffed me with the dinner bill.

Chapter Thirty: A Forward Step Back

PAYING THE CHECK AT LA OPCIÓN cleaned me out. Apparently the Taurians had been drinking rather heavily before I arrived (which explained their relative quiet during dinner) and run up a staggering bar tab three times the rest of the dinner bill. I handed the waiter all my money, save for two new pesos which I stuffed in my pocket. "I'm sorry, I don't have any cash left for your tip."

He shrugged. "The gratuity is already included. Did you enjoy your evening?"

"Oh yes, an excellent meal." I paused as thoughts of Reggie intruded on my mind again. "I only wish a friend of mine could have been here to share it. One last question, if I may. . ."

"¿Señor?

"The name of the restaurant. What does it mean?"

"¿La Opción? You would say . . . *The Choice*."

I rolled that one around in my head a moment. "Perfect. The one thing I'm lacking."

"¿Señor?"

"Never mind." I shook the waiter's hand and left La Opción. The evening had grown chilly, but a walk in the cool air cleared my head. I took stock of my situation. It looked pretty grim. All I had going for me was the local equivalent of two bucks burning a hole in my pocket.

I stopped walking and realized I was lost. I'd been too busy slipping into self-pity to pay attention to my surroundings and my walk had carried me beyond the neighborhood of well- maintained avenues, posh restaurants, and trendy art galleries. I had by no means wandered into a slum or shanty town, but the area around me now consisted mostly of small shops and businesses which had long since closed for the day. Apropos of this the streetlamps were spaced farther apart causing me to walk through gaps of shadow and gloom between pools of brightly lit sidewalk. I paused in one such gap where it coincided with the recessed entrance of a small pharmacy and leaned my back against the glass door.

Gazing out at the night, at the light and dark of this named and unknown street, I made a tally of all the things I'd lost in the last few days.

The weight of it threatened to crush me, until I recalled the one thing I had gotten. Somehow, the Arcturan's meld had restored in me the power of the Svenkali. It was small comfort compared to all the loss, but it was all I had.

"Fiona Katherine St. Vincent Wyndmoor." I whispered my great aunt's name, a gentle invocation, and opened myself to the memory as Kwarum had shown me, the way to think about her as I remembered her. I closed my eyes and saw her within my mind.

"Ah, boy, you had me worried, you know." I felt her hand reach out, a gentle and hesitant touch of my cheek, and then she pulled it away.

"Am I still just a boy in your eyes, Fi?" I said.

"Never 'just' a boy, not even when you were small. But you can scarcely blame me for seeing you through the eyes of my memory as you see me through yours."

"I suppose not. I hadn't really thought about it. This is all so new to me, so . . . impossible."

"Nephew, you of all people should know that possibility is a function of our perceptions. The last time we talked you had been entrancing people from a dozen different worlds and making them believe the impossible with no more concern than putting on your socks in the morning."

"I don't do that anymore, Fi."

"No? A shame. You seemed to enjoy it so."

"I did. I do. I just . . . I got sidetracked. I set up a business."

"Oh," she said. Only that one word. *Oh.*

"What does that mean?"

"When I was alive, whenever my travels would bring me back and I visited with your family, I always thought that of all of them, you and I were the most alike. And then, when you bespoke me on Hesnarj, and told me of your adventures, I was certain."

I nodded. "I've always thought of us as kindred souls."

"But you took root," she said. "If not settled down then at least settled in. There's dust on your fancy shoes, nephew. What do you think that means?"

And that was it, right there. My problem wasn't that I'd just lost my company and my fortune. My problem had begun years earlier when I'd acquired the corporate mantle and more wealth than I knew what to do with. My only loss of real worth was Reggie, and he had come to me when I was a rogue rather than rich. It was suddenly so clear. Fiona Wyndmoor had left hearth and home to wander the stars until the day she died, dedicating her life to the experience of new people and places. That spirit of adventure had resonated with me, but I'd let myself go out of tune. I'd stopped wandering. I'd returned to the world of my birth, but 'home' was out there in the darkness of space.

"Aunt Fiona, you've just saved me years of therapy. I wish there was some way to really thank you."

"Thank me by finding your way back to your true path. And after you've walked it awhile, now that you have the knack, bring me around again and tell me some stories."

"I promise," I said, and recast my thoughts, dismantling some connection that I alone knew how to make. She vanished as swiftly and silently as she'd arrived. I opened my eyes and sighed deeply. I merely slumped against the pharmacy door and slid slowly to the ground. The world slipped away from me, and in its place I dreamed I was lying in a comfortable hammock on some island shore, watching the waves and feeding bits of seashells to my buffalo dog as he balanced himself on my chest.

I woke to the morning sun warming my face. Dawn's light shone all rosy and gold from across the street where the top edge of the sun had begun to peek above the rooftops of buildings observable only in silhouette. I lay sprawled on my back looking like a well dressed vagrant. I'd woken up like this on more than one occasion in the past, but not since starting Buffalogic, Inc. That memory brought the events of the last few days to mind, and I ached as I thought of Reggie.

Self pity wouldn't help me. I had to move forward. The present sucked, and the pain of the past would consume me if I allowed myself to wallow in it. Pressing one hand against the pharmacy's outer wall, I levered myself slowly to my feet. I had a mild hangover without the satisfaction of having been drunk the night before. My cognitive fog dissipated as I got to my feet. Either I was getting better at channeling, or the talent grew easier with use, though it had sent me into a deep sleep. And yet, somehow I'd come up with a plan while asleep. Step one involved finding a phone.

Leaving the shelter of the pharmacy's entranceway I spotted a public globalink screen not twenty paces away. The screen was alight with some advertisement that cut off as I tapped the access bar. Smart sensors gave me a perusal and based on their minimal data a new commercial started up, one loosely tailored to the demographic I potentially represented. I waited through thirty seconds of refreshing and stimulating dental cream infotainment rendered in singsong Spanish, and then gained control of the screen. I tapped Betsy Penrose's emergency contact code into the touch screen, and waited. And waited. If Lisa or Eliza currently held sway, I was confident they'd allow Betsy access. Bess probably would too. Elly wouldn't, but I didn't want to talk to Elly anyway, not ever again. So I waited some more.

A message appeared on the screen indicating a connection in progress, audio only, no image.

Betsy's voice said, "Who's calling please?"

"Does anyone else have this particular number?" I asked.

"Boss? Where are you? Are you all right? You vanished from the hospital and I've been getting conflicting reports that you were abducted by eco-terrorists again, stolen away by a troupe of Arcturans, or taken into custody by one of half a dozen different government agencies with a claim on you."

"Nothing like that," I said. "I'm fine. I went out, met up with some friends, had a nice dinner. But I don't plan on going back. In fact, I'm thinking about leaving Earth for a while."

"Your yacht's been impounded, boss. And all of your funds are still frozen."

"Are yours?"

"Mine? Well, no, but I—"

"Betsy, here's the deal. I'm not going to accept your resignation. I was in the right place at the right time to start the company, but you and Lisa and Bess made it work. You believe that Buffalogic can survive, and I believe that with you in charge that's probably true. So here's what I want you to do: draw up some papers transferring any and all claim I have to your name. It's yours. I'm giving everything to you. I'll be the corporate scapegoat that Legal needs, and you can be the new CEO and rebuild."

There was silence and I thought that perhaps the connection had closed. Then she replied, her voice cracking as she said, "Mr. Conroy, I can't let you just give me the company."

"Betsy, right now I'm the majority owner of a worthless corporation; it's not like I'd be doing you any great favor even if I was handing it to you, but I'm not," I said. "I'm selling it to you. In exchange for my signing those papers, I need you to book me passage off Earth, ship me as freight if you have to. I'm not sure where I'm going, but I have a set of coordinates that I'm going to transmit to you."

I pulled the locator chit from my pocket and tapped the digits it displayed into the globalink's screen. I waited as Betsy received and processed them at her end. I could have used the globalink to learn the location of the transmitter myself, but I didn't bother. Knowing where I was going wouldn't change anything; I just had to go.

"What's there?" she said.

"My future. Can you do it?"

"I think so, boss. Can you meet me at the commercial spaceport in two hours? Cargo pad . . . twelve?"

"Two hours," I said. "Cargo pad twelve." I broke the connection and called up a map of Veracruz's public transit, hoping that two new pesos would be enough to get me into the subway.

Chapter Thirty-One: Two Person Hat

CARGO PAD TWELVE HAD BEEN ASSIGNED to Larkin Industries. I found Betsy Penrose in the company of Emilio Larkin, grandson of the president of the company and captain of the transport ship preparing to launch. Betsy introduced me as *Mr. Peaches*.

"Peaches?" I asked.

Larkin smirked. "You need to get to the Belt. I'm delivering preconstituted fruit to several mining communities, pineapples, pears, and peaches."

"Mr. Larkin has agreed to be distracted for a bit," said Betsy. "If someone were to sneak into the emergency pod in his ship, he wouldn't notice. And if he's questioned by authorities he can truthfully say—"

"That he's only carrying pineapples, pears, and peaches," I finished. "Is this going to work?"

"It should," she said. "The authorities are running around chasing phantoms. There have been more than a dozen reported sightings of you boarding outbound ships for as many worlds, or catching flights to the U.S., Europe, and Australia."

I nodded thinking about the Mocker's note. "Well then, with all that confusion, we're probably being overly cautious. Still, better safe than sorry. So, Did you bring the paperwork?"

"I did, but boss, are you sure about this?" She opened a small portfolio and handed me a freshly printed document.

"Very sure. It's something I should have done long ago. Face it, Betsy, I'm not cut out for corporate life. You've tried, I've tried, but we both know you've been carrying me." I signed and initialed a dozen different lines and handed them back.

She was crying. "I'll never forget all you've done for me, boss. For all of us."

"I'm going to go check my final manifest," said Larkin. "I won't be looking at the service tube that leads up to the main hold, or the left hand path that leads to the emergency pod. Nice meeting you, Mr. Peaches." And with that he turned and headed away.

"You'd better hurry, Mr. Conroy. He's filed for lift in half an hour."

I nodded and kissed her forehead. "Take care, Betsy. Give my best to the others in there." And with that I turned my back on the last link to the past five years of my life and climbed into the service tube.

The emergency pod was little more than an airtight hidey-hole with its own atmosphere controls and a wobbly jumpseat. I strapped in to await launch and pondered my options. No one in known space had any use for an out of work corporate leader with no practical experience, but someone might welcome a stage entertainer. With the rumble of engines and the press of acceleration I left my homeworld and the recent past behind. Conroy the entrepreneur might be done, but the Amazing Conroy still had the hypnotic juice to do three shows a night if need be.

Larkin hailed me over the ship's com once we were on course and I left the confines of the emergency pod to join him on the transport ship's tiny bridge. Over the next few days we played endless games of chess, engaged in pointless small talk, and watched the Clarkeson's locator chit count down the distance as we approached the Belt. I had one last bit of destiny to face, and then maybe, I could get on with starting my life anew.

The address identified by the chit was only a few thousand kilometers from where Larkin planned his first stop and drop as he resupplied several belter bases. I was to be dropped off first. We approached my destination, a roundish mass that had been sheered to create a flat space with room enough for a dozen ships and occupied by only a single, familiar vessel. The tiny transport slowed, swung closer, and efficiently set down on a spot no more than fifty meters from the Hat's ship.

Larkin ran through some piloting procedure on his control board; when he finished he swung around to face me. "Are you sure about this, Mr. Peaches?"

I smiled, but couldn't find the words that would make for a convincing answer. Instead I merely stood and said, "Thanks for the lift."

Larkin grunted, and turned back to his controls. He signaled the other vessel but received no reply. Nonetheless I stepped into the airlock and slipped on a disposable vacsuit. It was little more than an inflated bag with legs, but it only had to last long enough to cross to the other side. I cycled the hatch and tethered myself to the ship before exiting the lock. Then I crossed the vacuum to the Hat's ship, extending the line behind me as I bounded across the rockface, barely touched by microgravity. The ship looked no different than I'd seen it in the jungles of Mexico. I reached the entrance, stepped within, and attached this end of my tether to the ship's hull. The outer door closed and sealed on its own. The lock cycled, the inner portal irised open, and once again I saw a ribbed and ridged corridor filled with dustdevils and whirlwinds. Roils.

Lawrence M. Schoen

I pulled the tab on my vacsuit and stepped out as it deflated. Stepping down the corridor, I carefully placed my foot in the gaps between each rib. I kept my arms out to either side, my hands resting lightly upon a pair of ridges like boney handrails. I stayed to the left and wound around up the corridor for another full circle and then it opened onto a room.

"One last time," I said to myself as I stepped onto the Hat's bridge. "And after that, no more visions or fates, prophecies or purposes."

The Hat was waiting for me.

"Conroy, you're here," the vague figure of swirling vapors said, and the sound came at me from the walls of the ship.

"Don't pretend to be surprised," I said. "This is what you planned from the beginning." I would have said more, but my attention was drawn to a massive ball of stone standing beyond the Hat.

It followed my gaze and said, "The Clarkeson's machines are contained with this piece of rock. The heat did not disable them."

"Then why didn't they destabilize the tectonic plates?"

"Something else disabled them," said the Hat. "My buffalo dogs."

"Your buffalo dogs?" A point to the Hat; it had found one of my buttons and pushed it as surely as if it had regular fingers.

"Surely you don't believe such extraordinary creatures evolved naturally? They were constructed by a previous Hat."

"Last time you said you were the only Hat."

"And that is still true. At any time there is only one Hat. Each can last for a hundred thousand years, though some live only a few centuries if they grow bored too soon. Several of my predecessors have dabbled in biologic design; it can be a diverting hobby. One invented the buffalo dogs and left them for other races to find and make use of, charting and plotting how they were employed and exploited. Eventually, however, it too grew bored and passed on."

"What does that have to do with me?"

It gestured again at the alcove and the chunk of rock that had once been part or Orizaba. "Because of you, the buffalo dogs stopped the Clarkeson's machines."

"What? That's impossible. Nothing could survive that heat, not even buffalo dogs."

"They didn't have to survive," said the Hat. "Some of them merely had to last long enough, following their most primal instinct."

"You're kidding! They ate the damn machines?"

"Not all, but enough. They chewed through armor plating designed to resist temperatures found at a planetary core and shut off the machines."

252

"So, that was my destiny?"

"Perhaps the destiny the Taurian saw for you. But that was just a step to your coming here to answer a question I foresaw. Will you answer it for me?"

"That depends," I said. "What's the question."

"Simply this. What will you now give?"

I said nothing. I couldn't. I'd encountered alien gall before, but this was just too much. I probably should have just waked away, hurried back out, suited up, and hoped that by some fluke Larkin hadn't left yet. But I couldn't. Not after all I'd been through. Instead, I said what was on my mind.

"Are you insane? Why would I give you a anything?"

"I did not say your giving would be for me. In fact, I know it is not."

"I don't see anyone else here, do you?" I sighed. Human sarcasm was wasted on most aliens. "Besides, I have nothing I could give to anyone anyway."

The Hat lowered its head so that I could see the irregular grey flannel shape on top responsible for its name. "If that is so, then you are done. But, one thing more. In my vision, I saw that after asking you that question, it was *my* destiny to give you a gift."

"There's nothing you have that I want." I spat the words.

"There is one thing."

"Then give it to me and get this over with."

"I cannot until you first give your gift to another being."

I turned in a full circle. "Who?"

But in asking, I realized I knew the answer. At some level, I must have known it all along. I had nothing but contempt for the way in which the Hat manipulated me to its own ends, but I knew there was someone who would view the situation very differently.

"Hat, you're a smug, selfish bastard, but I'm going to help you and save your pathetic life."

"How could a mere human—?"

"I know why your predecessors died."

"I told you how they died. They pass on out of boredom."

"I don't think so. I think they pass on because of loneliness."

"You are showing your ignorance and your lack of perspective. I doubt you can truly grasp the nature of my existence."

"Maybe not. Maybe no human can. You're so alien to us. You live for millennia, you have access to more knowledge than my entire species could comprehend. But there are other alien races out in the galaxy that come

253

close, aren't there? Others that possess precognitive talents and longevity and knowledge. Why didn't your predecessors make contact with them to alleviate their boredom?"

Can an alien that resembles a body of boiling water and rising vapor frown? The Hat seemed to. "Attempts were made, in the distant past. They were . . . unsatisfactory."

"Why?"

"There are, as you suggest, other elder races, but they are aloof. They would have no contact with my predecessors."

"There is one who would welcome your company," I said, and hesitated. "If it were just you, I wouldn't give you a thing. But this will help him too."

"I don't understand."

"Of course you don't. You've always been alone. You've never had friends. But I do." I stepped closer, close enough to touch the Hat. "I hadn't seen one of them for years, not until a few days ago. His name is Kwarum Sivtinzi Lapalla."

As I said the name, I reached out and pressed my hands to the Hat's bowed head until my fingers made contact with that grey mass that to my touch felt nothing like flannel at all. I felt my focus on the outer world fade and saw the Svenkali in my mind's eye, the two of us standing face to face.

"Conroy?" Kwarum asked, "what are you doing?"

"Repaying a favor and a debt," I said. "Do you know what the Hat is?"

"I've heard only stories."

"Do you trust me?"

He smiled. His pebbly face looked lit up from inside. "I gave you my total trust when I spoke my full name to you years ago while I still lived."

"Good, then hold on." Barely a second had passed. The Hat was beginning to straighten up. My hands held his hat-organ and as he rose my arms pressed against and passed into the roiling substance of his head and shoulders. A warm roaring entered my body. I didn't know how to influence an alien brain, but I didn't need to. I only needed to form a bridge, and only for an instant.

The roaring felt like electrical noise. Like pins and needles calling out in fear. Like fire ants all over and through me screeching different operatic arias and all off key. I sobbed even as time slowed; my fingers were losing their grip. But the bridge formed, tenuous and shaky and collapsing almost as soon as it took on solidity.

"Go," I shouted inside my own mind. Kwarum stood at the near end of the bridge and the far end at the same time, and at every point along it at

254

once. And then he vanished, and the bridge along with him. I slumped to my knees, falling free of the Hat's substance, and gasped for air.

"There is someone here," said the Hat.

"Yes," I said, and tried to stop my body from trembling.

Kwarum's voice emerged from the Hat. "I am here, Conroy."

"Kwarum? The Hat can support you fully then?"

"Oh yes."

"Yes, Conroy," said the Hat's voice, "your Svenkali's presence does not tax me in the least."

"Good to know." I eased myself back up to my feet.

"This is your gift then?" said the Hat.

"To him, not you. He was promised immortality, that others would speak his name and channel his consciousness after he died. I've tried to give him some semblance of that, but you can host him. You don't have to be alone, and he can continue to exist through you."

"But what if he tires of me? He lacks the ability to bring me back."

"Then it was for nothing. I'm sorry, Kwarum. This brief taste must be worse than having nothing."

"It need not be," said the Hat. "What reason would I have to exile your friend?"

"You'll let him stay?"

"Yes. I now see an emptiness in myself that I did not know was there. And I see the error in my judgment of you and your race, Conroy. You have earned my gift to you. Will you accept it?"

"I didn't do this for you," I snarled.

"You may decline it, if you choose," said the Hat, "but know what it is you would refuse." It pointed its arms towards the chunk of Orizaba, and all the roils in the room threw themselves at the rock. A high pitched keening began, as they hurled themselves at it again and again. Flakes of stone floated in the air, and granitic curlings began to pile up all around the base of the rock, like delicate talus shavings. The noise continued and the debris pile grew. Tiny cracks appeared in the rockface. The cracks expanded to crevices and bits of gravel join the layer of shavings. Additional roils poured in from the corridor and enrolled in the assault. The keening increased in pitch and volume. Shavings became chips; gravel became pebbles; cracks gaped wider and ran deeper. Dust choked the room and I pulled my shirt over my mouth to breathe. Nestled in its alcove, the cooled slab of lava had lost nearly a fifth of its size.

The keening altered again. It acquired a tapping accompaniment. Slivers sputtered into the air with great force and I moved back to avoid being cut by them. I had a sudden memory of the dream on Titan and took a further step back. Amidst the glimpses of rock visible as the roils plunged forward I caught sight of something shiny and metallic.

"Quetzalcoatl and Tezcatlipoca," I said, though I could not hear myself over the noise. The roils changed their patterns and the sound changed. After a few more minutes, several square meters of polished metal lay revealed, and soon after a ragged edge to the metal was also exposed. The keening changed pitch again and the roils packed themselves tighter still, pressing themselves deeper into their work.

Something larger than any previous bit of stone, about the size of the proverbial breadbox, came flying out through the bodies of the roils directly at me. My hands came up and whether out of instinct or reflex I caught it. Burnt and crumbling I knew it at once by its shape and weight. I held a buffalo dog, presumably one of the last to dive into the lava. I let the tiny corpse fall from my hands even as other bodies, blackened and ruined, flew through the air at me. I tried to catch them. I couldn't, not all of them, and as their bodies fell around me I slid to my knees and sobbed.

"I apologize for your anguish," the Hat's voice spoke as if it stood directly behind my ear. "This is necessary."

"Why? Why is this necessary?" I screamed the question, not to be heard above the wild keening but for the sake of screaming alone.

"You have to see. In my vision, you witness all of this. Most of the buffalo dogs were consumed by the temperature; they could not dissipate or redistribute the heat elsewhere. But some had eaten their way deep enough into the machines that thermal release no longer mattered. The machines' own mechanisms had already begun attempting to cool the lava. This gave them enough respite to continue as they were led, and so they ate pathways still deeper."

The keening dwindled, became a hum. The roils packed themselves in a hole in the side of the rock, into a smaller hole in the side of one of the machines, and as each one fell back out it seemed to carry and provide a cushioned landing for an additional buffalo dog. The first of these were scarcely burned or blackened, and as more piled up upon the floor I saw no marks at all, only lifeless bodies coated with rock dust.

"These died of suffocation and asphyxiation," said the Hat. "Eventually, even buffalo dogs need to breathe and there was not sufficient oxygen in the raw materials they were eating to sustain them.

"They died to spare your world." It pointed at the rock. "Observe the funnel shape of this hole. Those at the outer and wider end of the funnel died soonest, while those further in, protected by their fellows and the machines' own housing lasted longer and thereby completed their task before succumbing. But one animal stood at the peak of this funnel, one led the assault, and indeed inspired the others. That one pushed and chewed and ate its way several lengths deeper into the Clarkeson's machines than any of its nearest fellows. Then that one estivated, slowed its biology down so low that it was undetectable."

I did not allow myself to hope. "How could you know such a thing then?"

"Because I saw it in my vision," said the Hat, and as it lowered its hands at last the roils poured from the hole, whirling like the pieces of a waterspout, and bringing with them on a cushion of their own bodies a single buffalo dog.

Tears sprang to my eyes. "Reggie? That's Reggie!"

He floated towards me and I lunged for him, plucking him from the air. His body was limp and cold. I hugged him to my chest.

"Is he alive? Is he alive?"

"Yes, but I cannot tell you how long before he will awake."

I knelt, Reggie cradled in my arms, pressing my face against his. His nose felt cold and dry.

"I have little else to give you, Conroy. You cannot remain here, nor I am sure would you wish to. A shuttle has been summoned for your use, and your passage paid to any world of your desire."

"That's it then? You're done?" I struggled to my feet, still clutching Reggie's body to me.

"My vision of you has reached its end. Your existence holds no additional purpose for me."

"I'm sorry, Conroy," said Kwarum. "I see how you have been sorely used in all of this. But may I offer you the advice of a friend?"

"Please."

"Travel to Hesnarj."

"The mourning world?"

"Are you not in need of mourning, Conroy? But moreover, it is the place where we met, where you set your foot upon the path of your life, at a time when you had nothing more than your grief and the clothes you wore."

Eighteen years had passed since I'd stood on Hesnarj, since I'd hypnotized my first audience participant. In that time I'd met many aliens and many humans, I'd heard stories and dreams and philosophies, from the grandiose to the absurd. Could I return to my beginnings? I had the clothes on my back, my grief, and more. I had Reggie. I had hope.

"I'll do that," I said.

I turned away, tucked Reggie's cold body under my arm as I'd done thousands of times before, and stalked back down the corridor and away from the Hat. Roils danced and whirled a few meters ahead of me. Silently, they led me down the right path to a shipboard dock where a nervous human pilot and his shuttle already waited for me.

Epilogue: A Scent of Wonder

HOWEVER THE HAT HAD ARRANGED IT, shortly after boarding his shuttle the pilot handed me papers for luxury class passage to Hesnarj aboard *The Mumby*, which would be leaving the solar system in just a few days. I didn't need the luxury accommodations, and I had other ideas. At my urging, the shuttle pilot beamed a communiqué to *The Mumby's* captain requesting some modifications. Gone was my reservation for a deluxe suite of rooms, and in its place was a much more modest cabin and a small bit of cash on account. That account would grow during the voyage, as I'd also hired on to provide some of the trip's entertainment. The Amazing Conroy lived again, and while the act might be a bit stale for the first few shows, I felt confident the patter and reflexes would come back quickly enough.

In the kind of coincidence I no longer believed in, *The Mumby* waited in orbit above the Jovian moon of Titan, the very placed I expected to find Left-John Mocker. My insystem shuttle got me there with most of a day to spare, and I found the Mocker seated behind a celebrity table at the posh Café Rhea that I'd last encountered in a dream. I pulled up a chair and sat down.

"I'm in your debt for those 'false trails,'" I said.

He waved it away. "It was the most amusing part of this whole trip"

"And the tux?"

"Wishful thinking on my part," he said. "It's good to see you in your old working clothes."

"They're my new working clothes now. I'm heading out beyond Human Space, and I'll be performing onboard ship."

"Ah. Do you have time for a bite? I've ordered us some meat pies. They're the specialty of the day."

I had Reggie tucked under my arm, wrapped in a blanket. He still hadn't moved a muscle.

The waiter appeared and placed plates before us both and I found myself looking at a kind of moussaka sandwich, seared on one side and lightly steaming. I repositioned Reggie under my other arm and carefully used my knife and fork to slice off a taste. As I cut into it an aroma of fragrant spices rose from within. A swirl of vapor enveloped me.

Reggie's nose twitched. Then it twitched again.

"Did he just. . ." said Left-John.

I said nothing. I didn't trust myself to speak at that moment. Instead I speared the bite-size morsel with my fork and brought it to my mouth. It had a delicate crunchy texture that almost immediately melted away. "Oh wow, that's good. It tastes even better than it smells."

"Doesn't it? That's got to be the best thing to be found on this moon."

I nodded, and looked down at Reggie, still snugged up tight in his blanket. "I think I'm going to need another favor."

"Name it," said Left-John, and then perhaps thinking better of the open offer he added, "and we'll see."

"I'm going to need as many of these as we can buy, wrap up, and pack away before my ship leaves."

Left-John gazed back at me blankly.

I scratched my fingers through the fur at the base of Reggie's neck. "I don't think he'd forgive me if he dreamed of the scent of them and didn't have them to actually eat when he wakes up."

About the Author

Photo: Nathan Lilly

Lawrence M. Schoen holds a Ph.D. in cognitive psychology, spent ten years as a college professor, and when not writing currently works as the chief compliance officer for a series of mental health and addiction treatment facilities. He's also one of the world's foremost authorities on the Klingon language, as well as the publisher behind Paper Golem, a new speculative fiction small press. He and his wife, Valerie, live in Pennsylvania.

LaVergne, TN USA
15 December 2009

166989LV00003B/142/P